First Daughter

BY ERIC VAN LUSTBADER

Sirens
Black Heart
Jian
Shan
Zero
French Kiss
Angel Eyes
Black Blade
Dark Homecoming
Art Kills
The Bourne Legacy
The Testament★
The Bourne Betrayal
The Bourne Sanction
First Daughter★

Nicholas Linnear Novels
The Ninja
The Miko
White Ninja
The Kaisho
Floating City
Second Skin

The Pearl Saga
The Ring of Five Dragons★
The Veil of a Thousand Tears★
Mistress of the Pearl★

The Sunset Warrior Cycle
The Sunset Warrior
Shallows of Night
Dai-San
Beneath an Opal Moon
Dragons on the Sea of Night

★Available from Tom Doherty Associates

FIRST
DAUGHTER

Eric Van Lustbader

A TOM DOHERTY ASSOCIATES BOOK

NEW YORK

FIRST DAUGHTER

A Forge Book
Published by Tom Doherty Associates, LLC
175 Fifth Avenue
New York, NY 10010

www.tor-forge.com

Forge® is a registered trademark of Tom Doherty Associates, LLC.

ISBN-13: 978-0-7653-2170-1
ISBN-10: 0-7653-2170-X

First Edition: August 2008

Printed in the United States of America

0 9 8 7 6 5 4 3 2 1

ACKNOWLEDGMENTS

From the very first day I started writing fiction, I've been influenced by many sources, but none as telling or important as Colin Wilson's brilliant book *The Outsider*.

As an Outsider myself, I never really understood who I was or how I fit in (or didn't!) until I read *The Outsider*.

For this, and especially for all the help and inspiration his body of work provided while mapping and unraveling some of the characters in *First Daughter,* a heartfelt thank-you to Colin Wilson.

This is for my cousin David.
With great love and affection.

And for my lost child . . .

January 20
Inauguration Day

ALLI CARSON sat in the back of the armor-plated limo, sandwiched between Sam and Nina, her Secret Service detail. She was just three days shy of her twentieth birthday, but with her father being inaugurated President of the United States today, she'd scarcely had time to think about what she might get in the way of presents, let alone contemplate what she was going to do to celebrate.

For the moment, it was all about her father. The inauguration of Edward Carson, former senior senator from the great state of Nebraska, was celebration enough. Even she had found it interesting that the media had made such a fuss over the exit polls showing that her father was the first president to be significantly helped by a massive African-American turnout. Those votes had been the result of a national campaign engineered by her father's formidable election machine in conjunction with the powerful black religious and political organization, the Renaissance Mission Congress. Her father had successfully run as the anti-Rove, basing his campaign on reconciliation and consensus building, for which the RMC had been the standard-bearer.

But for the moment, everything else was subsumed beneath the intricate and laborious plans for today, which had been ongoing for more than six weeks, as directed by the Joint Congressional Committee on Inaugural Ceremonies. The speeches, balls, cocktail parties, media ops, and shamelessly opportunistic sound bites had begun five days ago, and they would continue for another five days after her father was sworn in, an hour from now.

After eight years of the executive branch being at loggerheads with the legislature, today would usher in a new era in American politics. For the first time, a moderate Republican would be president—a man who, though a fiscal conservative, was unabashedly pro-choice and pro–women's rights, which put him at odds with many Republicans and the religious right. Never mind. His mandate had come from young people, Hispanics and African Americans who, finally deciding it was time for their voices to be heard, turned out in record numbers to vote for Edward Carson. Not only did they find him irresistibly charismatic, but they also liked what he said, and how he said it. She had to admit her father was clever as well as smart. Still, he was of a species—the political animal—that she despised.

Alli didn't even try to peer through the windows. The heavily smoked, bulletproof glass afforded only a glimpse of a world blurred in shadow. Inside, she was cushioned in a plush backseat, illuminated by the soft glow of the sidelights. Her hands were pale against the dark blue leather seat. Thick auburn hair framed an oval face dominated by clear green eyes. A constellation of freckles crossed the bridge of her nose like grains of sand, an endearing touch to a beautiful face. It said something important about her, that she deliberately didn't cover her nose with makeup.

An engine of anxiety thrummed in the pit of her stomach. She'd given her iPod to the driver to plug into the stereo. A wash of fuzzed-out guitars, thumping bass, and steaming vocals from a band called Kill Hannah made the air shimmer and sweat.

"I wanna be a Kennedy," the singer chanted, and Alli laughed despite herself. How many times had she had to endure the same question: "Are the Carsons the new Kennedys? Are you the political dynasty of the future?"

To which Alli would reply: "A Kennedy? Are you kidding? I don't want to die young." She'd said it so often, in fact, that it had become an iconic line, repeated both on hard news shows and late-night TV. It had even led to an appearance on *Saturday Night Live,* where they'd dressed her up like Caroline Kennedy. These antics didn't exactly thrill anyone else in the Carson family, most of whom were seriously deficient in the sense-of-humor department.

They turned west onto Constitution Avenue NW, heading for the Capitol, where, as convention dictated, the swearing in of Edward Carson and his vice president would take place.

"What about Random House?" Nina, on her right, said suddenly. She had to raise her voice over the music.

"What about it?" Alli said.

Sam, on her left, leaned slightly toward her. "What she means is, are you going to take the deal?"

Sam wore a dark suit of a conservative cut, starched white shirt, striped tie. He had thinning brown hair, soft eyes, and an oddly monkish air, was broad, tall, and powerful. Nina had a long, rather somber face with an agressive nose and large blue eyes. She wore a charcoal gray worsted suit, sensible shoes with low heels, a pale blue oxford shirt buttoned to the collar. Both Secret Service agents had earbuds so they could communicate with their brethren in the presidential motorcade.

"The memoirs of the First Daughter. Well, in this age, public humiliation is a badge of courage, isn't it?" Alli put her head back against the seat. "Ah, yes, the spellbinding saga of me. *I* can't wait to read that, so I can only imagine how everyone else will be clamoring for it."

"She's not going to take the deal," Nina said to Sam over her head.

"You think?" Sam said sardonically. Then he allowed a smile to creep onto his pock-cheeked face. "Right. She's no Paris Hilton."

Alli said: "Hey, listen, what Paris Hilton got before anyone else was the difference between exposing things about herself and being exposed. Why fight our tabloid culture, she asked herself, when I can make a mint from it? And that's just what she did. She made exposing yourself cool."

"You're not going to make a liar out of Nina. You're not going to take the deal." Sam frowned. "Are you?"

Alli screwed up her mouth. "Real men would take bets." She didn't like being so predictable.

The limo made a dogleg to the right, onto Pennsylvania Avenue NW, passing under the four lanes of Route 395, and onto the ring road that swung around the sprawling Capitol building.

Another song came on, "Neon Bible" by Arcade Fire, shaking the interior of the limo, and, strangely, Alli found herself looking at Sam's hands. They were square, callused, vaguely intimidating hands, reminding her of Jack McClure. She felt a quick stab deep inside her, and a darkness swept across her consciousness, like a veil lowered for a funeral. And just like that, the engine of anxiety morphed into a singular sense of purpose. She was looking at the world now as if through a telescope.

They were almost at the Capitol, rolling slowly, as if in thick, churning surf. She became aware of the press of people—dignitaries, politicians, security guards, military men from all the armed services, newscasters, celebrities, paparazzi—their heaving mass impressing itself on the smoked glass.

She was aware of the tenseness of her body. "Where's Jack?"

"My old buddy's on assignment," Sam said. But something in his voice alerted her.

"His assignment is here, with me," she said. "My father made me a promise."

"That may be," Nina said.

"You know how these things go, Alli." Sam leaned forward, grasping the inner door handle as they rolled to a stop.

"No, I don't," she said. "Not about this." She felt a sudden inexplicable fear invade her, and she felt the brush of the funeral veil. "I want to talk to my father."

"Your father is busy, Alli," Nina said. "You know that."

From out of her fear came a surge of outrage. Nina was right, of course, and this made her feel helpless. "Then tell me where Jack is," she demanded. Her green eyes were luminous in the sidelights. "And don't tell me you don't know."

Nina sighed, looked at Sam, who nodded.

"The fact is," Nina said, "we don't know where Jack is."

"He didn't check in this morning," Sam added.

Alli felt a small pulse beating in the hollow of her throat. "Why haven't you found him?"

"We've made inquiries, of course," Sam said.

"The truth is, Alli . . ." Nina paused. "He's vanished off the radar screen."

Alli felt a tiny scream gathering in her throat. She rolled the gold-and-platinum ring around her finger nervously. "Find him," she said tersely. "I want him with me." But even as she spoke, she understood the futility of her words. Jack was gone. If the Secret Service couldn't find him, no one could.

Sam smiled reassuringly. "Jack handpicked us to protect you. There's nothing to be concerned about."

"Alli, it's time to go," Nina said gently.

Sam opened the door, stepped out into the wan January sunshine. Alli could hear him whispering into his mike, listening intently to security updates.

Nina, half out of her seat, held Alli by the elbow. Alli smoothed down the skirt of the suit her mother had bought for her and insisted she wear. It was a mid-blue tweed with a hint of green in it that matched the color of her eyes. If she wore anything like this on campus, she'd never hear the end of it. As it was, her image would be plastered all over the papers and the evening news. She wriggled inside the suit, itchy and overheated. As was her custom, she wore a minimum amount of makeup—she had not given in on that one—and her nails were cut almost as short as a man's.

When Sam nodded, Nina urged her charge forward, and Alli emerged from the plush cocoon of the limo. She saw the Unites States Marine and Air Force bands standing at attention to either side of the inaugural platform and, on it, the Speaker of the House, who would make the Call to Order and the opening remarks; the Reverend Dr. Fred Grimes, from whom the invocation and the benediction would come; and two mezzo-sopranos from the Metropolitan Opera, who would sing arias during the musical interludes. There was the vice president and his family. And her father, chatting with the Speaker of the House while her mother, head slightly bowed, spoke in hushed tones with Grimes, who had married them.

Then, Alli was inundated by a swirl of people, voices, microphones, hundreds of camera shutters clicking like a field of crickets. Sam and Nina cut a protective swath through the straining throng, guiding her at long last up the steps of the inaugural platform, draped in the American flag, the blue-and-gold symbol of the president's office affixed to the center podium, where the speeches would be made, the swearing in would take place.

She kissed her mother as she was embraced; her father turned, smiled at her, nodding.

Her mother said, "Are you okay?" as they pulled away.

"I'm fine," Alli said in a knee-jerk reaction that she didn't quite understand. The breeze picked up and she shivered a little. As the marine band struck up its first tune, she put her hands in the pockets of her long wool coat.

Sunlight shone like beaten brass on the faces of the most important men in the Western world. She moved a step closer to her father, and he gave her that smile again. The I'm-proud-of-you smile, which meant he didn't see her at all.

The last bars of the fanfare had faded and the Speaker of the House took the podium for the Call to Order. Behind him rose the facade of the Capitol, symbol of government and freedom, its dome glimmering as if with Edward Carson's promise of a new tomorrow. Down below, among the pale fluted columns, hung three huge American flags, the Stars and Stripes billowing as gently as fields of wheat glowing in sunset.

Alli's right hand found the stitches in the satin lining of her coat, her nail opening the basting until there was a small rent. Her two fingers encountered the small glass vial that had been secreted there. As if in a dream, she lifted out the vial, closed her fist around it in her pocket. There was a ticking in her head as she counted to herself: 180 seconds. Then she would open the vial of specially prepared anthrax.

And like the contents of Pandora's box, out would come death in amber waves of grain.

PART ONE

One Month Ago

ONE

EXHAUSTED LIGHT from a winter sun swooned onto the black Ford Explorer as the vehicle crunched down the gravel drive toward the porte cochere of an impressive colonial mansion. A blaze of headlights from the armored vehicle momentarily sent a shiver of anticipation through the knot of reporters clustered around the mansion's columned entrance. They leaned forward, but could see nothing behind the bulletproof smoked-glass windows. News vans sprouting satellite feeds were drawn up as close as the squad of Secret Service agents would allow. These men—young, crew-cut, square-jawed individuals from Texas, Iowa, Nebraska—looked as sturdy as grain-fed steers.

The Explorer rolled to a stop. From its rear door, a Secret Service agent alighted, turned, tensely watched the crowd with hawk eyes as the POTUS, the President of the United States, emerged. As he climbed the brick steps, the front door opened and a distinguished-looking man emerged to vigorously shake his hand. At this moment, the news crush started, moving forward, the reporters trailing crews in their wake. Flashbulbs went off, reporters began calling out questions to the president, voices cawing urgently like crows discovering roadkill.

One of the reporters holding his microphone out toward the president had worked his way to the front of the press's storm surge, ostensibly to get himself heard over the rising din. No one took notice of him until he lunged forward. Pressing a button caused the fake mike to fall away, revealing a switchblade. Instantly, the alert agents converged on him, two of them disarming him, wrestling him to the top step before he could attack the president. Another had drawn the president into the relative safety of the open doorway, the man the president had come to see having retreated indoors and into the shadows.

All at once, shots rang out; the agent who had hold of the president instantly shielded his charge. Too late. Three, four red stains appeared on the president's shirt and lapels.

"I'd be a goner," the actual POTUS said, picking his way across the colonial mansion's reverse side in his small, quick, emblematic strides.

At his side, Dennis Paull, the Secretary of the Department of Homeland Security, who had also witnessed this latest Secret Service training session, said, "It's an unfortunate factor of the aftermath of the election, sir. The Service was obliged to hire an additional two hundred fifty agents to protect the candidates. There was very little time to train them to the depth usually required."

The president made a face. "Thank the good Lord none of them are in my detail."

"I'd never allow that to happen, sir."

The president was tall, silver-haired, possessed of the intangible trappings accruing from power. He had successfully faced down many a political opponent both at home and, increasingly, abroad. The secretary, barrel-chested, bearded, with ears as whorled as a cowrie shell, was the president's most trusted advisor. At least once a week, most often two or three times, the president saw to it that they spent private time together, chewing over both the increasingly slippery political climate and delicate matters known only to the two of them.

In companionable silence, they passed through the facade of the colonial mansion mock-up via the fiberboard front door. On the top step, the agent who had played the president was rising to his feet. The red paintball "hits" to his chest had ruined his shirt and suit. He was otherwise unharmed. His "assassin" came walking along the lawn, holding what looked like an assault weapon but was in fact a BT-4 Pathfinder paintball rifle.

"Assumptions kill," one of the Service instructors boomed to his charges with terrifying authority. "The lone assassin theory is antiquated. In this networked day and age, we have to prepare for cadres, coordinated attacks, tined and vibrating like tuning forks."

While the squad of Secret Service personnel was being debriefed—perhaps *criticized* was a better word for the severe dressing-down—by its chief instructor, the president and Secretary Paull, followed by their contingent of Secret Service personnel handpicked by Paull himself, moved off down the driveway. They were in Beltsville, Maryland, at the main Secret Service sanctuary, far away from everything and everyone—especially prying eyes and ears.

"I was afraid of this response, which is why I insisted on seeing the scenario myself," the president said. "When I meet with the Russian president, I want to be absolutely certain our people are prepared for anything, including whatever E-Two might throw in our faces."

"The latest manifesto we received from E-Two was a laundry list of the administration's so-called sins: lies, distortions, coercions, and extortions," Secretary Paull said. "They've also trotted out evidence of our ties to big oil and certain private defense contractors. Our counter has been to whip our usual mass media outlets and individual pundits into discrediting that laundry list as the ravings of a lunatic left-wing fringe."

"Don't make the mistake of taking this organization lightly," the president said. "They're terrorists—damnably clever ones."

"The relevant point as far as this discussion is concerned is that the manifesto didn't even hint at assassination."

The POTUS snorted. "Would you if you were planning to assassinate the President of the United States?"

"Sir, let me point out that terrorists thrive on taking credit for their disruptions of normal life. So I would think, yes, at the very least they'd hint at the violence to come."

The hubbub from the Secret Service debriefing had dispersed. Behind them, the elaborate state set was deserted, awaiting its next scenario. Their shoes crunched cleanly against the gravel. They kept to the wanly lit center, a narrow aisle between the massive bare-branched oaks and horse chestnuts that lined the driveway.

"The Service can do better," Paull said decisively, knowing what the president expected of him. "It *will* do better."

"I take that promise extremely seriously," the president said.

A bird twittered happily on a branch above their heads. Higher still, a parchment cloud floated away without a care. The early morning was free of mist, waxy as a spit-polished shoe. They navigated a turning and now, save for the Secret Service bodyguards, were absolutely alone.

"Dennis, on a personal note, how is Louise?"

"About as well as can be expected," Paull said stoically.

"Will she recognize me if I come to see her?"

Paull looked up at the bird and it flew off. "Truthfully, sir, I can't say. Sometimes, she thinks I'm her father, not her husband."

The president reached out, squeezed the secretary's arm. "Still, I want to visit her, Dennis. Today."

"Your calendar's full, sir. You have to prep for your meeting with President Yukin."

"I'll make time, Dennis. She's a good woman. I know inside she's fighting the good fight. We must strive to be inspired by her courage."

"Thank you, sir." Paull's head bent. "Your concern means the world to both of us."

"Martha and I say a prayer for her every night, Dennis. She's always in our thoughts, and our hearts. God has her in his hands."

They moved toward an old stone cottage, the gravel clicking under the soles of their shoes. The Secret Service detail, discreetly out of earshot, moved with them. The two men were like lightning bolts within a passing cloud.

"About Yukin."

The president shook his head, and they continued on in silence. At the president's behest, Paull unlocked the door of the stone cottage and they went inside. The praetorian guard took up station outside, backs toward the stone walls.

The president turned on lamps in the small stuffy room. The cottage was the original structure on the property. The government had turned it into a guesthouse for senior staff of other branches of the military intelligence community who were occasionally asked to lecture or teach a course here. The living room, low-ceilinged, bound by beams, was furnished simply, tastefully, masculinely in blacks and umbers. A leather sofa and easy chairs were arranged around a stone fireplace. A wooden Shaker sideboard held crystal decanters filled with a variety of liquors. Historical etchings were hung on the walls. There was no carpet to soften the colonial wide-plank floors.

It was cold inside. Both men kept their topcoats on.

"Yukin is a thieving, lying sonovabitch, if ever there was one," the president said with considerable venom. "It galls me no end to have to make nice to him, but these days it's all about commodities: oil, natural gas, uranium. Russia has them in spades." He turned to his secretary. "So what do you have for me?"

The president needed leverage in his upcoming meeting with Yukin. Paull had been tasked with providing it. "It's common knowledge within the intelligence community that Yukin's appointees are former KGB apparatchiks who once served under him, but what *isn't* common knowledge is that his new head of the newly state-owned RussOil used to be Yukin's personal assassin."

The president's head jerked around; his statesman's gaze bored into Paull. This was the look that had gotten him elected, that had bonded Britain's prime minister and France's new president to him. "Mikilin! You have proof of this?"

Reaching inside his coat, Paull produced a Black File. Across its top right-hand corner was a diagonal red stripe, a sign of its Most Top Secret status. "The fruits of six months of work. Your hunch about Mikilin was right on the money."

As he scanned the contents of the file, the president's face broke out into a huge smile. "So Mikilin ordered the poisoning of that ex-KGB agent because the agent had acquired a copy of Mikilin's KGB dossier and was about to sell it to the highest bidder in London." He smacked the file with the back of his hand, satisfaction in his voice. "Now I have Yukin—and Mikilin—just where I want them."

He tucked away the file, shook Paull's hand. "You did a stellar job on this, Dennis. I appreciate your support, especially in these waning days."

"I despise and mistrust Yukin as much as you do, sir. It's time he was taken down a peg or two." Paull's hand strayed to a bust of President Lincoln. "Speaking of which, have you read the brief I gave you regarding China?"

"Not yet. I was saving it for the long plane ride."

"I'd be grateful if we discussed it now, sir. Behind the scenes, there's a profound shift going on in the heart of mainland China. The regime in Beijing, having had to abandon communism in the new economy-driven international marketplace, has nevertheless decided that they dare not openly embrace capitalism. Yet they are in need of an ideology, because, as Mao showed them, a single ideology is the only way to unite an enormous nation with such a disparate population. Our veteran China watchers have had hints that Beijing has decided that ideology should be national atheism."

"But that's monstrous," the president said. "We've got to nip that in the bud."

"What worries our China-watchers, sir, is that the adoption of a new ideology may signal other changes in Beijing's policies—specifically an assault on Taiwan, which is why it's imperative for you to bring up the subject with Yukin. He has no love of Beijing or its aspirations."

"Thank you for that, Dennis. Beijing will be topic one once I get Yukin under my thumb." The president moved a curtain slightly, glanced out the window at their escort. "My praetorian guard," he said.

"The cream of the crop," Paull acknowledged.

"But what about afterward?" the president said softly. "What happens in twenty-one days, when I hand the reins of power over to God-less Edward Carson?"

"Begging your pardon, sir. Intelligence reports tell me that Edward Carson and his wife attend church every Sunday."

"A joke, surely." The president pursed his lips as he did when events ran away from him. "This is a man who has pledged to fund stem-cell research, stem cells from fetuses." He shuddered. "Well, what do you expect? He believes in abortion, in the murder of helpless innocents. Who's going to protect them if not us? And it gets worse. He doesn't understand, God help us all, the fundamental danger same-sex marriage poses to the moral fiber of the country. It undermines the very principles of family we as Americans hold dear." The president shook his noble head and quoted Yeats, " 'What rough beast . . . slouches towards Bethlehem to be born?' "

"Sir—"

"No, no, Dennis, he might as well be one of those First American

Secular Revivalists or E-Twos." The president gestured. "Those missionary secularists, who have what they call—can you believe this?—a zealous disbelief in God. Where in hell did they come from?"

Paull tried not to wince. No one else in the Administration was brave enough to tell the president, so as usual it fell to him to deliver the bad news reality was sending the president's way. Therefore, the guillotine was always hovering six inches above his neck. "I'm afraid we don't know, sir."

The president stopped in his tracks, turned to Paull. "Well, find out, damnit. That's your new assignment, Dennis. We need to wipe out this cancer of homegrown traitors PDQ because they're not simply atheists. Atheists, thank the good Lord, have a long history of keeping their traps firmly shut. They know their place, which is outside the clear-cut boundaries of God-fearing society. Are we not a Christian nation?" The president's eyes narrowed. "No, these sons-abitches can't stop yowling about the evils of religion, about how they're engaged in the final battle against theological hocus-pocus. Good Lord, if that isn't a sign that the devil walks among us, I just don't know what is!"

"Time is running out, sir." As he often did, laboring against the monolithic born-again tide of the Secretary of State and the National Security Advisor, Paull was trying to get the president to focus on reality-based decisions. "So far, E-Two has remained completely invisible, and as for the visible First American Secular Revivalists and other like-minded organizations who aren't radical—"

"Not radical?" The president was irate. "*All* those hell-bent bastards are radical. Goddamnit, Dennis, I won't countenance a bunch of homegrown terrorists. Find a way to wipe 'em out, find it pronto."

The president, hands deep in the pockets of his overcoat, stared up at the ceiling. Paull knew that look only too well. He'd seen it an increasing number of times over the past year as, one by one, members of

the president's inner council had left the Administration, as the enemy
took over Congress, as opposition mounted to the president's aggressive foreign policy. No matter. The president stood fast. There were
times when Paull forgot how long ago the president had sunk into a
bunker mentality, circling what wagons were left, refusing to listen to
any form of change. And why should he? He was convinced that the
success of his legacy depended on his unwavering belief that he was
carrying out the will of God. "I'm like a rock, pounded by the sea,"
he'd often say. "Yet steadfast, immovable." In these latter days, he'd
taken to calling himself the Lonely Guardian.

"To think that it's almost Christmas." The president made a noise
in the back of his throat. "Time, Dennis. Time betrays us all, remember that."

The president gripped the back of the sofa as if it were the neck of
his worst enemy. "I've spent eight years doing my level best to pull
America out of the pit of immorality into which the previous Administration had sunk it. I've spent eight years protecting America from
the most heinous threat it's every faced, and if that meant exercising
the power of this hallowed office, if it meant turning the country
around so that it would know its roots, know itself, see itself as the
righteous Christian nation it is, then so be it." His eyes were filled
with righteous pain. "But what do I get for my hard labor, Dennis? Do
I get the thanks of a nation? Do I get accolades in the press? I do not. I get
protests, I get excoriated in the liberal press, I get blasphemous videos
on YouTube. Does no one understand the lengths I've gone to to
protect this nation? Does no one understand the importance of
my legacy as president?" He rubbed the end of his nose. "But they
will, Dennis. Mark my words, I will be redeemed by history." He
regarded his companion. "I've made sure that we've become Fortress
America, Dennis, a stalwart redoubt against the fundamentalist Islamic
terrorists. But now we have to contend with traitors from within. I

won't have it, I tell you!" By way of punctuation, the president added his no-nonsense nod.

"Now let's pray." He got down on his knees and the Secretary followed suit while their cadre of bodyguards turned their backs. The two men bowed their heads, clasped their hands against their striped rep ties. Sunlight glittered off the president's polyurethane hair. *My hair's gone white, my beard is shot with gray. I feel the weight of the world crushing me,* Paull thought. *The expectation of greatness, the dread of making a mistake, of missing a vital piece of intel, of being one step late to the dance of death. Jesus, if he only knew. We've all aged a century since we came into power, all except him. He looks younger now than when he took office.*

"Lord, we humbly beg thee to come to our aid in our hour of need, so that we can continue your work and hold back the turning of the tide that threatens to overrun all that we've labored so hard for these past eight years."

A moment of silence ensued as the two men regained their feet. Before they took their leave of the guesthouse, the president touched his secretary's sleeve, said in a low but distinct voice, "Dennis, when on January twentieth of next year I step aside, I want to know that everything is in place for us to retain our grip on Congress and on the media."

Paull was about to respond when the sound of a helicopter sliced into the pellucid morning like a knife, exposing in him a sense of foreboding. And with that his cell phone rang.

It had to be important; his office knew whom he was with. He connected, listened to the voice of one of his chief lieutenants, his stomach spewing out acid in pulsarlike bursts. At length, he handed the phone to the president.

The president waved it away, clearly annoyed at having been interrupted. "Good Lord, just give me the gist, Dennis, like you always do."

This is why he hasn't aged, Paull thought. "I think you'd better hear this yourself."

The president's voice was querulous. "Why?"

"Sir, it's about Alli Carson."

The president reached for the phone.

Two

ARE YOU all right? Can you move?"

Jack McClure heard the voice, but he could see nothing. He tried to move, but between the seat belt and the airbag, he was held firmly in place.

"I've called nine-one-one," the familiar voice said. "There'll be an ambulance here soon."

Jack could smell hot metal, and the sickly sweet scent of fresh blood and gore.

"Bennett?"

"Yeah, it's me." Captain Rodney Bennett was his boss in the Falls Church, Virginia, ATF Group I, specializing in Arson and Explosives.

"I can't see."

"There's blood all over your face," Bennett said softly.

Jack lifted his right arm, which seemed to move okay. Using the cuff of his bomber jacket, he wiped his face clean. More blood trickled down his forehead into his eyes. Probing with his fingertips, he discovered a laceration at his hairline, put one hand over it. Then looked to the right. Part of the guardrail, ripped open by the impact of the crash, had twisted through the windshield, shearing off the passenger's-side headrest, which it would have done to Jack's head if he'd crashed a foot to the right.

Wind blew into the Escalade, drying the sweat on Jack's scalp to a salt crust. The rain had stopped. Clouds swirled high above, dirtying the white sky.

"Jack, what the hell happened?"

Disoriented, hearing the sounds of approaching sirens, his mind was cast back to other sirens, other flashing lights.

Another car crash.

SEVEN MONTHS ago he'd been in the office, a phone to his ear, coordinating a raid on a high-end cigarette smuggler, the end of a six-month sting operation for which Jack had been the front. He would have liked to be in the field, on the front line, but he was all too aware of his limitations, he knew Bennett placed him where he was invaluable, and that made all the difference to him. Bennett was one of the only people in his life who knew what Jack was and accepted it.

Jack, with a satellite map on the computer screen in front of him, barked out new locations to the team leaders. His cell phone buzzed; he ignored it. The buzzing stopped, then almost immediately, started again. While bellowing orders, redirecting one of the field units, he risked a glance at his cell. It was Emma.

The field units were redeploying in an attempt to take the high ground. He had a special talent for seeing the larger picture, for examining a situation in three dimensions—the more complex, the better, so far as he was concerned. His tactical expertise was unmatched.

The cell buzzed for a third time. Damnit, what mess had his daughter gotten herself into this time? Work phone pressed sweatily to one ear, he answered his cell.

"Dad, I've got a real problem, I've got to talk to you—"

"Honey," he said, "I'm in the middle of a crisis. I haven't got time for this now."

"But, Dad, I need your help. There's no one else—"

A harsh voice crackled in his other ear. "We're taking fire from the high ground!"

"Hold on," he said to his daughter. Then into the landline, "Get down and keep down." He manipulated the map on the screen. Lots of writing wriggled by like shining fish vanishing into an undersea cave. If he took the time, he could read the words, but . . . "Okay, take three men, move six meters to your left. You'll have cover from the stand of trees."

"Dad, Dad? . . ."

Jack, heart beating fast, said, "I'm here, Emma, but I don't have—"

"Dad, I'm leaving here." By here, she meant Langley Field College, where she was a sophomore.

"Honey, I'm happy to talk, but just not now."

Then the shit really hit the fan. "We're on top of 'em, Jack!" he heard in his other ear.

"Get the second team moving now!" Jack shouted. "You'll have them in a crossfire."

"I'm going to drive over to you."

Jack could hear the sudden crackle of automatic fire. His annoyance flared. "Emma, I have no time for your adolescent games."

"This isn't a game, Dad! This can't wait. I'm coming—"

"Jesus, Emma, didn't you hear me? Not now." And he hung up.

The cell buzzed again, but he'd already returned to the fray.

The raid was successful. In the hectic aftermath, Jack forgot all about the call from Emma. But that didn't last. Seventeen minutes later, Jack got another call. At high velocity, top light flashing blue and white, he sped to the scene of the accident, Saigon Road, off an isolated stretch of the Georgetown Pike at Dranesville District Park. The area—thickly treed, sparsely inhabited—had been cordoned off with yellow tape, a squad of uniforms was buzzing around a pair of state police detectives, and four burly EMTs were trekking back and forth between the crash site and the two ambulances, red lights flashing on their long white roofs.

Jack got out of the car and, for a moment, could do nothing, not even think. His brain seemed frozen. At the same time, his legs felt as if they would no longer support him. There was a large elm tree to which the car seemed attached. Tire marks, a laminate of rubber burned into the road behind the car, wove a crazy zigzag into the tree. Jack flashed on Emma's call. He'd been too immersed in the raid to register how distraught she was. Is that why she had lost control of the car? Had she plowed into the tree before she could regain control?

One of the uniforms approached him, hand outstretched to stop him. "What the hell happened?" Jack shouted into his face as if the crash were his fault.

The uniform barked something that Jack didn't hear. Mechanically, Jack showed his ID, and the uniform backed off.

When Jack saw the rear of the car—oddly pristine compared with the rest of it—he felt a chill pass through him. He recognized the tags on the vehicle—a blue '99 Toyota Camry. It was Emma's car, all doubt now erased.

"Will someone tell me what the hell happened?" he shouted again.

All during the drive he'd been telling himself that it had to be a mistake, that it wasn't Emma's car that had careened off the road at speed, ending in a head-on with a tree, that the dead girl driving it wasn't his daughter.

That was a fool's notion, a desperate attempt to alter reality. He saw her the moment he arrived at the crash site. Emma had been thrown from the car. He squatted beside her on hard ground blackened by oil and blood. His daughter's blood. Bending over, he cradled her head as he had on the day she was born. *My god, it's true,* he thought. It wasn't a nightmare from which he'd awake shaken but relieved. This was real; this was his doomed life. Why had she called him? What had she wanted? Where was she going in such a panic? He'd never know now. Her life, brief and bitter, came rushing at him like a locomotive, and she struck him full-on—a healthy pink baby he rocked to sleep, a toddler he helped navigate the obstacles in the living room, a little girl he regarded with a certain amount of awe as she climbed the playground jungle gym or whooshed down the slide, the beauty of her dark, liquid turned-up eyes as she waved to him on her way into first grade. Now came the wrecking ball that demolished them both in one cruel swing.

She was gone. In an instant. In a heartbeat. Like a cloud or the wind. After she broke away from his orbit, what had he ever done to take an interest in her, to show her that he loved her? Worst of all, where was he when she'd needed him the most? Where was she now? He wasn't a religious man, he held no illusions about heaven and angels, but it was inconceivable that she had vanished into nothingness. He was overcome by the horror that his time with her hadn't even begun. Wishful thinking, that's all his thoughts amounted to, because he had no beliefs, there was nothing to hold on to here but the battered head of his only child, his baby, his little girl.

Where had he been when she had been pushed out from between her mother's legs? Making sure a shipment of XM 8 lightweight assault rifles, stolen from Fort McNair, didn't fall into the hands of the Colombian drug-runners who very badly needed them. In the wrong place, just like today.

It was immensely difficult to keep looking at her, to absorb every burn, laceration, contusion, but he couldn't bear to turn away, because he was afraid that he would forget her. He was afraid that once this moment was over, she would be like a life only dreamed.

THREE

THREE CROWS rose from the empty field of grass that was being obliterated by the erection of four McMansions. The crows, wing feathers
iridescent, circled once and were gone. Maybe they knew where Emma
was now.

"I don't want to go to the hospital," Jack said.

"Fortunately, you don't get a say in this," Bennett said.

Jack turned his head as two EMTs lifted the gurney he was on into
the ambulance. Inside, one of them sat on a bench and monitored his
pulse. She was small, compact, dark, Latina. Eyes the color of coffee
unadulterated by milk. She smiled at him, showed even white teeth.
Bennett sat beside her.

JACK'S MIND seemed to drift, as if the jolt he'd received in the crash
had dislodged him from the present. He saw himself standing in National Memorial Park over the freshly dug hole in the ground into
which Emma's mahogany casket would be lowered as soon as Father
Larrigan ceased his interminable droning. Sharon was standing beside
him, but apart. There might have been a continent between them. For

her, he didn't exist, or rather, he existed in a world full of horror and death she could no longer inhabit. They'd yelled and screamed at each other, dishes had been hurled, a lamp that caused a flurry of flame that Jack quickly stamped out. No matter. The fight went on as if no bell had rung, until they came to blows, which was what they wanted or, at least, needed. Then all was still, save for Sharon's quiet sobbing.

Father Larrigan was done and the casket began its mechanical descent into the ground.

"No!" screamed Sharon, breaking to the casket. "My little girl! No!"

Jack made a move toward her, but Father Larrigan was closer. He put a sheltering arm around her.

Sharon leaned against his big Irish frame. "Why did Emma die, Father? It's all so senseless. Why did she have to die?"

"God works in mysterious ways," Father Larrigan said softly. "His plan is beyond human understanding."

"God?" Sharon shoved him away from her in disgust. "God wouldn't take the life of a young innocent girl whose life hadn't yet begun. No plan could be so cruel, no plan could excuse my daughter's death. Better to say it was the work of the devil!"

Father Larrigan looked like he was about to faint. "Mrs. McClure, please! Your blaspheming—"

But Sharon would not be denied. "There is no plan!" she howled to Father Larrigan, to the unfeeling sky. "There is no God!"

As JACK sucked in pure oxygen, his brain ceased its wandering. He opened his eyes.

"Ah, you're with us again," Bennett said.

He sat with only one buttock on the bench, tipped slightly forward. "D'you feel up to telling me what happened, Jack? Last I know you defused the packet of C-four the perp set in the basement of Friedland High School."

To the EMT woman's distress, Jack slipped off the oxygen mask. "The perp broke free of custody, I don't know how. I know my way around that basement, I knew he must be headed for the Bilco doors on the east side—besides the stairs, they're the only way out. I went after him. He hot-wired the principal's car, took off. I took off after him."

"You lost him?"

Jack tried to smile, but grimaced instead. In the aftermath of the crash, his head throbbed, but his body buzzed with the excess adrenaline it was still pumping out. "There's a steep embankment about a half mile back. He swerved into me there. I braked, swung into him, and he did a three-sixty while going off the edge."

The EMT strapped the mask back over Jack's nose and mouth. "Sorry, I need to get him back on oxygen."

Bennett shot her a glance. "Is he in shock?"

"No, but he will be if you keep this up."

Bennett frowned disapprovingly. "I mean, how's he doing overall?"

"There's no outward sign of concussion." She tightened the straps of the mask. "No broken bones, and the laceration to his scalp is superficial." Noting Jack's pallor, she recalibrated the flow of oxygen. "But I'm not a doctor. He needs to be properly evaluated."

The chief nodded vaguely. His face was fissured by hard decisions, painful failures, bureaucratic frustrations, cragged with the loneliness that only men like Bennett and Jack could feel. *We're a breed apart,* Jack thought. *We inhabit the world just like everyone else, but we walk through it as shadows. We have to in order to find the places where the vermin live, worm ourselves in to lure them out, or to chop them into tiny pieces. And after a while, even if we're extremely vigilant, we become so used to being shadows that we don't feel comfortable anywhere else but the darkness. That's when, like it or not, in order to save ourselves, in order to preserve our way of living, we sever our ties with normalcy, because it becomes more and more difficult to make that*

transition back from the shadows into the light, until it becomes impossible alto-
gether. And then here we find ourselves, deep in the places where only shadows
exist.

The ambulance came to a stop, and the EMT woman opened the
rear doors. Jack was rolled out of the ambulance, wheeled through the
automatic doors of the emergency room.

I'LL HANDLE all the paperwork," Bennett said to the admitting attendant.

"But the patient has to read and agree to—"

"I have power of attorney for the patient," Bennett said in his
brook-no-argument tone of voice.

The attendant bristled, gathered herself around her ample bosom.
"Do you have proof?"

Bennett whipped out a pad and pen, stared at her ID tag. "Ms.
Honeycutt, is it?" He scribbled on the pad. "Gimme the name of your
supervisor."

Ms. Honeycutt's glare was as sharp as a scalpel as she handed over
the clipboard, but whatever was on her mind she kept to herself,
which was all Bennett required.

Jack was sent down for X-rays and a CAT scan. Then his laceration
was cleaned and dressed while he was hydrated intravenously.

When Bennett pulled aside the opaque curtain that had been
drawn around Jack's cubicle, Jack said, "No breaks, no concussion. Are
you satisfied now? Can I get the hell out of here so I can get back to
work?"

"In a minute," the chief said. "Your ex is here."

Jack sat up in the bed. "Damnit, not now."

"Too late," a husky female voice said.

Jack, sliding off the bed and onto his feet, saw Sharon appear like a
fallen angel.

She smiled. "Hi, Roddy."

"Sharon." The chief leaned forward, pecked her on the cheek. "Good to see you again."

Looking at Jack frown, she said, "I'm glad someone thinks so."

She made her way past Bennett, who behind Sharon's back, gave Jack a small nod of encouragement before disappearing back into the holy hell of the ER, although at this precise moment, Jack didn't really know which was more of a holy hell, outside the curtain or inside.

It was as she stood silently contemplating him that Jack became acutely aware that he was without trousers. Her hair was lighter than it had been when they were married, and she wore different makeup. She looked both familiar and strange to him, as if she had gone through a mysterious transformation.

"What the hell are you doing here?"

"Rodney called me." She ran a hand through her hair, golden highlights glinting in the overhead fluorescents. "He said he thought you were okay but maybe I should come down and see for myself."

There was some shouting and the hasty squeaks of doctors' rubber-soled shoes on the ER's rubberized floor. The curtain rippled behind him as a patient was wheeled into the next cubicle. From the raised, rushed voice, Jack gathered that there was a lot of bleeding that needed to be stopped, stat.

"I don't know why you bothered," Jack said. "Aren't you too busy fucking Jeff?"

Color rose to her cheeks. "Your best friend is still in the hospital."

Jack felt the muck that had lain on the streambed of his mind being stirred up once again, and his heart began to shrivel. He could end this fight now, before it escalated out of control, but some part of him that was not finished punishing himself goaded him on. "He stopped being my best friend when he took you to bed."

"Neither of us meant it to—"

"Bullshit! Those things don't just happen. You both wanted it."

Her gray eyes stared placidly into his. "I wanted a shot at happiness,

Jack. Something I came to realize you know nothing about. After Emma died, I spent six months in mourning. I went on Prozac so I wouldn't tear my heart out."

He stood, stunned, rooted to the cold linoleum. "What? Why didn't you tell me?"

"Because you needed Prozac even more than I did. The difference is, you didn't get help. You wallowed in your pain, the self-flagellation became your reason to live. You became a black hole. I had to get out before you sucked me into it with you.

"I was so tired of you chasing criminals, of never knowing when you'd come home, *if* you'd come home." She took a step toward him. "Without you, our bed grew cold."

In the next makeshift cubicle, the doctors' voices rose. They were losing the patient. A spray of blood hit the other side of the curtain, which ballooned out briefly.

"Dear God," she started, "what's happening over there?"

"Forget it," Jack said. "There's nothing to be done."

Sharon's eyes turned back to him. All the fierceness had gone out of her. Like a tire running flat, she seemed suddenly wobbly, unsure of herself. "Anyway, I'm no longer seeing him."

"Found someone better already?" Jack snapped.

To her credit, she ignored his dig. "He's intent on pressing battery charges against you. I tried to persuade him he was making a mistake, but he wouldn't listen."

Jack felt his heart skip a beat. Is that why she'd broken up with Jeff? Had she sided with him? He stared at her, too many emotions flitting through him for him to recognize even one. After all that had happened, all that had come between them, she still had the uncanny ability to draw him like a flame. And yet he felt the gulf that lay between them: the broken promises, the lies, the guilt—the unforgiven. It had substance, the form of life. It felt like the holding of one's breath just before the onrush of a storm.

Beyond the stained curtain, there was silence, the activity had ceased, the doctors had gone on to the next urgent case. The patient was lost.

In a clumsy attempt to counteract the gulf, he moved closer to her. "Do you think I stopped loving you?"

Her lips parted, and her breath fanned his cheek. "No, I think you loved me. I know I loved you." Putting her hand on his biceps, she pushed herself away from him so gently, he didn't—couldn't—resist.

Despite his best intentions, he couldn't keep the bitterness out of his voice. She had kept so many things from him, even before they'd split up: the depths of her grief, her depression, taking Prozac. He lashed out in twisted fashion. "So you show it by spreading your legs for—"

She slapped him then.

He noticed that her lipstick was the same bloody color as her nails, which meant that she wasn't biting her nails anymore.

"Why did you make me do that?" Her voice was filled with sadness. "I didn't come here to rehash the past. I wanted . . . I want to offer you a bedroom, a good home-cooked meal, if you like."

He had no idea how to respond.

She gave him a nervous smile. "I went back to church, Jack."

He looked at her in bewilderment. He felt disoriented, as if he were in a forest of mirrors. Who was this woman standing in front of him? Not his ex-wife, surely.

"I suppose you think I'm either crazy or a hypocrite after the tongue-lashing I gave Father Larrigan." With a long finger, she swept a wisp of hair off her face. "The truth is, the Prozac didn't work. Nothing did. My heart was too damaged. The Prozac masked the pain, but it didn't take it away. In desperation, I turned to the Church."

He shook his head mutely.

"I've found a measure of peace there."

"Don't you see that all you're doing is running away from the world, Shar?"

She shook her head sadly. "You have a perverse way of turning something beautiful to ashes."

"So you've found religion," Jack said. "Great. Another secret revealed."

Sharon pulled open the curtain, said, not unkindly, "You need to get it into your head, Jack. We all have a secret life, not just you."

FOUR

AFTER RETURNING with Bennett to HQ, Jack took a long-overdue shower. In the locker room, he found a set of fresh clothes on hangers waiting for him, but was surprised they included a rather expensive suit of midnight-blue worsted wool, a pair of English brogues, a similarly expensive Sea Island cotton shirt, and a fashionable though decidedly conservative tie. He'd never worn such extravagant clothes; nor could he imagine his chief having an allowance for them in his budget.

He had just finished knotting his tie when Bennett returned.

Jack closed his locker door. "So tell me, what am I doing in this monkey outfit?" He tried and failed to straighten the knot in his tie. "Who am I going undercover as? A Secret Service agent?"

"Actually, you're not far off the mark." Bennett gestured with his head. "Come on."

He led Jack out the rear door, where a smoke-windowed limo idled. Bennett opened the rear door and they climbed in.

Jack settled into the backseat. The moment the chief sat down beside him, the limo took off at an almost reckless speed.

Jack stared at his boss. "Where are we going?"

Bennett was looking straight ahead, as if at a future only he could see. "To your new assignment."

Bennett, elbows on his bony knees, laced his fingers together. Jack felt his own muscles tense, because he knew that tell: Bennett's hands got busy when he was agitated, so he laced his fingers to keep an outward semblance of calm. But Jack wasn't fooled. During the time he'd been in the hospital, something very big and very nasty had landed in the chief's lap.

"Okay, give. What the hell's happened?"

At last, the chief turned to face him. There was something in his gray eyes Jack hadn't seen before, something that clouded them, darkening them in a way Jack hadn't thought possible. The chief's voice was dry and thin, as if the words gathered in his throat were choking him. "Alli Carson, the president-elect's daughter, has been abducted."

"Abducted?" Jack's stomach felt a drop, as if he were in a suddenly plunging elevator. "From where, by whom?"

"From school, from under the noses of the Secret Service," Bennett said dully. "As far as who took her, no one's been contacted, so we have absolutely no idea."

And then, with a shock like a splash of cold water, Jack understood. For the first time since he'd known the man, Rodney Bennett was frightened to death.

Truth to tell, so was he.

LANGLEY FIELDS was a private, closeted all-girl's college, very chichi, very difficult to get into. It was situated more or less adjacent to Langley Fork Park, which was just under seven and a half miles due north from the Falls Church location where the ATF had its regional headquarters.

The sun had broken through the overcast, throwing the passing buildings and trees into sharp relief. Telephone lines, black against the sky, marched into the vanishing point ahead.

"In just a few weeks from now, Edward Carson is going to be sworn in as President of the United States, so there is an absolute, airtight media blackout," Bennett said. "You can just imagine the intense feeding frenzy that would attach itself to the news. All the talking heads and bloggers in Medialand would speculate—wildly, perhaps recklessly, but in the end uselessly—about the identity of the perpetrators, from Al-Qaeda and Iran to the Russian Mafia and North Korea to god alone knows who else. These days, everyone has a reason to hate our guts."

Bennett, staring out the window as they barreled along the Georgetown Pike, frowned. "I don't have to tell you that the soon-to-be First Daughter's abduction has caused an intelligence mobilization of nine-eleven proportions." He turned to Jack. "The head of the special task force in charge of the investigation has requested you, not simply because you're my best agent by far, but I assume because of Emma."

That was logical, Jack thought. Emma and Alli both went to Langley Fields; they were roommates and good friends.

When the limo turned onto Langley Fields Drive from Georgetown Pike, it was met by a fleet of unmarked cars. There was not a police or other official vehicle to be seen. The limo stopped while the driver handed over his creds; then a grim-faced suit with an earful of wireless electronics waved them through the tall black wrought-iron gates onto the school grounds, which were guarded by a twelve-foot-high brick wall topped by wrought-iron spikes. Jack felt sure those metal points were more than decorative.

Langley Fields was the epitome of an exclusive, expensive women's college. The colonial-style white brick buildings were scattered across a magnificently groomed campus whose expansive acreage now revealed volleyball and tennis courts, a softball field, an indoor gym, and swimming facilities. They passed a professional dressage ring on their right, behind which was the long, low clapboard stable, its doors closed against the winter chill. Beside it, neat golden bales of pale hay were piled high.

The limo crunched over blue-gray gravel, moving along a sweeping drive toward the sprawling administration building. Jack pressed the button that rolled down his window and stuck his head out. At regular intervals, unmarked cars had been pulled unceremoniously onto the immaculately tended lawns, green even at this time of year. Beside them, more suits with ear candy consulted with the outdoor staff or were either setting out or returning in search parties of three or four.

Jack counted three sets of K-9 unit dogs straining at the ends of their handlers' leashes as they tried to catch a trace of Alli Carson's scent. High overhead a stationary helicopter whirred, no more than another bird with acute vision. With the president-elect's priority visits, the chopper wouldn't betray any unusual activity to the school's neighbors, Jack surmised.

The suits watched the limo's slow passage, their pale gimlet eyes narrowing as they spotted Jack. Their mouths turned down in disdain or outright hostility. He was an outsider come to take their Golden Fleece, make it his own. As they realized this change in the order of things, they bared their teeth slightly, and, aggrieved, their cheeks puffed up.

The car came to a stop under the porte cochere, held aloft by massive fluted Doric columns. Jack stepped out, but when the chief didn't follow, he turned, bent into the interior.

"This is as far as I go." Bennett's face was impassive, but his fingers were firmly laced together on his lap. "Your ass belongs to someone else now." His lips seemed to twitch in a grimace. "A word to the wise, Jack. This is a different arena. You go off the grid, they'll for damn sure make you wish you were dead."

FIVE

JACK, ID'D at the front door, was taken in through the vast echoing vestibule, with its domed ceiling, huge ormolu-framed mirror, and ornate spiral staircase to forbidden upper floors. A crystal chandelier hung like a cloud of tears caught in the moment before it's drops fall to earth.

The familiar polished mahogany console with its gold-tipped cabriole legs, delicate as a fawn's, stood to the left, a large bouquet of purple-blue hothouse irises rising from within its glass bed. To the right, through mahogany pocket doors, was the sumptuous drawing room used for teas given by the headmistress or for holiday parties. Jack stood for a moment, transfixed, as he stared in at the room's yellow walls, yellow flowered sofas and chairs, white trim. He saw himself with Sharon and Emma, having tea with the headmistress. He remembered their hostess had worn an unfashionable dress. In sharp contrast to Emma's shockingly short pleated skirt and formfitting V-neck sweater, the dress was ankle-length, covered with tiny Victorian flowers amid twining vines. In fact, it was Emma's alterations of the college's dress code—what the headmistress labeled subversive—that was the subject of the conference over tea, scones, and clotted cream. Jack had been proud of how his daughter stood up for her rights, though both the headmistress and Sharon had been scandalized. Inevitably, his gaze was magnetized to one of the sofas where Emma had sat, ankles primly crossed, hands in her lap, staring at a spot somewhere over the headmistress's left shoulder, her expression for once solemn as an adult's. She spoke respectfully when asked for an explanation, throughout seemed contrite. But this, Jack suspected, was merely a ploy to end the inquisition. Tomorrow, he was willing to bet, she would show up in class as outrageously dressed as before. The memory made him want to laugh and cry at the same time. From the moment the limo had entered the gates of Langley Fields, he was plunged into the past, and now he knew there was no escape.

He was about to turn away when his eye was caught by a slight rippling of the window drapes. His escort cleared his throat and Jack put up a hand. Quickly crossing the room, he pulled aside the drape. The window was firmly shut, but there came to him the hint of a smell: mascara, makeup, something Emma had used on her face. Behind him, he heard a whisper. Burnished light seemed to fall on the narrow space between the window and the drape. A shadow moved, a whisper like wind through a field of grass. Was it his daughter's voice?

A tiny thrill shot up his spine. "Emma?" he said under his breath. "Are you here? Where are you?"

Nothing. The smell had vanished. He stood for a moment, lost in time, feeling like an idiot. *Why can't you face it?* he told himself. *She's gone.* But he knew why. During the six months while Sharon was popping pills behind his back, while she and Jeff were finding shadowed corners to couple in, while his marriage was falling apart, he'd spent every minute of his spare time trying to piece together the hours before Emma's death. The truth was, he hardly slept, using the nighttime hours to prowl, run down leads, talk to snitches. Emma's cell phone, crushed in the accident, was no help, but he got a friend at the phone company to pull her records. He worked the list of numbers, building charts of her friends and acquaintances, but always the nodes and connectors circled back on themselves, like a snake eating its tail. He laboriously read the transcripts of her text messages for the previous two weeks, the longest the phone company kept such things. He scoured the hard drive of her laptop, looking for suspicious e-mails, links to Internet chat rooms, unfamiliar, possibly dangerous Web sites. It was like the dark side of the moon in there, the hard disk was clean of such ubiquitous detritus. If this had been a spy novel, he'd suspect it had been purged, but Emma was no spy and this wasn't a novel. He spent hours with Alli Carson, braced the faculty and staff at the school. He interviewed every neighbor of the school's in an ever-widening circle until even he understood he'd exhausted all possibilities. He'd run down all Emma's girlfriends until the father of one had taken out a restraining order on him. He'd followed every possible lead, even ones that appeared improbable. For his tireless and often frenzied efforts, he'd come up with nothing. After six months, he was no closer to finding out what had frightened his daughter so thoroughly. She'd always been something of a fearless creature. Not reckless, so far as he knew—though he'd finally had to admit to himself that he'd known Emma not at all. The bitter truth, as Sharon had said, was that their daughter had a secret life from which, even in death, they were excluded.

"Emma, I want to listen," he whispered into the space between the curtain and the window. "Honest I do."

Moments later, amid an eerie silence, he returned to his escort and was taken away, down the paneled corridor hung with photo portraits of the college's more illustrious alumnae, who had achieved fame and fortune in their chosen fields. Before he reached the end, the door to the headmistress's office opened and a woman came out. Jack's escort stopped, and so did he.

Closing the door firmly behind her, the woman strode toward him with her hand outstretched. When he took it, she said, "Jack McClure, my name is Nina Miller." Her clear blue eyes regarded him steadily. "I'm a special operative of the Secret Service and the Department of the Treasury," she said with exquisite formality. "I'm assisting Homeland Security First Deputy Hugh Garner. The president has appointed him to spearhead this joint operations task force."

Nina Miller was tall, slim, proper. She wore a charcoal gray man-tailored worsted suit, sensible shoes with low heels, a pale blue oxford shirt buttoned to the collar. All that was missing, Jack observed, was a rep tie. This one was trying too hard to fit into an old-boys network that obviously wanted no part of her. She had the narrow face of a spinster, with a rather long, aggressive nose and a pale, delicate complexion that seemed as translucent as a bowl of light.

She gestured. "This way, please," as she led him to the end of the hall, opened the door to the headmistress's three-room suite. It had been transformed into another world.

The first room contained the desks of a pair of administrative assistants, as well as file cabinets in which were stored meticulously maintained documents on each student, past and present. For the time being, at least, the assistants were sharing space in their boss's office. A forensics field crew laden with machinery Jack could only guess at, agents with the latest surveillance equipment, and what seemed like a battalion of liaison personnel now clogged the space. The room was sizzling with electronics from multiple computers, hooked up variously to satellite nets, closed-circuit TV cameras, and every terrorist and criminal database in the world. A battery of laser printers continuously spat out minute-by-minute updates from CIA, FBI, Homeland Security, the Secret Service, NSA, DOD, Pentagon, as well as the state and local police in Virginia, the District, and Maryland. Uniformed people were making calls, receiving them, barking orders, exchanging faxes, making more calls. Their pooled knowledge was like a living thing, a city of shadows being built out of the ether through which information traveled. Jack could feel the low-level hysteria that gripped everyone in the room, as if they had the jaws of a rabid dog clamped to their throats. Their shared concentration, like a stale odor, like sardines too long in the can, made him want to draw back to catch a breath.

Beyond, one could go left into the headmistress's office proper, or right into a room she used for private conferences. It was into the latter room that Jack was led. His silent escort left him at the door, disappearing presumably to handle other pressing concerns.

When Jack stepped into the room, a man looked up. He was perched impatiently on the edge of one of the two facing sofas separated by a glass-topped coffee table. Nina raised a hand, palm up, fingers slightly curled. "This is First Deputy Hugh Garner."

"Please sit down," Garner said with a smile as narrow as his retro tie. He was a tall man with prematurely gray hair, severe as his smile or his tie. He had a face Jack associated with a late-night TV pitchman—smooth of cheek, shiny of eye, his manner confident or glib, depending on your point of view. One thing Jack could see right away: He was a purely political creature, which put him at odds with Jack, and therefore dangerous. "You need to be brought up to speed as quickly as possible."

He offered a sheaf of papers—forensic reports, possible witness interviews, search results, photos of everything that had been vacuumed up from Alli and Emma's room. (Jack couldn't help thinking of it in that way.)

Nina Miller settled herself by scooping the sides of her skirt under her thighs. Her eyes were bright, inquisitive, completely noncommittal.

Garner said, "First thing: We've sent out a news brief on the reason for government agents here, as well as the whereabouts of Alli Carson."

Jack, preoccupied with the reports, did not immediately respond. He had stood up, moved over to the window so sunlight spilled across the pages. He kept his back to the others, shoulders slightly hunched. He tried to relax his body without much success. The letters, words, clauses, sentences on the pages swam in front of his eyes like terrified fish. They swirled like snowflakes, spiraled like water down a drain, pogoed like Mexican jumping beans.

Jack was having trouble finding his spot. Stress always did that to him, not only made his dyslexia worse but interfered with the techniques he'd been taught to work around it. Like all dyslexics, he had a brain designed to recognize things visually, not verbally. The speed of his thought processes was somewhere between four hundred and two thousand times faster than for people whose brains were wired for word-based thought. But that became a liability around written words, since his mind buzzed like a bee trying to find its way into a blocked hive. Dyslexics learned by doing. They learned to read by literally picturing each word. But there was a host of disorienting trigger words, such as *a, and, the, to, from*—words crucial to decipher even the most elementary sentences—for which no pictures existed. In his lessons, Jack had been asked to make those words out of clay. In fashioning them with his hands, his brain learned them. But stress broke the intense concentration required to read, stripped him of his training, shoved him out onto a rough sea of swirls, angles, serifs, and, worst of all, punctuation, which might have been the scratching of a mouse against a wedge of hard cheese for all the sense he could make of it.

"There's no way of knowing, however, how long our disinformation will hold up. On the Internet, where every blogger is a reporter, there's a limited time we can keep something like this a secret," Garner continued.

Jack felt the others' eyes on him as he crossed the room. He spoke up, more to distract himself from his growing terror than from a need to engage Garner. In fact, his fervent wish was for a sinkhole to open up under Garner and Nina Miller, swallow them whole, but no luck. When he looked, both of them were still alive and well. "How long do we have?"

"A week, possibly less."

Jack turned back to the gibberish that spitefully refused to resolve itself into language.

"You aren't finished yet?" Garner said from over Jack's right shoulder.

"I'm sure Mr. McClure needs a moment to orient himself to our standards of methodology," Nina said, "which are quite different from those of the ATF." She walked over to Jack. "Am I right, Mr. McClure?"

Jack nodded, unable to get his vocal cords out of their own way.

"ATF, yes, I see." Garner's laugh held a rancid note. "I trust our protocols aren't too difficult for you to follow."

Nina pointed to paragraphs on certain pages, read them aloud, as if to speed the process of familiarization by highlighting elements the team found of particular interest. Jack, his stomach clenched painfully, felt relief, but with it came a flush of secret shame. His frustration had morphed into anger, just as it always did. Trying to control that poisonous alchemical process was the key to maneuvering through the briar patch of his disability. He shuffled the papers as if scanning them for the second time.

"The reports contain no pertinent information, let alone leads or conclusions as to which direction the investigation should go," he said. "What about the private-security people, any last-minute changes in the night watchmen, and have you reviewed the CCTV tapes for last night?"

"We've interviewed the security personnel." Nina took the file from him. "No one called in sick, there were no sudden personnel substitutions. Neither the men on duty nor the tapes showed anything out of the ordinary."

Had Nina read off sections of the report to help him? Had she somehow found out about his secret? Bennett wouldn't have given him up, no matter the pressure, so how?

Garner said, "Edward Carson prevailed on the president to have you reassigned to us. I'm not one to beat around the bush, McClure. I think his interference is a mistake."

"A moron could understand president-elect Carson's line of reasoning," Jack said with a deliberate lack of edge to his voice. "I'm intimately familiar with the college grounds and the surrounding area. And because my daughter was Alli Carson's roommate, I'm familiar with her in ways you or your people can't be."

"Oh, yes," Garner sneered. "I have no doubt Carson considers those assets, but I have another take. I think this intimacy is a personalization, and will play as a detriment. It will distort your thinking, blur your objectivity. You see where I'm going?"

Jack glanced briefly at Nina, but her face was as closed as a fist.

"Everyone's entitled to his opinion," Jack said carefully.

The narrow smile appeared like a wound. "As the head of this task force, my opinion is the one that counts."

"So, what?" Jack spread his hands. "Have you brought me here to fire me?"

"Have you ever heard of 'missionary secularism'?" Garner continued as if Jack hadn't spoken.

"No. I haven't."

"I rest my case." Garner flipped the file onto the carpet. "That's about all those reports are good for—floor covering. Because they're built on old-school assumptions, we have to give those assumptions the boot or we'll never get anywhere on this case." He perched on the edge of the sofa again, linked his fingers, pressed the pads of his thumbs together as if they were sparring partners about to go at it. "It can be no surprise even to you that for the past eight years the Administration has been guiding the country along a new path of faith-based initiatives. Religion—the belief in God, in America's God-given place in the world—is what makes this country strong, what can unite it. Move it into a new golden age of global influence and power.

"But then there are the naysayers: the far-left liberals, the gays, the fringe elements of society, the disenfranchised, the deviants, the weak-willed, the criminal."

"The criminal—?"

"The abortionists, McClure. The baby killers, the family destroyers, the sodomites."

Again, Jack glanced at Nina, who was flicking what appeared to be a nonexistent piece of lint off her skirt. Jack said nothing because this argument—if you could call it that—was nonrational, and therefore not open to debate.

"There's a Frog by the name of Michel Infra. This bastard is the self-proclaimed leader of a movement of militant atheists. He's on record as claiming that atheism is in a final battle with what he terms 'theological hocus-pocus.' He's far from the only one. In Germany, a so-called think tank of Enlightenment, made up of Godless scientists and the like—the same dangerous alarmists proclaiming that global warming is the end of the world—are promulgating the devilish notion that the world would be better off without religion. The president is beside himself. And then there's the British, who haven't had a God-driven thought in their heads in centuries. *The God Delusion* is a book written by one of them." He snapped his fingers. "What's his name, Nina?"

"Richard Dawkins," Nina said, emerging from her near-coma. "An Oxford professor."

Garner waved away her words. "Who cares where he's from? The point is, we're under attack."

"What's further aggravated the Administration," Nina continued blandly, "is a recent European Union survey asking its citizens to rank their life values. Religion came in last, far behind human rights, peace, democracy, individual freedom, and the like."

Garner shook his head. "Don't they know we're in a religious war for our very way of life? Faith-based policy is the only way to fight it."

"Which is why this Administration is hostile to the incoming one." Having awoken, Nina now seemed on a roll. "Moderate Republicanism as represented by Edward Carson and his people is a step backward, as far as the president is concerned."

"Okay, this is all very enlightening," Jack said, "but what the hell does it have to do with the kidnapping of Alli Carson?"

"Everything," Garner said, scowling. "We have reason to believe that the people who planned and carried out the kidnapping are missionary secularists, a group calling itself E-Two, the Second Enlightenment."

"That refers to the ongoing—often violent—conflict originating in Europe's eighteenth-century Enlightenment," Nina said.

"A so-called *intellectual* movement," Garner sneered, making the word synonymous with *criminal*.

"Reason over superstition, that was the Enlightenment's battle cry, led by George Berkeley, Thomas Paine, who returned to the pioneering work of Pascal, Leibniz, Galileo, and Isaac Newton," Nina said. "And it's E-Two's credo as well."

"I never heard of them," Jack said before he could stop himself.

"No?" Garner cocked his head. "Your ATF office was forwarded the official memos Homeland Security sent around. The last one was—what?—but three months ago." He leered like a pornographer. "If you didn't see it, either you're negligent or you can't read."

"What makes you think this organization is involved?" Jack, the bile of anger feeding the heat of his shame, asked. "The most likely suspects are Al-Qaeda or a homegrown derivative."

Garner shook his head. "First off, the terrorist chatter's been elevated for about ten days now, but you know that ebbs and flows, and a lot of it is just trying to play with our minds. There's nothing there for us. Second, there have been no unusual movements in the suspected cells we have under surveillance."

"What about the cells you know nothing about?" Jack said.

Nina looked at Garner, who nodded.

"Show him," he assented.

Nina fanned out a handful of forensic photos of two men, naked from the waist up, with fatal wounds on their backs.

Jack studied the visuals with a relief only he could fully comprehend. "Who are they?"

"The Secret Service personnel assigned to guard Alli Carson," Garner said while Nina's lips were still opening.

Jack felt an unpleasant prickling at the back of his neck. The news just got worse and worse. The photos showed the respective bodies in situ.

"The killers are professionals," Garner said with an unforgivable degree of condescension. "They know how to kill quickly, cleanly, and efficiently." He pointed. "They took their wallets, keys, pads, cell phones. Just to rub our noses in it, I guess, because we've locked down everything belonging to or attached to these two individuals, so there's nothing the perps can do with the personal items. And see here."

Beside each body, partially wedged beneath their left sides, were what appeared to be playing cards.

He peered more closely. "What are those?"

Garner dropped two clear plastic evidence bags onto the photos. Each one contained a playing card. Drawn in the center of each card was a circle with a familiar three-pronged symbol: a stylized peace sign. "During the war in Nam, U.S. soldiers used to leave an ace of spades on the bodies of their victims. These E-Two sonsabitches are doing the same thing, leaving their logo on their victims."

Reaching down to his feet, he pulled a document out of a briefcase, read it out loud. "Faith-based initiatives and policies are spreading from America to Europe, where faith-based reasoning is taking root in the burgeoning Islamic populations of France, England, Germany, the Netherlands, et cetera. All too soon, Muslims will be running for office in these countries, and faith-based initiatives will begin there. . . ." There followed a list of statistics showing the alarming rise of Muslims into Europe, as well as increasing militance of certain sections.

"Here." Garner handed over the manifesto. "Read the rest yourself."

Jack, who was inordinately attuned to such undertones, wondered whether Garner suspected—or, worse, knew. Chief Bennett had gone to extraordinary lengths to keep Jack's secret under wraps, but with the Homeland Security geeks, one never knew. They were as zealous as a Sunni imam, and if they didn't like you—and clearly Garner didn't like Jack—and if they felt threatened by you—and clearly Garner felt threatened as hell—they would move heaven and earth to find the skeleton in your closet, even if it was an enigma wrapped inside a conundrum.

Jack stared down at the impassioned tract, which was signed "The Second Enlightenment." It contained a stylized peace sign identical to those on the playing cards found on the Secret Service detail.

"It's official now," Garner said. "E-Two are terrorists of the first rank. They won't hesitate to kill again—I can guarantee you that because E-Two's manifesto calls for a drastic change in the current president's faith-based policies before he leaves office. We believe that it is seeking to discredit him in front of the entire world, to sabotage his legacy, to force him to admit that his policies are wrong." He took the document back from Jack. "It's clear from the evidence that E-Two has abducted Alli Carson. I want all our energies concentrated on this organization."

"Sounds like a leap of faith, rather than a leap of logic," Jack said.

Garner squared around, bringing to bear every asset that had allowed him to climb the jungle gym of federal politics. "Do I look like I care what it sounds like to you, McClure? Goddamnit, you're in my army now. The President of the United States has tasked me with getting Alli Carson back, alive and as quickly as is humanly possible. I'm telling you how. Either you're with us or get out of our way."

"I'd like to see some hard evidence—"

"The E-Two cards on the bodies of our fallen soldiers aren't enough for you?" Garner rose and, with him, Nina.

The atmosphere had deteriorated from unpleasant to toxic. Jack went to the window, stood staring out at the neat manicured lawns.

He gathered himself. "I need to see where it happened."

"Of course." Nina nodded. "I'll take you."

"I know the way."

Garner's knife-edge smile just barely revealed the tips of white, even teeth. "Of course you do. Nevertheless, *I'll* accompany you."

SIX

LIGHT, MELANCHOLY as a ghost, tiptoed into the room through a pair of mullioned windows. It was northern light, dismal, vagrant, at this time of year almost spectral. Hugh Garner had peeled back the yellow-and-black tape that marked the boundary of the crime scene like an admonishing finger, but as he was about to step across the threshold, Jack blocked his way.

Jack snapped on latex gloves. "How many people have been through here?"

"I don't know." Garner shrugged. "Maybe a dozen."

Jack shook his head. "It looks like a shit disco in here. You sure took your time getting me over here."

"Everything in this 'shit disco' was tagged, photoed, and bagged without your expertise. You read the reports," Garner said with peculiar emphasis.

"That I did." Jack knew by now that the only thing keeping Garner from kicking his ass off the grounds was the president-elect. Even the president couldn't say no to Edward Carson without looking like something you picked up on the sole of your shoe.

"If you find anything—which I seriously doubt—it'll be analyzed by our SID division at Quantico," Garner said. "Not only is it the best forensic facility in the country, but the security is absolutely airtight."

"Is that where you sent the two bodies?"

"The autopsies were done by our people, but the bodies are housed locally." Garner took out a PDA, scrolled through it. "At the offices of an ME by the name of—" He seemed about to read off the name but, struck by a sudden idea, turned the face of the PDA so Jack could read it.

"Egon Schiltz," Jack said, his brain vainly trying to decode the scrawly squiggles on the PDA screen. Mercifully, his guess was more than a shot in the dark. Schiltz was medical examiner for the Northern District of Virginia. Despite sharp political differences, they had a friendship that went back twenty years.

Returning his attention to the present, Jack entered the room, carefully placing one foot in front of the other until he stood in the center. It was perhaps twenty by twenty, he estimated, not small by dorm standards. But then, Langley Fields wasn't a standard college. You got what you paid for, in all areas.

The floor was plush wall-to-wall carpet. Beds, dressers, chairs, lamps, desks, closets, sets of shelves—there were two of almost everything. Alli's laptop, its hard drive ransacked by IT forensics, sat on her desk. The shelf above her bed was a clutter of books, notes, pins, pennants, first-place trophies she'd won for horseback riding and tennis. She was an athletic girl and intensely competitive. He took several steps closer, saw the bronze medal for a karate competition, and couldn't help feeling proud of her. Owing to her diminutive size and with Schiltz's daughter in his mind, he'd convinced her to take it up in the first place. His eyes passed over the spines of the books—there were textbooks, of course, as well as novels. Jack had been taught to locate a spot outside himself on which to fix his rabbity mind. The point was fixed. Like a spinning dancer trained to concentrate on a single point in the distance in order not to lose his balance or grow dizzy, it was essential that Jack concentrate on the point and stay there to tame the chaos in his mind. Otherwise, trying to make sense of letters and numbers was as futile as herding cats. He couldn't always locate it. The more extreme the tension he was under, the less chance he had of finding the point, let alone holding on to it.

He located his center point, six inches above and behind his head, and the whirling hurricane inside his head dissipated, his disorientation melted away, and he was able to read the book spines with minimum difficulty: Neal Stephenson's *Cryptonomicon,* Natsuo Kirino's *Out,* Patricia Highsmith's *This Sweet Sickness,* Carlos Ruiz Zafón's *The Shadow of the Wind.*

Garner shifted from one foot to another. "After Emma's death, Alli Carson refused to have anyone else move in with her."

On what had been Emma's side of the room, nothing remained of her presence but a small stack of CDs. Everything had been taken by either him or Sharon, as if they were the contents of a house they were never going to share again. Seeing the CDs kindled a flame of memory: Tori Amos, Jay-Z, Morrissey, Siobhan Donaghy, Interpol. Jack had to laugh at that one. The day she moved in, he had given her an iPod—not a Nano, but one with a whopping big eighty-gigabyte drive. And as soon as she was able to rip tracks into MP3s, there went the CDs. Jack picked up the Tori Amos CD, and the first song his eye fell on was "Strange Little Girl." His heart, thumping and crashing like a drum set, threatened to blow a hole in his chest. His hand trembled when he put the CD back on the small stack. He didn't want them; he didn't want to move them either. Her iPod was living at home, untouched. He'd palmed it from inside the wrecked car without anyone seeing, the only thing miraculously undamaged. He couldn't count the number of times he'd promised himself he'd listen to the music on it, but so far he'd failed to work up the courage.

"So difficult," Garner continued, "I can only hope you can do your job with a clear head, McClure."

Jack was immune to the taunts. He'd been derided by eighteen-year-old professionals drawing on depths of sadism Garner got to only in dreams. He stood very still now, transferring his gaze from the specific, allowing it to sweep the room instead. He had what in the trade was called soft eyes. It was a phrase difficult to translate precisely but, more or less, soft eyes meant that he had the ability to see an area, a neighborhood, a house, a room as it was, not as it was expected to be. If you went into a crime scene with preconceptions—with hard eyes—chances were you'd miss what you needed to see in order to make the case. Sometimes not. Sometimes, of course, there was no case to be made, no matter how soft your eyes were. But that was a matter out of Jack's hands, so he never gave it a thought.

Jack walked straight down the center of the room, peered out and down through the windows. They were on the third floor, it was a straight drop down to a blue-gray gravel drive, no trees around, no hedges to break a fall, no wisteria trunk to climb up or down. He turned around, stared straight ahead.

Garner pulled ruminatively on the lobe of his ear. "So far, what? See anything we missed, hotshot?"

Soft eyes be damned. While Jack's dyslexia robbed him of his ability to see verbally, he received something valuable in return. His multisensory mode of seeing the world tapped into the deepest intuition, an area closed off to most human beings. This same strange quirk of the brain caused Einstein to fail at schoolwork yet become one of the greatest mathematical minds of his century. It was also what allowed Leonardo da Vinci to conceive of airplanes and submarines three hundred years before they were invented. These great leaps of intuition were possible because the geniuses who conceived of them were dyslexic; they weren't tied down to the plodding logic of the verbal mind. The verbal mind thinks at a speed of approximately 150 words a minute.

Jack's mind worked at a thousand times that rate. No wonder certain things disoriented him, while he could see through the surfaces of others. Take the crime scene, for instance.

Alli had slept here last night until just after three; then something happened. Had she been surprised, driven out of sleep by a callused hand clamped over her mouth, a cord biting into her wrists? Or had she heard a strange sound, had she been awake when the door opened and the predatory shadow fell on her? Did she have any time before being overpowered, before she was gagged, bound, and spirited out across the black lawn under the black sky? Alli was a smart girl, Jack knew. Even better for her, she was clever. Maybe Emma had been secretly envious of her roommate's ingenuity. The thought saddened him, but wasn't everyone envious of someone, wasn't everyone unhappy with who they were? His parents certainly were, his brother was, up until the moment the bomb took him apart on a preindustrial Iraqi highway, somewhere in the back of beyond. After the explosion and the fire, there wasn't enough left to make a proper ID, so he remained where he died, staring endlessly into the hellish yellow sky that seemed to burn day and night.

These disparate thoughts might have confused a normal mind, but not Jack's. He saw the room in a way that neither Garner nor any of the forensic experts could. To him what he was processing was a series of still frames, three-dimensional images that interlinked into a whole from which his heightened intuition made rapid-fire choices.

"There was only one perp," he said.

"Really?" Garner didn't bother to stifle a laugh. "One man to infiltrate the campus, soundlessly murder two trained Secret Service agents, abduct a twenty-year-old girl, manhandle her back across the campus, and vanish into thin air? You're out of your mind, McClure."

"Nevertheless," Jack said slowly and deliberately, "that's precisely what happened."

Garner could not keep the skepticism off his face. "Okay, assuming for a moment that there's even a remote possibility you're right, how would you know just from looking at the room when a dozen of the best forensic scientists in the country have been over this with a fine-tooth comb without being able to come to that conclusion?"

"First of all, the forensic photos of the Secret Service men showed that they were both killed by a single wound," Jack said, "and that wound was identical on both of them. The chances of two men doing that simultaneously are so remote as to be virtually impossible. Second, unless you're mounting an assault on a drug lord's compound, you're not about to use a squad of people. This is a small campus, but it's guarded by security personnel as well as CCTV cameras. One man—especially someone familiar with the campus security—could get through much more easily than several."

Garner shook his head. "I asked you for evidence, and this is what you come up with?"

"I'm telling you—"

"Enough, McClure. I know you're desperately trying to justify your presence here, but this bullshit just won't cut it. What you're describing is Spider-Man, not a flesh-and-blood perp." Garner, folding his arms across his chest, assumed a superior attitude. "I graduated second in my class at Yale. Where did you go to school, McClure, West Armpit College?"

Jack said nothing. He was on his hands and knees, mini-flashlight on, looking under Alli's bed—

"I've been Homeland Security since the beginning, McClure. Since nine-fucking-eleven."

—not at the carpet, which he saw had been vacuumed by the forensics personnel, but at the underside of the box spring, where there was a small indentation. No, on closer inspection, he saw that it was a hole, no larger than the diameter of a forefinger, in the black-and-white-striped ticking.

"What is it exactly you ATF people do again? Handcuff moonshiners? Prosecute cigarette smugglers?"

Jack kept his tone level. "You ever dismantle a bomb made of ammonium nitrate and fuel oil set in the basement of a high school, or defuse a half pound of C-four in a drug smuggler's lab while the trapped coke-cutter is trying to set it off?"

Garner's cell phone buzzed and he put it to one ear.

"You ever run down a psycho whose lonely pleasure is trapping girls and beating the piss out of them?" Jack continued.

"At least I can read without contorting my brain into a pretzel." Garner turned on his heel, walked out of the room, talking urgently to whoever was on the other end of the line.

Jack felt the heat flame up from his core, move to his cheeks, his extremities, until his hands began to tremble. So Garner knew. Somehow he'd burrowed back into Jack's past to discover the truth. He wanted to lash out, bury his fist in Garner's smug face. It was times like this when his disability made him feel small, helpless. He was a freak; he'd always be a freak. He was trapped inside this fucked-up brain of his with no chance of escape. Ever.

Something glimmered briefly as he shone the tiny beam of the mini-flash into the hole. Reaching in, he felt around, extracting a small metal vial with a screw top. Opening it, he saw that it was half-filled with a white powder. Tasting a tiny bit on his fingertip, he confirmed his suspicion. Cocaine.

SEVEN

NINA MILLER lit a clove cigarette, stared at the burning tip for a moment, and gave a small laugh. "Reminds me of my college days. I never lost my taste." She inhaled as slowly, as deeply as if she were drawing in weed, then let the smoke out of her lungs in a soft hiss. Behind her, the sun was going down over the low hills. A dog was barking, but the sound was high-pitched, from an adjoining property, not one of the K-9 sniffers.

She was standing outside of the west dorm, where Alli's room was, leaning against the whitewashed brick, her slim left hip slightly canted. Her right elbow was perched on the top of her left wrist, the left arm hugging her waist. The slow light placed her in the elongated shadow of the roofline.

"Find anything of interest?" she inquired.

"Possibly," Jack said.

"I saw Garner storming out. You got to him, didn't you?"

Jack told her about his single-perp theory.

She frowned. "It does sound hard to believe."

"Thanks so very much."

Her eyes slid toward his face. "Like Garner, I was trained to follow the forensic evidence. The difference between us, however, is that I won't simply dismiss your theory. It's just that I never had an intuition of how to unravel a case. I don't think real life works like that."

Jack felt sorry for her. It was a peculiarly familiar feeling, and then, with a start, he realized it was how he had felt toward Sharon most of the time they were married.

"One thing I will guarantee you," Nina said, breaking in on his thoughts, "that kind of argument won't fly with Garner."

That was when Jack handed her the metal vial. "I found it hidden in the bottom of Alli's box spring. There's cocaine inside."

Nina laughed. "So you found it."

"What?"

"Hugh owes me twenty bucks." She pocketed the vial. "He said you wouldn't find it."

Jack felt like an idiot. "It was a test."

Nina nodded. "He's got it in for you." Abruptly detaching herself from the wall, she threw down her cigarette butt. "Forget that sonovabitch." She moved off to the west, Jack keeping pace beside her.

"Back there," he said slowly, "when you read sections of that report . . ."

"I knew you were having trouble."

"But how?"

"You'll see soon enough."

They went along, paralleling the dorm. Just beyond it was a utility shed. At first it appeared that they were going to skirt the shed. Then, with a look over her shoulder, Nina opened the door.

"Inside," she said. "Quickly."

The moment Jack stepped through the narrow doorway, Nina closed the door behind them. The interior contained a plain wood table, several utilitarian chairs, a brass floor lamp. It was as sparsely furnished as a police interrogation cubicle. The small square window afforded a view down over the end of the rolling lawn to a tree-line beyond which was the wall that bordered the property.

Two people occupied the room. A cone of light from the floorlamp illuminated the sides of their faces. Jack recognized them: Edward Carson and his wife, Lyn. The soon-to-be First Lady, dressed in a dark, rather severely cut tweed suit, a ruffled white silk blouse held closed at the neck with a cameo the color of ripe apricots, stood at the window, arms wrapped tightly around herself, staring blindly at clouds shredded by the wind. Fear and anxiety drew her features inward as if every atom of her being were psychically engaged in protecting her missing daughter.

Jack glanced at Nina. She had learned about his secret from Edward Carson.

Though the president-elect looked similarly haggard, the moment Jack and Nina entered, his sense of moment forced his political facade back on. Back straight, shoulders squared, he smiled his professional smile, the sides of his mouth crinkling along with the corners of his eyes. Those eyes, so much a part of his extraordinary telegenic image, possessed, in person, a glint of steel that did not come through on the TV screen. Or, mused Jack, maybe he was in war mode, all the knives at his disposal being out.

He was sitting at the table, a Bible open to the New Testament. His forefinger hooked at a section of the text, he began to recite from Matthew chapter seven. "'For everyone who asks receives; he who seeks finds; and to him who knocks, the door will be opened. Which of you, if his son asks for bread, will give him a stone?'"

Edward Carson stood up, came around the side of the table. "Jack." He pumped Jack's hand. "Good of you to come. I have best wishes and Godspeed for you from Reverend Taske." He kept a firm grip on Jack's hand. "We've all come a long way, haven't we?"

"Yes, sir, we have, indeed."

"Jack, I never got a chance to thank you properly for your help when we needed to evacuate my office during the anthrax attack in 2001."

"I was just doing my job, sir."

Carson's eyes rested on him warmly. "You and I know that isn't true. Don't be modest, Jack. Those were dark days, indeed, marked by an unknown American terrorist who we never found. Frankly, I don't know how we would have gotten through it without the ATF's help."

"Thank you, sir."

Now the president-elect's other hand closed over Jack's and the familiar voice lowered a notch. "You'll bring her back to us, Jack, won't you?"

The president-elect stared into Jack's eyes with the intensity of a convert. Despite his big-city upbringing, there was something of the rural preacher in him, a magnetic flux that made you want to reach out and touch him, a call to arms that made your pulse race, rushed at you like a freight train. Above all, you longed to believe what he told you—like a father communicating with his son, or at any rate what in Jack's mind was how a father *ought* to communicate with his son. But that was all idealistic claptrap, a pasteboard cutout, a larger-than-life image from the silver screen, where happy endings were manufactured for captive audiences. Unlike reality, which had never been happy for Jack and, he suspected, never would be.

"I'll do my best," Jack said. "I'm honored you asked for me, sir."

"In all honesty, who better, Jack?"

"I appreciate that. Sir, in my opinion the first order of business is to create a plausible cover story." Jack's gaze swung to the woman by the window, who was holding herself together by a supreme force of will. He recalled Sharon in a similar pose, as Emma's coffin was slowly lowered into the ground. He'd heard a whispering then, just as he'd heard in the main building. Sharon said it was the wind in the treetops. He'd believed her, then.

He inclined his head slightly. "Mrs. Carson."

Hearing her name, she started, summoned back into this time, this place. She seemed thin, as if she'd lost her taste for food. For a moment she stared bleakly into Jack's face; then she came away from the window, stood in front of him.

"Ma'am, do your parents still have that olive farm in Umbria?"

"Why, yes, they do."

He looked at Edward Carson. "It seems to me that would be a good place for Alli to be 'spending the holidays,' don't you think?"

"Why, yes, I do." The president-elect put his cell phone to his ear. "I'll have my press secretary get right on it."

Lyn Carson moved toward Jack. "Now I know what you must have gone through, Mr. McClure. Your daughter . . ." She faltered, tears gleaming at the corners of her eyes. She bit her lip, seemed to be mentally counting to ten. When she had herself under control, she said, "You must miss Emma terribly."

"Yes, ma'am, I do."

Finished with his call, the president-elect signaled to his wife and she stepped away, turned her back on them to once again contemplate the world outside, forever changed.

"Jack, I have something to tell you. You've been briefed, no doubt, given the theories, the evidence, et cetera."

"About E-Two. Yes, sir."

"What do you think?"

"I think there's a hidden agenda. E-Two may be a prime suspect, but I don't think it should be the only suspect."

Lyn Carson turned back into the room. Her lips were half-parted, as if she was about to add something, but at a curt shake of her husband's head, she kept her own counsel.

When he spoke again, it was in the same tone, Jack imagined, with which he held sway over backroom caucuses—hushed and conspiratorial. "What's important, Jack, is that you not leap to judgment like these political hacks. I want you to follow your own instinct, develop your own leads. That's why I expended a great deal of political capital to have you reassigned."

Lyn Carson held out her hand. It was very light, very cold, no more than the hollow-boned wing of a bird, but through it pulsed the iron determination of a parent. The terrible agony in her eyes he recognized as his own.

"I'm so awfully sorry."

Her words had a double meaning, and he knew it. She was talking about both Emma and Alli.

"Bring our daughter back to us."

"I'll return her to you." When he squeezed her hand, the bones felt as if they truly were hollow. "I promise."

Tears overflowed from Lyn Carson's eyes, fell one by one at her feet.

EIGHT

YOU SHOULDN'T have promised," Nina said. "You can't guarantee you'll find Alli, let alone bring her back."

Jack found it interesting and enlightening that Nina Miller had been privy to his conversation with the Carsons. Garner's deliberate exclusion was an all-too-graphic example of the schism within the task force, behind which, of course, was the disagreement between the fundamentalist wing of the Republican Party currently in power and the moderate wing about to take that power away from them. It was no surprise that a political agenda governed the task force. This was precisely what Bennett had warned him about, and he knew there was no good news to be had here.

"What I can guarantee is hope," Jack said shortly. "Hope is her food and drink. Only hope will keep her going through the darkest hours."

"Hope dangles people from a slender thread," Nina said. "It's patently unfair."

They had been striding down the hallway. Now Jack stopped, turned to her. "Do you know anything about darkest hours?"

Nina stood staring at him. She didn't answer, because apparently she had nothing to say.

"I've had my darkest hours," Jack continued. "And now the Carsons are having theirs."

He stood very still, but there was so much energy coming off him that Nina, as if slapped in the face, took an involuntary step back.

His eyes glittered. "I *will* bring Alli back, Nina. You can make book on it."

JACK LED her to the right, skirting the shed. There was a swath of lawn, rather narrow by the standards of the rest of the property, beyond which lay a thick stand of fluffy pines and large, gnarled, very old oaks. By the time they reached the trees, Jack had determined that Nina had low-slung hips and a walk that, defying the odds, was distinctly sensual.

"I want you to know . . ." Nina stumbled over a stone as well as her words.

"What?"

"I've . . . had my darkest hours, too."

Jack, navigating through the rooty trees, said nothing.

"When I was a kid." Nina picked her way under tree branches, over exposed roots, the knuckles of angry fists. "My older brother . . . he molested me. . . ."

Jack stopped, turned back to regard her. He was startled at her admission, which couldn't have been easy to make. But then again, it was often easier to confess to a stranger than to someone you knew.

"And when I fought back, he beat me. He said I needed to be punished."

Jack felt a ping, like the ricochet of a steel ball bounding from bumper to bumper in his own shameful pinball machine. "You know that's not true."

Nina's face was pinched, as if she wanted to make the past disappear. "He's married, got two kids. Now he's got a whole new family to dominate. How I hate him. I can't stop." She made a little sound in the back of her throat that was either a laugh or a sob. "My parents loved God, they believed in his loving kindness. How wrong were they?"

"When we were growing up," Jack said, "parents were unconscious when it came to their effect on their kids."

Nina paused for a moment, considering. "Even if you're right, it doesn't make what they did better, does it?"

They resumed their trek through the stand of weeping hemlocks and pin oaks. He heard the rustle of the wind through brittle branches, the hiss of faraway traffic, the call of a winter bird. The melancholy sounds of winter.

At length, Nina said, "Where are we going?"

"There's a secret path." Jack pointed ahead. "Well, it isn't a secret to the juniors and seniors, but to the adults . . ."

They had reached the far side of the tree-line. He took three or four steps to his left, moved some brush away, revealing a narrow, well-trod earthen path through brambly underbrush and the occasional evil-looking hemlock.

"Except you."

He nodded. "Except me."

Nina followed him along the twisting path, at times half bent over in order to avoid shaggy low-hanging branches. Their shoes made dry, crunching sounds, as if they were walking over mounds of dead beetles. The wind, late for an appointment, hurried through the hemlocks. Grim bull briars and brambles pulled at them.

"With all the manicured lawn, why hasn't the school pulled this stuff out?"

"Natural barbed wire," Jack said.

"What do the kids do in here?" With a hard tug, Nina pulled her coat free of a tenacious bramble. "Drugs and sex, I expect."

"I have no doubt that drugs and sex are on the students' minds," Jack said, "but so is escape."

Nina frowned. "Why escape from the lap of luxury?"

"Well, that's the million-dollar question, isn't it?"

"Who told you about it? Emma?"

Jack's laugh held a bitter edge. "Emma never told me anything." Like so much in life, this was a matter of trust. Edward Carson certainly trusted Nina, and she had bravely trusted him with her secret, and that had touched him in a way she could never imagine. "It was Alli. She was worried about Emma."

"Worried? About what?"

"She never said. I got the impression there was only so much she was prepared to tell me. But she did say that several times when Emma thought she was asleep, she crept out of the room. Alli said the one time she followed her, she saw her vanish down this path."

"Did she go after Emma?"

"She didn't say."

"Didn't you ask?"

"I take it you don't have a teenager. I went after Emma myself."

"And what happened?"

They had reached the high brick wall that surrounded the property. It was guarded on this side by a double hedge: low, sheared boxwood in front of tall privet. Jack was already behind the boxwood, had found the slight gap in the stately privet. Pushing aside the sturdy branches, he vanished into the thicket.

When Nina tried to follow him, she found the privet was so thick, she was forced to leave her coat behind, press herself bodily into what she was sure had a moment before been a gap. Shouldering her way through, she found herself on the other side, almost flush up against the brick wall. Jack was on his haunches, hands pulling at the bricks. To Nina's astonishment, they came away easily until he had a pile of approximately twenty, which left a hole in the wall large enough for a human being of small to normal size to wriggle through.

"I followed her through here."

Crouching down, Nina saw a wedge of lawn, the bole of a tree, and beyond, a field at the end of which were stands of oaks, birches, and mountain laurels.

"I saw her meet someone; I couldn't tell who, it was just a shadow standing beneath that tree," Jack said. "Either she heard a noise or some instinct caused her to look back. She saw me, she came after me, pushed me back to this side, snarling like an animal." Jack sat back on his haunches, his eyes far away. "We had a real knock-down, drag-out shouting match. She accused me of spying on her, which was, of course, the truth. I told her I wouldn't have had to spy on her if she wasn't sneaking around in the dead of night. That was a mistake. She blew up, said what she did was no business of mine, said she hated my guts, said some things I don't think she really meant, at least I hope not."

Nina was kind enough not to look at him directly. "You never found out?"

Jack dived through the hole in the wall.

ON HANDS and knees they picked their way through. There was about the hole the stink of the grave, a sickly-sweet scent that reminded Jack of the time when he was a kid and the neighbor's black cat got stuck inside the wall of his room and died there, giving off the stench of slow decay. The neighbor, an old woman married to a male harem of feral cats, wanted the black one back, to bury it properly beneath her fig tree, but Jack's father refused. "It's good for the boy to smell death, to understand it, to know it's real," he explained to her papery face and sour breath. "He needs to know that his life isn't infinite, that death will come for him, like it does for everyone, one day."

In starless night, he lay in rageful silence, listening to the sound of his own ragged heart as he breathed in the stench that penetrated to the pit of his stomach until, unable to keep to inaction, he ran across the hall, there to violently lose his supper in the low porcelain bowl. In the adjacent room, his parents made love aggressively, raucous as sailors on shore leave, with no thought that they were not alone.

JACK AND Nina stood close together on the other side. Jack wondered whether Nina was thinking the same thing he was: *Is this how Alli's abductors smuggled her out of the school?* Over Nina's right shoulder, the hills rolled on, leading eventually to the Georgetown Pike.

Saigon Road, the site of Emma's crash, lay just five miles west down the Pike. He felt a stirring, as if a cold wind were blowing on the back of his neck. A prickling of his scalp. Was Emma here in some form or other? Was such a thing possible? In the course of his work, he'd come across a psychic who believed that spirits of the dead who had unfinished business couldn't cross over into the light or the dark until that business was finished. These thoughts sent his mind racing back to when Emma was alive.

At Sharon's fierce insistence, Emma had applied to Langley Fields. Jack saw no need for his daughter to be sequestered in what seemed like a four-year straitjacket, but Sharon had prevailed. The education was exceptional, she argued, and Emma would be exposed to a wide variety of students from all over the world. All Jack saw was the pretension of the consumerati: Mercedes, Bentleys, and tricked-out Hummers disgorging siliconed mothers, cell phones blaring Britney Spears, yapping dogs the size of New York City rats, the flash of platinum Amex cards held aloft. He had been obliged to take out a second mortgage on their house in order to pay the exorbitant tuition. He fervently wished he'd fought harder, insisted that she attend Georgetown or even George Washington, the other colleges to which she'd wanted to go, but Sharon had dug in her heels, wouldn't listen to either him or

Emma. She wanted her daughter to have the kind of education she herself had always dreamed of getting, but never had.

Nina said, "I feel I should warn you that if Hugh Garner got wind of our roles in his task force, he'd find some way to discredit us with the powers that be, so that even the president-elect couldn't save us. That's what a political animal would do."

"I don't concern myself with politics," Jack said, his mind still engaged by Emma.

"I'm with you on that, but you'd better give it some attention now." Without her coat Nina shivered against the advancing chill of evening. "Hugh Garner is a political animal, par excellence."

Jack took off his coat, but before he had a chance to sling it across her shoulders, Nina shook her head.

"Alli's life is beyond adversarial parties, beyond politics altogether."

"I suppose it would be," Nina said dryly, "in another universe."

Nina looked around at the thick stand of old oaks, gnarled into fantastic shapes, the sly shadows moving in and out beneath the cathedraled branches. "This place reminds me of something. I almost expect the devil to come bounding through the trees."

"Why d'you say that?"

Nina shrugged. "Ever since childhood, I've expected dreadful things to happen that I can't escape."

Jack inclined his head. "It's only the path the students take into the heart of the trees."

"Who knows what goes on here?"

They picked their way through the failing light into the clotted shadows of a dense copse of trees. The heavy rain had thickened the underbrush considerably, made the ground springy, in places almost marshy, impeding or slowing their progress. A moment later, ducking around a low-hanging tree limb, they burst out into a tiny clearing. The last rays of slanted sunlight turned the copse's heart a reddish gold, as if they had stumbled upon a coppersmith's workshop. An immodest west wind molded Nina's skirt to her well-muscled thighs, provoked eerie sounds from the interweaving of branches that spread weblike all around them.

At the base of a tree, where the root flare rose up just above the ground, was a mound of freshly dug earth.

"What have we here?"

She followed Jack as he knelt beside the mound of earth. Scooping the earth aside revealed a recently dug hole. Jack pulled out an odd-shaped item six or seven inches on a side wrapped in oilskin.

Nina's mouth opened. "What the hell—?"

Carefully, Jack brushed off the dirt and skeletal leaves that had adhered to the oilskin, peeled back the moist covering, revealed inch by inch what was inside.

Pale, almost opalescent flesh appeared to bleed in the ruddy sunset light. It was a hand, smallish, delicate of fingers, ringed, nails blunt-cut like a boy's. Nevertheless, it was the hand of a young girl—a young girl who had been immersed in water, judging by the deeply wrinkled flesh of the fingertips.

Nina looked at Jack, said, "Dear God, is it Alli Carson's?"

Without touching the hand, Jack scrutinized the gold-and-platinum ring on the pale, cold third finger.

"This is Alli's ring," he said. "I recognize it." He pointed. "Also, look at the nails, no polish or clear lacquer. Alli's nails are square-cut, like a boy's."

"God in heaven," Nina said. "She's been drowned."

NINE

I'VE JUST been reading over E-Two's latest manifesto," the president said when Dennis Paull entered the Oval Office. He had to make way for the National Security Advisor, who was just leaving.

Paull took a seat on the plush chair directly in front of the president's desk. The flags against the wall on either side of the thick drapes shone their colors in the burning lamplight. He felt as tired as they looked. Everyone around him did. In perpetual crisis mode, only the president, who leaned heavily on the advice of his close coterie of neo-conservative consultants, appeared sparkly eyed and rested. Perhaps, Paull thought, it was his faith, his vision, the absolute surety of the path his America was on, that made him burn so bright. Paull himself was ever plagued by doubts about the future, guilt about the past.

"The National Security Advisor brought it over himself." The president raised the sheets of paper. "This is pure evil, Dennis. These people are pure evil. They want to bring down the country, weaken it, make it more vulnerable to foreign extremists of every stripe. They want to destroy everything I've worked toward for eight long years."

"I don't disagree with you, sir," Paull said.

The president threw the papers to the carpet, trampled them underfoot. "We've got to root out E-Two, Dennis."

"Sir, I told you before that in the short time left us, I didn't think we'd be able to do that. Now I know it for a fact. We've been scouring the country for months without the slightest success. Wherever they are, we can't find them."

The president rose, came out from behind his desk, paced back and forth across the thick American blue carpet. "This reminds me of 2001," he said darkly. "We never found the people responsible for those anthrax attacks. That failure has stuck in my craw ever since."

Paull spread his hands. "We tried our best, sir, you know that. Despite millions of dollars and man-hours, we never even got to first base. You know my theory, sir."

The president shook his head. "Blaming a rogue element *inside* the government is mighty dangerous speculation, Dennis. Just the sort the National Security Advisor guards against. And he's right. We've all got to work together, Dennis. Circle the wagons. So let's not hear any more of that kind of treasonous talk."

"Yes, sir."

"All right, if we can't find even a trace of E-Two—" The president held up his hand. "We require a change in tactics. Forget about a direct assault on E-Two." His eyes narrowed. "We must make an example of these people. We'll go after the First American Secular Revivalists."

Paull was careful not to let his concern show. "They're a legitimate organization, sir."

The president's face darkened. "Goddamnit, in this day and age we no longer have the luxury of allowing terrorists to hide behind the banner of free speech, which is for good, honest, God-fearing Americans."

"It's not as if they're being funded by a foreign power."

The president whirled. "But maybe they are." His eyes were gleaming, always a dangerous sign. "President Yukin, who, as you well know, I'll be seeing in a few days, has just announced that he wants to stay on in power." The president grunted. "Lucky bastard. They can do that in Russia." He waved a hand. "With the evidence in the Black File you've provided me, I think I can get more out of him than concessions on oil, gas, and uranium."

Paull, truly alarmed, stood. "What do you mean, sir?"

"I think Yukin is just the man to provide whatever evidence we need that the Chinese are funneling funds to these missionary secularists."

Paull smelled the National Security Advisor all over this. The president didn't have the mind to come up with such a scheme.

"I mean, what could be more obvious?" the president went on. "You yourself told me that Beijing is in the process of setting up a Godless state. Americans have a long history of bitter antipathy toward mainland China. Everybody will be only too willing to believe that Beijing is attempting to export that Godlessness to America."

JACK HAD tried Egon Schiltz's cell, but it was off, and he knew better than to leave a message on his friend's voice mail.

Egon Schiltz was not an old man, but he sure looked like one. In fact, give him a passing glance and he might be mistaken for seventy, instead of fifty-nine. Like a hairstylist, he was round-shouldered, with prematurely gray hair so thick, he preferred to wear it long over his ears. In every other way, however, Egon Schiltz appeared nondescript. One curious thing about him: He and his wife had tied the knot in the ME's cold room, surrounded by friends, family, and the recently and violently departed.

He and Jack had become friends when Jack was asked to investigate missing cartons of fry, as embalming fluid was known on the District's streets, where it had become one of a number of increasingly bizarre drugs illicitly for sale. On anyone's list of bad drugs, fry was near the top, one of the long-term side effects of ingesting fry being the slow disintegration of the spinal cord. Certain bits of evidence were leading the police to suspect Schiltz himself of trafficking in fry, but after a long talk with Schiltz, Jack didn't like the ME as a prime suspect. Jack went looking for the middle man, in his experience usually the easiest to latch on to, since he was usually less off the grid than either the thief or the pusher. Using his contacts, Jack found this particular fence, put the hammer to him, and came up with a name, which he gave to Schiltz. Together, they worked out the way to trap the thief, a member of the ME's staff too impatient to wait for his state pension. Schiltz never forgot Jack's faith in him.

Schiltz's offices, sprawled on a stretch of Braddock Avenue in Fairfax, Virginia, were in a low, angular redbrick government building in that modern style so bland, it seemed to disappear. Using mostly the Innerloop of the Capital Beltway, it took Jack just over twenty minutes to drive the 16.7 miles from Langley Fields to Schiltz's office.

"Dr. Schiltz isn't here," the diminutive assistant ME said.

"Where is he?" Jack demanded. "I know you know," he added as her lips parted, "so don't stonewall."

The AME shook her head. "He'll take my head off."

"Not when he knows I'm looking for him." Jack leaned in, his eyes bright as an attack dog's. "You're new here, aren't you?"

She bit her lip, said nothing.

"Call him," he said now, "and tell him Jack needs to see him, stat."

The Indian woman picked up a cordless phone, dialed a number. She waited a moment, then asked to speak with Dr. Schiltz. In a moment, he came on the line, because she said, "I'm so sorry to bother you at dinner, sir, but—"

"Never mind," Jack said, hustling out of the office.

EGON SCHILTZ was an Old Southern type. His meals were sacred time, not to be interrupted for anyone or anything. A creature of habit, he always ate his meals at one place.

The Southern Roadhouse, set back in a strip mall as nondescript as Schiltz himself, was fronted by gravel ground down over the years to the size and shape of frozen peas. Its mock Southern columns out front only added to the exhausted air of the place. At one time, the restaurant had had a platoon of white-gloved attendants, all black, to greet the patrons, park their Caddies and Benzes, wish them good evening. It still had two sets of bathrooms at opposite ends of the U-shaped building, one originally for whites, the other originally for blacks, though no one connected with the place spoke about their history, at least not to strangers. Among themselves, however, a string of ascendingly offensive jokes about the bathrooms made the rounds like a sexually transmitted disease.

Jack walked in the kitchen door, showed his ID to the chef, whose indignation crumbled before his fear of the law. How many illegals were in his employ in the steamy, clamorous kitchen?

"Dr. Schiltz," Jack said as they made room for the expediter, bellowing orders to the line chefs. "Has he finished his porterhouse?"

The chef, a portly man with thinning hair and watery eyes, nodded. "We're just preparing his floating island."

"Forget that. Give me a clean dessert plate," Jack ordered.

One was produced within seconds. The chef nearly fainted when he saw what Jack put on the center of it. With a squeak like a flattened mouse, the chef turned away.

Holding the plate up high in waiterly fashion, Jack put right shoulder against the swinging door, went from kitchen to dining room with snappy aplomb, and immediately stopped so short, the hand almost slid off the plate. Egon Schiltz sat at his customary corner table, but he wasn't alone. Of course he wasn't. He made it a point to have dinner with at least one member of his family even when he was working late. Tonight was his daughter Molly's turn. *Same age as Emma,* Jack thought. *Look at them talking, laughing. Is that what it means to have a daughter?* All at once, his eyes burned and he couldn't catch his breath. *Jesus God,* he thought, *it's never going to get any better, I'm never going to be able to live with this.*

Molly, catching sight of him, leapt up, ran over to him so quickly that Jack had just enough time to raise the tray above the level of her head.

"Uncle Jack!" she cried. She had a wide, open face, bright blue eyes, hair the color of cornsilk. She was a cheerleader at school. "How are you?"

"Fine, poppet. You're looking quite grown up."

She made a face, tilted her head. "What's that?"

"Something for your father."

"Let me see." She rose on tiptoes.

"It's a surprise."

"I won't tell him. It's in the vault, I swear." She put on her most serious face. "Nothing gets out of the vault. Ever."

"He'd tell by your reaction," Jack said. *You can say that again,* he thought.

She waited a moment until she was sure Jack really wouldn't let her in on the surprise. "Oh, all right." She kissed his cheek. "I've got to go anyway. Rick's waiting for me."

Jack looked down into her shy smile. She still had her baby fat around her jawline and chin, but she was already a handsome young woman. "Since when have things become serious between you and Rick?"

"Oh, Uncle Jack, could you be more out of the loop?" She caught herself then. "Oh God, I'm so sorry."

He ruffled her hair. "It's okay." But it wasn't. He heard a sharp sound, was sure it was his heart breaking.

Molly turned. "Bye, Daddy." She waved and was off out the front door.

Schiltz sighed as he flapped a folded copy of today's *Washington Post*. "Speaking of Rick, I was just underscoring to Molly how religion and adherence to God's commandments will protect her against the wages of sin, which these days are all too evident. Senator George is the object lesson du jour. I suppose you heard that august Democrat has been exposed as an adulterer."

"Frankly, I haven't had time for Beltway gossip."

"Is that why I don't see you anymore? How long has it been?"

"Sorry about that, Egon."

Schiltz grunted as he slipped the paper into his briefcase. He nodded at the plate Jack was holding aloft. "Is that my floating island?"

"Not exactly." Jack placed the plate on the table in front of the ME.

Schiltz redirected his attention from Jack's face to the severed human hand on the dessert plate. "Very funny." He took up the plate by its edge. "Would you tell Karl I want my floating island now."

"I'm afraid that won't be possible. Your presence is needed elsewhere."

Schiltz glanced at Jack. Carefully, he placed the plate back down on the immaculate linen tablecloth. Not even a crumb of roll marred its starched white surface. The same could be said, in terms of emotion, for Schiltz's face. Then he broke out into peals of laughter. "You dog, you," he said, wiping his eyes. He stood up to briefly embrace his friend. "I've missed you, buddy."

"Back atcha, Slim." Jack disentangled himself. "But honestly, I need your help. Now."

"Slow down. I haven't laid eyes on you for months." Schiltz gestured for Jack to sit on the chair vacated by his daughter.

"No time, Egon."

"'No time to say hello, good-bye, I'm late, I'm late, I'm late!'"

Schiltz quoted the White Rabbit in Bugs Bunny's voice, which no matter his mood made Jack laugh.

"There's always time," he continued, sobering. "Give the hysteria of logic a rest."

"Logic is all I have, Egon."

"That's sad, Jack. Truly." He took a Cohiba Corona Especial out of his breast pocket, offered it to Jack, who refused. "I would have thought Emma's tragic death would have taught you the futility of a logic-based life."

Jack felt sweat break out at the back of his neck. His face was burning, and there was the same sick feeling in the pit of his stomach he'd had when he'd seen Emma in Saigon Road. In order to steady himself, he turned the chair around, pushed aside his holstered Glock G36, sat straddling the seat. "And you think faith is better."

"I *know* it's better." Schiltz sat back, lit the cigar, turning it slowly, lovingly between his thumb and first two fingers as he took his first tentative puffs. "Logic stems from the mind of man, therefore it's limited, it's flawed. Faith gives you hope, keeps you from despair. Faith is what picks you up and ensures you keep going. Logic keeps you lying facedown in the muck at your feet." He waved the gray end of the cigar. "Case in point: I'm certain you're convinced that Emma's death was senseless."

Jack gripped the table edge with both hands.

"I don't. She left us for a reason, Jack. A reason only God can know. I believe that with all my heart and soul, because I have faith."

Say what you want about Schiltz, he knew how to hunt and he smoked only the finest cigars. These attributes were sometimes all that kept Jack from strangling him.

"Jack, I know how much you're hurting."

"And you're not? You knew Emma as well as I know Molly. We had cookouts together, went camping in the Smokies, hiked the Blue Ridge together."

"Of course I grieve for her. The difference is that I'm able to put her death into a larger context."

"Egon, I need to make sense of it," Jack said almost desperately.

"A quixotic desire, my friend. The help you need you will find only in faith."

"Where you see faith, I see doubt, confusion, chaos. Situation normal, all fucked up."

The ME shook his head. "I'm saying this as a friend: It's time to stop feeling sorry for yourself."

Jack reflexively blocked that advice by going on the offensive. "So what is faith, exactly, Egon? I've never quite been able to get a handle on it."

Schiltz rolled ash into a cut-glass ashtray. "If you insist on reducing it to its basic elements, it's the sure and simple knowledge that there's something more out there, something greater than yourself, than mankind: a grand plan, a design that can't be comprehended by you or by any other human being, because it is numinous, it is God's design, something only He can fathom."

"What about the angels? Can they fathom God's plan?"

Schiltz expelled a cloud of highly aromatic smoke. "You see how logic binds you to the earth, Jack? It ensures you dismiss with a joke anything you can't understand."

"Like angels on unicycles, for instance."

"Yes, Jack." Egon refused to rise to the joke. "Just like angels on unicycles."

"Then Emma, up in heaven, must know God's plan for her."

"Certainly."

"She's content then."

Schiltz's eyes narrowed slightly behind the aromatic blue smoke. "All who are in heaven are content."

"Says who?"

"We have the Word of God."

"In a book written by men."

Egon gave Jack a look he might have reserved for the devil. "I suppose there's only one way to get rid of you tonight," he sighed.

WHAT DO you want me to tell you about the hand?"

"Whether or not it belongs to Alli Carson."

That got Schiltz's attention. His white eyebrows shot up, cartoonstyle. "The president-elect's daughter?"

"The same."

Jack and Schiltz faced each other in the autopsy room, lights low to cut down on the glare from all the stainless steel and tile.

Schiltz snapped on rubber gloves, placed a magnifying lens over his right eye. Then he adjusted a spotlight, the beam illuminating the hand. He bent over, his shoulders rolled forward, a hunchback in his ill-lit garret beside the stone belfry. "Waterlogged as hell," he said gloomily, "so you can forget about anything like DNA testing." His fingertips moved the hand. "Interesting."

"What is?" Jack prompted.

"The hand was sawn off, expertly."

"With a chain saw?"

"That would be a logical assumption." Was there a touch of irony in his voice? He held up the hand, stump first. "But the markings indicate otherwise. Something rotary, certainly. But delicate." He shrugged. "My best guess would be a medical saw."

Jack leaned in. The stench of formaldehyde and acetone was nauseating. "We looking at a surgeon as the perp?"

"Possibly."

"Well, that narrows it down to a couple hundred million."

"Amusing." Schiltz glanced up. "Here's what I do know: This was done with a sure hand, no remorse in the cut, no hesitation whatsoever. Plus, the immersion in water has made the pruning permanent. He's betting we won't be able to get fingerprints to make an ID."

"So—what?—the perp's done this sort of thing before?"

"Uh-huh."

Jack held up the gold-and-platinum ring in its plastic evidence bag. "I took this off the third finger. It belongs to Alli Carson."

"Which doesn't speak to her state of health." Seeing Jack blanch, he hastened to add, "All it means is your perp has access to her." Schiltz used a dental pick to scrape under and around the nails, one at a time. "Look." Holding aloft the implement so that the working end was directly in the light, he said, "What do you see here?"

"Something pink," Jack said.

"And shiny." Schiltz put the end of the pick close to his eye. "This is undoubtedly nail polish. Plus, the nails are newly cut, so my guess is that for whatever reason—"

"The perp cut this girl's nails and removed the polish," Jack finished for him. He stood up. "Alli Carson never wore polish; her nails were square-cut, like a boy's. This isn't her hand."

"You may be sure, Jack, but I'm a forensic pathologist. I need proof before I say yea or nay." He went to a sink, filled a pan with warm water. Immersing the hand in it, he gently loosened the skin, worked it off, starting at the wrist. The gray, amorphous jellyfish swam in the water. With the care of a lepidopterist working on a butterfly's wing, Schiltz unrolled the translucent material.

"Ami!" he called.

A moment later, the AME poked her head into the room. "Yes, sir."

"Got a fingerprint job for you."

Ami nodded, took a place beside him.

"Left hand," he said.

Ami put her left hand into the water. Schiltz rolled the skin over her hand like a glove. Ami air-dried the skin by holding her left hand aloft. Then he fingerprinted the human glove.

"You see," he said, rolling each finger on the ink pad, "wearing the skin smooths out the pruning." He held up the fingerprint card, nodded to Ami, who removed the skin, took the card, and went away. "We'll soon know whether or not this hand belongs to Alli Carson."

He took the severed hand out of its warm-water bath, laid it back on the metal examining tray, studying it once again. "Care to make a bet?" he said dryly.

"I know it's not hers," Jack said.

Several moments later, Ami popped back into the room. "No match in any system for the Jane Doe," she said. "One thing is certain, she isn't Alli Carson."

Jack breathed a huge sigh of relief, dialed Nina's cell, told her the good news. Pocketing his cell, he tapped a forefinger against his lips. "Alli's ring, the nails cut to Alli's length, the water pruning of the fingertips—clearly, someone wants us to believe this is her hand. Why play this grisly game? Why go to all the trouble?" Why had he taken her? What did Alli's abductor want? "What sick mind has maimed a girl Alli's age just to play a trick on us?"

"A very sick mind, indeed, Jack." Schiltz turned the hand over. "He cut the hand off while the girl was still alive."

RAIN MADE a stage set of the parking lot, beaded silver curtains slid down the beams of the arc lights. Jack walked through the glimmer of the near-deserted asphalt. After jerking open the car door, he slid in behind the wheel, fired the ignition. But he didn't pull out. The events of this morning overran him. His head pounded; every muscle in his body seemed to be screaming at once. Leaning over, he opened the glove box, shook out four ibuprofen, crunched down on them, wincing at the harsh, acidic taste.

He thought about the girl's hand. The abductor had immersed it in water so they wouldn't be able to ID her through fingerprints. But Egon had used it to prove that the hand didn't belong to Alli

Carson. And yet the abductor had sawn the hand off while the girl was still alive? Why had he done that? Everything else that Jack had seen led him to believe that this man was methodical, not maniacal. What if he wanted them to know that Alli was still alive? He'd made certain of that by cutting off the hand of a living girl. But he hadn't cut Alli's hand off. Why not? Jack's thoughts chased each other like flashes of lightning. He rubbed his forehead with the heels of his hands.

Beyond the lot, out on the interstate, an unending Morse code of lights flashed across his face, strobed against his eyes, doubling his headache. Neon signs flashed pink and green like bioluminescent creatures deep in the ocean's heart. A horn blared, carrying the diminishing sound behind it like a tail. The rhythmic thrash of the windshield wipers was like his father's admonishing finger. With a convulsive lunge of his hand, he turned off the ignition, watched the rain slalom down the glass.

Alli, he thought, *where the hell are you? What's happening to you?*

He was powerless to stop his thoughts moving toward Emma. His longing to talk with his daughter, so that she could spread the balm of forgiveness over him, brought tears to his eyes. His hands shook.

It's time to stop feeling sorry for yourself. Schiltz's advice came back to him like an echo in a cave. He knew his friend was right, but God forgive him, he couldn't stop. He was like an alcoholic with a bottle to his mouth. Every fiber in his being ached for the chance to say he was sorry, to tell Emma how much he loved her. Why was it, he asked himself despairingly, that he could acknowledge his love for her only now, when it was too late? He slammed his fist against the steering wheel, making the car shiver around him like Jell-O.

He looked up, unsure whether it was the rain or his tears he was seeing. He felt, rather than saw, a shimmer, as if the shadowy air at the corners of his vision rippled like the surface of Bear Creek Lake. Startled, he looked around and smelled Emma's scent. Was that her face he saw staring back at him in the rearview mirror? He whirled around, but his nose was filled with the cloying stench of hot metal, stripped rubber, and burnt flesh.

Gasping, he wrenched open the door, stumbled to his knees on the asphalt, head hanging down. The rain fell on him with an indifference that made him pound his fist against the car door. Pulling himself up on the door handle, he peered through the rain-beaded window. The backseat was empty. As he rested his forehead against the glass, his mind whirled backwards, into the dark whirlpool of the past.

He had taken Emma, Egon, and Molly to Cumberland State Forest to hike and fish in Bear Creek Lake. The girls were ten. He had bought Emma a Daisy air rifle. One afternoon she had come running back to camp, her eyes streaming with tears. She had aimed her rifle at a bluebird sitting on the branch of a pine and pulled the trigger. She'd never believed she would hit the bird, let alone kill it, but that's precisely what had happened.

She was heartsick, beyond consoling. Jack suggested that they have a funeral and burial. The physical preparations seemed to calm her. But she'd cried all over again when Jack shoveled the dirt over the pathetic fallen bird. Then Emma took the air rifle, hurled it with all her strength into the lake. It sank like a stone, ripples spiraled out from its grave.

That was the last time Jack could remember really being with his daughter. After that, what happened? She grew up too fast? They grew apart too quickly? He was at a loss to understand where the time had gone or how Emma had changed. It was as if he had fallen asleep on a speeding train. He might never have woken up if it hadn't been for the crash.

SCHILTZ OPENED the door in response to Jack's pounding. His rubber gloves were slick with unspeakable substances.

He moved away from the door so Jack could come in. "You look like roadkill. What happened to you downstairs?"

Jack, immersed in the horror of his own personal prison, almost told Schiltz about his ghostly visitations, but he had a conviction that they weren't visitations at all, merely wishful thinking, as if he could wish Emma back to life, or some transparent semblance of life. On the other hand, who but Egon, seeing God's hand in the incredible, the unexplainable, might understand. Nevertheless, Jack chose to keep silent on the matter. It was too personal, too humiliating—he'd seem like a child lost in a ghost story.

"I ran into something that disagreed with me." Sharon constantly accused him of hiding his true feelings behind sarcasm. What did she know?

The offices were shadowed, hushed. Carpeted and wood-paneled, they were a jarring contrast with the banks of stainless steel deathbeds, sluicing hoses, giant floor drains, vats of chemicals, rows of microscopes, tiers of body blocks used to elevate the cadavers' chests for easier entry, drawers filled with the forensic implements of morphology and pathology: bone saws, bread knives, enterotomes, hammers, rib cutters, skull chisels, Striker saws, scalpels, and Hagedorn needles to sew up the bodies when work was done. Jack and Egon skirted the X-ray room and the toxicology lab, went through the standards room, as refined as a Swiss watchmaker's, as blunt as a butcher shop, where cadavers as well as their major organs were weighed and measured. Even in the short corridor they felt the icy breath of the cold room, dim, blued, impersonal as a terminal, hushed as a library.

"So what brings you back? Nowhere else to go on a rainy December night?" Schiltz gestured at the wall of cadaver containers. "Since

I'm not full up, I could give you an overnight berth in my Japanese hotel. It's quiet as the grave and a gourmet continental breakfast is served in the autopsy room starting at eight. Would you like an upper or a lower berth?"

Jack laughed. Egon had the uncanny ability to dislodge his depressions.

"I'm interested in whichever berths the two Secret Service men are in."

"Ah, yes," Egon said. "The men in black."

Having a sense of humor—the darker the better—was essential for an ME, Egon once told Jack. "Professional detachment only gets you so far, because eventually someone gets under your skin," his friend had once told him. "After that, it's every macabre jokester for himself."

Schiltz moved Jack along the rows of gleaming stainless steel containers, opened two side by side at waist height. "In my fascination with your floating island, I forgot all about them. Maybe it's because I didn't do the original autopsies. The law now mandates that in cases of deaths of federal officials, pathologists from the Army Forces Institute of Pathology do the work." He shrugged. "Idiotic, if you ask me, but that's the government for you."

The two cadavers lay on their backs, even features waxy, doll-like, their chests cut and sewn back up in the autopsy T-scar that went from just beneath the collarbone to the lower intestine. "The pathology is yesterday's paper so far as your new compadres are concerned. They came, they saw, they were dead-ended."

"Nothing at all?" Jack said.

"I performed my own autopsies just to make certain. Not so much as a partial print, a stray hair, a scrap of skin, paint or dirt under the nails. No hint of anything that might lead you to ID the perps." Schiltz shrugged again. "Not much to see, either. One stab apiece—hard, direct, no hesitation whatsoever—interstitial, between the third and fourth dorsal ribs, straight into the heart." He paused. "Well, sort of."

Jack's own heart had begun a furious tattoo. "What d'you mean?"

Schiltz turned the first cadaver onto one side, shoved it to the far side of the deathbed, turned it on its stomach. As he performed the same procedure with the second body, Jack peered at the entry wound.

"See here. I peeled back the muscle so I could get a closer look at the interior wounds. Smooth as silk, so the assailant didn't use a serrated blade, but there was a slight curve to them. I can't quite make out what sort of blade would leave that signature."

But I can, Jack thought. He'd seen that odd, slightly arced wound before, once, twenty-five years ago. His subsequent investigation, all on his own, both dangerous and difficult, had unearthed the murder weapon: a thin-bladed knife, known as a paletta. It was used by professional bakers to spread batter or apply frosting. The truly odd part was this: A paletta had a rounded end. It was totally useless for a stabbing attack. This one, however, was unique among palettas: the murderer had ground the end into a mercilessly sharp point.

"You okay?" Schiltz peered into Jack's frozen face.

"You bet," Jack said in a strangled voice.

"Stole up behind them and bingo! No fuss, no muss." Schiltz's slightly bored tone indicated he'd been over this terrain numerous times in the past twenty-four hours. "Most professional, not to say impressive, especially in light of the victims' training. In fact, I would venture to say the stabs were surgical in their precision. To tell you the truth, I couldn't have done a better job of it myself."

Jack hardly heard his friend's last sentence. He was frozen, bent over in the space between the deathbeds, his gaze flickering back and forth between the two wounds. His galloping heart seemed to have come to an abrupt and terrifying halt inside his chest.

It's absolutely stone-cold impossible, he told himself. *I shot Cyril Tolkan while he was trying to escape over the rooftop where I'd trapped him. He's dead, I know he is.*

And yet, the evidence of his own eyes was irrefutable. These stabs were the hallmark of a killer Jack had gone after twenty-five years ago, after a murder that had left him devastated, sick with despair.

PART TWO

TEN

JACK, AT fifteen, often cannot sleep. It might be a form of insomnia, but most likely not. He has good reason to stay awake. He lives in a slope-shouldered row house so close to the border of Maryland, it seems as if the District wants it exiled. At night, bedeviled by a fog of anxious stirrings, he lies in bed, staring at the traffic light at the junction of New Hampshire and Eastern Avenues. He lives, eats, and breathes by the rhythm of its changing from red to green. Outside his window, at the eastern border of the District, the city roars, barks, whines, squeals, growls like a pack of feral dogs, glassy-eyed with hunger. Inside the row house, the darkness is filled with dread. It seems to grip his head like a vise squeezed tighter and tighter until he gasps, shoots up in a fountain of bedclothes. This moment is crucial. If the light is green, everything will be okay. But if it's red . . . His heart pounds; the roaring in his ears dizzies him. Disaster.

When he could bear to look back on those nights, he understood that the color of the traffic light didn't matter. The reliance on the pattern set by unknown city workers is an illusion of control over the parts of his life he dreads. But like all children, he relies on illusion to keep his terrors in Pandora's box.

Between the hours of one and three in the morning, his ears are attuned to the heavy tread of his father's footsteps as he returns from work. This particular night is no different. It is June and stifling, not even the smallest squares of laundry stir on the line. A dog lies wheezing asthmatically in the ashy buttocks of the empty lot next to the auto chop shop. An old man wheezes, coughs so long and hard, Jack is afraid he'll hawk up a lung.

The sounds creep in, as if the apartment itself is protesting his father's weight. Every one of the tiny but separate noises that mark his father's slow progress through it sends a squirt of blood into Jack's temples, causing him to wince in pain.

Sometimes that was all that happened, the sounds would gradually ebb, Jack would lie back down, his heartbeat would return to normal, and eventually, he'd drift into a restless sleep. But at other times, the first bars of "California Dreamin'" by the Mamas and the Papas creep into his room, and his heart starts to pound and he has to force himself not to vomit all over the sheets.

"I'd be safe and warm . . ."

The three slices of pepperoni pizza Jack had for dinner rise as if from a magician's wand.

". . . if I was in L.A. . . ."

Stomach acid burns his throat, and he thinks, *Oh God, he's coming.*

The melody takes on a life of its own. Like the notes of a snake charmer, it's filled with an ominous meaning at odds with its original sunny disposition. And like the cobra that hovers and strikes at will, digging its fangs deep into flesh, his father stalks him, the thick black belt he bought in a biker shop in Fort Washington, Maryland, held loosely in his left hand.

It was a time-honored ritual in the McClure household, this whipping. It would have been so much better if the cause had been alcohol because then it wouldn't have been Jack's fault. But it *is* Jack's fault. How many times has his father browbeaten the fact into him?

And Jack's mother, what is her part in this ritual? She stays in her bedroom, behind a tightly closed door that leaks "California Dreamin'" every time her husband wraps the belt around the knuckles of his left fist. Jack, a living example of Skinnerian psychology, prepares himself for the pain when he hears the first bars of flower power sweetly, innocently sung.

Fists aren't what frighten Jack, though his father possesses the big, knuckly rocks of a bricklayer or an assassin. By adult standards, his father isn't particularly big, but with his dark eyes, sullen mouth, and broken nose, he seems like a colossus to Jack. Especially when he's swinging the belt. Following Neanderthal instincts, he turned the biker belt into an ugly, writhing thing. Its armor of metal studs, its crown a buckle big as two fists are not enough. He filed the corners to points one sunny Sunday when Jack was out playing softball.

"Tell me a story, read me a book," his father says as he opens the door to his son's room. He looks around at the unholy mess of clothes, comics, magazines, records, bits of candy bars and chocolate. "Books, books, where are the friggin' books?" He bends down, swipes up a comic. "Batman," he says with a sneer. "How the fuck old are you?"

"Fifteen," Jack answers automatically, though his mouth is dry.

"And all you can read is this junk?" He shoves the comic in his son's face. "Okay then, brainiac, read to me."

Jack's hands tremble so badly, the comic slips through his fingers.

"Open it, John."

Dutifully, Jack flips the pages of the comic. He wants to read, he wants to show his father that he can, but his emotions are in turmoil. He's filled with fear and anxiety, which automatically extinguish what progress he's made in decoding English. He stares down at the comic panels. The speech balloons might as well be written in Mandarin. The letters float off like spiky sea creatures with a will of their own.

He sees them, but he cannot make heads or tails of what they might be. It's garbage in, garbage out.

"God almighty, it's a fucking comic. A six-year-old could read it, but not you, huh?" His father rips the comic from him, flips it into a corner.

"Hey, watch it," Jack says, leaping up.

His father sticks out his right hand, shoves him back onto the bed.

"That's issue number four."

"How the hell would you know?" His father stomps over to the corner, rips up the comic. Batman and his bat-cape are parted.

His father carefully removes his prized gold-and-diamond cuff links from his shirt, knocks a pile of comics off Jack's dresser with a backhand swipe, lays them down on the open space. Then the beating starts. The belt uncoils from his father's fist like an oily viper. It whips up, then down, striping Jack's rib cage. And as the lashing commences in earnest, his father punctuates each singing strike with a litany of words.

"You don't talk right." *Crack!* "You act like a goddamn zombie when I ask you to do something." *Crack!* "You fidget and procrastinate because you're too stupid to understand me." *Crack!* "Christ, fifteen years old and you can't read." *Crack!* "I was already hauling garbage when I was fifteen." *Crack!*

He is breathing hard, his chest rising and falling rapidly. "Where the fuck did you come from?" *Crack!* "Not from me, that's for damn sure!" *Crack!* "A hole in the ground, that's it." *Crack!*

His rage is immense, as large as the Lincoln Memorial, as large as the sky. He is a man who looks upon his son and is diminished. As if something in his seed is defective. He can't bear the thought. Having a son like Jack fills him with rage; the rage fuels his violence.

"Your mother must've fucked some sideshow freak—" *Crack!* "—while I was out trying to make ends meet, John." *Crack!* "John. They call the losers who go to whores johns." *Crack!* "You're a pinhead."

Crack! "A half-wit!" *Crack!* "You give morons a good name." *Crack!* "Stupid would be a big step up for you." *Crack! Crack! Crack!*

Jack's body absorbs the excruciating pain with its usual indifference. In fact, it grows hard and tough under the abuse. It's the words that penetrate to his inner gyroscope, fragile, delicately balanced in the best of times. The litany of hate knocks the pins out from under the gyroscope, the heavy machinery flattens Jack's tattered self-esteem, burying it in the muddy flats at the depths of his being. Belief is as ephemeral as a cloud, shape-shifted by invisible forces. How easily other people's beliefs masquerade as our own. The enemy outside invades, and we, young and impressionable, are vulnerable; the enemy is so insidious that we're changed without even being aware of it. Our cloud shape is altered as we are propelled onward through life.

AFTERWARDS, JACK lies on the blood-smeared sheets. His room is invaded by the howls at the edge of the city. The traffic light at the intersection of Eastern and New Hampshire blinks from red to green and back again. Once again, it has predicted his fate. But now the light is ignored. Jack's mind is busy continuing the punishment his father has meted out. He straddles a widening fault line. This fault line is his; he has manufactured it out of his dim brain, he has spun it from all the things he can't do, all the things he tried to do and failed. His father is right. His fault, his fault line, growing bigger and wider every day.

INSTEAD OF lying in a pool of sweat, waiting for the constellation of dreaded sounds, Jack takes to wandering the flyblown streets. Night shreds like smoke, manhandled by streetlights, neon signs blinking and buzzing like wasps, aggressive arc lights setting filling stations afire in blinding auroras. Shiny faces move in and out of his vision, crossing streets at a cocaine-induced angle, shuffling past him in a bog of alcohol fumes. Hands in pockets, shoulders hunched against wind or rain, he leans against a lamppost on Eastern Avenue, watches the world spin by without him.

It seems as if he has lost himself in the haze of the city. In shop-windows, he looks blurred, as if he is out of focus with the rest of the world. He realizes just how badly out of focus when he is taken behind the local discount electronics store by members of the local gang and beaten senseless for no particular reason save that he's white.

"Yo disrespected us, coming onto our turf." The gang leader spits into Jack's face as Jack sprawls in the filth of the back alley. He is tall—at least a head taller than Jack—and rangy. His eyes are buggy. "We find you here again, we pin yo pale mutherfuckin' ass to the rear end of a garbage truck." He kicks Jack insolently in the groin. "You listenin' t'me, whitey?"

Jack tries to nod, instead groans with the pain.

He must have passed out after that because when he opens his crusted eyes, dawn has crept into the alley. The gang leader and his cabal are nowhere to be seen, but Jack isn't alone.

A man of middle years with an angular face the color of freshly brewed coffee is crouched on his hams, regarding Jack with sympathetic eyes.

"Can you move, son?" He has a voice like liquid velvet, as if he is a singer of love songs.

Fully awake now, racked with pain, Jack pulls himself up against the slimy brick wall at the rear of the electronics shop. He sits with his legs drawn up, wrists resting loosely on his knees. Sucking in deep breaths, he tries to deal with the pain, but it covers so many parts of his body, he feels dizzy and sick in the pit of his stomach. All of a sudden, he rolls over and vomits.

The man with the velvet voice watches this without surprise. When he's certain Jack is finished, he rises, holds out his hand. "You need to get cleaned up. I'll walk you home."

"Don't have a home," Jack says dully.

"Well, I doubt that, son. Honest, I do." The man with the velvet voice pushes his lips out. "Mebbe it's a home you don't feature going back to at this point in time. Is that it?"

Jack nods.

"But you'll want to, I guarantee that." He bends a little, taking Jack's hand in his. "In the meantime, why don't you come with me. We'll mend what needs to be mended, then call your folks. They must be frantic with worry about you."

"They probably don't know I'm gone," Jack says, which probably isn't true, but it's what he feels.

"Still and all, I do believe they have a right to know you're okay."

Jack isn't sure about that at all. Nevertheless, he looks up into the man's face.

"My name's Myron. Myron Taske." Taske smiles with big white teeth. "Will you tell me yours?"

"Jack."

When Myron Taske realizes that's all Jack is going to say, he nods. "Will you let me help you, Jack?"

"Why would you want to help me?" Jack says.

Myron's smile deepens as it grows wider. "Because, son, that's what God wants me to do."

MYRON TASKE is minister of the Renaissance Mission Church farther down Kansas Avenue NE. The clapboard building that houses the church had once been a two-family attached house, but first one family defaulted on their mortgage, then the other. The building was put into receivership by the bank.

"Which was when we bought it," Taske says as he leads Jack through the side door into the rectory. "Lucky for us, one of the bank's vice presidents is a member of our congregation. We were searching for a new home and this became it." He winks. "Got it at a good price."

"But this area's filled with gangs, crime, and drugs," Jack says, and winces as Taske applies peroxide with a swab to his numerous scrapes, cuts, and lacerations.

"And where better to accomplish God's work?" Taske indicates that Jack should take off his shirt. "Which begs the question, what were you doing on that wild corner in the middle of the night?"

"Hanging," Jack says sullenly.

"Why weren't you home and in bed?"

Jack shrugs off his shirt. "I thought it would be safer out on the street."

The reverend stares at the black-and-blue marks across Jack's rib cage. Softly, he says, "You didn't get those tonight, did you?"

Jack bites his lip.

"Father or brother?"

"Don't have a brother, do I?" Jack says defensively. How would things go for him at home if he said his father is beating him? Anyway, it isn't his father's fault that Jack is so stupid.

Myron Taske, silent, contemplative, continues his work patching Jack up. As it turns out, he is a singer, every Sunday, leading the choir in three joyous songs at the end of his sermon. He loves to sing love songs of a sort, love songs to God's grace and goodness here on earth as in the heavens. This he tells Jack as he bandages him up.

"Everyone here is black?" Jack says.

Myron Taske leans back, regarding Jack over small eyeglasses he has set on the bridge of his nose for the close work. "Anyone who wants to be closer to God is welcome here, Jack."

Finished with his work, he packs up the first aid kit, stows it back in a large armoire that dominates one wall. On the opposite wall is a painting of Christ's face, resplendent within a golden aura.

"Do you believe in God, Jack?"

"I . . . I never thought about it."

Myron Taske purses his lips again. "Would you like to now?"

Before Jack can answer, a sharp series of raps comes on the door: three short, two long.

"Just a minute!" Taske calls, but the door swings inward anyway.

The doorway is entirely filled by a man of humongous height and girth. He must weigh close to 350 pounds. He is the color of a moonless night, his eyes yellow, teeth very large, very white, except for his left incisor, which is gold. Embedded in its center is a gleaming diamond. His hands are the size of other people's feet, his feet the size of other people's heads, his skull as bald as a bowling ball and twice as shiny.

"Jeremiah Christmas, Gus, didn't you hear me?"

Gus's face, scarred along both cheeks, is like a black lamp that sucks all the daylight out of the room. His gravelly voice is just as terrifying.

"Sure I heard you, Reverend." He walks into the room on legs whose thighs are so thick, they make him slightly bandy-legged. "I wanted to see for myself who you picked outta the gutter this time."

"News travels fast," Jack says, without thinking. He sucks in his breath as Gus's yellow eyes impale him on a stake.

"Good news travels fast," Gus rumbles. "Bad news travels faster."

"Gus is a storehouse of aphorisms," Myron Taske says for Jack's benefit. "A *vast* storehouse."

Gus's enormous belly shakes when he laughs. He moves into the room like a sumo wrestler, like a force of nature.

Still with his eyes on Jack, he says to Reverend Taske, "This one's different, though. He's white." He squints, addresses Jack without missing a beat. "That's one butt-ugly beating handed to you."

"It was my fault," Jack says.

"Yeah?" This seems to interest Gus. "How you mean?"

"I was standing on the corner over Eastern."

Gus nods his monstrously huge head as he circles Jack. "And?"

"And I got dragged into the alley and beaten. Guy said to me I disrespected him."

Gus appears on the verge of annoyance. "By doing what-all?"

"I was on his turf."

Gus's gaze swings to the reverend. "Andre," is all he says.

Taske nods sorrowfully.

"Shit, I told you the preachin' wasn't gonna work on him." Gus is clearly disgusted.

"How many times have I told you that kind of language has no place in God's house, Augustus," Reverend Taske says sternly.

"Apologies, Reverend." Gus looks abashed.

"Don't apologize to me, Augustus." He gestures with his head. "Do your penance, seek God's forgiveness."

With one last look at Jack, Gus lumbers out, slamming the door behind him.

There is a silence, out of which Jack struggles by saying, "I suppose now you're going to tell me not to worry, that his bark is worse than his bite."

Reverend Taske shakes his head ruefully. "No, son. You don't want to get in the way of Gus's bite." Slapping his palms against his thighs, he says, "Are you ready to go home now?" He looks at his watch. "It's already after eight."

"I'm not going home," Jack says stubbornly.

"Then I'll walk you to school."

Jack ducks his head. "Don't go to school. They don't want me."

There is a small silence. Jack is terrified Myron Taske will ask him why.

Instead, the reverend says, "I'll call Child Services at nine, make sure the beatings don't continue."

Jack bites his lip. Child Services. Strangers. No, then they'll find out how stupid he is, and his father will be even angrier. "Don't call anyone," he says in a voice that catches Taske's attention.

"All right, for the moment I won't," the reverend says, after a moment's pause, "on one condition. I'd very much like you to come back, because it seems to me that you're ready to talk about God."

Jack remains dubious, but he has no choice. Besides, Reverend Taske is so nice, there's a chance he'll get to like Jack, as long as Jack manages not to look or sound stupid around him. That means, among other things, keeping away from any printed matter the reverend might want him to read. Filled with anxiety, he nods his assent.

"Believe me, the first step is the most painful, Jack." Smiling, Myron Taske claps his hand gently on Jack's shoulder. "You're lost now— even you can't deny that. Consider that in finding God you will find yourself."

ELEVEN

THE FIRST Daughter awoke in a room of unknown size; the walls and ceiling, lost in shadows, seemed to mock her. She might have been in a bunker or an auditorium, for all she knew. Whether there were windows here was another mystery impossible for her to solve. A bare lightbulb, surrounded by the knife-edged penumbra of an industrial Bakelite shade, dropped a scorching bomb of light onto her head and shoulders.

She sat bound to a chair that seemed hand-hewn from the heart of a titanic tree. Its ladder back rose to a height above her head; its seat was of woven rush. Lacquered canary yellow, its surfaces were tagged in a graffiti of swooping red and purple, suggesting both bougainvillea and sprays of blood.

Her wrists were fastened to the muscular chair arms with thick leather straps, her ankles bound similarly to the chair legs, as if she were a madwoman in a nineteenth-century asylum. She was dressed in new clothes, not in the sleep shirt and boys' boxers she'd worn to bed. Her feet were bare. She felt the vague need to urinate, but she clamped down on it. She had far bigger problems.

Alli couldn't remember how she got here; she barely recalled the callused hand over her mouth, the nauseating odor of ether rising into her nostrils like swamp gas. After all, it could have been a nightmare. Now she smelled her own sweat, a stew of terror, rage, and helplessness.

"Hello? Hello! Is anybody there? Help! Get me out of here!"

Her straining voice sounded thin and strange to her, as if it were an elastic band pulled past its limits. Sweat rolled down her underarms, rank with fear. Tremors seized her extremities, held them hostage.

This is a dream, she thought. *Any minute I'll wake up in my bed at Langley Fields. If this were real, my bodyguards would have rescued me by now. My father would be here, along with a battalion of Secret Service agents.*

Then a mouse ran across her field of vision—a real, live mouse—and she shrieked.

BLACK HOODIES up over coffee-colored heads, the two young black men overran the block of T Street SE between Sixteenth Street SE and Seventeenth Street SE, the way dogs mark their territory. The Anacostia section of the District was not a good place to be if you weren't black, and even then if you were like these two big, rangy twenty-year-olds, you'd best be on the lookout for Colombians who, sure as hell if they caught you, would accost you, take all your cash, then, like as not, break your ass.

These two were searching for Salvadorans, runty little critters whom they could handle, on whom they could take out their rage, take their cash, then, like as not, break their asses. For years now, the Colombians, who owned the drug trade, had been muscling into the heavily black areas like Anacostia. Skirmishes had turned into battles, front lines fluid day to day. There had yet to be a full-blown turf war, though that level of hostility was in the air, corrosive as acid raid. In the Colombians' wake, slipstreaming like second-tier bicycle racers, came the Salvadorans, nipping at their heels, trying to dip their beaks.

That's the way things worked in Anacostia; that was the pecking order, written in broken bones and blood.

In any event, it was broken bones and blood these two were out for, so when they saw the big old red Chevy drawn to a stop at the traffic light at Oates, fenders sanded down to a dull desert hue, they sprinted in a pincer move, rehearsed and deployed scores of times. These two knew the timing of the lights in Anacostia as if they had installed them themselves; they knew how many seconds they had, what they had to do. They were like calf-ropers let loose in a rodeo, the clock ticking down from 120, and they'd better have made their move before then if they expected to get the prize. Further, they knew every car native to the hood—especially those owned by the Colombians, bombing machines with high-revving engines, ginormous shocks, astounding custom colors that made your eyes throb, your head want to explode. The sanded-down Chevy was unknown to them, so fair game. Inside, a young black male, making that mistake that outsiders made now and again, stopping in Anacostia instead of bombing on through like a bat out of hell, red traffic lights be damned. There wasn't a cop within three miles to stop him.

The truth of it was, he shouldn't have been here at all, so he deserved everything that came to him, which included being hauled out of his car, thrown to the tarmac, derided, pistol-whipped, and kicked until his ribs cracked. Then, tamed and docile, his pockets were ransacked, his cellie, watch, ring, necklace, the whole nine yards disappearing into deep polyester pockets. Took his keys, too, just to teach him a lesson, to be deftly whipped underhand into the yawning slot of a storm drain, there to *click-clack-click* derisively. The two thugs then fled, howling and whooping raggedly into a night with its head pulled in tighter than a turtle's.

RONNIE KRAY, drawn out of a back room by epithets and racial slurs hurled like Molotov cocktails, watched from behind a thickly curtained window as the two punks leapt down the street, whooping, guns raised, the flags of their gang, high on blood-lust. He knew those two, even knew where they had procured those guns, just as he knew every shadowy creepy-crawly of this marginalized neighborhood where civility had been mugged, civilization had fallen asleep and never woken up. He knew the lives they led, the lives they couldn't escape. He used that knowledge when he had to. Those guns, for in-stance, were as old and decrepit as the building stoops, no self-respecting District cop would be caught out on the street with one. But those guns—cheap, disposable, out of control—were all the young men had; in the way young white men in Georgetown had their parents to protect them, these thugs had their guns. And like parents, rich or poor, the weapons would probably fail you when you most needed them.

Ronnie Kray was curdled by these thoughts as he surveyed the graffitied row house fronts, the cyclone fences hemming in patches of dirt and half-dead grass across the empty potholed street. Fear had cleared the area as efficiently as a canister of tear gas. From the fumy gutter a sheet of newspaper lifted into the air, as if being read by one of the many mournful ghosts washed up on the shore of this waste-land. At length, his gaze settled on the one other moving thing in his field of view: the pulped young black man crawling along the gutter, this low thoroughfare the only one open to him. Even so, he quickly exhausted himself, spread-eagled like a starfish in spillage, much of it his own.

Ronnie Kray watched, observant as a hawk overflying a field of rabbit warrens. He could have gone out to help the young man, but he didn't. He could have called 911, but he didn't. In truth, those ideas never crossed his mind. Kray was a missionary, and like all good mis-sionaries, his mind ran along one track. Missionary zeal precluded any deviation whatsoever from his chosen path. So he stood behind the curtain, watching the world at its lowest, meanest ebb, and took heart, for only at the darkest depths, only when all hope is lost, does the catalyst for change raise a spark that turns into the flare of a thousand suns.

The moment was at hand; he knew it as surely as his heart beat or his lungs took in air. At last, when all movement had ceased, he turned and padded silently away, through a front parlor wrapped in the dust of ages. Everywhere lay teetering stacks of old books, abandoned magazines, forgotten vinyl phonograph records in colorful cardboard jackets. They weren't his, so he didn't feel the compulsion to categorize, alphabetize, catalog them, or even to align their edges so they wouldn't make his teeth grind every time he saw them.

On the paneled hallway walls were hung black-and-white photographs of a girl, not more than twenty, with intelligent, wide-apart eyes. The flattened, slightly grainy images of her face were the result of an extended telephoto lens like those used in police and DEA surveillance. In all the photos, the backgrounds were smeared and blurry. But in one or two could be made out a piece of the flag of the United States.

The kitchen was a cheery shade of yellow. It had wooden cupboards, painted a glossy white. Gaily striped café curtains were drawn across the windows. He paused at the soapstone sink, slowly drained a tumbler of cold water, then, after washing the glass with soap and steaming hot water he set it upside down in the precise center of the drainboard. He opened the refrigerator. Inside, all the metal racks had been removed to make room for the girl he'd curled into it, her knees kissing her chin. Her eyes were filmed, her blue-white skin a crush of crepe paper. Her arms were placed on her thighs. Her left hand was missing. Reaching into the triangular space between her heels and her buttocks, he removed a small cloth sack.

Off the kitchen was a small room. Once a pantry, the windowless room was outfitted with a small stainless steel sink, a cupboard straight out of a Grimm fairy tale, a beaten-up chest of drawers salvaged from the street and rehabbed with an exacting attention to detail. At the

chest, he opened drawers that were filled neatly with chemical re-
agents, gleaming scalpels, retractors, sterile syringes, vials of sera all in
perfectly neat rows set within mathematically placed metal dividers.
He took out a pair of surgical pliers, put it in the right-hand pocket of
his overalls.

Reaching up, he opened the cupboard. *Pseudocerastes persicus* coiled
around the semidarkness, neat as a sailor's rope. The light spun off
scales the pale pink of human flesh pulled inside out. The Persian horned
viper raised her head, body uncoiling slowly. The supraorbital horns
made her appear as sinister as a demon. Just below the horns, the ruby
eyes opened and the forked tongue flickered out. Then, catching sight
of the cloth sack, her jaws hinged wide, revealing erected fangs, hollow with venom.

"Ah, Carrie, you sense it, don't you?" Kray crooned softly. The
pink inside of her mouth was almost erotic. People were so predictable,
Kray thought bitterly. But you never knew about Carrie. That was the
delicious part of it, like a spice only he knew about. She could wind
herself lovingly about his wrist for years and then one day sink her
fangs into the meat between his thumb and forefinger. He felt—it was
a French word—a *frisson,* yes, that was it—he felt a frisson electrify his
spine.

"Dinner is served." Opening the sack, he dumped the contents
into his slightly cupped palm. The rat lay on its side, dazed, lethargic
from the cold. Out snaked Carrie's wide, triangular head, its tongue
questing. Coiling around Kray's wrist, the viper's demon head hovered
over the slowly stirring rat.

"That's right," Kray sang. "Eat your fill, baby."

The forked tongue quivered; the head reared back. Just as the rat,
warming, rolled onto its pink feet, Carrie struck, her flat head lanced
forward, her fangs sank to the root into the rat's neck. The rat's eyes
rolled, it tried to extricate itself, but so powerful was the nerve toxin
that it couldn't even move.

Now comes the most beautiful part, Kray thought as Carrie began the long process of swallowing her prey. The miracle of death overtaking life a centimeter at a time. Because, though paralyzed, the rat was still alive, its eyes rolling in terror as its hindquarters were sucked into the viper's throat.

Afterwards, Kray returned to the back room, where he drew out a key attached to a loop on his overalls by a stainless steel chain. Inserting the key in the lock, he walked through.

On the other side, he shut the door, locked it carefully behind him, turned, and said to Alli Carson, "What have they done to you?"

TWELVE

WHEN JACK walks out of Reverend Taske's rectory into the church proper, the first thing he sees is Gus sitting in a pew. His eyes are closed, his lips are moving soundlessly, but the moment Jack tries to glide past, his eyes open, and though he's staring straight ahead, he says, "First time in a place like this, kid?"

Jack feels a tremor run down his spine. "You mean a black church?"

Very slowly, Gus turns his head. His eyes are boiling with rage, and Jack shrinks back into the shadows. "I mean a church, kid."

Jack, hovering, doesn't know what to say.

"I'm talkin' God here."

"I don't know anything about God," Jack says.

"What *do* you know 'bout?"

Jack shrugs, dumbfounded.

"Huh, smart white kid like you. Think you got all the perks, right?" His lips purse. "What you doin' in these parts, anyway? Why ain't you tucked away nice an' cozy in yo' own bed?"

"Don't want to go home."

"Yeah?" Gus raises his eyebrows. "Rather be beaten up in a alley-way?"

"I'm used to being beaten."

Gus stares at him for a long time; then he lumbers to his feet. "Come outta there, kid. Only rats stick to the shadows."

Jack feels like an insect stuck on flypaper. His muscles refuse to obey Gus's command.

Gus squints. "Think I'm gonna hurt you? Huh, that already been done real good."

Jack takes a tentative step forward, even though it means coming closer to the huge man. He smells of tobacco and caramel and Old Spice. Jack's frantic heart lurches into his throat as Gus lays a hand on his shoulder, turns him so that the early morning sun, colored by the handmade stained-glass windows in the church's front, falls on him.

"That little muthafucka Andre."

He looks up into Gus's eyes and sees a curious emotion he can't quite identify.

"Past time someone taught him an' his crew a lesson, what d'you think?"

Jack feels a paralyzing thrill shoot up his spine.

Gus puts a thick forefinger across his lips. "Don't tell the rev. Our secret, right?" He winks at Jack.

MEAN STREETS flee before the grilled prow of Gus's massive Lincoln Continental, white as a cloud, long as the wing of a seagull. Jack, perched on the passenger's seat, feels his heart flutter in his chest. His hands tremble on the dashboard. Below them, dials and gauges rise and fall. Gus is so huge, his seat has been jacked to the end of its tracks, the back levered to an angle so low, anyone else would be staring at the under-side of the roof.

Beyond the windshield, the climbing sun bludgeons blue shadows into gutters and doorways. The wind sends sprays of garbage through the early morning. Soot rises into miniature tornados. An old woman in garters pushes a shopping cart piled high with junk. An emaciated man, fists clenched at his side, howls at invisible demons. An empty beer bottle rolls into his foot and he kicks it viciously. The old woman scuttles after it, stuffs it into her cart, grunting with satisfaction.

But this ever-changing scene with all its sad detail nevertheless seems distant and dull compared with the interior of the car, which is alive with Gus's fevered presence. It is as if his inner rage has frightened the very molecules of the air around him. It feels hot in the car, despite the roar of the air conditioner, and Jack somehow intuits that this unnatural heat is exceedingly dangerous.

Jack went once to the zoo with his class at school, while he was still going to school. He was both drawn to and terrified by the bears. In their black bottomless eyes he saw no malice, only a massive power that could never be harnessed for long, that could turn instantly deadly. He imagined such a bear in his room at night, raising its snout at the small sounds his father made, its wet nostrils flaring at the scent of his father's approach. The music would mean nothing to the bear; it ignored Mama Cass and the others. And when the door to the bedroom swung inward, the bear would swat the man down before he could raise the belt. Of course, no such creature existed—until the moment Jack stepped into the white Lincoln Continental, felt the electricity sizzling and popping as it had through the bars of the bear's cage.

"You know where Andre hangs out," Jack says because he has a desperate need to banish a silence that presses on him like a storm descending.

"Don't know, don't care," Gus says as they round a corner.

Jack is trying hard to follow, but everything that's happened to him over the last several hours is so out of his ken, it seems a losing battle. "But you said—"

Gus gives him a swift look, unreadable, implacable. "It's not for me to punish Andre."

They drive on in silence, until Gus flicks on the cassette player. James Brown's umber voice booms from the speakers: "*You know that man makes money to buy from other man.*"

"It's a man's world," Gus sings, his voice a startling imitation of Brown's. "True dat, bro, it fo' damn sho is."

At length, they draw up in front of the All Around Town bakery on the ground floor of a heavily graffitied tenement. Through the fly-blown plate-glass window, Jack can see several men talking and lounging against shelves stacked with loaves of bread, bins of muffins, tins of cookies.

When he and Gus walk through the front door, he is hit by the yeasty scents of butter and sugar, and something else with a distinct tang. The men fall silent, watching as Gus makes his way toward the glass case at the far end of the narrow shop. No one pays any attention to Jack.

"Cyril," Gus says to the balding man behind the counter.

The balding man wipes his hands on his apron, disappears through an open doorway in the rear wall, down a short passageway lined with stacks of huge cans, boxes, and containers of all sizes, into a back room. Jack observes the men. One curls dirt from beneath his fingernails with a folding knife, another stares at his watch, then at the third man, who rattles the pages of a tip sheet he's reading. None of them look at Gus or say a word to each other or to anyone else.

The balding man returns, nods at Gus.

"C'mon," Gus says, apparently to Jack.

Jack follows him behind the counter. As he passes by, the balding man plucks a chocolate-chip cookie off a pile in the case, gives it to him. Jack chews it thoughtfully, staring at the containers as he walks by.

The passageway gives out onto a cavelike room with a low ceiling the color of burnt bread. It is dominated by a line of enormous stainless steel ovens. A cool wind blows from a pair of huge air-conditioning grilles high up in the wall. Two men in long white aprons go about their laconic task of filling the kneading machines, placing pale, thin loaves into the ovens in neat rows.

Standing in the center of the room is a squat man with the neck of a bull, the head of a bullet. His wide, planular olive-gray face possesses a sleekness that can come only from daily shaves at a barbershop.

"Hello, Cyril," Gus says. He does not extend his hand. Neither does Cyril.

Cyril nods. He takes one glance at Jack, then his round, black eyes center on Gus. "He looks like shit, that kid." He's got a curious accent, as if English isn't his first language.

Gus knows a put-down when he hears one. He chews an imaginary chaw of tobacco ruminatively. "He looks like shit 'cause a Andre."

Cyril, divining the reason for the visit, seems to stiffen minutely. "What's that to me?"

Gus puts one huge hand on Jack's shoulder with an astonishing gentleness. "Jack belongs to me."

The bakers are looking furtively at the two men as if they are titans about to launch lightning bolts at each other.

"I would venture to say Andre didn't know that."

"Andre an' his crew beat the crap outta Jack." Gus's voice is implacable. The inner rage informs his face like heat lightning.

Cyril waits an indecent moment before acquiescing. "I'll take care of it."

"I warned you 'bout that muthafucka," Gus says immediately.

Cyril shows his palms. "I don't want any trouble between us, Gus."

"Huh," Gus grunts. "You already been through *that* bloodbath."

THE LINCOLN Continental is singed with invisible fire as Gus drives them away from the bakery. Gus, brooding, is like a porcupine with his quills bristling.

"That muthafucka," he mouths, his eyes straight ahead. And Jack doesn't know whether he means Andre or Cyril.

"You know that bakery isn't a bakery," Jack says. "First off, there were no customers, just some men standing around." He's afraid of what he's said, afraid that Gus's seething will find its outlet in him. But he can't help himself; it's part of what's wrong with him. His brain is exploding with everything he saw, heard, intuited, extrapolated upon.

"Course it ain't only a bakery. Fuckin' Cyril runs drugs 'n' numbers outta there."

Times like now, when he can focus on what his own brain has recorded, when it shows him the big picture, when he can "read" the signs and from them build a three-dimensional model in his mind, he has a clarity of thought he finds exhilarating. "I mean they're making something more than bread there."

Brakes shriek as all at once his words sink in. Gus pulls the Continental over to the curb. The engine chortles beneath them like a beast coming out of a coma. Gus throws the car into park. His seat groans a protest as he twists around to stare at Jack.

"Kid, what the *hell* you talkin'?"

For once Jack isn't intimidated. He's in his own world now, secure in what he has seen, what he knows, what he will say.

"There was the smell."

"Yeast and butter and sugar, yah."

"*Underneath* all those things there was another smell: sharp and blue."

"*Blue?*" Gus goggles at him. "How the fuck can a smell be blue?"

"It just is," Jack said. "It's blue, like the smell when my mother takes off her nail polish."

"Acetone? Nail polish remover is all acetone. I use it to take glue spots offa stuff people bring in to my pawnshop." Gus's expression is thoughtful now. "What else, kid?"

"Well, that cookie the guy gave me was days old. It should've been fresh. Plus which, whatever he had on his hands wasn't flour or yeast, because his fingertips were stained orange by what he had on them."

Gus appears to think about this revelation for some time. At last he says, as if in a slight daze, "Go on. Anything else?"

Jack nods. "The room with the ovens should've been hot."

"Course it wasn't hot," Gus says. "It's hugely air-conditioned."

"Still," Jack persists, "no heat came from inside when they opened the oven doors. The loaves were too thin to be bread. That wasn't dough they were putting in, it was something that needed drying."

"How the hell—?"

"Also, that guy Cyril is scared of you."

"Huh, you betta believe he is."

"No," Jack says, "I mean he's scared enough to do something about it."

Gus frowns. "You mean he actually wants to move against me?" He shook his head. "No way you could know that, kid."

"But I do."

"Cyril an' I have a treaty—an understanding. Between us now it's live an' let live."

"No, it's not."

Something in Jack's voice—some surety—gives Gus pause. "What are you, kid, a oracle?"

"What's an oracle?" Jack says.

Gus stares out the side window. "You like fried pork chops an' grits?"

"I never had grits."

"Shit, that figures." Gus makes a disgusted face. "White folk."

He puts the car in gear.

THIRTEEN

ALLI CARSON saw the handsome man smile, remove himself from the doorway, pull a folding chair from the shadows. He straddled it, arms folded across the metal-tube back. He radiated a kind of magnetism, strong as her father's, but entirely different: steely, opaque. All she saw when she looked into his face was her own reflection.

"They tied you up, poor girl," he said gently. "I asked them not to do that, but do they listen to me?"

"Who—?" Alli's tongue felt thick and gluey. "I'm so thirsty," she managed to choke out.

The man stepped into the shadows, returned with a glass of water. Alli stared at it, desire flooding her, but fear, too, because there was an unknown world all around her. What horrors lurked there, waiting?

Leaning over her, he tipped the glass against her lower lip. "Slowly," he said as she gulped. "Sip slowly."

Despite her aching thirst, Alli obeyed him. When at last the glass was drained, she ran her tongue around the inside of her mouth. "I don't understand," she said. "Who are 'they,' who are *you*? Why have you brought me here, what do you want?"

He had soft eyes and such a large masculine presence, it seemed to fill the entire lit space.

"Be patient," he said. "In time, all your questions will be answered."

She wanted to believe him. That way lay hope. Hope that she'd soon be freed. "Then can't you at least untie me?"

He shook his head sadly. "That would be most unwise."

"Please. I won't run away, I swear."

"I'd like to believe you, Alli, really I would."

She began to cry. "Why won't you?"

"The others might come in at any time, you see, and then who would be punished? Me. You wouldn't want that, would you?"

She felt desperation fluttering in her breast like a caged bird. "For God's sake, before they come!"

"Are you kidding me?" He said in a voice that lashed her like a whip, "You can't be trusted. You're a liar—and a cheat."

Alli, confused as well as disoriented, said, "I—I don't understand. What are you talking about?"

He produced a thick manila folder, which he opened on his lap. With a shiver, she saw a snapshot of herself stapled to the top sheet of paper. Wasn't this a scene from a film she had seen? And then with an internal shriek she realized that her mind and body had parted company, that she was looking at herself from a distance, or another dimension, where she was safe, would always be safe because nothing could touch her.

She heard someone with her voice say, "What are you holding?"

"Your life." He looked up. "You see, Alli, I know everything about you."

The schism inside her deepened—or widened, whichever. "You don't . . . You couldn't."

His eyes flicked down, skimming information with which she could see he was clearly familiar. "You were born Allison Amanda Carson—Amanda was your maternal grandmother's name—on January twenty-third, daughter of Edward Harrison Carson and Lyn Margaret Carson, née Hayes, married thirty-seven years this past September fourteenth. You were born in Georgetown University Hospital, your blood type is O-negative. You attended Birney Elementary, Lincoln Middle, and—let's see—Banneker High School. At age five you fractured the ulna in your right forearm. At age eight you twisted your left ankle so severely, you were required to wear a cast for seventeen days. Neither injury had a lasting effect.

"In ninth grade you were diagnosed with Graves' disease by your pediatrician—what's his name?" He turned a page. "Ah yes, Dr. Hallow. He recommended you for treatment at Children's Hospital, where you stayed for six days while tests were being performed, medication prescribed and evaluated in your system."

He looked up into Alli's stricken face. "Have I left anything out? I thought not." Returning to the file, he struck himself lightly on the forehead and a smile spread over his face like taffy melting on a July afternoon. "But of course I have! I've failed to mention Barkley. Philip Barkley. But you called him—what? Help me out here, Alli. No? All right, all on my own then. You called him Bark, isn't that right? Bark was your first love, but you never told your parents the truth about you and Bark, did you?"

"There was a reason."

"Of course. There's always a reason," Kray said. "Human beings are so good at rationalization. Did you or did you not tell your parents the truth about Philip Barkley? A simple yes or no will do."

Alli gave a little moan, appearing to sink as much as she was able into the chair.

"You see the futility of your current predicament?"

It was a measure of her mental paralysis that it wasn't until this moment that the thought occurred to her. "How could you possibly know about Bark? I never told anyone about—"

"That night on the raft?"

She gasped. "It's impossible! You *couldn't* know!"

"And yet I do. How to reconcile this seeming impossibility?" He cocked his head. "Would it help if I tell you that my name is Ronnie Kray?"

Some inarticulate sound got caught in the back of Alli's throat, and she almost gagged.

I'M A PRISONER, Lyn Carson thought for the first time in her life. She, her support staff, and her bodyguards were in a motorcade, on their way from a luncheon, where she'd spoken to the Washington Ladies' something-or-other, to a fund-raiser where she was standing in for her husband, who was God knew where, doing God knew what. This morning, she had been on *Good Morning, America.* She barely remembered what she'd said.

Normally, she loved these functions; they allowed her to feel senatorial—and now presidential—all on her own without feeling like Edward's elbow. But these days, she was so preoccupied with thoughts of Alli that the luncheons, fund-raisers, photo ops . . . these days what an effort it was to keep her smile intact, the tasks that usually filled her with joy dragged by like a ragged filmstrip. *What a useless process life is,* she thought as the armored limo sped her crosstown, traffic peeling away, pedestrians peering briefly, wondering which member of the government was passing by. *Without Alli, my life is without purpose.*

In desperation, she pulled out her cell phone, dialed an overseas number. Checking her watch, she calculated it would be just after dinnertime in Umbria. Blue shadows would have already fallen over the olive groves, the ancient stone house would be lit by warm light and the smells of tomato sauce and roasted meat would have permeated the thick-walled rooms. Perhaps music would be playing softly.

"Hi, Mom," she said when the familiar voice answered. "Yes, I'm fine, everything's fine. Of course, Alli misses you, too."

She listened for some time to the melodious drone. Not that she was uninterested in what was fresh in the market that day or the old man who pressed their olives into fragrant green oil, the one who was teaching her to speak like an Umbrian. It was simply that her parents' world seemed so far away, so carefree it was almost criminal. She felt suddenly older than her own mother, who continued rabbiting on about this year's oil, the *cinghiale* they'd eaten for dinner, the series of paintings her father was completing.

Suddenly, she realized that this was no respite. As long as Alli was missing, there was no respite for her. She could run herself ragged with daily tasks, mindless work, but it wouldn't change reality one iota. The nightmare descended on her once again, roosting on her shoulder like a vulture.

"I've got to go now, Mom." She almost choked on her emotions, had to bite back the words that threatened to keep tumbling out: *Mom, Alli's been abducted. We don't know whether she's alive or dead.* "Our love to you and to Dad."

She snapped the phone shut, bit down on it until the metal showed the marks of her small white teeth.

ON THAT note, maybe we should talk about Emma, your best friend," Ronnie Kray said. "Our mutual acquaintance." He slipped a photo out of the file, held it up for Alli to see. It was a snapshot, slightly grainy, of two girls walking across the Langley Fields campus. "Recognize the two of you? You and Emma McClure."

Alli, staring at the photograph, remembered the moment: It was October 1, just after noon. She remembered what they were talking about. How could she forget! Seeing that intimate moment preserved, knowing that she and Emma had been spied upon gave her the willies. Then it hit her like a ton of bricks: The surveillance had been going on a long, long time. Someone—maybe the man facing her— had wormed himself into her bed, under her skin, wrapped himself around her bones, lying out of sight while she, unknowing, went about her life. She had to fight the queasy churning of her stomach.

Having read both *1984* and *Brave New World,* having her own life so tightly controlled, she was under the impression that she knew the meaning of intrusion. But this invasion was monstrous, Big Brother on steroids.

"I told Emma about Bark." Her mind was racing so fast, she grew dizzy, even more disoriented. "Emma told you?"

"Did she? What do you think?"

"What do I think?" she echoed stupidly. She felt as if she were in an elevator whose cable had been cut, was now in free fall. "I knew her. She couldn't, she wouldn't."

He cocked his head. "May I ask what might seem an impertinent question? What in the world were you doing slumming? Emma McClure wasn't from your socioeconomic class. She was rough-and-tumble, from the wrong side of the tracks, as we said back in the day. Not your kind at all."

Alli's eyes blazed. "That just shows how much you *don't* know!"

His face hardened like a fist. "I thought we were friends. I was even thinking of untying you, despite the danger it would put me in. But now . . ."

"Please untie me. I'm sorry I talked to you that way." Her cresting fear made her voice quaver like a glass about to shatter. "I'll never do it again, if only you'll untie me."

He shook his head.

The pain congealed with outrage into an intolerable barb inside her. "You can't treat me like this! My father will move heaven and earth to find me!"

Abruptly, Kray took out surgical pliers. Alli thought she was going to pass out. What was he planning to do to her? She'd seen plenty of films filled with scenes of torture. She tried to remember what happened in those scenes, but her mind was blind with panic. Her terror mounted to unbearable heights.

She watched him stand up. She was shaking now, couldn't take her eyes off the pliers, which, glowing, swung in a short arc, back and forth. Then, without any warning, Kray disappeared into the blackness.

Alli couldn't believe it, but she actually began to weep. She tried to stop, but her body wouldn't obey. Some animal part of her nervous system had been activated. What she was feeling she could neither believe nor abide: She wanted him back. The feeling was so powerful, it was as physical as the pliers.

He was her only connection to the outside world, to life. "Don't leave me alone!" she wailed. "I don't care what you do to me, I'll *never* tell you about Emma," she said through her tears.

"Quite the little loyalist, aren't you?" His voice came from the darkness. "No matter. As it happens, I already know all I need to know about Emma McClure."

She felt a wave of nausea as her terror ratcheted up.

"No, no! Please!"

She wanted to shrink into the chair, to disappear like him, but she remained in the cone of light. She hung her head, the blood pounding in her temples.

"What is it?" Kray said, his voice suddenly soft. "I'm a reasonable man. Tell me."

She shook her head. Her fear clouded her eyes.

Kray stepped into the light. "Alli, please speak to me." His features took on a rueful cast. "It's not my fault. You forced me to frighten you. I didn't want to, believe me."

For a moment, utter stillness held her in its grip; then she began to weep, her breath fluttering like a spent leaf. "I need . . . I need to go to the bathroom."

Kray expelled a tender laugh. "Why didn't you say so?"

He unstrapped her from the chair, and she whimpered.

"There," he said.

She stared at him, wide-eyed, so stunned, her brain refused to function.

He brought over a bedpan.

"This can't be happening," she said more to herself than to him. "I won't." She was sobbing and begging all at once. "I *can't*."

He stood in front of her, arms crossed like a corrections officer, detached, observant, his smoke-colored eyes on hers.

"Please!" she begged. "Don't look. Please, please, please turn away. I'll be good, I promise."

Slowly, he turned his back on her.

Stillness overcame her then, as her mind tried to accommodate. But it was so hard. Each time she thought she had a handle on her new reality, it turned upside down: good was evil, kindness was pain, black was white. She felt dizzy, alone, isolated. Terror crept into her bones, freezing the marrow. But, oh, her bladder would burst unless she peed, peed right now! But she couldn't.

"Emma didn't tell you a thing." She was trembling, the muscles in her thighs jumping wildly. "How do you know about me and Bark?"

"I'll tell you, Alli, because I like you. I want you to trust me. I know because there was a microphone in your dorm room. When you confessed to Emma, you were also confessing to me."

Alli closed her eyes. At last, head bowed, shivering, she let go, the sound like rain spattering a tin roof.

FOURTEEN

THE POTUS and Secretary Paull sat together in the backseat of the president's heavily armored limo on the way from the White House to where Air Force One was waiting to take the president and his small party to Moscow to meet with the Russian president, Yukin. In the briefcase that straddled the president's knees was the Black File Paull had provided, proof that Yukin's handpicked head of the state-owned RussOil was his still-active ex-KGB assassin.

The president could have taken Marine One, his helicopter, to the airfield but with its privacy shield between the passenger compartment and the driver, the limo provided absolute privacy, something with which the president, in the waning weeks of his Administration, had become obsessed.

"This abduction business," the president said, "how is it progressing?"

"We're following every lead," Paull said noncommittally.

"Ach, Dennis, let's call a spade a spade, shall we?" The president stared out the bulletproof smoked-glass window. "We've been blessed with a bit of great good luck. This business, unfortunate as it may be for the Carsons—and God knows every day I pray for that young woman's safe release—has provided us with the excuse we need to excise the missionary secularists—*all* of them." He turned back, his eyes burning with the fire of the devout. "What I want to know is why hasn't that already happened?"

"The president-elect's agent—Jack McClure—has been following a very promising lead."

"Well, you see, Dennis, now you've just put your finger on the nub of the problem."

Paull shook his head. "I don't understand, sir," he said, though he was quite certain he was reading the president all too well.

"It appears to me that Jack McClure is gumming up the works."

"Sir, I believe he's on to a lead that could bring us Alli Carson's abductor. I was under the impression that our first priority was her safe return."

"Have you forgotten our previous discussion, Dennis? Give the order to Hugh Garner, and let's get on with it. By the time I return from Moscow, I want the First American Secular Revivalists in custody. Then I'll address the nation with the evidence he'll have trumped up from his FSB security force."

"I'll inform Garner as soon as you board your flight, sir," Paull said with a heavy heart. He wondered how he was going to finesse this ugly—and quite illegal—situation the president had dropped into his lap. At the moment, he saw no alternative to turning Garner loose on the FASR, but he held out hope that if he insisted that Jack McClure assist in the operation, the president-elect's man could find a way to mitigate the damage. Of course, that would put McClure squarely in everyone's line of fire. He'd take the heat if he got in Garner's face, but that couldn't be helped. Agents in the field were designed to deal with whatever heat was thrown at them. Besides, McClure was expendable; Paull's agent in the Secret Service wasn't.

During the secretary's ruminations, the limo had arrived at Andrews

Air Force Base. Paull, who had been debating all morning whether or not to bring up an extremely delicate subject, finally made his decision as the presidential limo rolled to a stop on the tarmac twelve yards from the near-side wing of Air Force One.

"Sir, before you leave, I have a duty to inform you . . ."

"Yes?" The president's bright, freshly scrubbed face seemed blank, his thoughts already thousands of miles away in bleak, snow-driven Moscow. He was, no doubt, licking his chops at the prospect of putting Yukin in his place.

"Nightwing missed his last rendezvous." Nightwing was the government's most productive deep-cover asset.

"When was that scheduled for?" the president snapped.

"Ten days ago," Paull replied just as crisply.

"Dennis, why on earth are you telling me this moments before I leave for Moscow?"

"He missed his backup dates four days ago and yesterday, sir. I felt it prudent not to bother you before this, hoping that Nightwing would surface. He hasn't."

"Frankly, Dennis, with your plate so full, I don't understand why you're even bothering with this."

"Assets are a tricky lot, sir. We ask them to do a lot of dodgy things—wet work. There's a certain psychology to people who kill without remorse. They tend to think of themselves as the center of the universe. This is what makes them successful, it's what keeps them going. But I've seen it happen before—every once in a while some developmental aspect becomes arrested. Their urge to be someone—to be special, to become known—overrides their self-discipline."

"What is this, psychology one-oh-one?" the president said testily.

"Sir, I want to make my position clear. When an asset's self-discipline disappears, he becomes nothing more than a serial killer."

The president's hand was on the door handle. His expression revealed that he already had one foot on Russian soil. "I'm quite certain that isn't the case with Nightwing. My goodness, he's been an invaluable asset for upwards of thirty years now. Nothing's changed, I assure you. Stop jumping at shadows. I'm quite certain there's a good reason for his silence." He smiled reassuringly. "Concentrate on the missionary secularists. Let Nightwing take care of himself."

THE TROUBLE with the president's suggestion," Paull said, "is that no asset—even one as productive and, therefore, sacrosanct as Nightwing— should be allowed to be so independent. In my opinion, that's a recipe for lawlessness and, ultimately, the corruption of basic moral principles."

"The president came to see me." Some wavering spark inside Louise's mind had roused her from her stupor. "Isn't that nice?"

"Very nice, darling."

Paull sat with his wife on the glassed-in porch of the facility where she lived. He could feel the radiant heat coming up through the flagstone floor.

"Daddy," she said, "where am I?"

"Home, darling." Paull squeezed her hand. "You're home."

At this, Louise smiled blankly, lapsed back into her mysterious inner world. Paull stared at her face. The dementia had not dimmed a beauty that still made his heart ache. But now there was this glass wall between them, this horrifying divide he could not bridge no matter how hard he tried. She was as lost to him as she was to herself. He couldn't bear the thought, and so as he'd done before, he'd come and talk to her as if she were the close confidante she never could have been when she'd been young and vibrant. He had of necessity shut her out of his work life; now, to fashion his time with her into a memory he could take back with him into the real world, he spoke his mind to her.

"I inherited Nightwing eight years ago, Louise. What troubles me most is that though I'm his handler, I've never laid eyes on the man. Can you believe it? The rendezvous are dead letter drops, always in a different District hotel designated by Nightwing himself, a sealed message left for 'Uncle Dan.' "

He shook his head, becoming more concerned as his thoughts were made concrete by his words. "At first, Nightwing provided us with intel on Russia and mainland China. More recently, he's widened his field to include priceless datastreams of intelligence regarding decisions being made behind closed doors in key Middle Eastern states, some of which are our purported allies. These datastreams invariably proved reliable, invaluable, so you can see why the president insists on treating him with extreme kid gloves. But Nightwing has been involved in questionable assignments; he's a law unto himself. Is it any wonder I'm disturbed that I know virtually nothing about him? His file is unusually thin. I have an unshakable suspicion that the information it contains is more legend than real. Who created the legend and why remains a mystery. Nightwing's previous handler is dead, so there's no one else to ask, and believe me I've spent many fruitless nights poring through the Homeland Security database—it incorporates those of the CIA, FBI, and NSA now—without finding any mention of Nightwing whatsoever. More than once it's occurred to me that the file was written by Nightwing himself."

Louise's hand in his was cool, as if he were addressing a marble statue, marvelously carved but, for all that, still stone. He wondered whether she heard him, whether his voice was familiar to her, like a favorite radio station one listened to when one was young. He liked to think his voice made her feel safe, secure. Loved. Tears welled in his eyes, temporarily blinding him. He plowed on with his discussion, more determined than ever to make of this visit something private and intimate he could savor later, when out in the bustling world, he'd think of her here, entombed in the labyrinth of her own mind.

"In fact, Louise, only two men know more about the asset than me: the president and the National Security Advisor. Given the president's nonchalant attitude toward the asset suddenly falling off the grid, I'm beginning to suspect that against all protocol, one of those two men has been in touch with Nightwing without my knowing. However, I'm all too aware that trying to confirm that suspicion is a sure way to commit political suicide."

No, he decided, as he pressed the speed-dial key for Hugh Garner's cell, he'd have to take the president's advice and concentrate on Alli Carson's abduction and the FASR. For the moment, he had no choice but to leave Nightwing—file name Ian Brady—to his own devices. However, if the National Security Advisor now had the inside track with the president, it was time he himself made contact with his own powerful ally, because all at once the political landscape had turned to quicksand. Despite the danger, he had to make a decisive move before it sucked him under.

The call completed, he freed his hand from Louise's limp grasp. When he leaned over, kissed her pale lips, a tremor of love and yearning passed through him as he thought of her, rosy-cheeked and laughing, her long hair glinting in sunlight, lifted through the air by his strong arms.

FIFTEEN

WELL DONE, McClure," Hugh Garner said. "As if we didn't have enough trouble, you've given us another girl—approximately the same age and weight as the First Daughter—who's also missing. She's either dead or wishes she was; at the very least, she's severely maimed." He slapped three sheets of paper he was holding. "But according to the ME's report, we have no way of identifying her." He smirked, looking from Jack to Nina. "Which one of you lovelies is going to volunteer to tell Edward Carson and his wife this bit of inspiring news?"

"I will," Jack said. "I call him on an hourly basis, anyway."

"One of these days I trust you'll surprise me, Jack." Garner tossed aside Schiltz's chilling report. "But, no, I need you with me, so, Nina, it'll be you who provides the Carsons with this morning's update."

Nothing on Nina's face betrayed what she might be feeling. She was dressed today in a smart suit over a blouse with pearl buttons up to her neck, where a tasteful cameo was pinned. How a woman could appear demure and sexy at the same time was beyond Jack.

They were grouped around a desk in the makeshift command center at Langley Fields. The desk was littered with the day's early dispatches from the FBI, CIA, DIA, NSA, as well as every regional and municipal law enforcement agency that had been dragooned by Homeland Security into the search for Alli Carson.

The trio was the eye of a carefully controlled storm of activity that raged around them. No less than thirty operatives were crammed into the headmistress's outer office, working the computers that were hooked into the nation's deepest surveillance networks. Many were simultaneously on the phone, distributing phoned-in leads that other operatives in the field needed to run down. Bags from McDonald's, KFC, barbecue joints, along with half-empty boxes of subgum chow mein and moo goo gai pan were strewn about. Garbage cans were piled high with empty soda cans. The greasy odors of stale food, sweat, and fear made a permanent fug impossible to escape.

One of these drones had accessed the national missing persons database for the entire District, Virginia, and Maryland, but the printout was useless. Save for the usual slew of runaways from Omaha to Amarillo who had disappeared into the bowels of the District, there was nothing to help them.

"Let's get to work," Garner said to Jack as Nina left them.

He led Jack out via the rear exit that gave out onto a dimly lit corridor, down a short flight of concrete steps to the custodian's area. Here was a warren of workshops and storerooms containing all the many implements and supplies required to keep an upper-tier college like Langley Fields looking shipshape for the parents who paid tens of thousands for the education of their sons and daughters. No fine school could afford to look shabby, and with a large campus like this one, the maintenance was constant.

Clearly, however, the custodial staff was elsewhere because when Garner led Jack into the largest of the workshops, it was deserted, save for two hooded men and their armed guards. They were sitting on opposite sides of the room, facing away from each other. Between them, along the wall, was an oversized soapstone sink and several workbenches above which hung pegboards thick with handsaws, hammers, awls, levels, metal rulers, and planes. Screwdrivers, chisels, pliers, and wrenches of every imaginable size were clustered in one area. Some of the benches had vises bolted to them. The smells of glue and oiled metal were strong in the air. Between the pegboard sections were windows that afforded a peaceful view out over the rose garden, now an army of thorny miniature stick soldiers on a half-frozen parade ground.

"What is this?" Jack said, alarmed.

Garner pulled him back into the hallway for a moment.

"We've brought in the co-leaders of the First American Secular Revivalists," he said in a low voice. "A number of FASR members have vanished, only to resurface as part of E-Two. At the very least, FASR is a training ground for E-Two terrorists. In our estimation, it's a legit front for the revolutionary group."

"Brought in? Are these men criminals?"

Ignoring Jack's question, Garner concluded: "Keep your mouth shut, bright boy, and you just might learn something."

Returning inside, Garner signaled to the guards, who jerked the prisoners' chairs around, pulled off their hoods. The men blinked, disoriented. They stared at each other, then at Garner and Jack, their eyes wide open. They were clearly terrified.

"Who are you?" one of the men asked. "Why are we here?"

Garner strode over to the soapstone sink, inserted a rubber stopper in the drain, turned on the cold-water faucet full-blast. As the water began to fill the sink, he said, "Peter Link, Christopher Armitage, you're members of E-Two, the missionary secularist terror group."

"What?" both men said nearly simultaneously. "We're not!"

Garner stared down at the rising water. "Are you telling me you're not missionary secularists?"

"We believe that organized religion—*all* organized religion—is a danger to modern-day society," Chris Armitage, the man on the right said.

"But we're not terrorists," Peter Link said from the opposite side of the room.

"You're not, huh?" Garner signaled to Link's guard, who unshackled him, hauled him up by the back of his collar, frog-marched him over to where Garner was standing. Garner turned off the cold-water tap. The sink was filled to the brim.

Link stared from Garner's face to the gently rippling water. "You can't be serious. . . . What do you think this is, a police state?"

Garner slammed his fist into Link's stomach. As the man doubled over, Garner grabbed both sides of his head, jammed it into the sink. Water fountained up, foaming as Link began to thrash.

"You can't do this!" Armitage shouted. "This is America—we're guaranteed the right of free speech!"

Garner hauled the sputtering, choking Link out of the water. The guard grasped his arms as Garner turned to Armitage, dug in his jacket pocket, flipped open his ID for the other man to see. "As far as you and your pal here are concerned, I *am* America."

Stowing his ID, he got back to work torturing Peter Link. But as Link went under for the second time, Jack put a hand on Garner's arm.

"This isn't the way," he said softly. "You're being foolish."

He sensed that was the wrong thing to say. Garner kept his hands on the back of Link's submerged head as he glared into Jack's face.

"Get your fucking hands off me, or I swear to God you'll be next."

"You brought me in for my help," Jack said quietly. "I'm giving you my opinion—"

"I didn't bring you in, McClure. In fact, I fought to keep you out. But the new president will have his way, even if it's the wrong way."

Using the edge of his hand, Jack struck Garner's elbow at the ulna nerve, breaking his grip on Peter Link. Jack hauled him out of the water. Tears streamed out of Link's eyes, and he vomited water all over himself.

"Jesus Christ!" Armitage shouted, terrified.

Garner broke away from Jack, stalked over to Armitage, yelled in his face, "You don't get to use those words!" He was seething, his shoulders bunched, his hands curled into tight fists. A pulse beat spastically in his forehead.

Jack, seeing that Link was semiconscious, laid him down on the floor. He knelt beside him, checked his pulse, which was erratic and weak. Looking up, he said to Garner, "I sure as hell hope you have a doctor on premises."

Garner opened his mouth to say something, apparently thought better of it, hauled out his cell phone. Not long after, the door swung open and a physician appeared. He hurried over to where Peter Link lay in a puddle of water and his own vomit.

Jack rose and said to Garner, "Let's take a walk."

THE SKY was piled with ugly-looking clouds, ready for a fight. A stiff wind hit their faces with a chill edge, making their noses run, their eyes water.

"I'll have your career for this," Garner said as they walked past the dormant rose garden.

"You'd do best to cool down," Jack said, "before you make threats."

Garner stalked ahead, then whirled on Jack. "You challenged my authority in there."

"You exceeded your authority," Jack said quietly. "We're not in Iraq."

"We don't have to be," Garner said. "This is a matter of national security. We're dealing with homeland terrorists, traitors to their own way of life."

Jack peered into Garner's face. He was determined to keep his voice calm and steady. Someone had to be rational in this discussion. "Because they don't think like you or the current Administration?"

"They kidnapped the First Daughter!"

"You don't know that."

"Quite right. Thanks to you, I don't. Not for certain, anyway. On the other hand, we have E-Two's signature at the scene of the crime."

"Someone else could have left those," Jack pointed out.

Garner laughed bitterly. "You don't really believe that, do you?"

"To be honest, I don't know what to believe, because we don't yet know what's going on."

Garner began to walk back the way they had come. "Right. Let's get back to the interrogation so we can find out."

Jack turned, blocked his way. "I won't let you continue torturing these people."

"You can't stop me."

Jack flipped open his cell phone, put it to his ear. "I'm due to call the president-elect anyway."

Garner put up his hands. "Look, look. I'm here to find the people who snatched the president-elect's daughter. What's your excuse?"

"Torture doesn't work," Jack said. "Either the subject clams up till he dies or, more likely, he lies. He tells you exactly what you want to hear, but it's not the truth. Fortunately, there's a better way to determine if these guys are the perps."

Garner licked his lips. Jack could see his ire ebbing slightly.

"So what's your bright idea?"

Jack folded his cell phone, put it away. "I go back in there, talk to Chris Armitage. Then I let him go."

"Are you insane? I won't allow it!"

"We release him and, when he's recovered, Link as well," Jack said. "We follow them. Put them under twenty-four–seven surveillance. If they're involved, we'll know it soon enough."

After considering a minute, Garner nodded. "This is your idea, you do the surveillance yourself."

Too late, Jack saw how Garner would make him pay for challenging him. Though Jack wanted more than anything to detach himself from Garner, run down his own lead with regard to Cyril Tolkan, he knew he couldn't wriggle out of this assignment, so he nodded his assent.

"I'll need help keeping an eye on the two men."

"That's your problem. Take care of it."

As he was walking away, Garner called after him, "You have forty-eight hours, bright boy. And after you fail, I *will* have your career."

SIXTEEN

WHY IS the light out?"

From out of the absolute darkness, Alli Carson felt the air against her face and she shrank away, certain that he was going to hit her. In the days she'd been here, he'd never struck her, but the threat of violence was always in the air, keeping her immersed in a sea of terror. She was too frightened not to sit in it.

"What have I told you?" Kray's voice seemed disembodied, the heart of the darkness itself. "No talking except at mealtimes."

She kept her head up. He didn't want to hurt her, merely to teach her a lesson not yet learned; she knew this now.

"You need to focus your mind, Alli."

She could tell by the placement of his voice that he had sat down in front of her. She felt a little thrill of accomplishment at her newfound ability to discern the nuances of movement in sounds. This was Ronnie Kray, the same man Emma had met, whom Emma wanted to know more about. Now it was her turn. She had to keep that thought in the forefront of her mind. Emma had taught her how to be tough, how to go her own way. Emma was also fearless, a trait Alli had never been able to grasp. Perhaps now was her chance. *Be brave,* she told herself. *Fate has put you in the same hands as Emma. You have the chance to finish what she started. You have a chance to understand this enigmatic man.*

"You have a keen mind," Kray continued, "but it's been dulled by your sheltered life. You've been taught to believe that you live a pampered life, but that's a lie. The truth is you live the life of a prisoner. You're forbidden to go where you want, you're forbidden to say what you want. You can't even make friends without your father's knowledge, so that their private lives can be invaded by the Secret Service, just as yours is. You don't own yourself, Alli. You're a puppet, dancing to your father's tune."

A chair creaked, and Alli knew that he had sat back. A whisper of cloth told her that he'd crossed one leg over the other. *I can see,* she thought, *without seeing.* She was grateful to him for having kept the light off, grateful for the opportunity he'd given her to sharpen her senses. For the first time since she'd known Emma McClure, she had stepped outside herself—the self, as Kray had so accurately said, that had been created for her.

As if divining her thoughts, Kray said, "You exist at the pleasure of your father. The Alli Carson the country—the world—knows is a confection, a Hershey bar: an all-American girl, with all-American values, all-American ideals. When have you ever been allowed to say what's really on your mind? When have you been allowed to voice your own opinion? Your lot in life has been to further your father's political career."

She heard his voice, and only his voice.

"Isn't that right, Alli?"

The darkness made it grow in power, until she could see it glowing like a jewel in her mind.

"You have your own opinions, don't you?"

For a long moment she said nothing, though she felt the answer fizzing in her throat, clamoring to be exposed, to have its own life at last. Still, she bit it back, afraid. She realized just how familiar this fear was, how she had been afraid for years to say what was really on her mind, as opposed to what her father's handlers had insisted she say publicly. Only Emma had known her real mind, only Emma could have taught her how to be fearless, but Emma was dead. She lowered her head and felt a great sob welling up in her breast, and hot tears leaked out of her eyes, ran down her cheeks, dropped onto the backs of her hands. It was so cruel, so unfair that her one true friend had been taken from her. . . .

"Focus, Alli," Kray said in the manner of a professor to an inordinately bright student with ADD. "It's important that you focus your mind, that you shake off the dullness of the old automaton Alli Carson, that you hone your mind to a diamond edge. Now, tell me, do you have your own opinions?"

"I do," Alli said, her throat unclogging as the words she'd been wanting to say flew out. She felt herself transported back to campus, walking with Emma, who had more or less asked her the same question: Do you have your father's opinions, or are they your own?

He sighed, it seemed to her with pleasure.

"Then perhaps there's a chance I can reach the real Alli Carson. There's a chance I can undo what's been done to you."

The creak of the chair. "You wish to speak."

How did he know that? she wondered. What marvelous power he possesed!

"You have my permission."

"Why are you doing this?" she asked.

"Because I have to."

He said it in a way that shook her. She didn't know why yet, she was too stunned by her own reaction, but she was beginning to have faith now that she would come to understand what was happening to her, and why.

She felt him lean in to her, felt the aura of his warmth as if she held his beating heart in her hands.

"I want to share something with you, Alli. I have absolute faith in what I'm doing. Beyond that, I'm a patriot. This country has lost its way. There's a shadow over democracy, Alli, and its name is god—the Christian god in whose name so many ethnic people have been attacked, decimated, or destroyed: the Aztecs, the Inca, the Jews of Spain, the caliphs of Constantinople and Trebizond, the Chinese, blacks, our own American Indians. Sinners all, right?"

She could hear his breathing, like the bellows fanning a fire, expelling a hard emotion with each word. This emotion was familiar to her; she understood it without being able to define it. And she felt Emma close beside her, whispering in the nighttime dorm room in Langley Fields, so far away now, so very far. She began to weep again, silently—for Emma, absolutely, but also for her own fractured self, for the life she had been forced to live, for everything she had missed: friends, laughter, goofing around, being silly. Being herself, whatever that might be. That thought brought yet more tears and a weight in her chest she could scarcely bear.

Through it all, Kray remained silent, holding her hands in the dark, keeping contact. She was unspeakably grateful for the silence, the human contact.

"For more than a decade," he said when her tears had at last subsided and her breathing returned to normal, "there has been a conspiracy to hijack democracy. It's only in the last eight years that it's crawled into the light. Under the guise of knowing what's best for America, a cabal of right-wing fanatics has made a pact with religious fundamentalists whose fervent wish is for a pure and Christian America. This alliance is a new twist on what Eisenhower ominously called the military-industrial complex. He feared it would take over the running of the country, and those fears were realized. Big Oil runs America, Big Oil determines our foreign policy. If the Middle East wasn't filled with oil, we wouldn't care one bit about who kills who there. We wouldn't even know what a Sunni is, let alone why he wants to kill his Shiite neighbor.

"But now the religious right has forced itself into the mix, now we have a president who believes he's doing the work of god. But I and millions like me all over the world don't believe god exists. Then whose work is the president doing?"

Alli listened to him with all her senses. She felt taut as a drumhead, taken out of herself, given the privilege to emerge from her own body, to hover like a ghost above the human proceedings below. And with this sensation came a feeling of energy, and of power.

"You and me, Alli, we're being trampled by this religious stampede masquerading as a democratic government. How many times does this president have to say that he doesn't care what the people or the Congress think, he knows what's best for us, he knows what's right? He means his god knows, but his god doesn't exist. His morality is a delusion invented by the so-called righteous to bolster their claim that every decision they make is right, that all criticism directed at them comes from a radical left-wing element. They've tried to make an unswerving belief in god synonymous with patriotism, a healthy skepticism in god synonymous with treason. We have to fight this false morality; we have to stop it before its infection goes too far."

With one last squeeze, he let go of her hands. "Now you know me. I haven't said any of this to another living human being."

He stood up; she felt his presence receding. She wanted to cry out for him to stay, but she knew she mustn't. She'd learned her lesson.

"I want to trust you, Alli. That's my most fervent wish. But you've still got to prove yourself worthy of trust." His voice was growing fainter. "I believe you can do it. I have faith in you."

SEVENTEEN

JACK NEVER went home again. But he is afraid that his father will try to find him, that he will use the authorities to drag Jack back to the room with the stoplight blinking outside the window, hostage to the creaks and groans of his father's nighttime footsteps. He knows he needs to disappear.

Where do you go when you disappear off the grid the authorities have constructed? Back in the day, you joined the army; before that, if you had a romantic soul, it was the Foreign Legion. But those gilded days have been long drained to black-and-white. Off the grid for Jack means staying with Gus.

Gus owns the Hi-Line, a pawnshop on Kansas Avenue, where the sidewalk is sticky with spent body fluids, and at any time of the year a dank and gritty wind rattles folding gates on dilapidated storefronts.

Jack shows up outside the gated storefront at 7 A.M. the day after the incident at the All Around Town bakery and waits there until Gus arrives.

Gus shows no surprise whatsoever. "Huh, white boy develop a taste for grits." He unlocks the gate, rolls it up. "I mightta known."

"I'm not going home." Jack follows Gus into the Hi-Line, a long, narrow space with glass cases to the right, a wall of mirror to the left. It's impossible to do anything in the Hi-Line, even pick your nose, without Gus seeing it. "I want to work for you."

Gus turns on the fluorescent lights, then the air conditioner, which begins to rumble like an arthritic pensioner.

"Well, I mightta said no, despite what Reverend Taske tol' me." More lights come on at the rear of the store. "Huh, he thinks he knows everything 'cause he's got a direct pipeline t'God." Now the lights in the glass cases flicker once before illuminating the pawned goods. "I made some calls after I dropped you off yesterday. Now I gotta better line on Cyril."

Gus steps behind the line of counters, checks the till, puts in a stack of bills. He looks up, an expression of mild surprise on his face. "My name's Augustus Turlington the Third, no lie. My name alone would get me into any country club in America. Until they see my black-ass face, that is." He grunts. "So what a you doin on the customer's side a the counter, anyways? You never gonna learn the business from there."

THE HI-LINE is habituated by tattooed bail-bondsmen, furtive pornographers, rough-and-tumble Colombians, burly pimps, sallow-faced pushers, and beat cops on the take preceded into the fluorescent-lit shop by their bellies.

At first, Jack's job is simply to follow Gus's orders, or so it seems to his clients. But what Jack is really doing is observing them, in the way only he can, absorbing the nature of the up-front business deals.

"I want you familiar with what I do here," Gus says that first morning. "I want you familiar with the folks who run in an' outta here on a reg'lar basis, got me?"

GUS LIVES in a large house at the end of Westmoreland Avenue, just over the Maryland border. Improbably, it's surrounded by trees and thick shrubs. Jack has his own room on the top floor. When he looks out his windows, he imagines he's in a tree house, all leafy bower, safely green. There is a bird's nest dotted with bits of fluff and droppings in the crook of a branch, as empty now as it was full in the spring. In the mornings, the green bower is spangled gold; at night, it's frosted by a silvery glitter. Except for the birds and, in August, the cicadas, it's quiet.

Sometimes, though, Jack hears music. There is a part of him that quails deep inside, but it's the music itself—slow, sad, resigned even in its seething anger that draws him. Gradually, he conquers his inner fear enough to creep downstairs. Now he hears the male voice, deep, richer, more burnished than James Brown's. He sits down on the bottom riser, arms clasped around his bony knees, rocking slightly to the rhythm. For an hour or more, he is inundated by the river of sorrow, soaking up sounds that seep into his bones, that in their sadness seem to lift him up on a golden chariot, transport him over the gummy rooftops, the blinking traffic lights, the blaring horns, screeching brakes, the drunken shouts, into a realm of pure bliss.

After the last notes die away, Jack climbs back up the stairs, crawls into bed, and falls into a deep, dreamless sleep.

Every night he hears the music, the ritual is the same: the soft creeping down the stairs, sitting alone, but not alone, connected to an invisible world by the music, by the lyrics, by the voices of men who've seen things he can't even imagine.

WEEKENDS JACK is being taught the ways of God by Reverend Taske. His weekdays are spent at the Hi-Line observing, cataloging, and collating the sad parade of used bric-a-brac that down-at-the-heels customers bring in for Gus to evaluate and, if he deems them desirable, shell out meager cash payment. Most never return for their pawned goods, Jack learns soon enough, though they may be dear to them in ways no one else understands. Every month Gus holds an auction to sell what's been there for a half year, the term of the Hi-Line agreement. Always there are several treasures among the old guitars, Timex watches, cameos, and gold lockets. He makes money on these transactions, to be sure, though after less than a week on the job, Jack is quite certain his living is made in the back room.

During one such auction, Jack comes across a box of comics. Excited, he begins to paw through them, until he realizes that these are his comics. His father must've come in one weekend while he was with Reverend Taske, pawned them. At once, Jack knows that his father never had any intention of coming back for them. A terrible sense of freedom overwhelms him, a sorrow and a joy commingled precisely like that curious emotion that draws him to the bluesy music Gus plays at night.

For a moment, he contemplates asking Gus to take the cost of the comics out of his salary. Then he opens one, begins to read it. Almost immediately, he puts it aside, opens another, then another and another. He puts them all aside. Then he takes the box, puts it on the auction counter to be sold.

It's only when he looks up that he sees that Gus has been watching him all along.

ONE MORNING about a week after the auction, there's a present waiting for him when he comes down for breakfast.

He stands staring at the large package resting on the kitchen table. Gus, in a chef's apron, his fingers white with flour, says, "Well, go on, kid, open it."

"It's not my birthday."

Gus expertly pours four circles of batter into a smoking cast-iron skillet. "You don't want me t'have t'give it to someone else, do you?"

Jack feels himself being impelled by Gus's words. His fingers tremble as they rip open the paper. Inside is a square box with a grille on one side. He opens the top: it's a record player. Inside are three albums, one by Muddy Waters, one by Howlin' Wolf, one by Fats Domino.

Gus, flipping corncakes, says, "Life without blues music, now that's a sin. Blues tells all kinds o' stories, the history of the people composed it."

He slides a plate of corncakes onto the table. "Eat yo' breakfast now. Tonight we'll listen to these records together. No sense you sittin' all by yo'self on them hard stairs."

AFTER SIX weeks, Gus decides Jack is ready to observe the backroom deals. The back room is a frigid twelve-by-twelve bunker outfitted with a sofa and two La-Z-Boy easy chairs, between which rests a sideboard on which sits an array of liquor bottles, old-fashioned and highball glasses of sparkling cut crystal. A girl comes in once a day to clean, dust, and vacuum. Gus is extremely particular about the environment in which his deals get hammered out.

Jack fears that these deals somehow involve drug-running because that is one of the businesses Cyril Tolkan is into, and it seems clear to him that Cyril and Gus are rivals. He needn't have worried. The deals are of another nature altogether.

His first day in the back room, Gus tells him, "All my life I was a outcast, someone who wanted t'be happier'n my daddy, but every time I tried, there was a white man standin' in my way. So finally I gave up, went back here t'my own world where I'm the king of the castle."

Through the back door of the Hi-Line come a succession of police detectives. Although they all look different physically, they seem the same to Jack's brain: they're hard, flinty-eyed, dyspeptic. To a man, they've seen enough—often too much—of the streets they are sworn to protect: too much rage, too much bitterness, too much jealousy and envy, too much blood. They inhabit a swamp eyeball-deep in orga-nized prostitution, drug smuggling, murder for hire, turf warfare. They have murder in their sleep-deprived eyes. Jack can see it; he can smell it, taste it like the tang of acrid smoke.

They all want the same thing from Gus: shortcuts to turn their perps into collars. They want to make arrests, no fuss, no muss, arrests that stick, that won't blow back in their faces like street litter. This Gus can do, because what Gus trades in, what makes him his living, is information. Gus's castle may be at times too small to suit his taste, but it's populated by a battalion of corner snitches, gang informants he set in place, embittered turncoats, ambitious politicos—the list seems endless.

Whatever these detectives want, Gus usually has or, if not, can get in a matter of days. All for a price, of course. They pay, with reluctance and a show of crankiness. They know the value of the goods.

One of Gus's regulars is a detective by the name of Stanz. His face is as crumpled as a used napkin; his shoulders as meaty as a veteran boxer. His nose is a mess, broken in street brawls when he was Jack's age and never properly fixed. He smokes like a demon, speaks as if his throat is perpetually clogged with tar and nicotine.

Decades on the force haven't dimmed his clothes sense. He opens the button on his smartly tailored suit jacket, lifts his trouser legs fractionally before he sits down on the sofa. He lights an unfiltered Camel, inhales mightily.

"You did good on the Gonzalez thing." He hands a thick white envelope to Gus. "That particular sonovabitch won't be making money off coke or anything else for the foreseeable future."

"We aim to please." Gus stuffs the envelope in a pocket without opening it. Obviously, he trusts Stanz.

"Speaking of which." The detective picks a piece of tobacco off the tip of his tongue. "My boss is on my ass like you wouldn't believe about the deuce murders over McMillan Reservoir."

Gus frowns. "I tol' you. I'm workin' on it."

"Working's not good enough." Stanz hunches forward, perching on the edge of the sofa. "These past three weeks my life's been a living hell—no sleep, no downtime—I can't even get my usual tug-and-tickle, for fuck's sake. You know what that does to a man my age? My prostate feels as big as a goddamn softball."

The ash trembles precariously at the end of his Camel. "My tit's in the fire, Gus. Three weeks of interviewing, reinterviewing, poring

over old cases, canvassing the neighborhood, scouring every fucking
trash can and Dumpster for the knife or whatever the fuck sharp in-
strument was used to kill the vics. I feel like I've run the marathon,
and what do I got to put in the report to my loo? What's he gonna
report to the chief of detectives? What's the chief gonna say to the
commish and the mayor? You see the bind I'm in? All that goddamn
pressure has more than a trickle-down effect. I'm the guy where the
shitstorm's gonna hit."

He grinds out his Camel, stands. "Get me the name of the perp."
He points at Gus. "Otherwise I'm pulling my business, and where I go
everyone else is gonna follow."

Gus's eyes go hooded, and Jack, feeling the dangerous crackle of
heat lightning in the room, involuntarily takes a step back.

Gus says in the lazy voice that Jack has already determined means
trouble, "You been on the force—what?—thirty years now?"

"Thirty-three, to be exact."

"No." Gus shakes his head. "Thirty-three years, eight months,
seventeen days."

Stanz stares, blinking. He has no idea where this is going, the lug.
But Jack does, and he can't help smiling a secret smile.

"That's a long time," Gus drawls. "Lotta shit piles up in those
years."

Understanding comes at last to Stanz. "Now, wait a minute."

"Five years ago, the Ochoa takedown," Gus continues as if Stanz
hasn't said a word. "Along with the thirty kees of coke, twenty-five
mil was found with him, but only twenty-three made it into the police
evidence room. Eighteen months ago, a Hispanic down. Forensics
found a gun in his hand, but we both know that when you shot him he
was unarmed, 'cause you bought the gun from me. And, my goodness,
I have the paperwork to prove it."

Stanz's face is flushed red. "Hey, you told me—"

"This's a game you don't wanna be playin' with me." Gus's inner rage has boiled up into his eyes.

Stanz turns away for a moment, gathering himself. At length, he says, "I'd never threaten you, Gus. You know that, we go back a long way."

Gus's bulk fills up the space; his rage seems to have sucked all the oxygen out of the room.

Stanz is trying his best not to breathe hard. "We good now?" he asks.

It looks like he can't wait to get the hell out of there.

EIGHTEEN

Is PETE going to be all right?"

"The doctor says he will be," Jack said. "He's been taken to Bethesda Medical. He'll get the best of care."

Jack had volunteered to drive Chris Armitage home. A fine mesh of sleet slanted down from a pewter sky. The car's tires made a hissing noise as they slithered along the road.

Armitage shivered. "Until they torture him again."

"He won't be tortured again."

"Damn straight he won't." Armitage was huddled against the passenger's-side window, as far away from Jack as he could get. "I'm filing a complaint with the Attorney General's office."

"I'd advise against it." Jack got on the George Washington Memorial Parkway, heading toward the District. "If you do, Garner will haul you in again. I also guarantee the Attorney General won't ever see the complaint."

"Then I'll take it public—any one of the news outlets would jump at this story."

"Garner would love that. In the blink of an eye, he and his people will prove you're a crank, and whatever credibility you're trying to build for your movement will be shot to hell."

Armitage regarded him for a moment. "What are you? The good cop?"

"I'm the good guy," Jack said. "The only one you're likely to meet in the next few weeks."

Armitage appeared to chew this over for some time. "If you're such a good guy, tell me what the hell is going on."

Jack maneuvered around a lumbering semi. "I can't do that."

Armitage's voice was intensely bitter. "This is a nightmare."

Every twenty seconds, Jack's eyes flicked to the rearview mirror. "Tell me about your organization."

Armitage grunted. "For a start, we're not E-Two. Nothing like it, in fact."

A gray BMW 5 Series had taken up station two cars behind theirs.

"But you know about E-Two." Jack was careful to keep whatever tension he was feeling out of his voice.

"Of course I do." Armitage pointed. "Can we get some more heat? I'm freezing."

Jack turned up the heater. "It's the fear draining out of you."

"Who says it's going? I feel like it'll be a part of me for the rest of my life."

Jack switched to the center lane. The gray BMW waited several minutes, then followed.

"Every movement has its radical element," Armitage was saying, "but to tar us with the same brush—well, it's like saying all Muslims are terrorists."

There was an exit coming up. Jack switched to the left lane. "You'd be surprised at how many Americans believe that."

"Fifty years ago, most Americans believed that Jews had horns," Armitage said. "That's part of what's wrong with this country, what we're fighting against."

Here came the gray BMW, nosing into the left lane.

"I can imagine Garner and his people still believing that," Jack said tartly.

"Why do you say 'Garner and his people'? Aren't you one of them?"

"I was brought in to keep them honest." That was one way to look at it, Jack thought. "Their philosophy isn't mine."

"Anyway, thank you. You probably saved Peter's life."

Jack was aware of Armitage studying his face.

"Unless it was all an act. Was it?"

"No, it wasn't."

"How do I know you're not lying?" Armitage said.

Jack laughed. "You don't."

"I don't see what's funny," Armitage said in a wounded voice.

"I was going to say, you have to take it on faith that I'm telling the truth."

Armitage managed a smile. "Oh, I have faith—faith in mankind, faith in science, faith that reason will win out over the engines of reinforcement built up by religion. Reason doesn't require a priest or a rabbi or an imam to exist."

"You sound very sure of yourself."

"I ought to," Armitage said. "I used to be a priest."

This interested Jack almost as much as the gray BMW did. "You fall out of bed?"

"I know what you're thinking—but, no, it wasn't a girl. It was more simple than that, really, and that made the revelation ever more profound. I woke up one day and realized that the world of religion was totally out of sync with the world I was living in, the world all around me, the world I was administering to. The bishops and archbishops I knew—my spiritual leaders—didn't have a clue about what was happening in the real world, and furthermore, *they didn't care.*"

Armitage put his head back; his eyes turned inward. "One day, I made the mistake of voicing my concerns to them. They dismissed them out of hand, but from that moment on, I could tell that I was a danger to them. I was shut out of policy decisions even within my own parish."

They continued to move south on the parkway. "So you left."

Armitage nodded. "Whatever ties I'd felt with the irrational, faith-based world were severed. I found myself drawn instead to physics, quantum mechanics, organic chemistry—not as a scientist, per se, but as a means of understanding the world. I discovered that all these disciplines are empirical absolutes. They can be defined. Even better, they can be quantified. They're not subject to interpretation.

"Look, organized religions poison everything. They keep people superstitious, ignorant, and intolerant of anyone who's not like them. They also falsely bestow power on people who have no business being in power."

"Speaking of which," Jack said, "hold on."

He had been keeping to just under the speed limit, but with the off-ramp just over a hundred yards away, he floored the gas pedal. The car jumped forward. Jack hauled the wheel over, entering the center lane to an angry blare of horns. He slowed abruptly to allow a truck to get in front of him, then wedged the car into the right lane, onto the off-ramp at a frightening rate of speed.

Behind them, he could hear the shriek of rubber being flayed off the BMW's tires, the scream of horns, squeals of brakes being jammed on.

Armitage twisted around as far as his seat belt would allow. "You didn't lose them," he said.

"When I want to lose them," Jack said, "I will."

He prepared to turn off Dolley Madison Parkway almost immediately, making a left onto Kirby Road, but up ahead he saw one of those wheeled temporary signs with a grid of tiny lights blinking a message. The problem was, he couldn't read it. The array of lights swarmed like a hive of bees. He was coming up on it fast, there was no time to find his set point, to command his dyslexic brain to read what it refused to read, so he made the left off the parkway.

"What the hell are you doing?" Armitage shouted, bracing his hands against the dashboard.

Jack could see what he meant. The access to Kirby Road was blocked off. They sliced through a pair of wooden barricades, hit a potholed roadbed partially stripped to the bone. Workmen scattered, shouting and gesticulating wildly. The car dipped into a pothole, then bounced upward, coming down hard on its shocks.

The wheel vibrated under Jack's hands. "What did the sign say?"

"What d'you mean?" Armitage was bewildered. "You could read it as well as I could."

"Just tell me what it said!" Jack shouted.

"It said Kirby Road was under construction for the next half mile."

There was no help for it now. "Hang on," Jack said grimly.

They jounced over the rutted roadbed, Jack swinging the car back and forth in order to avoid the deepest holes. The bone-jarring half mile seemed to take forever; then the car reared up onto smooth tarmac. Jack could see the gray BMW negotiating the road behind them.

Swiveling back around, Armitage said, "Why is someone following us?"

"Damn good question."

Jack flicked open his phone, dialed his ATF office, which was not five minutes away. "It's McClure; get me Bennett," he said as soon as someone answered. Chief Rodney Bennett came on the line right away.

"How's it hanging, Jack?"

"I'll know in a couple of minutes, Chief. I've got a high-powered tail on me. Late-model gray BMW Five Series. Three minutes from now I'll be on Claiborne Drive. I need a stop 'n' shop."

"I'm all over it," Bennett growled.

"Right. Later." He folded away his phone.

"Open the glove box," he said to Armitage. "Take out a pad and pen."

Armitage did as he was told.

Precisely three minutes later, Jack took a left onto Claiborne Drive. This was a high-rent district with large, gracious homes, spacious front lawns, expensive landscaping.

Jack, one eye on the rearview mirror, saw the gray BMW corner after them, its distinctive front end just entering Claiborne.

"Why are you slowing down?" Armitage was truly alarmed now. "They'll be on top of us before—!"

"Shut up and take down the BMW's tag number," Jack snapped.

"Got it," Armitage said, scribbling hurriedly.

Jack heard sirens on Kirby, heading straight for them.

With the BMW close enough to rear-end him, he suddenly veered to the left. The BMW jumped the curb, plowed over a lawn, through a low hedge of boxwood, veered out of sight around the side of the house just as a pair of ATF cars, lights flashing, sirens wailing, tore up Osborne Drive, bracketing Jack's car.

NINETEEN

THE MAN we got t'see, he don't like people he don't know," Gus says. "Plus, he don't like whitey, so that makes two strikes against you."

"You want me to stay in the car?" Jack says.

Gus turns the wheel over, rolls slowly down T Street SE. "Huh. You stay in the car, the Marmoset he liable to come over, shoot you through the head. He don't ask me, should I do sumthin'. It don't smell kosher to him, he acts."

"What's a marmoset?" Jack asks.

"Some kinda monkey, I think, likes the treetops in forests, sumthin' like that, anyway."

"You ever see one? I mean a real marmoset."

"Me, no."

Gus's eyes are scanning the street. Jack can feel something in Gus condensing with concentration.

"When you think I got time t'go to the zoo?"

Between Sixteenth and Seventeenth Streets, Gus pulls into the curb, turns off the engine.

"This here's Anacostia, no place fo' you, okay? So jes' keep close t' me, don't say a word, and do yo' thing, got me?"

"Gotcha," Jack says.

The Continental's enormous engine ticks over like a clock winding down. The heat of the early evening seeps in, begins to weigh on the air-conditioned air. Gus grunts, opens the driver's door.

They're on a street of narrow row houses sided with peeling wooden slats. Tiny overgrown front yards are divided by cyclone fencing. A huge German shepherd starts to bark, throwing itself against the fence as its jaws snap.

"Hey, Godzilla." Gus strolls over to the fence, Jack right behind him. "Marmoset's neighbor keeps Zilla half-starved so he'll go for anybody gets too close." Gus digs in his pocket, pulls out a handful of dog biscuits, launches them over the fence. "Can't stand to see a animal mistreated."

As Godzilla cracks down on the first biscuit, Gus and Jack approach the next house. "My father, he was a dogcatcher," Gus says. "Man, he hated his job—dealing with 'em alla time—the rabies, the mistreatment, he come up against it all."

Gus leads them up the steps of a house painted the color of the evening sky. It has neat white shutters and a roof without the tar paper patches of its neighbors.

"This it here." He raps on the door.

There's a short pause, then, "Come on in," a male voice calls.

The instant Gus opens the door, three gunshots ring out, and Gus throws Jack unceremoniously back out onto the stoop. Jack's ears ring, he can't hear a thing, but from his prone position he sees Gus pull a Magnum .357 from his jacket, bang open the door. He shouts something to Jack as he vanishes into the interior, but Jack can't hear what it is.

Jack pushes himself up and runs inside. As he passes the door, he sees three bullet holes ripped clear through the wood. It's strange to feel himself moving, but to hear nothing except the ringing in his ears, beneath which is a dead, all-encompassing silence. It's as if the world has been stuffed solid with cotton balls.

Sprinting after Gus, he finds himself in a dimly lit room, so cluttered with books, records, magazines, strewn clothes, hats, shoes, sneakers that it seems like a maze. The ceiling fixtures have been removed, leaving bare patches like the hide of a mangy dog. Instead, a multitude of lamps on tables, chairs, the floor provide weird colored light. It's a moment before Jack realizes that all the lampshades are draped with colored bits of fabric, dimming the illumination as well as dyeing it.

Across the room he sees Gus lumber back toward him from a butter-yellow kitchen. The Magnum is pointed at the floor. Gus says something to him, gesturing emphatically with his free hand, but Jack is still deaf from the aftermath of the gunshots, possibly in shock, and keeps on coming.

He sidesteps a precariously stacked pile of books, stumbles clumsily over another, larger mound. It has one red mark on its back, like a chalk mark or a brand. Then it hits him. First, his balance deserts him, then his legs turn watery, and he falls.

On his hands and knees, he finds himself not six inches from a thin, scarred face. The eyes, open wide, stare back at him. Then he becomes aware of the trickle of blood leaking from the corner of the half-open mouth, the horrific stench of offal, and he screams, leaping backwards, tripping over a pair of boots, tumbling onto his backside, his legs in the air. It would be funny if Jack weren't so terrified. He pushes himself to his feet, smacks blindly into the wall in a desperate attempt to run out of the house. His only thought is to get as far away from the dead man as he can.

He's crying, and he's sick, vomiting onto the floor. He can't get the sight of those staring eyes out of his mind. He wants only to have time run backwards, to be back in Gus's air-conditioned Continental, safe and secure, before this all began.

Then Gus grabs him by the collar, hauls him off his feet. Jack is hysterical, kicking and screaming, and the fact that he's still half-deaf makes everything worse, as if he's living out a nightmare from which he can't pinch himself awake. Nothing is real, and yet everything is all too real: those eyes, the blood drooling out of the half-open mouth, the stench of excrement and death, of a human body letting go of life. It's all too much. His fists beat a silent tattoo against Gus's shoulders; his shoes swing back and forth into Gus's shins.

Then he's outside and Gus has let him go and he doubles over, gagging and retching, feeling as if every atom in his body is exploding in pain and terror. He is empty inside. His guts feel as if they have been turned inside out. Every nerve in his body is firing at once, making his limbs jump, his torso twitch.

The night enfolds him, or is it Gus? Gradually, he comes down from the precipice where shock and terror pushed him. Gradually, he becomes aware that Gus has gathered him into his arms and is rocking him like a baby.

Then he hears the sirens start up and knows his hearing is coming back. At first they're a long way off, but quite rapidly they come nearer and nearer.

"You okay t'go?" Gus asks.

Jack clings to him tightly, his face buried in Gus's massive chest.

With Jack in his arms, Gus gets to his feet. He takes Jack back to the Continental, fires the ignition. They're just turning the corner onto Sixth Street NE when the rear window is briefly awash in red and white flashing lights. Sirens scream close at hand, then rapidly diminish as Gus puts on speed.

A dozen gray blocks later, Gus pulls up to a phone booth.

"I gotta make a call," he says. "On'y be a minute, kid, 'kay?" His eyes study Jack slowly, carefully. "You'll be able to see me the whole time."

Jack watches Gus squeeze half his bulk into the phone booth, feed the slot. His teeth start to chatter. Chills run through him, and as he imagines that that horrific stench has invaded the car, he starts crying again.

It's only when he sees Gus striding back that he wipes his eyes and nose. He hiccups once as Gus slides behind the wheel. They sit in silence for a time. Gus stares straight ahead. Jack tries to piece himself together, but every now and again a half-stifled sob escapes him.

Finally, he manages, "Was that . . . was that . . . ?"

"The Marmoset?" Gus nods. "Yeah, that was him."

"What . . . what . . . ?"

Gus sighs. "Remember that double murder at McMillan Reservoir Stanz wants me t'help him with? The Marmoset was my man onna case." Gus looks around. "He got close to the bone, seems like."

"Too close," Jack says with a shiver.

Gus puts his arm across the seat back. "Anyway, ain't nuthin' fo' you t'worry yo'self 'bout." His brows converge in worry. "Don't you believe me?"

"I was thinking of the Marmoset," Jack says. "I was thinking that he should be buried, not pawed at by people who never knew him."

For a long time nothing more is said. At last, Gus fires the ignition. After putting the car in gear, he eases out into the street.

Jack doesn't know where they're headed; he doesn't care. He has sunk back into the world he knew through newspapers, TV, and the movies must exist, yet could never have imagined. It has come upon him too soon, its implications too much for him to handle. He wonders at all the tears he's shed because he can't remember shedding even one before this. He made it an iron-bound rule never to cry when his father beat him, not even when his father slunk back across the apartment and the strains of "California Dreamin'" winked out like a fearful light. He never cried when Andre and his crew took him into the alley behind the electronics store. Tonight, it seems, he can't stop.

It takes Gus just eleven minutes to get to 3001 Connecticut Avenue NW, the front entrance to the National Zoo.

Jack turns, peers out the window. "Gus, it's night. The zoo isn't open at night."

Gus opens the door. "Who says it ain't?"

Looka how small he is." Gus stares up through the branches at the tiny black-and-white face staring down at them. There are other marmosets elsewhere in the large cage, but this one, having taken notice of them, has come the closest. The others are busy eating fruit held in their claws or gnawing at the tree with startlingly long lower incisors.

Jack studies the black eyes staring down at him. The face looks so full of intelligence and insight, as if the marmoset sees a world at once smaller and bigger than he does.

"What's he thinking?" Jack says.

"Who knows?"

"That's just it." Jack's voice is full of wonder. "No one knows."

Gus puts his arm protectively around Jack's shoulders. "Don't get too close now, kid," he says gruffly. "Mebbe these things bite."

Jack doesn't think to ask Gus how he managed to get the zoo open at this hour, because he knows Gus won't tell him. Anyway, he doesn't want to spoil the magic of the moment, which has temporarily banished all thoughts of death, thousand-mile stares, the stench of death. There is life here, strange and beautiful, its strangeness making it all the more vibrant. Jack feels his heart beating strongly in his chest, and a kind of warmth suffuses him.

"Hello, marmoset," he says. "My name is Jack."

TWENTY

ALLI CARSON, being fed a hamburger, rare, with mustard and slices of crisp Mrs. Fanning's bread-and-butter pickles, looked into Ronnie Kray's face, so close to hers. His expression was altogether unthreatening. He might have been a mother bird feeding her chick.

She savored the tastes in her mouth, then, almost reluctantly, she swallowed. In his other hand he held a coffee milk shake with one of those bendy straws stuck into its thick foam. He brought the straw to her lips and she sucked down the sweet drink.

"How do you know my favorite foods?" she asked quietly. She didn't fear him now. She had learned that she was allowed to speak without permission during mealtimes.

Kray smiled in a way that somehow drew her to him. "I'm like a parent," he said in a voice as quiet as hers. "I'm the father you always dreamed of having, but never thought you would."

She made a motion with her head, and he gave her more burger. While she chewed, her eyes never left his face.

"I know what you like," he continued. "And what you don't. Why would I want to know that, Alli? Because I value you, because I want to please you."

Alli sucked down more of the coffee milk shake, swallowed. "Then why am I bound to this chair?"

"I bought that chair in Mexico seven years ago, at the same time I purchased a painted sugar skull, on the Day of the Dead. The chair is my most prized possession; you're privileged to sit in it. Up until I put you into it, only I have sat in it."

Intuiting her hunger, he fed her the last of the hamburger. "Do you know about the Day of the Dead, Alli? No? It's the one day of the year when the door between life and death is open. When those alive may talk to those who are dead. If they believe." He cocked his head. "Tell me, Alli, what is it you believe in?"

She blinked. "I . . . I don't know what you mean."

He hunched forward, forearms on his knees. "Do you believe in god?"

"Yes," she said immediately.

"Do you truly believe in god—or are you parroting something your parents believe?"

She looked at him for a moment, her mouth dry. Once again, it was as if he had peered down into the depths of her soul; it was as if he knew her from the inside out.

"I'm . . . I'm not supposed to say."

"There you have it, Alli. All your life you've been walled away from the rest of the world. You've been told what to say and what to think. But I know you better. I know you have your own thoughts, your own beliefs. I won't judge you the way your parents do. And there's no one here, except you and me."

"What about the others?"

"Ah, the others." Leaning in, Kray wiped the corners of her mouth. "I'll tell you a secret, Alli, because you've earned it. There are no others. There's only me. Me and my shadow." He chuckled.

"Why did you lie to me?"

"Lessons need to be learned, Alli. You're beginning to understand that now. Lessons learned obviate the need for lying. And, here's another secret I want to share with you: I don't enjoy lying to you." He sat back. "You're special, you see, but not in the way your parents have hammered into your head."

Loosening the bonds on her wrists, he took her hands in his and said, "You and I, Alli, together need to undo all the senseless hammering, all the disservice that's been done to you. Welcome to the beginning. In this place, you're free to speak your heart. You're freer than you've ever been in your life." He let go of her hands. "Now, will you tell me the truth? Do you believe in god?"

Alli studied him. After the whirl of confusion, doubt, and fear, her mind seemed clearer than it had ever been. How could that be? she asked herself. Looking into Kray's face, she saw that in time she'd have the answer.

"No," she said, her voice firm. "The idea that there's an old bearded man somewhere in heaven who created the world, who listens to our prayers, who forgives us our sins makes no sense to me. That Eve was made from Adam's rib, how stupid is that?"

Ronnie Kray regarded her with a contemplative air. "And do you believe in your country—in the United States?"

"Of course I do." She hesitated. "But . . ."

Kray said nothing, and his absolute calmness soothed her.

Now the dam broke, and out gushed feelings she'd been holding inside ever since Emma, her only confidante, had died. "I hate how the country's become a fortress. The president and his people have nothing but utter contempt for us. They can do anything, say anything, wriggle out of any wrongdoing, sling every kind of mud, hire people who slander their political enemies, and no one has the guts to stand up and say they're wrong, they're killing hundreds of people every day, they've trampled all over due process, they've blurred the separation of church and state, because anyone who dares oppose them is immediately branded a traitor, a dangerous left-wing lunatic, or both."

"They've done that to your father."

"Yes."

"But he's survived their slings and arrows to become the next president."

"Yes."

"Yet he hasn't spoken out, he hasn't denounced the alliance between the Christian fundamentalists and the Administration. Does that mean he agrees with the present Administration? Did the Administration's media attack dogs pull their punches in return for his lack of criticism?"

She could sense him preparing to leave, and she felt a sharp pang of imminent loss.

"What do you think he prays for when he and your mother attend church every Sunday?"

"I . . ." All at once confusion overwhelmed her again. "I don't know."

"Now you have surprised me," Kray said.

She heard the sharp disapproval in his voice, and her blood ran cold.

"I—"

Kray put a forefinger across his lips. "Mealtime's over."

Retying her wrists, he rose, vanishing into the gloom.

TWENTY-ONE

NINA MILLER caught Jack's call while she was in the middle of the Potomac.

"Excuse me, sir," she said.

"One moment," Dennis Paull said. "I need to see the Mermaid."

Nina squinted into the wind. "Are you sure that's wise?"

"Just set it up," Paull said brusquely.

She gave him a curt nod as she walked aft, away from the Secretary of the Department of Homeland Security. They were on his 185-foot yacht, big enough to contain an aft upper deck that served as a pad on which the small private helicopter that had brought Nina sat, its rotors quivering and flexing in the wind gusts. The pilot inside the cockpit was ready to lift off at a moment's notice.

Paull watched Nina out of the corner of his eye as she lit a clove cigarette, her back to him, cell phone to her left ear. He worried about her. He worried whether he could trust her. But then, Dennis Paull worried about every person he spoke to or came in contact with during his grueling twenty-hour days. He was playing a dangerous game, and no one knew it better than he did. Over the years, how many people had he or his people uncovered who were playing their own dangerous games? Of course, he was at the eye of the storm, the calm center from which, like an Olympian god, he could look in all directions at once. But he didn't fool himself; he didn't allow his exalted position at the right hand of the president to dull his caution or dim his vigilance.

He'd been living on a knife-edge for almost two years now, the midpoint of the president's second term in office. His stomach always hurt; his nerves vibrated so badly that he couldn't recall the last time he had slept soundly. Instead, he'd taught himself the art of catnapping—five minutes here, fifteen there—during the day. In the dead of night, as one of his days bled into the next, he sipped strong black coffee and carried out the spinning of his web. For good or ill, he was in too deep now to have second thoughts, for if he were to succeed, he needed to commit to his plan absolutely. Any waver of intent would be lethal.

He put on the smile he used for intimates—if one could use that word for those in his inner circle, because Secretary Paull had no true intimates. This the job had taught him a long, painful time ago.

His thoughts threaded away on the spume purling from the sleek bow of his yacht as Nina walked back to where he stood just forward of the cabin. It was a blustery day, spitting intermittently. Not a fit day for a boat ride, which was why Paull was here on the water instead of in an office that might very well be bugged or an open space where whatever he said was at the mercy of a parabolic microphone on the top of some innocuous-looking van. His yacht was swept three times a day for bugs, and that included the entire hull. Plus there were sophisticated jamming devices fore and aft installed by a friend of his at DARPA, the Department of Defense's advanced weapons program.

To the uninitiated, Paull mused, these precautions might seem the product of paranoia, but as William S. Burroughs aptly said, *Sometimes paranoia's just having all the facts.*

"That was McClure," Nina said, folding away her phone. "He

wants me to meet him at the headquarters of the First American Secular Revivalists."

Paull didn't like the sound of that. "What's he doing there? FASR is supposed to be Hugh Garner's responsibility."

"Garner's got it in for McClure."

They were into the wind, no one who wasn't in spitting distance could hear them, not even the crew, who Paull had made certain were all inside. "What the hell is McClure up to?"

"I don't know," Nina confessed, "but it seems clear he doesn't believe E-Two is behind the kidnapping."

"Then who the hell is?"

"I don't know, sir, but I have a feeling McClure is closer to finding out than we are."

The secretary looked thoughtful. "From now on, I want you to stick close to him."

Nina took a drag on her clove cigarette. "How close?"

The secretary's eyes bored into hers. "Do whatever it takes to keep him close. We're rapidly running out of time and space to maneuver."

Nina's gaze was cool and steady. "How does it feel, I wonder, to pimp someone else out?"

He waved a hand dismissively. "You'd better get over there pronto."

Nina turned, headed aft.

"And Nina," he called after her.

She turned back, pulled her hair off her face.

"Make sure you start thinking of him as Jack."

INSIDE THE polished mahogany cabin, the yacht's captain ignored the helicopter as its rotors started up. A moment later, it had lifted off with the woman passenger aboard. The captain didn't know her name, didn't care what it was. His job was simple and he was doing it now, transcribing onto the tiny keypad of his BlackBerry from scribbled notes he'd taken of the conversation Secretary Paull had just had with the visitor.

Growing up with a deaf sister had made him proficient in lip-reading. Finished with the transcription, he pressed the SEND key, and the e-mail was instantaneously transmitted directly to wherever the president was at the moment, no doubt eagerly awaiting its arrival.

His job concluded for the time being, the captain set his Black-Berry down beside the pair of powerful binoculars through which he'd viewed the conversation in question. Then he got back to maneuvering the yacht through the wind-tossed afternoon. He'd never had an incident at sea aboard any of the yachts he'd captained, and he wasn't about to start now.

TWENTY-TWO

EVERY ACTION invites a reaction. No, no." Kray rocked slightly from one foot to the other. "Every action *causes* a reaction. The religious right's infiltration of the federal government finally has had its proper reaction: us, the enemy. The missionary secularists, the Army of Reason." He laughed. "It seems ironic, doesn't it, that without *them* there would be no *us*. They created us; every extreme gives rise to the opposite extreme."

He bent down, untied Alli's wrists. "Hold your arms over your head."

It was phrased as a suggestion rather than a command. Nevertheless, Alli complied, but after only a few seconds she was obliged to fold them in her lap.

"I . . . I can't," she said. "I don't have the strength."

"I have a cure for that."

Kneeling, Kray unbuckled her ankles and legs. With his arms around her waist, he helped her to her feet. She stood, wobbly as a toddler, her weight against him from her hip to her shoulder.

With his coaxing, she took one tentative step forward, then another, but her legs buckled and Kray had to hold her firmly lest she collapse onto the floor like an invalid.

"I think you might have to teach me to walk all over again," she said with an embarrassed laugh.

"You won't need me to do that, I promise." He took her out of the room that had been her home for several days. He helped her shower and dress, and she felt neither embarrassed nor ashamed. Why should she? After all, he had watched her defecate and urinate; possibly he'd watched her sleep. Could there be anything more intimate?

There was not an inch of her he didn't know. It had taken just over a week for him to become a part of her.

In the kitchen, he pulled out a chair for her. She sat with one arm on the table, where cartons of orange juice and milk, and several water tumblers stood in a precise cluster. He poured her a glass of orange juice with pulp, the kind she liked best.

He waited until she had drained the glass. "After lunch, we'll go for a walk around the house. You'll get your strength back in no time, you'll see," he said. "Now, what would you like to eat?"

"Eggs and bacon, please."

"I think I'll join you." Kray opened the refrigerator so that the door to the interior was outside of Alli's field of vision. The other girl sat folded, as if she were performing a contortionist's trick. He pulled out a carton of eggs and a stick of butter from the shelf on the door. A pound of thick-sliced bacon was on the lower shelf near the girl's stiff, blue feet. Her skin looked bad now; it was starting to slough off like snakeskin. Very soon now, Kray knew, he'd have to move her, either to the freezer in the basement—though that would necessitate cutting her up into sections—or somewhere else, a landfill or an empty lot, perhaps. But not yet. He was reluctant to let her go. She'd been so useful to him. He'd sedated her while he cut off her hand so as not to cause her pain. She didn't deserve that; she had a home here now, and he didn't want to abandon her. It wasn't her fault that he'd needed her to make sure the authorities knew Alli wasn't dead and buried. He was on a strict timetable. He required the urgency only a search for a living girl would bring.

Arms full, Kray kicked the refrigerator door closed, lined up the ingredients on the counter next to the stove, placed a cast-iron skillet on the burner, turned on the gas. So as not to expose his fingers to grease, he used one of the gleaming knives on a magnetic wall rack to peel off six slices of bacon, then laid them side by side in the skillet. Turning up the heat made them sizzle. The rich scent permeated the kitchen.

When the bacon was golden brown, he set the slices on a paper towel, drained off the fat from the skillet. Without washing it, he sliced off a thick pat of butter, plopped it in the skillet to melt. Then he put the carton of eggs, a stainless steel bowl, and a whisk on the table.

"How about you scrambling the eggs?"

Once again, it was a suggestion rather than a command. Alli knew she was free to say no. But she didn't want to say no. She opened the carton, broke six eggs one by one on the rim of the bowl, poured in a dollop of milk, then began to whisk the mixture.

"I don't know how anyone can eat those Eggbeaters," she said idly.

"Or an egg-white omelette, for that matter," he answered.

Quite quickly her arm began to tire. But she rested it briefly, then began again, bringing a pale yellow froth.

"Ready," she said.

Kray took the bowl from her, added three twists of salt, two of pepper, then tipped the contents into the skillet. He stirred the eggs a bit with a white plastic spatula.

"White bread?"

"Whole-wheat today, I think," Alli said.

"In the pantry." He put down the spatula, went into the small room. Immediately he turned around, stood watching her from the shadows.

She rose, one hand supporting herself on the tabletop. Then she walked over to the stove. Her hand passed the knives in the wall rack, picked up the spatula. She stirred the eggs in the skillet. She hummed to herself.

Satisfied, Kray found a fresh loaf of whole-wheat bread, tucked it under his arm. Then he reached up, opened the cupboard. Carrie was curled and winding in her dark cave. Her red eyes stared at him enigmatically.

He put a finger across his lips, whispered to her, "Shhh."

Kray closed the cupboard door, returned to the kitchen.

Alli turned her head. "Almost done," she said.

Was that the ghost of a smile on her face?

They ate, sitting across from each other.

"I was right about you," he said at length. "Despite your hothouse upbringing, you're not a fool. You despise privilege."

Alli swallowed a mouthful of egg and bread. "Fear and loathing."

He nodded. "Hunter Thompson."

She looked up, not for the first time surprised by him. "You've read him?"

"Because he's a favorite of yours."

A shiver went through her—of pleasure, not fear.

"Tell me what you liked most about Thompson."

Alli didn't hesitate. "He was a subversive. He thought civilization was hypocritical, he loved to show how good people were at rationalizing their actions."

Kray bit off a piece of bacon. "In other words, he was like us—you and me."

"What do you mean?"

Kray wiped his mouth, sat back. "From my point of view, the civilization Thompson was writing about is inextricably entwined with religion. And what is religion, after all, but totalitarianism? The strictures god presented to Adam and Eve, that both the Old and New Testaments describe, are nothing more than a series of laws so extreme,

so prohibitive, they're impossible to adhere to. In the so-called beginning, in the garden of Eden, god tells Adam and Eve that he's provided
them with everything they could possibly desire or ever will desire.
The only thing is, see that tree over there? That's the Tree of Knowledge. If you want to find out what's really going on, you need to eat
the fruit. But hey, wait a minute, eating the fruit is forbidden, so forget
that knowledge thing, who needs it anyway when I've given you everything you want. So, in essence, religion insists we live in ignorance—
but that's perfectly okay, because we have our priests and ministers to
tell us what to do and what to think.

"Shall I go on? Okay, how about 'Thou shalt not covet thy neighbor's wife.' The commandment doesn't say don't screw another man's
wife, that would be doable. Instead, it gives you an impossible task: It
forbids you even to *think* about screwing another man's wife!

"You see what's happened here? Religion was invented by men in
order to *create* sin. Because without sin there can be no fear, without
fear how do you control large numbers of human beings? Add to that
an elite theocracy that periodically issues edicts as it sees fit, in order to
keep itself in power, and the definition of totalitarianism is complete."

Alli took a moment to absorb what Kray said before replying:
"What about the totalitarianism of Hitler and Stalin?"

A knowing smile spread across Kray's face. "The Vatican acqui-
esced to Hitler. In fact, it rushed to knuckle under in 1933, signing a
treaty with Hitler forbidding German Catholics to participate in any
form of political activity that criticized the regime. After the war, it
provided documents, false passports and the like, enabling Nazis to flee
to South America, and no German was ever excommunicated for war
crimes. The historical connection of the Christian churches with fas-
cism is undeniable and a matter of public record. Hardly surprising,
when you think about it. Totalitarianism attracts totalitarianism. Its
members are absolutists—by definition, they cannot apologize for their
transgressions. Think about it for a moment. Totalitarianism whether

it be religious in nature like the Christian church or political in nature like history's fascist states is all faith-based. Absolute faith in one's infallible leaders.

"At least we secularists have the freedom—and the duty—to admit our mistakes, and to correct them."

Alli, eyes turned inward, was lost in thought. She was absorbing everything, like a sponge. "It's true. I see things that frighten me," she said at length. "A group of people with tremendous power and inflexible views, everyone else afraid to speak up, more limits put on personal freedoms." She pursed her lips. "What does it mean? It's unthinkable, but could it be that we're inching away from democracy?"

"The very fact that you're asking the question is cause for celebration." Kray pushed his plate to one side. "Now you tell me. Your opinion is as important as mine."

Her lips curled in an ironic smile. "Even though I've lived a life of privilege?"

"Precisely because you've lived a life of privilege," Kray said seriously.

She rose, gathered the plates and cutlery.

"You don't have to do that," he said.

"I'm stronger now." Her hands full, Alli walked over to the sink with decidedly less difficulty. Her back to him, she began to wash the dishes.

Kray stood. "Alli?"

"Yes?"

"You're free to go any time you want."

Alli scrubbed a plate free of yolk and grease, placed it with great deliberation on the drainboard rack. "If I go home," she said without turning around, "I'll stop learning."

TWENTY-THREE

STOP 'N' shop," Armitage said, "what's that?" He was even more jittery now. His face was as white as the sleet bouncing off the car's windshield.

Jack turned down Kirby Road about five miles from Claiborne. "It's when you intercept a perp—a suspect—grill him about where he's going, why he's in the area, what he's got in his vehicle."

"Where's your probable cause?"

Jack pulled out his gun. "Here's my probable cause."

"You can't just—"

"What are you, an ex-priest *and* an ex-lawyer?"

Armitage fell silent. While he tried to gather himself, Jack said, "Give me the BMW's tag number."

Armitage showed him the pad, but Jack's emotions were running too high, he was under too much stress for him to be able to get to the mental place where he could concentrate enough to make sense of what Armitage had jotted down.

"Read it to me."

Armitage looked at him quizzically.

"I can't take my eyes off the road," Jack lied. He'd never get over the shame of his disability.

Armitage read off the license tag.

Jack called Bennett back. "I need a check on a gray late-model Five series BMW, tag number two-four-nine-nine CXE. Right. Thanks."

Jack closed the connection. They drove awhile in an uneasy silence.

At length, Armitage said, "I didn't sign on for this."

"You want out?"

Armitage looked at Jack, seemed abruptly ashamed.

"Tell me more about the FASR."

Armitage ran a hand through his soaking hair.

"Come on," Jack urged, "the talking'll do you good."

"All right." Armitage licked his lips nervously. "What we believe, first and foremost, is that an ethical life can be led without religion. In fact, it's religion of all stripes that most batters the ethical life into submission. The word of the lord God is the best method devised by man to twist ethics, morality, to escape the consequence of your actions. The pious can get away with all manner of heinous crimes—burning people at the stake, quite literally turning their guts inside out—all in the name of God. The so-called laws of religion have been rewritten over and over in order to justify the actions of the religious elders."

It was at that precise moment that Jack felt a slight prickling at the back of his neck. The hair on his forearms stirred as if magnetized, and his eyes were drawn to the rearview mirror. For a moment, he thought he was losing his mind, for there sat his own beloved Emma looking back at him with her clear eyes, as alive as she had ever been.

"*Dad—*"

He heard her voice! It was definitely her voice, but when he glanced over at Armitage, it was clear that the other man had heard nothing. Jack scrubbed his face with his hand, glanced again at the rearview mirror, which now showed the road behind, traffic moving in normal locomotion. No one was in the backseat.

He swallowed hard. What was causing these hallucinations? he asked himself. They had to be hallucinations, right? What else could they be?

With an enormous effort, he returned his attention to the man sitting beside him. He had been going to ask him another question entirely, but what came out of his mouth was, "Does that mean you don't believe in God?"

"God doesn't enter into it," Armitage said matter-of-factly. "It's what religion has done in god's name that we're rebelling against."

"Then you have in common with E-Two their desire for a Second Enlightenment."

Armitage sighed. "We do. But we strenuously disagree with their methods. They're extremists, and like all extremists, they're wholly goal-oriented. They see only the shortest distance, the straight path to victory, and that invariably involves violence. As with all extremists the world over and down through history, the means to their goal is of no interest to them."

"That much I get." Jack was watching the side mirror, but nothing suspicious showed itself. His cell buzzed. It was the president-elect. Jack must have missed his hourly check-in. He answered the call, assured Edward Carson that in pursuing his own line of investigation he was making progress. There was nothing more he could say with Armitage sitting right next to him. Carson seemed to understand that Jack wasn't in a position to speak freely and he rang off.

"What I don't understand is why Garner and his people think you're an E-Two training ground," Jack said.

"That's a sore point, I admit." Armitage folded his arms across his chest. "Over the past months—I don't know how many, but certainly it's under a year—a number of our younger members have left. In fact, they've dropped out of sight. We've heard rumors that some of them surfaced in E-Two, but so far as we know, that's all they are—rumors."

At least Garner has something right, Jack thought.

"If we're a training ground," Armitage went on, "it's totally inadvertent. This is still a free country—" He looked pointedly at Jack. "—more or less. Neither Pete nor I nor anyone else can control what our members do. Unlike the Church, we've no wish to."

Jack's phone buzzed. It was Bennett.

"You sure about the number you gave me?"

"Two-four-nine-nine CXE," Jack said.

"Then you've got a problem, my friend." The voice was tight, whispered.

"How serious?"

"That BMW is a Dark Car."

"What the hell is that?" Jack said.

"There's no registration attached to that particular tag, no info in the data bank whatsoever." There was a slight pause. "Which means it belongs to a government black ops division. They have no official oversight."

Jack's mind was racing. "Which means they can do pretty much whatever they want."

"And here's why: Only four people are authorized to send out a Dark Car," Bennett said. "The president, the National Security Advisor, and the Secretaries of Defense and Homeland Security."

"How would you know that?" Jack asked.

"Same way I know that all Dark Cars are foreign because no one would think of U.S. government agents using anything but an American vehicle." Bennett chuckled. "I guess the time when you thought you knew everything about me is over."

"Thanks," Jack said.

"For what?" his contact said before hanging up. "We never spoke about this."

"What?" Armitage said. "Who can do whatever they want?"

"Whoever was in the car." Jack paused for a moment, thinking the situation through. "It's not registered. Officially, it doesn't exist. Neither do its occupants."

Armitage moaned. "This really *is* a nightmare."

"Not if you keep your head." Jack turned to Armitage. "I'm going to tell you what this is all about. At this point, I think you deserve some context."

Armitage's eyes were wide and staring. Jack wondered whether he'd be able to keep his wits about him.

"A few days ago, two Secret Service agents were murdered. The E-Two logo was found at the scene of the crime. That's why Garner and his people came down on you. This is the opening they've been praying for to discredit the entire missionary secularist movement. I'm afraid this Administration is going to do its best to paint your people as criminals—worse, actually, they'll say you're homegrown terrorists. They want to destroy you." Jack paused. "But there is a way out."

Armitage's bitter laugh dissolved into a sob. "You must be seeing something I'm not."

"Very likely," Jack said. "If you can marshal your resources to help me find the killer, you'll have the best weapon you can hope for to fight the media firestorm the Administration is planning to rain down on you." He watched a speeding car pass by. "The problem, as you can see, is that you don't have much time. I can hold these people off for a day, maybe three, but that's it."

Armitage groaned. "What d'you need from me?"

"For starters, a list of your defectors," Jack said. "Then you and I are going to have to run them down."

Armitage stared out the window at the low sky, the driving sleet. "I don't have a choice, do I?"

"You tell me."

Armitage pointed. "We'd better get to my office then, as quickly as possible, so I can access the encrypted database."

"Where are we going?" he asked.

"Kansas Avenue. Just south of the junction of Eastern and New Hampshire," Armitage answered. "You ever heard of the Renaissance Mission Congress?"

Jack said he had.

"Back in the day, before it moved to larger, more luxurious quarters, it was known as the Renaissance Mission Church. We moved into its original building two years ago. Ironic, isn't it?"

Armitage didn't know the half of it, Jack thought.

His phone beeped. It was Chief Bennett.

"How did the stop 'n' shop go?" he asked with no little apprehension.

"It didn't," Bennett said. "I don't know what the hell you've gotten yourself into, Jack, but I got an official reprimand and a strict 'stay clear' order from the commander."

"Sorry, Chief, but you also got them off my tail."

A blur at the corner of Jack's eye made him reach for his Glock. There was a loud crack, the car swung on its shocks as the bullet entered the car's metalwork, and Armitage screamed. A second gunshot shattered the windshield, and Jack used the butt of his gun to punch out the crazed sheet of safety glass. Wind and sleet filled the interior, half-blinding him. But his mind had already formed the three-dimensional picture of his car, the road, the BMW. He could see the angles, feel the shifting vectors even as they formed and re-formed.

Just ahead of them, off the driver's-side fender, rode the gray BMW. Jack could see that the expert driver was jockeying for the perfect position, to enable the shooter to have a clear line of fire. The professionals were leaving nothing to chance.

The scenario was clear in his mind, the playing field existed in his world, and there was no one better at its mastery.

Jack's eyes flicked to the rearview mirror, his mind performing a thousand calculations in the blink of an eye. He braked suddenly. The Toyota behind them screeched to slow down, rear-ended them at a reduced speed, jouncing them sharply against their seat belts, then back against the seats. In the following moment, when most people would be in shock, Jack's brain figured vectors, speeds, distances. Then he slammed the BMW's right rear fender.

The BMW spun clockwise; then everything happened very quickly. Jack put on speed. The BMW careened out of control, veering sharply to the left, its rims sparking off the wet tarmac. Jack caught a glimpse of the driver desperately scrambling to regain control, the shooter off-balance, white-faced. Then the BMW struck the left-hand guardrail at speed, its rear end rose up angrily before the car punched through the rail, spun crazily down the slope at the side of the parkway.

A moment later, flames flickered and an explosion of debris geysered up as the gas tank cracked. Jack floored the car, heading for Kansas Avenue NE, smack in the middle of his past.

PART THREE

TWENTY-FOUR

ALLI CARSON lay drowsing in the pantry, on the folding cot Kray had provided for her. The sheets and blanket were tucked up around her chin. Her face was flushed but calm. Kray, standing over her, emptied a syringe into the crease behind her left earlobe, where the puncture would never be noticed. On the counter below Carrie's lair was a full syringe, capped to keep the needle sterile. Kray dropped the empty syringe in the hazmat waste bin, bent over Alli, began to whisper in her ear.

Alli's mind was adrift on a cloud that shape-shifted first into her favorite toys as a child: Splash the dolphin, Ted the giraffe, and Honey the teddy bear. They romped and laughed as she played with them, before dissolving into other images. At first, these images were jumbled, smeary, and confusing, but presently they resolved themselves into scenes intimately familiar to her. Specifically the incidents that more or less defined her life up to the moment she was abducted.

Her mind brought her back to just before she was diagnosed with Graves' disease. At thirteen, she suffered moods so black, her mother took her to a psychologist. She referred Alli to her physician, who in turn referred her to an endocrinologist, who finally made the diagnosis. Her pituitary gland was affected, her eyes bulged slightly, her mood swings were vicious, the bouts of anxiety left her limp and exhausted, drenched in her own sweat. There were times when she was sure she was losing her mind. Lying on her bed, she would stare up at the ceiling, lost in the blackness of the universe, the essential futility of life. Future, what future? And why would you want one, anyway? Her heart galloped faster and faster until it seemed as if it would burst through her chest. Methimazole prevented her thyroid from producing too much hormone, so gradually the anxiety loosened its grip on her, her heart rate returned to a normal trot, her eyes ceased to bulge.

These memories, running one over the next, vanished into a pearly mist, only to be replaced by visions of the summer when she went to camp for the first and only time. She was fifteen. She'd begged her parents to let her go, not only to separate herself from the suffocating atmosphere of a senior senator's entourage but also in order to get a sense of how she'd do on her own. She needed a venue where she could explore who she was. She met a boy—an unutterably handsome boy from a wealthy family in Hartford. His father owned a huge insurance firm that generated obscene profits. His mother was a former Ford model. All this Alli learned from the boy, whose name was Barkley, though with the particular cruelty of teens, everyone called him Bark. Well, almost everyone; the kids on work programs at the camp in order to pay for the privilege of being there had another name for him, Dorkley.

That a portion of the community—so tight-knit, it was incestuous—reviled Barkley only endeared him to Alli. He was a misfit just like her; she could relate to his being marginalized. After dinner, they took walks in the long cobalt twilight, hanging at the edge of the softball field or on the sloping muddy shoulder of the lake. Often they stared as one at the raft moored in the center of the lake. They sat close together, but they never brushed shoulders, let alone held hands. And yet a certain magnetism, plucked out of the droning summer air, drew them, caused them perhaps to feel the same longing, an ache deep down in a place they could not identify. Once, they spoke about the raft in an argot they understood better than anyone else at camp—as Oz, Neverland, the other end of the White Rabbit's hole, heavily romanticized worlds that were home to Others, the people so special or different, they didn't belong in Kansas or London or the English countryside.

That night they spoke while the last smears of color faded under the onslaught of darkness. The air grew chill and damp, and still they did not move. Their talking had come to an end; there seemed nothing left to say. It was difficult for Alli to remember who began to strip first. In any event, there came a time when they stood in their underwear side by side, feet in the cool, still water. They heard a bullfrog out on the lake, saw water spiders skimming the surface. All the lights were behind them, up the hill where the buildings were situated. Here their own world began, and Alli, with a shiver of intent, pushed aside her anxiety about her nude body as she slipped out of undershorts and bra.

Wading into the water, arms held high, they lay down in the deliciously cool water, as if it were a bed. Alli did an excellent crawl out to the raft, arrived there seconds before Barkley. She hauled herself, dripping, from the water; he was right behind her.

At first they lay on their stomachs, out of modesty perhaps or because this was the way most children slept. They were still more children than adults, knew it, clung to its safety.

As a certain fear flooded her mind, Alli said, "I don't want to do anything. You know that."

Barkley, head on folded forearms, smiled slowly. "Neither do I. We're just here, right? Just us. We've left all the knuckleheads behind."

Alli laughed softly at how sweetly he used words that were so, well, dorky. It occurred to her that his very unhipness was another reason she liked him. Preening boys, showing off their cool in the most obvious and ostentatious manner, had a tendency to buzz around her because they wanted something from her father, if only to bask in the penumbra of his celebrity. Proximity to power was a potent aphrodisiac for boys of that age, and would be, until they had gathered their own. Later in life, it would be the women who'd be buzzing around these boys' moneyed hives.

They lay side by side on their softly rocking island, silent, listening to the slap of rope against the raft's pontoons, the lap of water, and in the humming night the occasional bellow of the bullfrog, the call of a skimming loon on its way to nest for the night, the eerie hoot of an owl high overhead. Who turned first? Alli couldn't recall, but all at once they were lying on their backs, their eyes focused on the spangled blackness of the sky, not on the pale flesh beside them, a blobby blur in the corners of their eyes.

"I wish we were up there," Barkley said, "on a spaceship heading for another planet."

He was a sci-fi nut, reading Heinlein, Asimov, Pohl. Alli had read them also, saw through them. They were men from the dying pulp-magazine world—men with amazing ideas, granted, but they weren't writers, not when you compared them with her current favorites, Melville, Hugo, Steinbeck.

"But the planets have no breathable atmosphere," Alli said. "What would we do when we got there?"

"We'd find a way to survive," Barkley said in a very grown-up tone of voice. "Humans always do." He turned his head, looked at her. "Don't we?"

Alli, mute, felt paralyzed beneath his serious gaze. Trying to put herself in his head, she wondered what he thought of the body stretched out before him. She herself had not looked at his.

He rose up on his side to face her, head propped on the heel of one hand. His hair was golden, his skin glowing. All of him seemed golden. "Don't you want to fly far, far away, Alli?"

A moment ago, she would have said yes, but now, forced to make a decision, she didn't know what she wanted. She thought she'd miss her family, no matter how annoying and stifling they sometimes could be. She didn't want to be without them, and then the revelation hit her: She was a conventional girl, after all. The thought depressed her momentarily.

"I want to go back."

She sat up, but Barkley put a hand on her forearm. "Hey, it's early yet. Don't get spooked, no one can see us, we're safe."

Reluctantly, she lay back down, but a subtle shift had occurred inside her, and she was unable to keep her thoughts at rest.

As if sensing her unease, Barkley wriggled up behind her, put one arm gently around her. "I'll just hold you close, I'll protect you, then we'll swim back, okay?"

She said nothing, but her body nestled back against his and she gave an involuntary sigh. Folding one arm beneath her cheek, she closed her eyes. Her thoughts, like fireflies, darted this way and that against the blackness of her lids. Eventually, though, she felt a warmth spread from Barkley to her, the fireflies dimmed, then vanished altogether as she fell into peaceful slumber.

She was awakened slowly, almost druggily, by a repeating rhythmic sound and a persistent sensation. Drawn fully out of sleep, she realized that it was pain she felt, pain and pressure in a localized area, the place between her buttocks. It was then that she realized that the rhythmic sound and the pressure were connected. Barkley, grunting, held her tight against him. Sweat slicked the surface of her back, spooned against his front, and a peculiar musky scent dilated her nostrils, roiled her insides.

"What are you doing?" Her voice was thick, still slurry with sleep.

His grunting became more intense.

All at once, she snapped fully awake. She felt something rubbing against her bare buttock.

"Have you lost your mind?"

For what seemed like an eternity, she struggled silently in the prison of his arms.

It was only later, in the relative safety of her bunk, that she began to realize that she had been the victim of violence. At the moment, she was defeated by shock and terror. Her little body shook and quivered with each masculine thrust. She wanted to curl up into a ball, a crushed and discarded paper bag. She wanted to cry, she wanted to beam herself to another planet like they did in *Star Trek*. *Beam me up, Scotty,* she thought despairingly. But she remained locked in the sweaty embrace of this monstrous octopus that had risen up from the muck of the lake to entwine her in its tentacles.

Suspended time ticked away like taffy being pulled in slo-mo. She was no longer there, on the bucking raft, pinned to sun-beaten wooden slats. Pine trees on the shore ruffled; a sinister cloud, spreading like mist, masked the bone-white moon. An owl hooted, and a squadron of bats winged low over the water like Darth Vader's TIE fighters. But she was deaf and blind to the world around her. Her mind fled down pitch-black hallways that smelled of him, of them, of sweat and fear, of wood-rot and despair. But this place wouldn't do, so she went deeper, to a fortress her mind made impenetrable, and there she pulled up the drawbridge, locked herself away like a princess in a fairy tale, retired to the keep in the still center.

Without knowing how, she wormed her way to the edge of the raft. Perhaps Barkley was done and simply let her go. Rolling into the still, black water, she gasped, wept as she swam back to shore.

She never told her parents what had happened that night. In fact, she scarcely spoke a sentence to them in the aftermath, preferring to grunt or not to respond at all to their probes. In those months when autumn strode confidently after summer, her mother badgered her about dating Barkley, who, she felt certain, was the perfect match for her daughter. In fact, Alli was boxed into going to dinner with Barkley and both their parents. What seemed to her in summer handsome was now in autumn reptilian. She felt her stomach heave at first sight of him, and when forced to sit beside him, all appetite fled her like a mouse at the pounce of a hungry cat. What followed was an excruciatingly awkward, secretly embarrassing evening. Over ashy coffee and cloying flourless chocolate cake, Barkley, his nose firmly up her father's ass, contrived to tell him a joke. At the same time, hidden beneath the table, he slithered his hand between her thighs. Alli leapt up and fled the restaurant, for which, later, she was severely reprimanded. She'd broken her mother's strict rules of social engagement, and that was that.

That might have bothered the old, proper Alli, her mother's clone, but that girl was dead, left at the mercy of the sweaty octopus on the raft. When she'd dropped into the lake, the black water closing over her head, swirling her hair across her face, there had come a breach. Her old self turned to misty cloud that masked the illumination of the moon. She left behind everything she had felt or believed. In the process, she shriveled, closed up like a clam inside its striated shell. But alone with herself she was safe.

In time, even her mother came to dimly realize that something was wrong. Since neither tough love nor punishment worked, she sent Alli to a psychologist, which made Alli retreat even further into her citadel of solitude. She was reduced to weaving lies in order to avoid being sucked into that cold, impersonal office furnished with psychobabble. She never once considered what the solemn man sitting across from her made of those lies; she didn't care. She had already developed a healthy cynicism about males, and as for trust, forget about it.

Within six weeks, unable to make any headway, the shrink recommended a meds psychiatrist, who met with Alli for twenty minutes.

Diagnosing her depression, he handed her a smile along with a prescription for Wellbutrin XL.

"We'll give the Wellbutrin several weeks. If it doesn't do the trick there's a whole galaxy of medications we can try," he said. "Worry not, we'll have you right as rain in no time."

She promptly threw the little cream-colored pills into a trash bin at the pharmacy.

In Alli's drugged mind, it was now three years later. She heard "Neon Bible" by Arcade Fire as if from a long distance away. Superimposed over it was the drone of a familiar voice, repeating instructions she found so rudimentary, a half-wit could follow them. Still, they were repeated to the cadence of "Neon Bible" until they became as much a part of her as her lungs or her heart.

Presently, on a cloud of memory, she drifted off again, into her past. She had met Emma McClure on her first day at Langley Fields, and from that moment on she knew she wanted Emma to be her roommate. The college had assigned her someone else—a blonde from Texas, whom she loathed on sight; her accent alone set Alli's teeth on edge, not to mention her obsessions with high-end clothes and imported beauty products. Alli lobbied for a switch, for she and Emma to be together, and finally the administration acceded to her request. It wasn't that she'd demanded they do as she asked; she didn't have to go that far, merely point out that she'd mention the "stressful" situation to her father. The headmistress didn't want Edward Carson on her case; no one would, not even the president.

There were reasons Alli liked Emma. Emma came from the wrong side of the tracks, from a family that had to take on debt to send her to Langley Fields. She was smart, funny, and, best of all, utterly without pretensions. Born into a family with, it seemed to her, nothing but pretensions, Alli lived in fear that this trait lay buried in her DNA, sealing her fate, would at any moment turn itself on like a geyser, humiliate her to tears. And when, at Emma's insistence, she read Hunter

S. Thompson's *Fear and Loathing in Las Vegas,* she understood that Emma was a kind of talisman, her subversive bent a magic charm that could immunize Alli against her screwed-up hereditary disease.

Plus there was an edge, a toughness to Emma, the hardy scuff picked up in the street. She was fearless. Privilege, Alli had reason to understand, made you soft, vulnerable, fearful, as if your body had been turned inside out, pink and pulsing. It was a hateful disfigurement, one she felt powerless to reverse until Emma came into her life.

Then everything changed.

TWENTY-FIVE

IT'S A total blackout," Chief Bennett said, "as if the Dark Car never crashed."

"What about the gunshots on Kirby Road?" Jack asked.

Bennett shook his head. "Only a small item about a milk truck that caught fire."

The two friends sat in Tysons Corner in a small coffee shop with a striped awning out front and bistro tables inside. From where Jack sat, he had a good view through the front window of the leafy side street and the occasional passing car. As soon as he had dropped a thoroughly rattled Armitage off at his office, he called Bennett. Then he ran every red light to get here. The pursuit by the Dark Car, the shooting, and its aftermath had shaken him more than he cared to admit. He felt as if he had entered a new and far more dangerous arena.

Bennett turned his coffee cup around and around as if something about its symmetry made him uncomfortable. "Someone very high up in the government food chain is spinning the news at a furious clip," Bennett said.

"According to your information, that would be the president, the

Secretaries of Defense and Homeland Security, or the National Security Advisor. Why in the world would any one of them want me dead?"

Bennett watched a middle-aged man enter, then slide into a booth where a young woman waited for him. She smiled, took his hand in hers. Bennett lost interest in them.

"I've been in this business thirty years," he said. "I've never run up against a brick wall like this. Jack, I've made a career of getting around the brick walls of various government agencies, but this one's different. None of my contacts can help me—or they won't."

"Too scared?"

Bennett nodded. "I'm sorry, Jack. I should have followed you, should have protected you."

"It's not your job."

"I agreed to have you seconded to Hugh Garner's band of merry men." He gave Jack a lopsided grin. "I knew more or less I was throwing you to the dogs."

Jack nodded. "You warned me. But it was Edward Carson who asked for me. I don't see how you could've refused."

There was an unhappy pause while the waitress refilled their cups. Bennett's eyes strayed out through the side window, across the avenue. Following his gaze, Jack saw the bottles of wine, whiskey, designer vodkas, aged rums artfully displayed in the window of the shop across the street.

"I suppose it doesn't get any easier."

Bennett shook his head. "It's like a siren's call."

"As long as you're securely lashed to the mast like Ulysses."

Bennett's gaze swung back to him. "I lost my wife because I was drunk all the time; I'm not about to go off the wagon now."

"I'm happy to hear it."

Bennett poured half-and-half into his cup, along with lots of sugar. That was his treat. "Speaking of wives, you ought to get back with Sharon."

"I was wondering why you insisted she come down to the hospital."

"To be honest, Jack, she was glad I asked. I think she wanted to come."

Jack sipped his coffee, said nothing.

"I know you're still pissed about her and Jeff."

"You could say that. He was my best friend."

"Jack, what he did—he was never your friend."

Jack's eyes slid away, staring at nothing.

"Sharon did it to get back at you, because she blamed you for Emma's death. She made a mistake." Bennett's voice was low, urgent. "Jack, don't fuck things up with this girl. She loves you." He gave a little laugh. "Shit, you're not the hard-hearted bastard you think you are."

As JACK turned onto Kansas Avenue NE, he saw Nina waiting for him. He'd called her while walking out of the coffee shop in Tysons Corner. She leaned against her black Ford, smoking one of her clove cigarettes. She looked unaccountably fetching in boots with sensible heels, dark slacks, and a navy peacoat buttoned up to the chin. She seemed oblivious of the sleet.

The Hi-Line had been transformed into the Black Abyssinian Cultural Center. The electronics shop behind which Andre and his crew had beaten the crap out of him was now a ninety-nine-cent store. Otherwise Kansas Avenue looked much the same. It was still filthy and decrepit, no place for the Renaissance Mission Congress. But the old clapboard building, still peeling, still deeply tarnished with mildew, did seem peculiarly appropriate for the First American Secular Revivalists.

Jack got out of the car and led Nina into the building that held so many memories for him.

Where there had once been pews and pulpits was now a large work space divided into cubicles by cheap, movable half walls, each equipped with a desk, cordless phone, computer terminal, and the like. A soft murmur of voices filled the area where once a choir had opened up their throats and their hearts to God.

The cubicles were filled by an eclectic army of men and women whose ages Jack judged to be from their early twenties to their late sixties. They all looked extraordinarily busy. Only a young girl glanced up as they went past.

Armitage—and presumably Peter Link—occupied a separate office, what had once been Reverend Myron Taske's rectory. Jack, in the center of the room, looked around. The huge armoire was still against one wall, Taske's battle-scarred desk was opposite, but everything else was different—modern, sleek, gleaming. Maybe it was the new furniture that made the room look so small, Jack thought. Or perhaps it was his memory playing tricks on him. Either way, as in the Langley Fields buildings, Jack felt a dislocation—as if he were both here and not here. He wondered if that was how Emma felt when she appeared in the backseat of his car.

By this time, Armitage was behind his desk. "You said you wanted a list of members who had defected over the last eighteen months."

Jack cleared his throat. "That's right."

Armitage nodded. "I can do that."

His fingertips flew over his computer keyboard, typing in the algorithm that would decrypt the FASR database. A moment later, he was scrolling down a list, cutting and pasting into a new document. He pressed a key, and the printer began to hum. Then it spit out two sheets of paper. Armitage leaned over, pulled them out of the hopper, handed them to Jack.

Jack was aware of Nina very close beside him, leaning in to read the list so easily, so effortlessly, he felt a stab of envy. For him it was a struggle of the first order. He concentrated in the way Reverend Taske had taught him, remembering the three-dimensional letters Taske had made for him, so Jack could feel them, understand their individual nature in order to recognize them in two dimensions, make sense of their sequences. The letters stopped swimming away from him, began to gather like fish around a coral reef. Jack began to read the names, slowly but accurately.

"See anyone you know?" Armitage asked.

Jack, concentrating fully, shook his head.

Nina looked around, said to Armitage, "Honestly, I don't get what you're all about."

"It's not so mysterious, despite what the talking heads on Fox News claim," Armitage said. "I and people like me don't want to live in a 'Christian nation,' we don't want members of the Administration to be anointing themselves with holy oil. Above all, we don't want a president who believes he's doing the will of God. We simply want the freedom to explore the unknown, wherever that might lead."

"Where d'you stand on the human soul?"

"Several leading scientists around the world who are missionary secularists believe that what we call a soul is in fact electrical energy, that when the body dies, that energy lives on. That's one of the mysteries they're trying to solve."

"And God?"

"God is a personal matter, Ms. Miller. Many of us believe absolutely in God, in whatever form. It's not God that we're fighting against. It's what's done in God's name by all the 'systems of religion.'

"Here, let me give you an example from history." He rummaged around his desk until he found a hardcover book titled *Marriage of Heaven and Hell*. "These are the words of William Blake, the eighteenth-century English visionary:

> 'All Bibles and sacred codes have been the cause of the
> following errors:
> That man has two really existing principles, viz., a body
> and a soul.

That Energy, called Evil, is alone from the body, and
Reason, called Good, is alone
from the soul.
But the following contraries to these are true:
Man has no body distinct from the Soul—for what is
called body is that portion of the soul
discerned by the five senses . . .
Energy is the only life, and is from body, and Reason is
the bound or outward
circumference of energy.'"

Armitage closed the book, set it aside. "What William Blake is saying is that there is no evil inherent in human beings. I believe him. The story of the poisoned apple from the Tree of Knowledge is a fiction created by men who, from the first, sought power over others by keeping them ignorant."

Nina said, "Still, I don't understand your preoccupation with finding the meaning of things. What if there is no meaning?"

"Keeping yourself in ignorance is the Church's idea," Armitage said calmly. "Knowledge is wisdom, Ms. Miller. Wisdom is power. Power provides individuality."

"It also feeds the ego," Nina said. "An excess of ego breeds chaos."

"Come on." Jack took Nina by the elbow, moved her toward the rectory door. "This guy can debate you until Gabriel comes calling." As he hustled her out the door, he said, "Thanks for your help, Armitage."

"Anytime." Armitage was already back to work, scanning his e-mails.

"I just may take you up on that." Jack closed the door softly behind him.

As soon as Jack and Nina left the FASR offices, a young woman in her early twenties got rid of her current call. She was pretty, dark of hair, fair of cheek. In fact, in looks, size, and age she was remarkably similar to the homeless girl Ronnie Kray had picked up off the street for the use of her left hand, the girl who was now moldering in his refrigerator.

The pretty FASR worker dialed a local number. Almost immediately, she heard the familiar male voice on the other end.

"Yes, Calla."

"He just left," Calla said into the receiver.

"You're certain it's him," Kray said.

Calla looked down into the open drawer of her desk. Among the pens, pencils, erasers, paper clips, and spare staples was the small photo of Jack McClure Kray had given her. It had the same flat, slightly grainy look as the photos of Alli Carson that hung on the wall of Kray's house in Anacostia.

"Absolutely," Calla said.

"Tonight. Same time, same place." Kray broke the connection.

TWENTY-SIX

GODDAMNIT!"

Secretary Dennis Paull rarely lost his temper, but as those who worked closely with him could attest, when he did fly into a rage, it was best to say, "Yessir!" and get out of his way.

"Goddamnit to hell!" The Secretary of Homeland Security had his cell phone jammed so tightly to his head, circulation was being cut off to his ear. "The occupants were roasted alive, then."

He listened intently to the harried voice on the other end of the line. The call had come in just as he was about to go into a debriefing with the POTUS, the Secretary of State, and one of the ranking generals—he forgot who, they all looked, spoke, and thought alike—who had just returned from the successful arm-twisting of the Russian president, Yukin. The POTUS was jubilant. He told Paull to get his fanny over to the West Wing, that they were all going to gorge themselves on beluga caviar, a parting gift from Yukin, who had knuckled under to the president's agenda.

Paull had been on his way to see his wife, not that she would recognize him. But when he failed to see her during the week, his heart broke all over again, and thoughts of their courtship and early years together would flood through him like a riptide, threatening to spin him away on whatever mysterious current had snatched her away from him. For an insane moment, he had contemplated the unthinkable: defying the president, sitting with Louise, holding her hand, willing the puzzlement out of her eyes and mind, willing her back to him. But then his survival instincts, honed by decades inside the Beltway, came to the fore and saved him.

Paull was about to say something but caught himself in time. He was standing on the blue carpet that led to the Oval Office. He was surrounded by polished wood paneling, cream paint, and the hushed sounds of a staff that ran like a well-oiled machine. Like the emanations of magnetic north, he felt the waves of power so close to the Oval Office. He was not fooled, however; the power lay in the office, not in the man who temporarily inhabited it. He strode down the hall, and then ducked into a small room, an extra office that was deserted. His phone was specially designed by the magicians at DARPA, ensuring that his conversations would sound like gibberish to anyone picking up the bandwidth. Nevertheless, he was cautious about his own voice being overheard.

"You're sure they're dead," he said into the phone.

"They had no time to get out," the man on the other end of the line said. "And believe me, no one short of Superman could have survived that blaze."

"How the hell did this happen?"

"The best I can tell, McClure pissed them off. He got on to them; he sicced his ATF pals on them. They couldn't believe it, so they went after him."

Paull rolled his eyes. Why did he have to suffer these incompetents? But he already knew the answer. Incompetents were who this Administration hired. "And," he prompted.

"They got a little overzealous."

Paull had to count to ten before he could say in a low voice, "You call firing handguns on the parkway 'overzealous'? This wasn't a termination mission, for the love of Mike."

Silence on the line.

Paull felt as if his eyes were bugging out of his head. "It sure as hell wasn't a termination mission."

"Sir," the disembodied voice replied, "they sure as hell thought it was."

What about your car?" Nina said.

Jack drove south on Kansas Avenue. Considering the gray BMW, he thought it best not to be driving his car the rest of the day. "After we're done, you can drop me back here."

"It may be nothing but a burned-out husk by that time," Nina said.

"Or it might not be there at all and I can requisition a new one."

"Har-har." Nina banged down her door lock. "Where are we going, anyway?"

"Take a look at the list."

Nina took up the two sheets Armitage had given them, her eyes scrolling down the list of names. "What am I looking for?"

"Known criminals."

"Let's see." Nina ran her forefinger down the list on both sheets. "Nope. Nothing shouts out at me."

Jack made another turn, onto Peabody Street NW. He checked the rearview mirror. He was justifiably paranoid about tails. "Try the second sheet, fourth name from the bottom."

"Joachim Tolkan? What about him?"

"Twenty-five years ago, his father, Cyril, was a notorious criminal in this section of the District." Jack put on some speed. "Ran numbers, drugs, and explosives out of the All Around Town bakery."

Nina laughed. "That's where I get my croissants and coffee. There are maybe a dozen of them throughout the District."

"Back in the day," Jack said, "there was only one."

Perhaps Nina heard something in his tone. "You knew the father, this Cyril Tolkan."

"He murdered someone." Jack slowed as they approached the old tenement, home of the original All Around Town bakery. "Someone close to me."

Nina frowned as Jack pulled to a stop on Fourth Street NW between Kennedy and Jefferson. "This isn't some kind of personal vendetta, is it, because we have no time for extracurricular activities of any nature whatsoever."

Jack was sorely tempted to describe in detail Hugh Garner's manhandling of Peter Link, but decided against it. Instead, he said, "I have a hunch. If it doesn't pan out, I'll drop it and we'll be back to square one."

He knew he was on edge. Why would any of the four order him tailed and attacked? Was it Armitage they wanted silenced? The state of unknowing was not a pleasant one for him. He resisted the urge to call Bennett; he knew the chief would contact him as soon as he had dug up anything of substance.

A bell sounded as they entered the bakery. The place was much as he remembered, full of the delicious swirl of butter, sugar, yeast, baking bread. He remembered in vivid detail the first time Gus had taken him here. In his mind's eye, he could see Cyril's goons standing around, reading the racing forms, waiting for their orders to dispense drugs or weapons, pick up payments, and if the envelope was a little light, to deliver a bloody payment of their own. He remembered the balding man behind the counter who gave him a chocolate-chip cookie. And Cyril himself, with his dark, olive eyes, his Slavic cheekbones, and his sinister air. Today, however, there were only a couple of elderly ladies buying their daily bread. They

smiled at him as they walked out with their sweet-smelling purchases.

"Name's Oscar. Can I help you?"

A short, squat man in a baker's apron, with a monkish fringe of
hair around the circumference of his milk chocolate scalp and a wide
flat nose that must once have been broken regarded them with curious
eyes and a welcoming smile. The current All Around Town bakery
was a couple of light-years from the shop Cyril Tolkan had presided
over.

"I'll take a square of crumb cake." Jack turned to Nina. "And you,
sweetheart?"

Nina, unfazed, shook her head.

Jack grinned at Oscar. "The missus is a bit shy in this neighborhood."

"I understand completely." Oscar had a spray of freckles over the
flattened bridge of his nose. He placed Jack's crumb cake in a square of
paper on the top of the glass case. Addressing Nina, he said, "How
about a chocolate-chip cookie?" He picked one out of the pile, held it
out. "No one can resist one of our chocolate-chip cookies."

Jack remembered. Even stale it was good.

Nina gave a tight smile, took the cookie.

Jack took out his wallet.

"The cookie's on the house," Oscar said.

Jack thanked him as he paid. He bit into the crumb cake, said,
"Delicious." As he chewed, he said, "I wonder if Joachim is around."

Oscar busied himself arranging a tray of linzer tortes. "Friend or
business?"

"A little of both."

Oscar seemed to take this nonanswer in stride. "The boss'll be
back tomorrow. He's in Miami Beach, for his mother's funeral."

Jack looked around the room, munched on his crumb cake. "You
know what time he'll be in?"

"First thing in the morning," Oscar said. "I just got off the phone with him." He took a tray of butter cookies from a thin lad who'd appeared from the oven room. "Any message?"

"No." Jack finished off the crumb cake, brushed his fingertips together. "We'll be back."

Oscar held aloft a couple of cookies. "Something for the road?"

Jack took them.

TWENTY-SEVEN

THE RENAISSANCE Mission Church is more than a place of worship for Jack; it's his schoolhouse. It doesn't take long for Reverend Taske to unearth the root of Jack's reading difficulties. As it happens, he's studied a bit about dyslexia, but now he studies more. Every evening when Jack arrives after work at the Hi-Line, Taske has another idea he's found in some book or other pulled from libraries all over the District.

One evening Jack is particularly frustrated by trying to read a book—this one is of poems by Emily Dickinson. He lashes out, breaks a glass on Reverend Taske's desk. Immediately ashamed, he too-quickly picks up the shards, cuts the edge of his hand. After throwing the glass into the wastepaper basket, he goes over to the armoire, takes out the first aid kit. As he does so, his eye is caught by something on the floor of the armoire. Pushing aside some boxes, he sees what looks like a door.

Just as he's pushing the boxes back in place, Reverend Taske comes in. Within the blink of an eye, he seems to take in the entire scenario. He holds out his hand, and once Jack gives him the first aid kit, gestures for Jack to sit down. He looks at the cut on Jack's hand.

"What happened?"

"I was having trouble reading," Jack said. "I got angry."

Taske searches to make sure no tiny bit of glass has lodged itself in the wound. "The glass means nothing." He begins to disinfect the wound. "But your anger needs tending."

"I'm sorry," Jack says.

"Before you allow your temper to flare, think about why you're angry." Taske bandages the cut, then indicates the armoire. "I expect you're wondering where that trapdoor leads." He regards Jack sternly. "I can trust you, can't I?"

Jack sits up straight. "Yes, sir."

Reverend Taske gives him a wink. "You see, back in the thirties, when liquor was outlawed, these buildings were under the control of bootleggers—people who dealt in illegal liquor. There's a tunnel under here that leads into Gus's back room." He closes up the kit, puts it away. "Now, let's get back to Emily Dickinson."

"I'll never be able to get it," Jack says in despair.

Taske bids him put down the slim volume. "Listen to me, Jack. Your brain is special. It processes things in a way mine can't—in three dimensions." He hands Jack a Rubik's Cube. "The idea here is to get a solid color on each side of the cube. Go on. Give it a try."

As Jack turns the cube, understanding comes to him full-blown, and he manipulates the mind-bending puzzle. He hands the cube back to Taske. Each side is a solid color.

"Well, I can't say I'm surprised," Taske says. "All the current literature claims you wouldn't have trouble solving Rubik's puzzle, but four minutes!" He whistles. "No one else I know can solve this, Jack, let alone so quickly."

"Really?"

Taske smiles. "Really."

Though it's in a run-down neighborhood that could charitably be called marginal, the Renaissance Mission Church attracts a high level of media coverage and, therefore, attendance from local politicos. This is due to the benevolent work Reverend Taske does, rehabilitating hardened criminals of thirteen or fourteen, turning them into citizens of the District who make tangible contributions to their neighborhood. Taske's admirable goal is to rehab the entire area, not by inviting white entrepreneurs to take over failing black businesses, but by creating black entrepreneurs who have the tools to turn these businesses into moneymaking operations. Unfortunately, in his neighborhood, the businesses that make the most money are those that run numbers, deploy prostitutes, deal drugs. Old habits are hard to break, especially those that have proved painlessly lucrative for their bosses. No schooling is needed, no learning to abide by the laws of the Man. No need to become civilized—or even civil, for that matter. All that's required is muscle, guns, and a pair of brass balls.

That includes Andre. After taking his lumps from his boss, Cyril Tolkan, for beating up on Jack, Andre has moved up Tolkan's crooked corporate ladder with alarming rapidity. Part of his motivation, of course, was to get out of Tolkan's doghouse, but far more worrying is the flame of his ambition, which is burning brighter than even Gus had imagined. Andre never comes to the church anymore, and ever since Reverend Taske returned from Andre's new lair with a black eye and a lacerated cheek, he doesn't even mention his name. Gus, enraged, wanted to go after Andre himself, but Taske wouldn't let him. Jack happens to overhear their conversation early one Sunday morning, which takes place in the rectory, where Jack is laboriously working his way through *The Great Gatsby*. The novel is interesting because, like Jack himself, Gatsby is an outsider. But it becomes downright fascinating when Jack, thumbing through a biography of F. Scott Fitzgerald he takes out of the local library, learns that the author was, like Jack himself, dyslexic.

"I've had enough standin' aside while Andre goes off on ev'rybody," Gus says.

"You just can't abide him taking business from you," Reverend Taske responds.

"Huh! Looka whut he did to you!"

"Occupational hazard," Taske says. "You're not my daddy, Augustus. I can take care of myself."

"By turnin' the other cheek."

"That's how I was taught, Augustus. That's what I believe."

"Whut you believe ain't nuthin' but a jackass's brayin'."

Jack sucks in his breath. He is compelled to get up, creep down the hall, put his eye to the crack between door and jamb he makes by pulling with his fingertips. In his limited line of vision, the Reverend Taske is eclipsed by Gus's planetary shape.

"Because your ire is up, I'm going to ignore your insult to me, Augustus, but I can't overlook your blasphemy toward God. When we're done, I want you to make penance."

"Not today, Reverend. I gots no truck with turnin' the other cheek. Moment I knuckle to that, I'm shit outta business. You-all gonna tell me that if I don't do fo' myself, God will?"

"I am concerned for your immortal soul, Augustus," Taske says slowly and carefully.

"Huh, you best be concerned with things that matter, like whut you gonna do 'bout expenses round here now that yo' famous bank vice president got indicted for embezzlement. Reg'lators gone pulled the plug on all his deals, including the one that's been keeping this place afloat fo' three years."

Jack hears the creak of a chair, figures the reverend has sat heavily down. "You do have a point there, Augustus."

"Now, you know I make a lotta money, Reverend, an' I'll give you as much as I can."

"The church isn't here to drain you of every penny you make."

"Still an' all," Gus perseveres, "whatever I can muster won't be enough. You gotta think long-term."

"If you have a suggestion," Taske says.

It's at that point that Jack knocks on the door. There is a short startled silence, at the end of which Taske's voice bids Jack enter.

Jack stands in the doorway until the reverend beckons him into the room. "What can I do for you, Jack? Having trouble decoding Fitzgerald's prose?"

"It's not that." Jack is for a moment at a loss for words. Taske looks weary, older. Why hasn't he noticed this before? Jack asks himself.

"Augustus and I are in the middle of a discussion, Jack," Taske says kindly.

"I know, that's why I came in."

"Oh?"

"I couldn't help overhearing."

"Huh, you betta close that door good," Gus says, "so you the on'y one."

Jack shuts the door firmly, turns around. "I heard about the money crisis."

"That's none o' yo' business," Gus says darkly.

"I think I have a way out," Jack says.

The two men seem to hang suspended between disbelief and raucous laughter. The thought that a fifteen-year-old has seen a way out of the fiscal quicksand the Renaissance Mission Church has unceremoniously found itself in is, on the face of it, ludicrous. Except, as both men know, each in his own way, this is Jack—and Jack is capable of extraordinary leaps of logic that are beyond either of them.

So Taske says, "Go ahead, Jack. We're listening."

"I was thinking of Senator Edward Carson."

Taske frowns. "What about him, son?"

"He was here last week," Jack says. "I read the papers—you assign me to do that every day, and I do."

Taske smiles. "I know you do."

"I noticed that Senator Carson got a lot of great press out of his visit here. He even spent some time with the parishioners before and after the service. He said he used to sing in his choir back home in Nebraska. I heard him accept your invitation to sing with our choir today."

"All true," Taske agrees. "What exactly is your point, Jack?"

"There's an election coming up this fall. Senator Carson's campaign war chest is big. According to the papers, he's the party's great future hope. The bigwigs are rumored to be grooming him to run for president one day. Him being here last week and this, I think the rumor's true. But to make a successful run, he's going to need every vote he can get. Last time I looked, there weren't too many blacks living in Nebraska, which is where the Renaissance Mission Church comes in."

"Huh. Sounds like the kid's on to sumthin'," Gus says. "Yes, indeed."

Taske's mouth is half-open. Jack can just about see the gears mesh in his mind, the wheels begin to turn.

"I don't believe it," Taske says at length. "You want me to offer him votes for funding."

Jack nods.

"But we're one small community church."

"Today you are," Jack says. "That's the beauty of the idea. You're always talking about expanding beyond the neighborhood. This is your chance. With Senator Carson's backing, the Renaissance Mission Church could go regional, then national. By the time he's ready to make his run at the presidency, you'll be in position to offer him the kind of help he'll need most."

Gus laughs. "This here boy thinks as big as the sky."

"Yes," Taske says slowly, "but he has a point."

"Carson's gotta go for it," Gus cautions.

"Why won't he?" Jack says. "He's a successful politician. His livelihood depends on him making deals, accommodations, alliances. Think about it. There's no downside for him. Even if you should fail, Reverend, he gets a ton of national press for helping a minority raise itself off its knees."

"Jack's right. The idea makes perfect sense," Taske says. He's chewing over the idea, looking at it from all angles. "And what's more, it just might work!" Then he slams his palms down on the desk as he jumps up. "I knew it! The good Lord bringing you to us was a miracle!"

"Here we go," Gus growls, but Jack can see he's as proud of Jack as Taske is.

"My boy, who would have thought of this but you?" The Reverend Myron Taske takes Jack's hand, pumps it enthusiastically. "I think you just might have saved us all."

TWENTY-EIGHT

LYN CARSON stood at the bedroom window of the suite high up in the Omni Shoreham Hotel. Dusk was extinguishing the daylight, like a mother snuffing out candles one by one. Ribbons of lights moved along Massachusetts Avenue, and the skeletal structure of the Connecticut Avenue Bridge was lit by floodlights. She and her husband were here for a few days to escape the depressing reality that each hour of each day pressed more heavily in on them.

Alli was somewhere out there. Lyn tried willing her into being, to stand here, safe beside her.

Hearing Edward moving about in the sitting room, she turned. She knew why he liked this storied hotel above all others in the District. Though its architecture was blunt to the point of being downright ugly, it was downstairs in room 406D that Harry Truman, whom Edward so admired, had often come to play poker with his friends Senator Stewart Symington, Speaker of the House John McCormack, and Doorkeeper of the House Fishbait Miller.

Just then, her husband's cell phone rang and her heart leapt into her throat. *My Alli, my darling,* she thought, running through the open doorway. Her thoughts swung wildly: *They've found her, she's dead, oh my God in Heaven, let it be good news!*

But she stopped short when Edward, seeing the look on her face, gave her a quick shake of his head. No, it wasn't news of Alli, after all. Churning with disappointment and relief, Lyn turned away, stumbled back to the sitting room, half-blinded by tears. *Where are you, darling? What have they done to you?*

She stood by the window, watching with a kind of irrational fury the indifferent world. How could people laugh, how could they be driving to dinner, having parties, making love, how could they be out jogging, or meeting under a lamppost. How could they be carefree when the world was so filled with dread? What was wrong with them?

She clasped her palms together in front of her breast. *Dear God,* she prayed for the ten-thousandth time, *please give Alli the strength to survive. Please give Jack McClure the energy and wisdom to find her. God, give my precious daughter back to me, and I'll sacrifice anything. Whatever you want from me I'll gladly give, and more. You are the Power and the Glory forever and ever. Amen.*

Just then she felt Edward's strong arms around her, and her shell of toughness—hard but brittle—shattered to pieces. Tears welled out of her eyes and a sob was drawn up from the depths of her. She turned into his chest, weeping uncontrollably as black thoughts rolled through her mind like thunderheads.

Edward Carson held her tight, kissed the top of her head. His own eyes welled with tears of despair and frustration. "That was Jack. No news yet, but he's making progress."

Lyn made a little sound—half gasp, half moan—at the back of her throat.

"Alli's a strong girl, she'll be all right." He stroked her back, soothing them both. "Jack will find her."

"I know he will."

They stood like that for a long time, above their own Washington, the world at their feet, the taste of ashes in their mouths. And yet their hearts beat strongly together, and where hearts were strong, they knew, there was fight yet left. There was hope. Hope and faith.

A sharp rap on the door to the sitting room caused them both to start.

"It's okay." Edward Carson kissed her lightly on the lips. "Rest a little now before dinner."

She nodded, watched him cross the bedroom, close the connecting door behind him. Rest, she thought. How does one rest with a heart full of dread?

THE PRESIDENT-ELECT pulled the door open, stood aside so Dennis Paull could enter, then shut and locked it behind him.

"Nina delivered your message," Carson said.

"The Secret Service agents outside?"

"Absolutely secure. You can take that to the bank." He walked over to a sideboard. "Drink?"

"Nothing better." Paull sat on a sofa that faced the astonishing view. "What I like most about flying is that you're so high up, there's nothing but sky. No woes, no uncertainty, no fears."

He accepted the single-malt with a nod of thanks. Carson had no need of asking what Paull drank. The two men had known each other for many years, long before the current president had been elected to his first term. Two years into that first term, when Paull had been faced with carrying out yet another semi-legal directive he found personally abhorrent, he was faced with a professional dilemma. He might have tendered his resignation, but instead he'd gone to see Edward Carson. In hindsight, of course, Paull understood that he'd already made his choice, which was far more difficult and dangerous than simply throwing in the towel. He'd decided to stay on, to fight for the America he believed in in every way he could. His plan began with the alliance he and Edward Carson formed.

This was surprisingly easy. The two men held the same vision for America, which included returning the country to a healthy separation of church and state. Though fiscal conservatives, they were moderates in virtually every other area. They both disliked partisan politics and despised political hacks. They wanted to get on with things without being encumbered with pork barrel politics. They wanted to mend fences overseas, to try to undo the image of America as bully and warmonger. They wanted their country to be part of the world, separated from it only by oceans. At heart, each in his own way, had come to the same inescapable conclusion: America was at a critical crossroads. The country had to be healed. To do that, it had to be resurrected from the little death of the current administration's policies. Otherwise, intimidation, divisiveness, and fear would be the legacy of the last eight years.

Neither of them was a starry-eyed idealist; in fact, over the years, they'd each brokered difficult deals, made compromises, some of them painful, in order to achieve their goals. But both did believe that the country was on the wrong path and needed to be set right. So they had agreed. Whenever he could, Paull would secretly work against the Administration's weakening of democratic freedoms, and in return, Edward Carson would name him Secretary of Defense.

The two men sat in what under other circumstances would have been a comfortable silence. But between them now was the specter of Alli's abduction and possible death.

"How are you two holding up?" Paull had noticed the president-elect's reddened eyes the moment he walked through the door.

"As well as can be expected. Any news from Jack?"

"Jack is doing everything he can, I've made certain of that," Paull said. "And he's protected."

"Protected." Carson's head swung around. "From who?"

Paull stared down into the amber drink, watching the light play off the surface. Only amateurs drank single-malt with ice. "I'd like to say I knew for certain, but I don't."

"Give me the next best thing, then."

Paull had been told that no bodies had been found in the wreck, which meant that Jack had somehow survived the attack. He thought for a moment. "The knives are out. All signs point to the National Security Advisor." He lifted his eyes. "Trouble is, I suspect he's not in it alone."

Paull, staring into the president-elect's eyes, knew Carson understood he'd meant the president.

After a moment, Carson said very deliberately, "Can you get proof?"

Paull shook his head. "Not before January twentieth. Given time, I think I'll be able to find a chink in the National Security Advisor's armor, but I very much doubt I'll get further."

Maintaining plausible deniability was any president's first priority, his most potent line of defense. Carson nodded, sipped his drink. "Getting one will have to suffice, then. It'll be your first order of business come January twenty-first."

"Believe me, it'll be a pleasure."

The ship's clock on the mantel chimed in the new hour. Time lay heavy on Edward Carson's shoulders.

"Look at them down there, Dennis. It's that hour when the workday is over, when everyone lets out a sigh of relief on their way home. But for me, does evening bring darkness, or the end of my daughter's life?"

"Do you believe in God, sir?"

The president-elect nodded. "I do."

"Then for you everything will be all right, won't it?"

IT WAS late when Nina dropped Jack off. His car, windshield replaced, was waiting for him at the lot of the repair shop. Jack climbed into it warily as well as wearily. He felt as if he'd been beaten with a nightstick for the past few days. Had he slept in all that time? He couldn't remember. He opened a bottle of water, drank it all down in one long swallow. Speaking of essential functions, apart from the crumb bun he'd wolfed down, when had he last eaten? He vaguely recalled scarfing down an Egg McMuffin, but whether that was this morning or yesterday, he couldn't say.

It occurred to him that he was hungry. He held the sugar cookies from the All Around Town bakery in his hand, but he didn't eat them.

Instead, he methodically checked out the environment. He was looking for another Dark Car. No word yet from Bennett on who had sent out the first one. He didn't know whether that was good news or bad news. He was almost too tired to care.

Finally, he admitted to himself that what he really wanted to do was look in the backseat to see if Emma had magically appeared once more. A flicker of his eyes told him that he was alone in the car. He set the sugar cookies on the seat beside him. An offering or an entice-ment?

"Emma," he heard himself say, "are you ever coming back?"

He was appalled at the sound of his own voice. Frightened, too. What was happening to him? Was he cracking up? Surely he hadn't seen Emma, surely he hadn't heard her voice. Then what had he seen, what had he heard? Was it all in his head?

All of a sudden, these questions were too big for him. He felt that if he sat with them any longer, his head would explode. He started the car, headed for Sharon's. She lived in a modest house, one of many identical in shape and size, in Arlington Heights. It took him thirty-five minutes to get there. During that time, he had ample opportunity to make sure an Audi or a Mercedes hadn't taken the place of the gray BMW.

The lights were on when he pulled into the driveway, and now that he thought about it, he didn't know whether that was a good or a bad thing. Before he left the car, he checked to see if the cookies had been eaten. They lay against the crease where the seat met the back. They looked sad, forlorn, as if they knew no one would enjoy them. Jack, halfway out of the car, licked his forefinger, picked up a small constellation of crumbs that had formed around the cookies, let them melt on his tongue. He could feel the tears well hotly, so close did he feel to Emma.

He rang the bell, his heart hammering in his chest. Sharon pulled the door open. The scent of chicken and rice wafted out with her, making his mouth water. She regarded him with an unreadable expression. She wore a skirt that clung to her thighs, a sleeveless blouse that showed off her beautiful golden shoulders. Nina would have appeared pale and wan beside her, anorectic instead of willowy. She said nothing for a moment.

"Jack, are you okay?"

"Yeah, sure, it's just that I can't remember the last time I had a decent meal."

"You were on your own so long, I often wondered why you never learned to cook for yourself."

"The tyranny of shopping makes me anxious."

She gave him a tentative smile as she moved aside so he could enter.

Jack closed the door behind him. He took off his overcoat, slung it over the back of the living room sofa. Unlike the old house with its familiar creaking he'd moved into when they split, Sharon preferred a modern place. She had busied herself repainting walls in colors she chose, picking out warm carpets, filling each room not only with furniture but accessories as well—scented candles, a log cabin quilt hanging on the wall, small dishes filled with lacquered shells and gaily striped marbles. No unicorns, thankfully, but a variety of other knick-knacks and souvenirs, along with keepsakes and photos of Emma and Sharon as a child in handmade frames. None of this, however, made up for the house's complete lack of character. Unlike his house, it was a two-story box to live in, nothing more. He found being here disorienting and overwhelming. He'd never get used to Sharon living here, living without him.

What did he have of Emma's? He thought of her iPod, pushed to the back of his ATF locker. One night he took it home and couldn't sleep. Then again, he must have because at one point he started up from a horrific dream of standing paralyzed and mute as Emma's car hurtled into the tree. He could hear the crack of the wood, the explosion of glass, see the twists of metal spiraling inward. The car door snapped open, and a shape already curled in death shot out, struck him full in the chest. Then he was sitting up in bed, screaming and shivering, sweat pouring off him like rain. He spent what was left of the night commiserating with Nick Carraway in the pages of his beloved, tattered copy of *The Great Gatsby,* and was never so glad to see the first blush of dawn turn the darkness gold.

IN SHARON'S new digs, he picked up one of the photos of Emma, but the image seemed flat and empty, a shell of what once had been a vibrant and mysterious girl. As for photos of other people in Sharon's life, he knew there would be none.

Sharon had no past, and so couldn't understand what appeal it could possibly hold for Jack. She had parents, but she never saw or spoke to them. A brother, as well, in Rotterdam, where he was an international lawyer. For reasons he'd never been able to fathom, Sharon had cut herself off from her family, her past. When they were dating, she told him that she had no family, but after they were married, he found photos in the trash, spilled out of an old cigar box. Her mother, father, and brother.

"They're dead to me," she'd said when he'd confronted her. She'd never allowed the subject to come up again.

Did that mean, he often wondered, that Sharon didn't dream? Because he dreamed only of his past, iterations of it with intended outcomes, or not, bizarre twists and turns that he often remembered after he awoke, and laughed at or puzzled over. It seemed to him that there was a richness in life that came with the years, that only your past could provide. It was unbearable to him to think, as Schopenhauer had written, that no honest man comes to the end of his life wanting to relive it. But it seemed possible to him that Sharon believed just that, that her erasing of her past was an attempt to relive her life.

He put the photo back, turned away, but his mood didn't improve. The house's aggressive homeyness produced a hollowness in the pit of his stomach. As for his heart, it had gone numb the moment she appeared at the door.

Below her short skirt, Sharon wore little pink ballet slippers with teeny bows and paper-thin soles. They made her movements around the house elegant and silent, even on the hard tile of the kitchen floor. No matter which way you looked at them, her legs were magnificent. Jack tried not to stare, but it was like asking a moth to ignore a flame.

Sharon opened a glass-fronted cabinet over the sink, stretched up to reach a pair of stemmed glasses. Her figure was highlighted in such a way that Jack felt the need to sit down.

She uncorked a bottle of red wine, poured. "Fortunately, I made enough food for two."

"Uh-huh," was all he could muster because he'd bitten back one of his acerbic replies.

She brought the glasses over, handed him one. "What?"

"What what?"

She pulled a chair out, sat down at a right angle to him. "I know that look."

"What look?" Why all of a sudden did he feel like a felon?

"The 'Baby, let's get it on' look."

"I was just admiring your legs."

She got up, took her wineglass to the stove. She stirred a pot, checked the chicken in the oven. "Why didn't you say that when we were married?" Her voice was more rueful than angry.

Jack waited until she paused to take a sip of wine before he said, "When we were married, I was embarrassed by how beautiful you are."

She spun around. "Come again?"

"You know how you see a hot movie star—"

Her face grew dark. "Where do *you* live, Beverly Hills?"

"I'm talking about a fantasy figure, Shar. Don't tell me you don't have fantasies about—"

"Clive Owen, if you must know." She took the bird out, set it aside to allow the juices to settle. "Go on."

"Okay, so I'm alone with . . . Scarlett Johansson."

Sharon rolled her eyes. "Dream on, buddy."

"I'm alone with her in my mind," Jack persevered, "but when I try to—you know—nothing happens."

She dumped the rice into a serving bowl. "Now that's just not you."

"Right, not when I'm with you. But Scarlett, when I think about her—really think about her—well, it's too much. I'm wondering why the hell a goddess like that would be with me. Then the fantasy goes up in smoke."

She stared intently at the steaming rice. Her cheeks were flushed. After a time, she seemed to find her voice. "You think I'm as beautiful as Scarlett Johansson?"

If he said yes, what would she do? He didn't know, so he said nothing, even when she turned her head to look at him. Instead, he got up, rather clumsily, and helped her serve the food.

They sank back down into their respective chairs. Wordlessly, she handed him the carving utensils and wordlessly he took them, parting the breast from the bony carcass, as he always did. Sharon served them both, first slices of the chicken, then heaping spoonfuls of rice, and broccoli with oil and garlic. They ate in a fog of self-conscious silence, sinking deeper and deeper into their own thoughts.

Finally, Sharon said, "You're feeling okay now?"

Jack nodded. "Fine."

"I thought . . ." She put her fork down. She'd hardly eaten anything. "I thought maybe after the hospital you might call."

"I wanted to," Jack said, not sure that was the truth. "There's something I want to tell you."

Sharon settled in her chair. "All right."

"It's about Emma."

She reacted as if he'd shot her. "I don't—!"

"Just let me—" He held up his hands. "Please, Shar, just let me say what I have to say."

"I've heard everything you need to say about Emma."

"Not this you haven't." He took a deep breath, let it out. He wanted to tell her, and he didn't. But this time seemed as good as any—better, in fact, than any of their recent meetings. "The fact is—" He seemed to have lost his voice. He cleared his throat. "—I've seen Emma."

"What!"

"I've seen her a number of times in the past week." Jack rushed on at breakneck speed, lest he lose his nerve. "The last time she was sitting in the backseat of my car. She said, 'Dad.'"

Sharon's expression told him that he'd made a terrible mistake.

"Are you insane?" she shouted.

"I tell you I saw her. I heard her—"

She jumped up. "Our daughter's dead, Jack! She's dead!"

"I'm not saying—"

"Oh, you're despicable!" Her brows knit together ominously. "This is your way of trying to weasel out of your responsibility for Emma's death."

"This isn't about responsibility, Shar. It's about trying to understand—"

"I knew you were desperate to crawl out from under your guilt."

Her wildly gesticulating hands knocked over her wineglass. Then she deliberately knocked over his. "I just didn't know *how* desperate."

Jack was on his feet. "Shar, would you calm down a minute? You're not listening to me."

"Get out of here, Jack!"

"C'mon, don't do that."

"I said get out!"

She advanced and he retreated, past the seashells and the colored glass, the postcards Emma had sent to them from school, the photos of her as a child. He scooped up his coat.

"Sharon, you've misunderstood everything."

This, of course, was the worst thing he could have said. She flew at him with raised fists, and he backed out the front door so quickly that he stumbled over the top step. She got to slam the door on him once again. Then all the downstairs lights were extinguished and he knew she was sitting, curled up, fists on thighs, sobbing uncontrollably.

He took a convulsive step up, raised his fist to hammer on the door, but his hand flattened out, palm resting on the door as if by that gesture he could feel her presence. Then he turned, went heavily down the steps, returned to his car.

TWENTY-NINE

JACK THOUGHT he was heading home, but instead he found himself pulling into Egon Schiltz's driveway right behind Candy Schiltz's Audi A4 Avant wagon. He got out, walked to the front door, pushed the bell. If Sharon wouldn't talk to him about Emma, maybe Egon would. Jack checked his watch. It was late enough that he was sure to be home by now.

Schiltz lived in the Olde Sleepy Hollow area of Falls Church. His house was a neat two-story colonial the family had lived in for decades. Schiltz had paid just north of $100,000 for it. Back in the day, that wasn't exactly cheap, but these days it was worth conservatively fifteen times that.

Molly came to the door, gave an excited shriek as he whirled her up and around.

"Molly Maria Schiltz, what is going on!"

Candy came bursting into the entryway, but as soon as she saw Jack, the look of concern on her face changed to a broad smile.

"Jack McClure, well, it's been too long!" she said with genuine pleasure.

He kissed her on the cheek as Taffy, their Irish setter, came bounding in, tongue lolling, tail wagging furiously.

"We've finished dinner," Candy said, "but there's plenty of leftovers."

"I just ate, thanks," Jack said.

While he and Candy went into the family room, Molly trooped upstairs to do her homework.

"I have cherry pie," Candy said with a twinkle in her eye. "Your favorite, if memory serves."

Jack laughed despite his black mood. "Nothing wrong with your memory."

Seeing no way out, he allowed her to bustle around the open kitchen, Taffy happily trotting at her heels. She was a statuesque woman with ash-blond hair and a wide, open face. In her youth, she'd been a real beauty. Now, in later middle age, she possessed a different kind of beauty, as well as an enviable serenity. She cut a slice of pie as generous as her figure, took a bowl of homemade whipped cream out of the refrigerator, piled on a huge dollop.

"Milk or coffee?" she said as she plunked the plate and fork down on the pass-through. Taffy came around, sat on her haunches, her long, clever face turned up to Jack.

"Coffee, please." Jack rubbed Taffy's forehead with his knuckles, and the dog growled in pleasure. He picked up the fork. "How many people is this portion supposed to feed?"

Candy, pouring his coffee into a mug she herself had made in pottery class, giggled. "I can't help it if I still consider you a growing boy, Jack." She padded over with the mug. She remembered he liked his coffee straight. "Anyway, you're looking far too gaunt to suit me." She put a hand over his briefly. "Are you getting along all right?"

Jack nodded. "I'm doing fine."

Candy's expression indicated she didn't believe him. "You should come over here more often. Egon misses you." She indicated with her head. "So does Good Golly Miss Molly."

"Molly's grown up. She's got her own friends now."

Candy pulled a mock face. "D'you think she'd ever stop loving her uncle Jack? Shame on you. That's not how this family works."

Jack felt as if he were dying inside. Here was a picture of his own family life . . . if only so many things had happened differently. "The pie's delicious." He smacked his lips. "Is Egon upstairs? I'd like a minute of his time."

"Unfortunately, no," she said. "He called to say he was staying extra late at the morgue, some kind of hush-hush government case. But you should go on over there. He'll be happy for the company. And you know Egon, he can lend an ear with the best of them."

Candy flattened down the front of her dress. "I wish you and Sharon would patch things up."

Jack stared down at the remains of crust. "Well, you know how it is."

"No, I don't," Candy said rather firmly. "You love each other. It's obvious even to a nonromantic like my Egon."

Jack sighed. "I don't know about love, but Sharon doesn't like me very much right now. Maybe she never will again."

"That's just defeatist talk, my dear." Candy put away the pie and washed the whipped cream bowl. "Everything changes. All marriages survive if both of you want it to." She dried her hands on a green-and-white-striped dish towel. "You've got to work at it."

Jack looked up. "Do you and Egon work at it?"

"Goodness, yes." Candy came over, leaned on the pass-through. "We've had our ups and downs just like everyone else, I daresay. But the essential thing is that we both want the same thing—to be together." She looked at him with her wise eyes. "That's what you want, isn't it, to be with her?"

Jack nodded mutely.

Candy pushed the plate aside and began to shoo him out of the family room. Taffy barked unhappily. "Go on now." She kissed him warmly. "Go see my man, and I hope he makes you feel better."

"Thanks, Candy."

She stood at the door. "You can thank me by showing up on my doorstep more often."

QUIET AS *a morgue,* Jack thought as he entered the ME's office. In times past, that little joke would have put a smile on his face, but not tonight. He walked down the deserted corridors, hearing only the soft draw of the massive air conditioners. There was a mug half-filled with coffee on Schiltz's desk, but no sign of the man himself. The mug was inscribed with the phrase WORLD'S BEST DAD, a years-ago present from Molly. Jack put his finger into the coffee, found it still warm. His friend was here somewhere.

The autopsy room was similarly still. All the coldly gleaming chrome and stainless steel made it look like Dr. Frankenstein's lab. All that was needed were a couple of bolts of lightning. A dim glow came from the cold room. Jack stood on the threshold, allowing his eyes to adjust to the darkness. He remembered the time he'd taken Emma here. She was writing a paper on forensic medicine during the year the vocation had fired her interest. He'd been here many times, but he found it enlightening to see it through her eager, young eyes. Egon had met them, taken them around, explained everything, answered Emma's seemingly endless questions. But when she said, "Why does God allow people to be murdered?" Egon shook his head and said, "If I knew that, kiddo, I'd know everything."

Jack saw that one of the cold slabs had been drawn out of the wall. No doubt holding part of the hush-hush work that chained Egon to the office so late at night. Jack stepped forward, was on the point of calling out Egon's name when he heard the noises. It sounded as if the entire cold room had come alive and was breathing heavily. Then he saw Egon.

He was on the cold slab, lying facedown on top of Ami, his assistant. He was naked and so was she. Their rhythmic movements acid-etched the true nature of Egon's hush-hush work onto Jack's brain.

Jack, his mind in a fog, stood rooted for a moment. He struggled to make sense of what he was seeing, but it was like trying to digest a ten-pound steak. It just wasn't going to happen.

On stiff legs, he backed out of the cold room, turned, and went back down the corridor to Egon's office. Plunking himself into Egon's chair, he stared at the coffee. Well, that wasn't going to do it. He pawed through the desk drawers until he found Egon's pint of single-barrel bourbon, poured three fingers' worth into the coffee. He put the mug to his lips and drank the brew down without even wincing. Then he sat back.

For Egon Schiltz—family man, churchgoing, God-fearing fundamentalist—to be schtupping a cookie on the side was unthinkable. What would God say, for God's sake? Another of Jack's little jokes that tonight failed to bring a smile to his face. Or joy to his heart, which now seemed to be a dead cinder lying at the bottom of some forgotten dust heap.

He thought about leaving before Egon came back and saw that his "hush-hush work" was now an open secret, but he couldn't get his body to move. He took another slug of the single-barrel, reasoning that it might help, but it only served to root him more firmly in the chair.

And then it was too late. He heard the familiar footsteps coming down the corridor, and then Egon appeared. He stopped short the moment he saw Jack, and unconsciously ran a hand through his tousled hair.

"Jack, this is a surprise!"

I'll bet it is, Jack thought. "Guess where I just came from, Egon?"

Schiltz spread his hands, shook his head.

"How about a clue, then? I was just treated to the best cherry pie on God's green earth." Was that a tremor at the left side of Schiltz's head? "And speaking of God . . ."

"You know."

"I saw."

Schiltz hid his face in his hands.

"How long?"

"Six months."

Jack stood up. "I just . . . what the hell's the matter with you?"

"I was . . . tempted."

"Tempted?" Jack echoed hotly. "Doesn't the Bible tell us again and again, ad nauseam, how God deals with the tempted? Doesn't the Bible teach you to be strong morally, to resist temptation?"

"Those . . . people didn't have Ami working next to them every day."

"Wait a minute, if *that's* your excuse, you're nothing but a hypocrite."

Schiltz was visibly shaken. "I'm not a hypocrite, Jack. You know me better than that." He sank into a visitor's chair. "I'm a man, with a man's foibles." He glanced up, and for a moment a certain fire burned in his eyes. "I make mistakes just like everyone else, Jack. But my belief in God, in the morals he gave us, hasn't changed."

Jack spread his arms wide. "Then how do you explain this?"

"I can't." Schiltz hung his head.

Jack shook his head. "You want to cheat on Candy, go right ahead, I'm the last person to stop you. Except I know from personal experience how affairs fuck up marriages, how they poison the love one person has for another, how there's no hope of going back to the love."

Schiltz, elbows on knees, looked up at him bleakly. "Don't say that," he whispered.

"Another truth you don't want to hear." Jack came around the desk. "If you want to risk a broken marriage, who the hell am I to stop you, Egon? That's not why I'm pissed off. I'm pissed off because you go to church every Sunday with your family, you're pious and righteous—you denounce so-called sexual degenerates, ridicule politicians—especially Democrats—who've had affairs exposed. It's been easy for you to identify sinners from your high pedestal. But I wonder how easy it'll be now. You're not one of God's chosen, Egon. By your actions—by your own admission—you're just one of us sinners."

Egon sighed. "You're right, of course. I deserve every epithet you hurl at me. But, my God, I love Candy, you have to know that. I'd rather cut off my right arm than hurt her."

"I feel the same way, so don't worry. I'm not going to tell her."

"Well, I'm grateful for that. Thank you, Jack."

An awkward silence fell over them.

"Weren't you ever tempted, Jack?"

"What does it matter? This is about you, Egon. You and Candy, when you get right down to it. You can't have her and Ami, too, because if you do, you'll never be able to hold your head up in church again. I doubt even God would forgive that sin."

"Feet of clay." Schiltz nodded. "I've been laid low."

There was a rustling in the corridor and a moment later Ami entered, a clipboard in one hand, a pen in the other. She froze when she saw Jack. "Oh, I didn't know you were here, Mr. McClure."

"You must have been away from your desk." Jack saw her eyes flicker.

She was about to hand her boss the clipboard when she saw his stricken face. "Is everything all right, Dr. Schiltz?"

"Egon," Jack said. "You should call him Egon."

Ami took one look at Jack, then at Schiltz's face, and fled the room.

"Go on, make jokes at my expense, Jack." Schiltz shook his head ruefully. "God will forgive me."

"Is this the same god that was supposed to look after Candy, or Emma?"

I REMEMBER," Schiltz said. "I remember when everything was different, simpler."

"Now you sound like an old man," Jack said.

"Tonight I feel old." Schiltz sipped his bourbon and made a face. It wasn't single-barrel or anything close.

They were sitting in a late-night bar off Braddock Avenue, not far from the office. It was attached to a motel. While the interior was not quite so seedy as the motel itself, the clientele was a whole lot seedier. A low ceiling with plastic beams, sixty-watt bulbs further dimmed by dusty green-glass shades, torn vinyl-covered banquettes, a jukebox ringing out Muddy Waters and B. B. King tended to attract a fringe element right at home with the bleak dislocation of midnight with nowhere to go, no one to be with.

"Think of your daughter, then."

Schiltz shook his head. "I can't think of Molly without thinking of Emma."

"Actually, it's Emma I came to see you about," Jack said.

Schiltz's face brightened considerably.

"It's something . . . well, something I can't explain."

Schiltz leaned forward. "Tell me."

Jack took a deep breath. "I'm seeing Emma."

"What d'you mean?"

"I heard her talk to me from the backseat of my car."

"Jack—"

"She said, 'Dad.' I heard her as clearly as I'm hearing you."

"Listen to me now, Jack. I've heard of these manifestations before. Actually, they're not uncommon. You think you're seeing Emma because your guilt is too much to bear. You feel you're complicit in the tragedy, that if you'd been able to pay more attention—" Schiltz held up a hand. "But we've been over all that too many times already. I'm genuinely sorry that nothing's changed for you, Jack."

"So you don't believe me, either."

"I didn't say that. I fervently believe that you saw Emma, that she spoke to you, but it was all in your head." Schiltz took a breath. "We die, we go to heaven . . . or to hell. There are no ghosts, no wandering spirits."

"How d'you know?"

"I know the Bible, Jack. I know the word of God. Spiritualism is a game for charlatans. They play on the guilt and the desperate desire of the grieving to speak to their loved ones who've passed on."

"It isn't just life and death, Egon. There's something more, something we can't see or feel. Something unknown."

"Yes, there is," Schiltz said softly. "His name is God."

Jack shook his head. "This is beyond God, or the Bible, or even his laws."

"You can't believe that."

"How can you not even accept the possibility that there's something out there—something unknowable—that isn't God-based?"

"Because everything is God-based, Jack. You, me, the world, the universe."

"Except that Emma's appearance doesn't fit into your God-based universe."

"Of course it does, Jack." Schiltz drained his glass. "As I said, she's a manifestation of your insupportable grief."

"And if you're wrong?"

Schiltz presented him with an indulgent smile. "I'm not."

"See, that's what I think gets you religious guys in trouble. You're so damn sure of yourselves about all these issues that can't be proved."

"That's faith, Jack." Egon ordered them another round. "There's no more powerful belief system in the world."

Jack waited while the bourbons were set in front of them, the empty glasses taken away.

"It's comforting to have faith, to know there's a plan."

Schiltz nodded. "Indeed it is."

"So if something bad happens—like, for instance, your nineteen-year-old daughter running her car into a tree and dying—you don't have to think. You can just say, well, that's part of the plan. I don't know what that plan is, I can't ever know, but, heck, it's there, all right. My daughter's death had meaning because it was part of the plan."

Schiltz cleared his throat. "That's putting it a bit baldly, but, yes, that's essentially correct."

Jack set aside the raw-tasting bourbon. He'd had more than enough liquor for one night.

"Let me ask you something, Egon. Who in their right mind wants a fucked-up plan like that?"

Schiltz clucked his tongue. "Now you sound like one of those missionary secularists."

"I'm disappointed but hardly surprised to hear you say that." Jack made interlocking rings on the table with the bottom of his glass. "Because I'm certainly not a missionary secularist."

"Okay. Right now because of Emma's death you're cut off from God."

"Oh, I was cut off from that branch of thinking a long time ago," Jack said. "Now I'm beginning to think there's another way, a third alternative."

"Either you believe in God or you don't," Schiltz said. "There's no middle ground."

Jack looked at his friend. They'd spent so many years dancing around this topic, holding it at bay for the sake of their friendship. But a line had been crossed tonight, he felt, from which there was no turning back. "No room for debate, no movement from beliefs written in stone."

"The Ten Commandments were written in stone," Schiltz pointed out, "and for a very good reason."

"Didn't Moses break the tablets?"

"Stop it, Jack." Schiltz called for the check. "This is leading us nowhere."

Which, Jack thought, was precisely the problem. "So what happens now?" he said.

"Frankly, I don't know."

Schiltz stared into the middle distance, where a couple of dateless women who had given up for the night were dancing with each other while Elvis crooned "Don't Be Cruel."

His eyes slowly drew into themselves and he focused on Jack. "The truth is, I'm afraid to go home. I'm afraid of what Candy would do if she found out, afraid of the disgrace I'd come under in my church. I can tell you there are friends of mine who'd never talk to me again."

Jack waited a moment to gather his thoughts. He was mildly surprised to learn that whatever anger he'd felt toward Egon had burned itself out with the bourbon they'd thrown down their throats. The truth was, he felt sad.

"I wish I could help you with all that," Jack said.

Schiltz put up a hand. "My sin, my burden."

"What I can offer is another perspective. What's happened tonight is a living, breathing test of your iron-bound faith. You live within certain religious and moral lines, Egon. They allow for no deviation or justification. But you can't fall back on any religious fiction. God didn't tell you to have an affair with Ami, and neither did the devil. It was you, Egon. You made the conscious choice, you crossed a line you're forbidden to cross."

Schiltz shook his head wearily. "Would Candy forgive me? I just don't know."

"When I saw her earlier tonight, she told me in no uncertain terms just how strong your love is for each other. You've been through bad patches before, Egon, and you've managed to work through them."

"This is so big, though."

"Candy's got a big heart."

Schiltz peered at Jack through the low light, the beery haze. "Have you forgiven Sharon?"

"Yes," Jack said, "I have." And that was the moment he realized that he was telling the truth, the moment he understood why her unreasoning outburst had cut him so deeply.

Jack cocked his head. "So who are you now, Egon? You see, I can forgive what you've done, I can look past the part you play, the lies you've maintained, and still love the man beneath, despite your betrayal of Candy and Molly—and of me, for that matter. You're my friend, Egon. *That's* what's important in life. Friends fuck up, occasionally they do the wrong thing, they're forgiven. The religious thing—well, in my view, it's not relevant here. It's what you do now as a man, Egon, as a human being, that will determine whether you live the rest of your life as a lie, or whether you begin to change. Whether or not that includes telling Candy is entirely up to you."

The Everly Brothers were singing "All I Have to Do Is Dream." The two listless women on the dance floor seemed to have fallen asleep in each other's arms.

"This is a chance to get to know yourself, Egon, the real you that's been hidden away for years beneath the Bible. I've seen bits of him out in the woods with our daughters, fishing, looking up at the stars, telling ghost stories."

Schiltz downed the last of his bourbon, stared down at the table with its empty glasses, damp rings, crumpled napkins. "I don't believe I fully understood you, until tonight."

He turned away, but not before Jack caught the glimmer of a tear at the corner of his eye.

"I don't . . ." Schiltz tried to clear the emotion out of his throat. "I don't know whether I have the strength to get to know myself, Jack."

"Well, I don't know either, Egon." Jack threw some money on the table. "But I'd lay odds that you're going to try."

THIRTY

THE SPANISH Steps, running on Twenty-second Street, between De-
catur Place and S Street NW, was part of the luxe, lushly treed Dupont
Circle area of Washington. Its formal name was the rather dull Deca-
tur Terrace Steps, but no one, especially the residents of the Circle,
called it that. They preferred the infinitely more romantic name that
conjured up the real Spanish Steps in Rome. By any name, however, it
was a delightful stone-and-concrete staircase guarded on either side by
ornamental lampposts and crowned at its summit by a leonine fountain. By day, children could be seen running and squealing around the
mouth of the great beast from whose mouth water spewed in a constant stream. At night, it gathered to itself a certain Old World charm
that made it a favorite assignation spot of young lovers and adulterers
alike.

Calla stood waiting for Ronnie Kray at the top of the steps. She
had arrived a few minutes before midnight so that she could drink in
the nighttime glow that illuminated the steps in a sepia tint. One of
the lamppost lights on the right was out, and the resulting pool of
shadows spilled across the stairs in a most pleasing manner. Couples

strolled arm in arm, perhaps kissed chastely, then ran across the street laughing or stood on the corner, waiting for their radio-dispatched taxis to arrive.

Though she worked long and hard for the First American Secular Revivalists, and was as rational as the members who sat on either side of her, she was, at heart, a true romantic. Perhaps this was why she was drawn to Ronnie. Though she knew he was in his mid-fifties, he looked a decade younger. Perhaps that was because he was possessed of a romantic streak with which she could identify. Besides, he treated her like a lady, not like a kid, the way many at FASR did, especially Chris and Peter. She hated that they never took her suggestions seriously. Ronnie did. Ronnie got her, and she loved him for that.

She couldn't help furtively watching a young couple sitting on the steps, perhaps halfway down, necking. Calla imagined herself in the girl's place, her lover's hands on her warm flesh, and envied her. She'd come to Washington three years ago from Grand Rapids in search of a husband with a good job and solid family values. But finding that kind of man proved more difficult than she had imagined. She'd dated men who were either windbags or hopeless narcissists. And she'd deflected a number of married men who wanted to bed her, sometimes desperately. Switching to plan B, she'd thrown herself body and soul into FASR, a cause she believed in—fine for her sense of justice, bad for her love life.

As if from an invisible vibration, her head swung around and she saw him coming, stepping off the street onto the rectangular plaza at the top of the stairs where she waited for him.

"Hello, Ronnie," she said softly as he bent, his lips brushing her cheek.

"You came."

"Of course I came!" She looked deep into his dark eyes. "Why wouldn't I?"

"You could have changed your mind," Kray said. "People do, at the last minute."

"Well, I don't," Calla said firmly. He had taught her to stand up for what she believed, even with Chris and Peter. Terrifying and exhilarating all at once, like being on a roller coaster.

She shivered in the gusts of wind swirling around the fountain. The lovers on the steps had left, no doubt for a warm bed somewhere. The steps were clearing of people.

He put his arm around her. "Are you cold?"

"A little."

"Then let's get some hot coffee into you. Would you like that?"

Calla nodded, rested her head on his chest. She liked the bulk of him, the heft. She often thought of him as a sheltering cove.

He began to lead her down the steps.

She tugged against him gently, almost playfully. "Don't you want to go to Cafe Luna?"

"This is a special night." He continued to steer her down. "I've got a special place in mind."

They entered that area of the Spanish Steps where, because of the burned-out bulb, shadows billowed out across the stone and concrete like ink from an overturned bottle.

"Where are you taking me?" Calla asked. "Have we been there before?"

"It's a surprise," was all he said to her. "I promise you'll like it."

Huge trees rose far above their heads, the skeletal branches scratching the sky, as if trying to dig the diamond-hard stars out of a setting made milky by the District's million lights. In among this winter bower Calla shivered again, and Kray held her tighter, one arm around her waist.

All of a sudden, he lurched against her, as if his left ankle had turned over on a stone. She stumbled against the trunk of one of the trees and, as she did so, Kray stabbed her once in the back. So precise was the thrust, so practiced the hand, so unwavering the intent, the wickedly sharpened paletta did the rest.

Kray held her lifeless body and glanced around. Had anyone been looking, they'd have seen a man holding his drunk or ill wife, but as luck would have it, no one was about. Kray slowly laid Calla's body at the bole of the tree. With quick, practiced movements, he snapped on surgeon's gloves, pulled out the cell phone he'd taken from one of Alli's Secret Service guards, put it into her hand, pressed her fingers around it, then threw it into a nearby evergreen bush. Then he picked up the paletta. It was such a superb implement; it had penetrated through cloth, skin, and viscera with such ease, there was hardly any blood on it. He pocketed the weapon and, his mission accomplished, vanished into the shadowy forest of swaying trees.

THIRTY-ONE

IT'S A universal law of teenhood that the bully always returns for more. Maybe he's drawn to what he perceives as weakness, because other people's weakness makes him stronger. Maybe he's a sadist and can't help himself. Or maybe he just can't leave well enough alone. In any event, Andre returns to Jack's life, stronger, meaner, more determined than ever.

It's as if he's been biding his time, accumulating power, calculating his return like a general who's been forced to make a strategic retreat from the field of battle. The source of his newfound power isn't only his patron, Cyril Tolkan, but a supplier he's found on his own—a man named Ian Brady.

"One thing fo' sho," Gus says with a fair amount of scorn, "Ian Brady ain't no black man. Shit, Ian Brady ain't no American name, no way, no how. But, shee-it, he a ghost, that man, 'cause none a my snitches know shit 'bout him. I mean, who the fuck is he? Where he come from? Who's his contacts? He got so much fuckin' juice, he could light up alla D.C."

This tirade occurs one evening when Jack and Gus are at home, listening to James Brown. Jack has made a couple of purchases at the local record store and is eager to both hear them and share them with Gus. In the wake of Gus's rant, he wonders whether he should keep the LPs under wraps, but having brought up the subject during dinner, he has no choice.

"Huh! I mighta known!" Gus says, holding the cardboard sleeves in his massive hand. "Elvis Presley an' the Rolling Stones. White boys, jus' like you. And some of 'em look like they ain't eaten in weeks!"

"Just listen, will you? You're such a hard-ass!"

"Well, I heard Elvis, an' he ain't half-bad. So play this here other, so's I can see whut yo' taste in music's like."

Jack carefully slides the James Brown disc back in its sleeve, then rolls out the black vinyl disc of *Out of Our Heads,* puts the needle down, and out blasts "Mercy, Mercy." After the last jangling bars of "One More Try" fade into the walls, Gus turns to Jack, says, "Play dat again, son."

Jack puts the needle back on the first cut, and Mick Jagger starts it up.

Gus shakes his head in wonder. "Shee-it, fo' skinny little white boys, they sho-nuff do shout."

JACK NOW goes regularly to the library on G Street NW. At first, he went because Reverend Taske urged him to, but lately he's realized that he likes going. Because of Taske's training, he's tamed his fright of reading new texts; it's become more of a challenge, a way out of the strange little world his dyslexia shoved him into.

He loves the dusty air, golden with motes of history. He loves opening books at random, finding himself engrossed, so that he goes back, starts at page one and doesn't stop until he's devoured the last word. Unlike movies and TV that show him everything, even if he doesn't like it, books transport him into the world of his own imagination. As long as he can create pictures from the words he reads—scenes filled with characters, conflict, good and evil—he can build a world that's in many ways closer to the one other people inhabit. And this makes him feel less like an outsider. He feels he is that much closer to rubbing shoulders with the passersby on the street. This is the atmosphere that draws him day after day into the dusty quietude, calm as a still lake. But in those depths something waits for him, as it does almost every teenager: the fear that recurs, the fear that needs to be faced.

Jack comes face-to-face with his one Monday afternoon. He's back in the stacks, pulling down massive treatises on his latest passion: criminal psychology. A head in the book precludes vigilance. But who would think to be vigilant in a District public library? That's how Andre thinks, anyway. He's been following Jack to G Street every day for a week, until he's familiar with the schedule. It says something about just how deep his feelings of vengeance run that he's been on surveillance for five straight days when he could be negotiating his next shipment of smack from Ian Brady.

But some things are more important than H, more important than greenbacks, because they cry out to be resolved. And, frankly, Andre can't rest easy until this particular matter is resolved to his satisfaction.

Jack doesn't hear him as Andre creeps up from behind. Andre, in crepe-soled shoes he's bought for the occasion, approaches slowly, relishing the end to the ache that's been inside him ever since Cyril Tolkan delivered his punishment.

At the very end, he makes his rush, silent, filled with the power of righteous rage. He grabs Jack by his collar, lifts him bodily into the air, slams him against the rear wall. Shelves tremble; books spill onto the floor. Andre, his eyes alight with bloodlust, jams a forearm across Jack's windpipe both to silence him and to subdue him as quickly as possible. Though he's filled with a desire for vengeance, Andre is nothing if not pragmatic. He doesn't want to get caught in here with a dead or dying body. He has no intention of going into whitey's slammer, either now or ever.

With a tiny *snik!* he flicks open his switchblade. His victim seems so stunned, his hands aren't even up, trying to pry his forearm away. Maybe he doesn't have enough oxygen to act. Either way, it doesn't matter to Andre, who jabs the point of the blade in toward Jack's diaphragm. He's aiming for the soft spot just below the sternum, to drive the long, slender blade upward into Jack's heart.

JACK'S HANDS, down by his sides, have not, however, been idle. His left hand has kept its grip on the thick hardcover book he's been reading, and now, as he hears the telltale *snik!* of the switchblade, he reflexively presses the tome to his chest. The point of the knife encounters cotton, pasteboard, and paper instead of flesh. Andre's eyes widen in surprise, then squeeze shut as Jack's knee plows hard into his testicles.

As Andre begins to double over, Jack's windpipe is freed. He sucks in a great lungful of air, brings the book up, jams its edge into Andre's neck. To maintain the maximum force, he's obliged to keep both his hands on the spine of the book and so lacks the means to force Andre to drop the switchblade. This weapon now swings back and forth like a pendulum with a razor's edge, grazing first Jack's ear, then his shoulder. With each wild pass, Jack feels searing pain, and hot blood begins running down him. The next arc could find his carotid artery.

Gritting his teeth, he jams the book harder into Andre's throat, hears a crackle like a sheet of paper being crumpled prior to being thrown away. Then Andre's mouth opens wide, emits a sound like a grandfather clock about to break down.

Jack, staring into Andre's bloodshot eyes, begins to cry. Part of him knows what's happening, what the outcome will be, but that part must stand aside while the organism is in danger. Andre, in a last, desperate attempt to kill, brings the edge of the switchblade up to the level of Jack's ear. He points it inward, aiming for the canal opening. Jack, terrified, shifts his weight. The corner of the book penetrates into the hole made by the fracture of Andre's cricoid cartilage. All air is cut off.

Andre's knife hand moves. The point of the switchblade is almost at the canal opening. Jack leans in with all his weight; more of the book pushes inside Andre. Andre's knife hand begins to tremble; the momentum falters. Tears are streaming down Jack's cheeks. They fall onto Andre, into his wound. Andre's eyes stare at him. They are unreadable.

There is now a contest of wills. Andre can no longer breathe, but he holds the knife. All he has to do is summon the strength to jam it point-first into Jack's ear. There is a moment of stasis, when the power, the wills of both boys are held in balance. Nothing moves. The small sounds of the library, the occasional whisper, the soft pad of footfalls, the tiny, very particular sound of a book being slipped out from between its neighbors, all seem exaggerated, like the sounds of insects deep in the forest. All the trappings of civilization have become irrelevant, useless. All that remains are the tiny symphony of sounds and the beating of your own heart.

Nature abhors stasis; like fame, it's fleeting, though its seconds may seem like minutes. Jack feels the point of the knife enter his ear canal, and he twists the corner of the book. Andre's eyes roll up; his lips are drawn back in a rictus. He has nothing left, only a helpless rage that ushers him rudely from life to death.

Jack, panting like a sick dog, lies against Andre's crumpled form. He feels as if a light has gone out in the depths of his soul, as if he has lost a part of himself. He is in shock, stunned at what has occurred. There are no words, no thoughts in his head adequate to what he's feeling. Soon enough, he begins to shake with a profound chill. The strong copper taste of blood is on his tongue, but whether it's his blood or Andre's or both is impossible to say.

In a dim dead-end of the library where no one comes, he lies in a daze, in a kind of trancelike state, remembering an Indian parable from *The Gospel of Sri Ramakrishna* he came across weeks ago. It happened that a tigress, large with an unborn cub, attacked a herd of goats. As it sprang forward to grip in its teeth a terrified goat, the goatherd shot it.

The tigress fell, and in that moment before she expired, she gave birth to her cub. The cub grew up with the goats, eating grass and, mimicking its adopted brothers and sisters, bleating. Until the day a male tiger found the herd. It quite naturally attacked the youngster, who did not fight back, but only bleated. The male tiger gripped the adolescent by the scruff of his neck, dragged him to the river.

"Look at our reflections," the male tiger said. "You and I are as brothers. Why do you bleat like a goat? Why do you live with them instead of feasting on them?"

"I like grass," the adolescent replied.

"Because grass is all you know."

Whereupon the male tiger leapt upon a goat, tore out its throat. The adolescent was close enough to the feast to taste the goat's blood. Then he put his head down and bit into the flesh, which he discovered he liked much more than the taste of grass.

The male tiger lifted his head, watching the adolescent gorge himself on goat meat. With his great muzzle covered in blood, he said, "Now you and I are the same. Now you know your true Self. Follow me into the forest."

Jack, weeping still, gets to his feet. He dries his eyes and, finding his shirtfront bloodied, grabs his jacket off the back of a chair, puts it on. He finds that if he buttons the jacket up to his neck, the blood is hidden.

On the verge of leaving, he turns to regard Andre. What has happened has affirmed a notion embedded in his subconscious for a number of years: It isn't simply his dyslexia that's made him an Outsider. He won't bleat and run like a goat. He won't ever rub shoulders with the passersby on the street; he doesn't want to. Like the tiger, he stands apart. The jungle is his home, not the cultivated field.

THIRTY-TWO

ONCE EVERY two weeks or so, Secretary Dennis Paull scheduled a senior staff meeting at dawn, much to the grumbling of those closest to him. There was no obvious reason for doing this except to keep them on their toes, which is what pissed off his senior staff because it cut into their social lives. God forbid they should attend one of Paull's senior staff meetings with a yawn or, worse, hungover. The secretary would hang them out to dry in front of their colleagues.

The meetings were held at Fort McNair, which was a building that didn't look like a fort and was in the heart of downtown Washington. No one understood why the meetings were held at an army base and not at Homeland Security HQ, but no one had the intestinal fortitude to query Secretary Paull. Consequently, people thought he was simply eccentric and this behavior, along with numerous other peccadilloes, simply became part of the Beltway lore concerning him.

This was precisely what Dennis Paull had in mind. He never did or said anything without a specific reason, though that reason, like the moves of a chess player, was not always readily apparent. The reason Paull scheduled the meetings at the crack of dawn was because virtually no one was around. The reason he held them at Fort McNair was that it was a place within which even the president couldn't track him.

This particular morning, at precisely 0617, Secretary Paull called a ten-minute break, pushed his chair back, and strode from the conference room. He walked down a number of halls, went down a flight of stairs, up another just to reassure himself that he was absolutely alone. Then he ducked into the men's room at the rear of the third floor. No one stood by the row of sinks; no one was using the urinals. He went down the row of stalls, opening each door to ensure no one was in temporary residence.

Then he banged open the door to the last stall in the row and said, "Good morning, sir."

Edward Carson, the president-elect, who had been reading the *Washington Post,* stood up, folded the paper under one arm, and said, "No need to call me sir yet, Dennis."

"Never too early to get started, sir."

The two men emerged from the stall. "Imagine what the Drudge Report would say about this," Carson grunted. "We're all alone?"

"Like Adam before Eve."

Carson frowned. "What news of Alli? Lyn is beside herself."

Paull knew it wasn't presidential for Carson to add that he was also beside himself. Presidents never lost their cool, no matter how dire the straits. "I believe we're closer to finding her today than we were yesterday."

"Knock off the media-speak," Carson said testily. "This is my daughter we're talking about."

"Yessir." Paull rubbed his chin. "The ball is in your man's court. I've given McClure every ounce of freedom I possibly can without showing my hand to the POTUS."

Carson's frown deepened. "But is that going to be enough, Dennis?"

"I'd be lying if I said I knew for sure, sir. But you and McClure go back quite a ways, from what you tell me, and you've said he's the best man for the job."

"And I stand by that," the president-elect said stiffly.

"If it makes you feel any better," Paull went on, "my agent agrees with you."

"The only thing that's going to make me feel better is the safe return of my daughter."

There was a sudden noise outside, and both men went completely still. Paull held up a finger, crossed to the door, pulled it open quickly. One of the cleaning personnel was turning a corner. When he was out of sight, Paull ducked back into the men's room, shook his head in the negative.

"I had to deliver Yukin into the POTUS's hands," Paull said. "I had the evidence against Mikilin, and I gave it to the POTUS before he left for Moscow. I attended a celebration of sorts following the POTUS's return. He's got the Russian president in his back pocket now, so does he demand exports from RussOil, as I suggested? Does he forge a pact to create a joint strategic uranium reserve, as I also suggested? No, of course not. Instead, he's spent the ammunition I gave him obtaining Yukin's promise to back the POTUS when he makes his final national-policy address to the nation. In it, he's going to charge that the government has direct evidence that Beijing is funding E-Two, and that the First American Secular Revivalists are, in fact, a front for E-Two. And where d'you think that bogus evidence will come from? Moscow, of course. And no one will be able to say it's false." Paull crossed to the door once again, put his ear to it. Satisfied, he returned to where Carson waited for him. "The POTUS is going to declare war on the missionary secularists of any and every stripe."

"I want to help you, Dennis, but until Alli is returned to me safe and sound, my hands are tied. As long as there's a suspicion that either

E-Two or the FASR is behind her abduction, I can't make a stand against the president."

"I understand your overriding concern here, sir, but we've had a complication."

Carson's blue eyes bored into the secretary's. "What kind of a complication?"

"The men I sent to keep McClure safe were compromised."

He'd caught the president-elect's full attention.

"Compromised in what way?"

"The POTUS's people gave them orders to terminate."

A deathly silence overtook them. "Jack's safe?"

"Yessir, he is."

"I don't want another incident like that," Carson said. "Am I being clear?"

Paull stiffened. He knew a rebuke when he heard one, and this one was well deserved. "Absolutely, sir." Somewhere along the line, his careful security net had been breached. He had to find out where with all possible haste.

Carson stepped away, regarded his pale, lined face in the mirror, then turned around. "Dennis, if the POTUS got on to your men, then he knows. Jack's not the only one in terrible danger. We are, too."

"Yessir." Paull nodded. "That's the goddamned truth of it."

THIRTY-THREE

IT HAD been a long time since Jack woke up with a splitting headache. He clambered out of bed with the unusual care of a mountain climber with vertigo. Crawling into the shower, he turned on the cold water full-blast so that no one would hear him screaming.

Ten minutes later, when Nina called, he had crawled out of the muck of the sea and had grown a spinal cord. He figured by the time she showed up, he had a chance of being halfway human.

Still, he insisted on driving them over to the All Around Town bakery. The day was cool but sunny, which made a welcome change of pace. But according to AccuWeather, there was another front coming in that wasn't afraid of dumping three inches of rain or something worse on them.

He was in no mood to talk, but soon enough he noticed Nina repeatedly glancing at him out of the corner of her eye.

Finally, she ventured an opinion on his physical state. "You look like crap."

"That's what a week without sleep will do to you." He eyed her speculatively. She was dressed in a gray flannel suit over a cream-colored cashmere sweater. "On the other hand, you look as fresh as a plate of sushi."

"And just as cool." Nina laughed. "I'll bet good money you were thinking that."

"Actually," Jack said, "I was thinking about what we'll do if Joachim Tolkan hasn't shown up from his sad trip to Miami Beach. Or, even worse, if the story he fed Oscar was a lie."

"Since when did you become a glass-half-empty guy?"

"Since last night," Jack said, more to himself than to her.

"What happened?"

"My ex happened," Jack said bitterly.

"I'm sorry, Jack." Nina put a hand briefly over his. "I once tried to get back with an old boyfriend. All that did was make me realize why we broke up in the first place."

Wanting to get off the subject of exes, Jack said, "I grew up around here. A lot of memories, good and bad. Mysteries, too."

"What kind of mysteries?"

"A double murder up at McMillan Reservoir, for one."

"It went unsolved?"

Jack nodded. "Not only that, I remember there was no info at all on who was killed."

"That *is* odd," Nina acknowledged.

Jack turned a corner. "Then there was Ian Brady."

"Who was he?"

"No one knew who he was or where he came from. But he had a huge amount of juice—too much, I'd say, for a local drug dealer. He was supplying heroin, God alone knows what else. Other suppliers were caught or killed, but not Brady. No one could lay a finger on him."

There was a sporty cabernet-colored Mercedes coupe parked in front of the All Around Town bakery, and Jack took this as a good sign. The bell rang as they walked in, and there was Oscar behind the counter.

"Boss just got here," he said as soon as he saw them enter. "Wait right there." He disappeared into the back. A moment later, he returned with a man whose only genetic connection with his father was his olive-gray complexion. He was tall and slim, dapper as his dad, though.

His expression was quizzical, curious, free from his father's dark guile. "Oscar said you wanted to see me."

"That's right."

Nina produced her Homeland Security ID. Jack made the introductions, gave their condolences for his loss.

Joachim Tolkan held out his hand.

Jack hadn't expected this. He didn't want to shake Joachim Tolkan's hand, the son of a murderer, but he saw no way out. The moment he took Joachim's hand, he felt an electric shock travel up his arm. It was as if he'd made contact with Cyril Tolkan from beyond the grave.

"Are you all right, Mr. McClure? You went white there for a moment."

"I'm fine," Jack lied.

"We just need a couple of moments of your time, Mr. Tolkan," Nina said in her best neutral voice.

"No problem." Joachim Tolkan lifted an arm. "Why don't we continue this discussion in my office? That way we can all sit down and relax." He turned to Oscar. "How about some coffee for our guests?"

As Nina passed Oscar, he handed her a chocolate-chip cookie, along with a wink.

Tolkan led them back through the oven room, hotter than Hades despite the exhaust fans and air-conditioning. To the right was a door through which he took them.

Jack found himself in a surprisingly large, pleasantly furnished office, complete with an upholstered sofa, coffee table, a pair of lamps. A full bathroom was to the right and beside it a short hallway that led to what appeared to be a bedroom.

"I stay here to all hours," Joachim Tolkan said, noticing Jack's scrutiny. He shrugged. "Anyway, no point in going back to the house these days. It's become the soon-to-be ex's territory."

As Tolkan settled himself behind his desk, Oscar arrived with a tray filled with mugs and a carafe of coffee. Oscar slid it onto the low table in front of the sofa and left, closing the door behind him.

"Help yourselves." When neither Jack nor Nina made a move to the tray, Tolkan said, "I'm curious. What does the Department of Homeland Security want with me?"

"Were you a member of FASR?" Jack said.

"So far as I know that's not a crime."

"You dropped out three and a half months ago," Nina said.

"Again, not a crime." Tolkan laced his fingers together. "Where, may I ask, is this going?"

Jack walked slowly around the room, studying everything. "E-Two."

Tolkan blinked. "I beg your pardon?"

"You can," Jack said, turning to him, "but it won't do any good."

Tolkan spread his hands. "What's an E-Two?"

"Doesn't read the paper, apparently." Nina, perched on the arm of the sofa, took a tiny bite of her chocolate-chip cookie. "My, this *is* good."

"Listen." Jack advanced toward the desk. "We're not in the mood for lies."

Tolkan shook his head. "Lies about what?"

Was it Jack's imagination, or was Joachim Tolkan becoming more and more like his late father, Cyril? He found the thought intolerable. He was just about to lunge at Tolkan when, entirely without warning, Nina skimmed her cookie right at Tolkan's head. The edge struck him just over the left eye, the impromptu missile shattering on impact.

Tolkan's hand flew to his face. "What the hell—!"

Jack reached over, grabbed Tolkan by his lapels, dragged him up off his comfortable chair so that he was half-hanging over his desk. Cookie crumbs and bits of chocolate were strewn across his Hermès tie.

"You haven't been listening to us, Joachim." Jack's face was flushed; there was a murderous look in his eye. "We don't have time for your fun and games." Jack hurled him back into the chair. "Tell us about your involvement in E-Two."

Now it was Tolkan's face that was white. He looked visibly shaken. "I was sworn to secrecy."

"Your allegiance is admirable," Nina said with a chill Jack could feel, "but misplaced."

"Spill it, Joachim!" Jack thundered.

Tolkan expelled a little squeak. "All right, but there really isn't much to tell." With a trembling hand, he pushed his hair off his forehead. "I heard about E-Two through someone I worked with at FASR. I quit when he did because he said FASR was too slow and poky, too conservative to get anywhere. He said if I was really serious about change, there was another group we could join, one that would get things done. Sounded good to me, so I said okay. Then I come to find out that E-Two's methods are violent."

"That didn't attract you?" Jack said.

"What? No."

"But your father was a violent man."

Joachim regarded Jack with the proper amount of fear. "What does my father have to do with it?"

Jack said, "The rotten apple doesn't fall far from the poisoned tree."

Tolkan shook his head. "You've got it wrong."

Nina crossed her arms. "So enlighten us."

Tolkan nodded. "The truth is once I was old enough to understand how my father could afford all the luxuries I enjoyed as a kid, I stayed as far away from him as I could. It sickened me the way he'd take us all to church on Sunday, how he'd kneel, say his prayers to Jesus, quote from the Bible, and then go out and do . . . the things he did. I wanted no part of him, his contacts, his blood money. I worked my way through college, got an MBA from Georgetown."

Nina came down off the sofa arm. "So how come you wound up here?"

"I worked for Goldman Sachs for a year and hated every minute of it. When I quit, I decided I wanted to be my own boss. The bakery was still going, more or less. I saw an opportunity. I stepped in, invested in advertising, in a community-outreach program. Gradually I built up the business to the point where I needed to expand."

"And look at you now," Nina said.

Jack put his fists on the desk. "So you expect us to believe that you never joined E-Two."

"I didn't," Tolkan said, shying away. "I swear it."

"What happened?" Nina asked.

"I felt ashamed of myself. I went back to FASR, but they wouldn't have me. Chris said I could no longer be trusted."

Jack said, "This friend of yours—"

"He isn't a friend."

"Colleague, whatever." Jack pulled himself up. "Does he have a name?"

"Ron Kray."

Nina checked the printout Armitage had given them. "He's here," she said, and read off his home address.

"That's a phony. Kray told me. He's very private."

Jack wondered why the name seemed familiar to him. He racked his brain, but the answer remained frustratingly out of reach. "So where does Mr. Kray live?" he said.

"He never told me and I never asked," Tolkan answered. "But he said he works at Sibley Memorial Hospital."

"I've heard of it," Jack said. "It's a rehab place for the elderly. Physical and psychiatric."

Tolkan nodded. "Ron's a nurse there. A psychiatric nurse."

THE MODERN layer cake of Sibley Memorial occupied a wide swath of real estate on Sleepy Hollow Road outside of Falls Church. Nina suggested they call to see if Kray was on duty, but Jack disagreed.

"First off, I don't want to take any chance of him being tipped off we're coming. Secondly, even if he's not there, the HR department is bound to have a current photo of him."

As it turned out, Kray wasn't on duty. In fact, the head of the psychiatric department told them he hadn't worked there for over two years.

They were directed to the HR department, where they obtained Kray's last known address, which matched the one on the list Chris Armitage had given them. Kray's photo ID, however, had been destroyed.

KRAY LIVED on Tyler Avenue, not more than six minutes away. Nina was silent during most of the drive. At length, she turned to Jack.

"You must think I'm quite the neurotic."

Jack concentrated on his driving. This was somewhat of a new area for him, and he wanted to make sure he read every road sign.

Nina took his silence for assent. "Yeah, you do."

"What do you care what I think?"

"For one thing, we're working together. For another, I like you. Your mind doesn't work like anyone else's I've ever met."

"I'll take that as a compliment."

She offered a nod of assent. "In a very short time, I've come to trust what you call your hunches."

"Would you call them something else?"

She nodded. "I would, yes, if I had a word to describe them. Whatever they are, they're far more than hunches, though." She put her head back. "You know, if I spend any more time with you, I'll start to doubt everything I thought was true."

She put a hand over his. "We had a moment there under the old oaks where Emma escaped from school at night." Her forefinger curled, the nail scratched lightly, erotically along his palm. "Why don't we take it from there?"

He braked until he could decipher a street sign. Also, to clear the air between them.

"Listen, Nina, I'm flattered. But just so there's no misunderstanding, I'm not into on-the-job screwing."

"Too many complications?"

The image of Sharon was beside him, with her long tanned legs, hair swept across her face, that mysterious look in her eyes he loved because he never quite knew what it meant or foretold. "Among other things."

"What if we weren't partners? I could arrange—"

"It wouldn't matter."

"Well, that's candor for you." Nina removed her hand. "Your ex still under your skin?"

He swung onto Tyler, slowed to a crawl.

"Okay, forget it. Privacy's something I respect. There is, in any case, a kind of privilege in loneliness. It makes you feel alive, introduces you to yourself."

Jack felt annoyed. "I didn't mean that."

"You just didn't say it." She took out a clove cigarette, lit up. "I have a question. D'you have any idea who Emma met underneath the oaks?"

"My daughter's life was a closed book to me. It was as well hidden as a spy's dead drop."

"You never followed up on it?"

"With who?" A nerve she had nicked flared up. "My daughter's dead."

THIRTY-FOUR

JACK WENT up the flagstone path, knocked on the door. Immediately, a dog began to bark. He heard a scuffling inside, then the patter of feet. The door opened, revealing a middle-aged woman in a housecoat. A cigarette was dangling from her mouth.

"Yeah?" She looked Jack square in the eye without a trace of apprehension.

Jack cleared his throat. "I'm wondering if Ron Kray is home."

The dog continued barking inside the house. The woman squinted through the smoke trailing up from her cigarette. "Who?"

"Ron Kray, ma'am." Nina stepped up.

"Oh, him." The woman expelled a phlegmy cough. "He used to live here. Moved out about, oh, six months ago."

"Do you know where he went?"

"Nah." The dog's barking had become hysterical. The woman ducked her head back inside. "For God's sake, Mickey, shut the fuck up!" She turned back. "Sorry about that. People make him nervous. He's probably gonna leave a deposit on the kitchen linoleum." She grunted. "At least the carpet'll be spared."

"You wouldn't happen to still get any of Kray's mail," Jack said.

"Not a one." The woman took a mighty drag on her cigarette, let out a plume of smoke like Mount Saint Helens. "Sorry I can't be of more help."

"You did fine," Jack said. "Can you tell me the address of the local post office?"

"I'll do better than that." The woman pointed the way, giving him detailed directions.

Jack thanked her, and they picked their way back down the flagstone walk.

"The post office?" Nina said as they climbed back into the car.

Jack glanced at his watch. "We just have time to get there." He pulled out, drove down the street. "Tolkan said that Kray was a private man. He wouldn't have wanted anyone else getting his mail. I'm betting he filed a change-of-address form before he left."

They headed east on Tyler, while Nina finished her cigarette, turned right onto Graham Road, right again on Arlington Boulevard, then a left onto Chain Bridge Road. The post office occupied a one-story pale brick building. It looked like every other post office Jack had been to, outside and in.

He walked up to the counter, asked to see the postmistress. Ten minutes later, a hefty woman in her mid-fifties appeared, walking none too quickly. It seemed to Jack that all postal employees were constitutionally incapable of moving at anything but a sluggish pace. Then again, maybe they learned it at some secret government academy.

Jack and Nina showed their credentials, asked for a forwarding address for Ron Kray. The postmistress, who had a face like a boxing glove, told them to wait. She disappeared into the mysterious bowels of the building. Time passed, people walked in, got on line, waited, inched forward. Forms were filled out, packages were rubber-stamped, more forms were filled out, letters and more packages were rubber-stamped. People who failed to fill out the proper forms were sent to the corner stand to correct their mistakes. Jack was at the point of risking a federal offense by hurdling the counter to go after the postmistress, when she reappeared, inching snail-like toward them.

"No Ron Kray," she said in her laconic manner. She spoke like a character straight out of a Raymond Chandler novel.

Jack took a pad and a pen, laboriously wrote down Kray's last known address, the house they'd just come from. Tearing off the top sheet, he handed it to the postmistress, who looked as if her recent labors had tired her out. "How about a forwarding from this address?"

The postmistress peered down at the slip of paper as if it might possibly do her harm. "I don't think I can—"

"From six months ago, give or take a week."

The postmistress looked at him bleakly. "Gonna take some time, this."

Jack smiled. "We'll be waiting."

"I get off work in twelve minutes," she pointed out.

"Not today, you don't," Nina said.

The postmistress glared at her, as if to say, *Et tu, Brute?* Then, in a huff, she shuffled off.

More time passed. The line gradually dwindled down, the last customer finally dealt with. A collective sigh of relief could be felt as the postal workers totaled up, locked their drawers, and followed their leader into the rear of the building.

"I wouldn't be surprised if she was having a cup of tea back there," Jack said. "She looks the vindictive type."

"Jack, about Emma—I was just trying to help."

He looked away, said nothing.

She bit her lip. "You're a hard man."

She waited a moment. They were alone in the front of the post office, the entry doors having been locked.

She peered into his face. "Could we start over?"

Jack returned slowly from the black mood of last night. "Sure. Why not?"

She caught the tone of his voice. "You're not very trusting, are you?"

"Trust has nothing to do with it," he said, a wave of leftover anger washing over the wall of his normal reserve. "Life has taught me how not to love."

At that moment, shuffling footsteps forestalled further discussion. The postmistress had reappeared and was heading straight toward them. She was holding a handful of forms. Nina snatched them out of her hand just as she was saying, "There are six—well, I never!"

Nina was scrutinizing them, for which Jack was grateful. Considering the tense circumstances and the watchful eyes of the postmistress, he'd have had a difficult time focusing.

Nina went through the forms one by one, shook her head. "We're going to have to run all of these people down." Suddenly, her eyes lit up. "Wait a minute!" She flipped back to the fifth form. "Charles Whitman. Now that's odd. Charles Whitman was the name of the sniper who climbed the University of Texas tower in August of 1966 and in an hour and a half killed fourteen people and injured a whole lot more. Someone at the scene, I forget who, said, 'He was our initiation into a terrible time.'"

"I remember, that was a local shopowner. I saw him interviewed." Then Jack snapped his fingers. "*That's* why Ron Kray sounded familiar to me. Ronnie Kray and his twin brother, Reggie, were a pair of notorious psycho killers in the East End of London during the fifties and sixties."

"We've got him!" Nina said. "Our man's using both Kray and Whitman as aliases."

Jack took Kray/Whitman's change-of-address form from her. Concentrating hard, he began to read the new address. It was in Anacostia; that much he got right away. But the street and the number eluded him, swimming away on a sea of anxiety. Of course, the street name was simplicity itself, and part of his brain had recognized it at once. The problem was, it had shied away from recognition.

"He's at T Street SE," Nina said.

Then she read off the number, and Jack's hand began to shake. Their target, Ron Kray, Charles Whitman, whatever his real name was, the man who might very well have abducted Alli Carson, was living in the Marmoset's house.

THIRTY-FIVE

FEW PEOPLE know where Gus and Jack live; even fewer come to visit. So when Detective Stanz shows up one evening at the Maryland end of Westmoreland Avenue, Jack has cause for a certain degree of alarm. For a time, Stanz and Gus stand out on the porch, jawing away. Stanz lights a Camel, and smoke comes out his nostrils. He looks like a bull in one of those Warner Bros. cartoons, except there's nothing funny about him. He seems to carry death around with him under his left armpit, where his service revolver is holstered.

Jack, lurking inside, hears the words "McMillan Reservoir," so he's reasonably certain that after the Marmoset's murder, whoever Gus put on the double murders hasn't come up with enough to satisfy Stanz. But apparently he's come up with something, because Jack hears Stanz say, "I say let's go now. There're questions I want to ask him."

Gus nods. He walks into the house, uses the phone out of Jack's hearing. He returns to tell Jack that he's going off with Stanz, that he'll be back in a couple of hours. As he watches the two men step off the porch, Jack hurries to the desk where Gus keeps an extra set of car keys. Slipping out of the house, he just has time enough to start the white Lincoln Continental, put it in gear as he's seen Gus do, roll out after Stanz's dark-colored Chevy. Jack deliberately keeps the headlights off until there's enough traffic so that neither man will pick up the Continental. He's only ever driven around the near-deserted streets of the house, with Gus beside him talking softly, correcting his errors or overcompensations. The sweat rolls into his eyes, pours from his armpits. His mouth is dry. If a cop stopped him right this moment, he wouldn't be able to say a word.

With a desperate effort, he finds his equilibrium. Thankfully, he only has to concentrate on the Chevy and the colors of the traffic lights. If he needed to read street signs, he'd be completely lost. He pushes a button on the dashboard, and James Brown starts shouting "It's a Man's Man's Man's World." Singing along, he thinks fleetingly of how far he's come since "California Dreamin'" sent ugly shivers up his spine.

He notices that the Chevy is heading more or less toward the reservoir area and wonders who it is that Gus recruited to take the Marmoset's place. It's an unenviable position, one that almost certainly requires a higher degree of compensation than Gus is used to paying. But then, that expense will no doubt be borne by Stanz and the Metro Police.

They are traveling north on Georgia Avenue NW, overshooting the reservoir. When Stanz's Chevy turns right on Rock Creek Church Road, Jack switches off his lights, feeling he knows where the rendezvous with Gus's snitch is going to take place. His hunch is confirmed when he follows the Chevy onto Marshall, and then Pershing Drive. They are now skirting the west side of the flat black expanse of the U.S. Soldiers' & Airmen's Golf Course. Bare trees loom up in groups that no doubt vexed the duffers making their slow rounds during daylight hours. Now, however, the trees have the course to themselves.

After flicking its headlights twice, the Chevy rolls to a stop on a section of road hemmed in on both sides by trees. Immediately, Jack sees Stanz and Gus emerge from the Chevy. Stanz has kept the head-lights on, and the two men follow the twin beams that cut through eerie shadows, straight down the road. Pale moths flutter, spending themselves in the glare.

Cautiously, Jack emerges from the Continental, making sure the door swings shut noiselessly but doesn't latch. Keeping to the side of the road, he creeps from tree to tree, stepping from shadow to shadow to make sure he won't be seen.

He's close enough now to see that Stanz and Gus have been joined by a male figure. He stands just outside the beams of light, and Jack moves forward to try to get a look at his face. He still isn't sure why he felt compelled to follow Gus. He knows he's worried. Someone murdered the Marmoset because he got too close to whoever killed those two men at the McMillan Reservoir. Jack read the news story, was mildly surprised to find that there was no information about who the victims were. The article said that the identities were being withheld pending notification of the respective next of kin. But in the increasingly smaller follow-ups, no mention was ever made of the victims' names.

As he inches closer, Jack can see that the three men are in animated discussion. Stanz's hands are hewing the air like axes. His mouth is going a mile a minute.

"—you mean, you can't get a name? I need a goddamned name!"

"I haven't got one," Gus's snitch replies.

"Then I'll damn well find someone who—"

"I guarantee you'll never get the name of the murderer," the snitch says, "either from me or anyone else."

Jack starts as he sees Stanz pull his service revolver. If it isn't for Gus's intervention, Jack feels certain Stanz would have shot the snitch. As it is, Stanz leaps at him, gets in a roundhouse right before Gus grabs him around the waist, holds him bodily in check.

"Get outta here," Gus growls. "Go on now!"

"That's right," Stanz howls in fury, "run away with your tail between your legs, you good-for-nothing nigger!"

Gus hurls Stanz to the ground, stands over him with the detective's gun in his huge hand. "I'll take alotta shit from you, but not this." He empties Stanz's service revolver, throws away the bullets. Then he drops the gun. "Don't come round my place no more, heah?"

As he stalks away, Stanz yells, "Don't expect to be paid for this!" And then as Gus squeezes behind the wheel of the Chevy and drives off, "Hey, are you leaving me here? What the fuck!"

GUS IS waiting for Jack in the side yard under the shadows of the big oak. Jack, rolling in with the lights off, doesn't see him until he steps out. Jack brakes and Gus looms up to the driver's window, which Jack rolls down.

"Since you got yo'self used t'drivin' the boat, you can follow me t' the precinct so I can drop off this piece-o'-shit Chevy."

Gus lets Jack drive on the way home, as well. He says, "Whut you 'spect t'do, out there onna golf course?"

His voice isn't pissed off; it isn't even querulous. If Jack didn't know better, he'd think there was a note of tenderness.

"I was worried."

"Huh, 'bout me?" Gus pulls out his Magnum .357.

Jack says nothing, concentrates on making it home without getting lost. He supposes this to be a lesson, what's behind Gus's decision to let him stay behind the wheel.

"You bring a weapon, kid?"

Jack is startled out of his thoughts. "Uh, no."

"Why the hell not?" Gus puts away the enormous gun. "Whut you think you could do out there if things got ugly?"

"They almost did," Jack says, happy now to speak up.

"Huh, don' take no chances like that again, heah?"

Jack nods.

"They's a key behin' the kitchen door."

"I've seen it."

"Bottom right-hand drawer of my desk. They's a snub-nosed .38. Jus' right for a young feller like you. It's loaded, but there's a coupla boxes of ammo inna back."

"I don't like guns," Jack says.

"Huh, who the fuck does?" Gus shifts in his seat. "But sometimes there jes' ain't no substitute."

JACK WANTS to stay awake. In fact, with all the excitement, he's certain he will. But Gus turns on the stereo. Music, familiar, earthy, shuffling, comes from his room, wraps Jack in a cocoon of melancholy history, and soon he's in a deep sleep.

He opens his eyes to see a bird on the branch of the oak outside his window. It's perched near the empty nest. Its head swivels as it looks in, peers around. It's morning. A thin, milky light stretches across the bare plank floor. Jack throws the covers off, stumbles to the bathroom to empty his bladder and splash cold water on his face.

He wonders what Gus is going to make for breakfast this morning. He hopes it's wild-blueberry pancakes. Since he doesn't smell anything cooking from downstairs, he knows there's time enough to put in his request with the chef.

Padding out into the hallway in just his underwear, he yawns hugely, scratches his stomach. He knocks on the partly open door of Gus's bedroom, calls his name, and walks in. The curtains are drawn and it's dim, still night here.

Gus is lying on the bed, the sheets and blanket rucked beneath his huge frame. He's facedown, his arms splayed wide. Jack assumes he's in a drunken stupor, calls his name more loudly. Getting no response, he pulls the curtains. Morning steps into the room, floods the scene.

Jack sees the bedclothes are black and shiny. He sees Gus's mouth half-open, as if he's about to yell at someone. He's staring right at Jack.

"Gus?"

Then Jack sees a knife with an odd-looking hilt jammed into Gus's back.

Much later, after the police have come and gone, after he's given his statement, after Reverend Taske has come, prepared food for Jack, after the house empties of light and life, Jack goes to the stereo, puts on *Out of Our Heads*. As Mick Jagger begins his aural strut, Jack stands fixed, staring at nothing at all. He knows he'll spend the night down here—maybe many nights to come. He can't bring himself to go upstairs, either to his room or to Gus's. But he wonders if that bird is still in the oak. He wonders what he was looking for.

Nearly a month after that, Detective Stanz comes to see him at the Hi-Line, the running of which Jack has taken over. Stanz walks slowly along the length of the glass cases, as if he's in the market to buy one of the odds and ends displayed there. But Jack knows why he's here. The only mystery is what took him so long to show up.

At last, he gets to where Jack is standing behind the register. He clears his throat. "You have some, uh, documents that Gus was keeping for me. I'd, uh, I'd like to have them back."

Jack considers for a moment. "I know what documents you mean. They belonged to Gus; now they belong to me."

Stanz's face looks like a fist. "Why, you little—!"

Jack reaches under the counter, pulls out a plain manila envelope. "I have one of them here."

He opens it, so Stanz can see the photocopies of the paperwork Stanz signed when he got his safe-deposit box at the Riggs National Bank.

Stanz snorts. "So what? Most everybody has a safety deposit box."

Jack slides a photocopy of another document from under the paperwork. "Not when two million dollars of Luis Arroyo Ochoa's money goes from the box to this offshore account in the Caymans."

Stanz goes white. He grips the display case so as not to lose his balance. "But this is impossible! Those accounts are sealed."

Jack nods. "So I understand, but that tax lawyer you went to who set up the account? He works for Gus."

Stanz wipes his sweating face. He moves to gather in the damning evidence against him, but Jack is quicker. He spirits the folder away.

"There's a price for everything," he says.

Shooting him a bleak stare, Stanz says, "What's yours?"

"I want to know who murdered Gus."

Stanz breathes a sigh of relief, and Jack knows why. He was terrified that Jack would demand half of the two million he stole. But Jack wants no part of Ochoa's blood money, and he's quite certain neither would Reverend Taske. Besides, Gus provided generously for Renaissance Mission Church in his will, just as he provided for Jack.

The detective licks his lips. "What about the other one?"

"The receipt for the gun you used to kill Manny Echebarra is safe with me, Detective Stanz. No one needs to see it."

Stanz ponders the unexpected situation he finds himself in. At length, he nods. "As it happens, I can help."

He holds out his hand. Jack gives him the folder and he stashes it away.

"The knife we took out of Gus's back is so unusual, it took the ME two weeks to track it down," Stanz says. "It's called a paletta. It's used in bakeries. Gus introduce you to any bakery-store owners? Yeah, I thought so. His calling card, right?" His glittery eyes regard Jack without even the smallest measure of sympathy. This is a business transaction, pure and simple. "The thing of it is, there's no prints, so we can't prove anything. The Metro Police's hands're tied, know what I mean?"

Jack, his mind already fixed on Cyril Tolkan, knows precisely what he means.

THIRTY-SIX

UNLIKE OTHER places in his past Jack had visited recently, the Marmoset's house looked just as he remembered it, with its deep-blue exterior and white shutters. It must have been repainted recently, he thought.

With the real possibility of a kidnap victim inside, along with her abductor, Jack wasn't prepared to take any chances of some overeager idiot tipping Kray/Whitman off. He got no argument from Nina. What he didn't tell her was that, incredible as it seemed, he was now quite certain that Kray/Whitman was the same person who had killed the two nameless men at McMillan Reservoir, the Marmoset, and Gus twenty-five years ago. He was also the man who had abducted Alli Carter, and Jack had little doubt that he would slip his paletta into Alli Carter's back if he was given the slightest hint his lair had been compromised. What he couldn't work out as yet was the overarching pattern into which all these terrible offenses fit, because there was absolutely no doubt in his mind that all the crimes were somehow connected. He was drawing close, however, because he could sense its color in his mind: a cold, neon blue, as beautiful as the developing pattern was ugly.

There was something else the developing pattern told him: In gunning down Cyril Tolkan for Gus's murder, he'd gone after the wrong man. Now, as his mind rolled all the emerging facts around, he had to wonder whether his stalking Tolkan was a case of deliberate misdirection. After all, it was the unique murder weapon that both Stanz and Jack had found most incriminating. The paletta was used in bakeries; Cyril Tolkan owned one: the All Around Town bakery. But though Jack had killed Tolkan twenty-five years ago, the strange filed-down paletta was being used again as a murder weapon. Jack didn't believe the paletta turning up again was a coincidence, nor did he think it was a copycat killer, simply because twenty-five years ago the murder weapon had never been revealed to the public. That meant Gus's murderer had been alive all this time. But why surface now, and why abduct Alli Carson?

Jack sat stunned, trying to regain his equilibrium as past and present rushed headlong at each other.

At last, he roused himself. "I know this place," he said as they sat in the car where they'd parked down the block. "I'll take the back, you take the front."

They synchronized their watches. It was dusk, the light grimly fading from the sky as if whisked away by a sooty broom. The air was cold but still. Dampness lay on the ground like trash.

"Give me ninety seconds from the time we split up to get into position," he continued, "okay?"

Nina nodded and they both got out of the car. Together, they glanced at their watches as they parted company on the pavement. Jack counted to himself as he made his way down the side of the house, past a couple of garbage cans on his right, a chain-link fence on his left. Jack thought of Zilla, the huge German shepherd Gus treated so well.

He arrived at the back door with sixteen seconds to spare. On his way, he'd passed three windows. Two were heavily curtained, making it impossible to see in. The third looked past lacy curtains to a kitchen, yellow as butter. It was deserted.

Inserting a pair of hooked picks into the lock, he manipulated them so that they simulated the turn of the proper key. The door popped open at almost the same time Nina was knocking on the front door. Glock drawn, Jack went from room to room, listened for any human sounds in between Nina's insistent knocking. It was dim, gloomy, full of bad memories that seemed to vibrate through the floorboards. In the hallway, he paused at the line of photos. His hair stood on end—they were all of Alli Carson. They had the telltale flatness associated with a long telephoto lens. Then his breath caught in his throat, for there in the middle was a photo of Alli and Emma walking together on the Langley Fields campus. As he stared at the two girls, Emma's image seemed to flicker, grow wavy, and move toward him. He could swear she knew he was here; he thought the smile on her face was for him.

As if from the wrong end of an amplifier, he heard her call to him. He wanted to answer her, but the fear of Kray/Whitman being in the house kept him silent.

Nina's renewed banging on the front door caused him to jump, but that was hardly the source of his fright. He passed into the foyer, reached out and opened the door to let her in. A quick negative shake of his head let her know he hadn't found anyone, but he led her silently to the photos in the hallway.

With his left hand, he indicated that she should check the second floor. He went room by room: the cobwebby basement, smelling of raw concrete and damp, the living room with its astounding volcanoes of books, magazines, papers of all kinds. The bathroom was clear, as was the kitchen. It was curious, though. The living room and foyer were just as he remembered them, cluttered and musty, but the kitchen and bathroom were neat and spotless, shining like a scientist's laboratory. It was as if two completely different people inhabited the same place: the ghost of the Marmoset and Kray/Whitman.

To the left, he found a closed door. Trying the knob, he ascertained that it was locked. His picks were of no help here. The lock was of a kind he hadn't encountered before. He stood back, aimed, then shielded his eyes as he fired the Glock at it. The resulting percussion brought Nina at a dead run.

He kicked in the door, found a room with only a huge painted wood chair. At one time, probably when the Marmoset had lived here, the room had had a window. Since then it had been bricked up and painted over. It reeked sourly of sweat, fear, and human excrement.

The two of them returned to the hallway, went down it until they found themselves back in the cheerful kitchen.

"Check everything," Jack said.

They opened closets, drawers, cabinets. All the utensils, bottles, cans, mops, brooms, dustpans were arranged in order of utility and size. The oven was empty inside. Nina pulled open the door to the refrigerator.

"Look here."

She knelt in front of the open refrigerator. All the shelves had been removed. She pointed to the bottom, where something translucent was wedged between sections.

"I think that's a piece of skin."

Jack nodded, his heart thudding in his throat. "Let's bag it, get it over to Dr. Schiltz. I have a feeling it belongs to our Jane Doe who had her hand amputated."

Nina donned a pair of latex gloves. "Let's pray it doesn't belong to Alli Carson."

As she produced a plastic bag and tweezers, Jack moved to the pantry door. It was closed but not latched. Gingerly, he pulled it open.

He expelled a long sigh of relief. The First Daughter was wedged into a corner, her back against the far wall where it met a set of cabinets.

Her knees were drawn up to her chest, her arms wrapped around her shins. She was rocking gently back and forth, as if to comfort herself.

Jack squatted down to Alli's level.

"Alli?" He had to call her name three or four times before her head swung around, her eyes focused on him. By this time, Jack could hear Nina speaking to HQ. She was asking for an ambulance, the Carson family doctor, who was standing by at Langley Fields, and an armed escort. She had initially asked for Hugh Garner, but for some reason Jack couldn't make out, wasn't able to speak with him.

"No sirens," Jack said softly, and Nina relayed the message.

Jack edged closer, and Alli shrank back. "Alli, it's Jack, Jack McClure. Emma's father. Do you remember me?"

Alli regarded him out of depthless eyes. She hadn't stopped rocking, and Jack couldn't help thinking of the room with the monstrous chair, the straps, the smell.

"Don't be afraid, Alli. Nina and I were sent by your father and mother. We're here to take you home."

Something in what he said put the spark of life into her eyes. "Jack?"

"Yes, Alli. Jack McClure."

Alli suddenly stopped rocking. "Is it really you?"

Jack nodded. He held out one hand until Alli reached out, tentatively took it. He was prepared for her to draw back, but instead she launched herself into his arms, sobbing and shaking, holding on to him with a desperation that plucked at his heart.

He rose with her in his arms. She was trembling all over. Nina moved in beside him. She was opening the drawers in the cabinet, one by one. All were empty, save the top one, which held an assortment of the usual handiwork tools: hammer, level, pliers, wire-cutter, a variety of screwdrivers and wrenches.

Alli began to whimper again, and Jack put one hand at the back of her head in an attempt to calm her. With the other, he fumbled out his cell phone, pressed a button. A moment later, president-elect Edward Carson came on the line.

"Sir, I have your daughter. Alli is safe and sound."

There was a brief rustle at the other end of the line that could have been anything, even Carson brushing away some tears. "Thank God." His voice was clotted with emotion. Then Jack heard him relay the news to his wife, heard her shout of relief and joy.

"Jack," Carson said, "Lyn and I don't know how to thank you. Can we speak with her?"

"I wouldn't advise it, sir. We need to extract her fully and assess her health."

"When can we see her?"

"The ambulance is on its way," Jack said. "You can meet us at Bethesda."

"We're on our way," the president-elect said. "Jack, you made good on your promise. Neither Lyn nor I will forget it."

At the same moment Jack put away his cell, Nina opened the cupboard over the small sink. Nina recoiled when she saw the horned viper slither down onto the countertop. The evil-looking wedge-shaped head with its demon's horns quested upward. The viper was hungry, and she was annoyed. Her tongue flicked out, vibrating, scenting living creatures.

Jack dug the pliers out of the drawer. The head moved forward, far faster than he could follow, but midway toward him a shadow fell across it, slowing it. Jack felt a breath of cool air brush the nape of his neck. With a well-aimed swipe of the pliers, he stunned the snake. Gripping the viper's head between the ends of the pliers, he squeezed as hard as he could. Though its brain was pulped, the viper's body continued to thrash, slamming itself this way and that in a random fury for a long time.

Nina struggled to regain her equilibrium. "Jack, are you all right?"

Unable to find his voice, he nodded.

"It was coming straight at you; I was sure it would bite you."

"It would have," Jack said, a little dazed himself, "but something slowed it down."

"That's impossible."

"Nevertheless, something did. A shadow came between the snake and me."

Nina looked around. "What shadow, Jack?" She passed her hand through the space Jack indicated. "There's no shadow here, Jack. None at all."

Alli twisted in his arms, taking her face out of his shoulder. "What happened?" she whispered.

Jack kicked the snake's body away. "Nothing, Alli. Everything's fine."

"No, it isn't, something happened," she insisted.

"I'm taking you out of here, Alli," he whispered as he took her back out through the kitchen and down the hall. "Your folks are coming to meet us."

The Marmoset's house was crawling with the heavily armed detail Nina requested. Along with them came two EMS attendants with a rolling stretcher, a nurse, and the Carson family doctor. But Alli refused to be parted from Jack, so he and Alli, with Nina at their side, strode out of the house with the escort.

Alli put her lips to his ear. "I felt something, Jack, like someone standing beside us."

"You must have blacked out for a minute," Jack said.

"No, I felt someone breathe—one cool breath on my cheek."

Jack felt his heart lurch. Could it be that Alli had felt the shadow, just as he had? His mind lit up with possibilities.

He climbed into the ambulance with her clinging to him. Even when he managed to get her onto the stretcher so that the doctor could examine her, she wouldn't let him go entirely. She was clearly terrified he'd leave her alone with her living nightmare.

He gripped her hand, talking of the good times when she and Emma were best friends, and gradually she relaxed enough for the doctor to take her vitals and administer a light sedative.

"Jack . . ." Alli's lids were heavy, but the abject horror was sliding off her face like a mask. "Jack . . ."

"I'm here, honey," he said with tears in his eyes. "I won't leave you."

His voice was hoarse, his breathing constricted. He was all too aware that this is what he should have said to Emma a long time ago.

PART FOUR

THIRTY-SEVEN

THE EARLY January sunset was painting narrow bands of gold and crimson across the low western sky when Jack met with Dr. Irene Saunderson on the wide, Southern-style veranda of Emily House.

"I've tried every way I can think of—and any number of new ones—to get through to Alli," Dr. Saunderson said. She was a tall, stick-thin woman with dark hair pulled severely back into a ponytail, accentuating a high forehead and cheekbones, bright, intelligent eyes. She looked like a failed model. "She either can't or won't tell us what happened to her."

"Which is it?" Jack said. "Can't you at least tell that much?"

Dr. Saunderson shook her head. "That's part of what's so frustrating about the human mind. I have little doubt that she's suffering from a form of posttraumatic stress syndrome, but at the end of the day, that tells us next to nothing. What's indisputable is that she suffered a traumatic episode. But what form the trauma took or what the actual effect on her is, we can't determine."

She sighed deeply. "Frankly, I'm at a dead end."

"You're the third shrink to say that." Jack unbuttoned his coat. A thaw had set in with a vengeance. "What about physical damage?"

"The exhaustive medical workup shows that she wasn't raped or physically harmed in any way. There wasn't even a superficial scratch on her."

"Is there a possibility of Stockholm syndrome?"

"You're thinking of Patty Hearst, of course, among many others." Dr. Saunderson shrugged. "Of course it's possible that she's come to identify with her captor, but she's shown no indication of hostility toward us, and given the relatively short amount of time she was with her abductor, it seems unlikely. Unless, of course, he used drugs to accelerate the process, but there was no sign of chemical markers in her blood workup. As you know, the president's own medical team at Bethesda took charge of her when you brought her in."

"It's been three days since I asked to see her," Jack said.

"You can see her right now, if you like," Dr. Saunderson said, brushing aside his complaint with a shrink's easy aplomb.

They always know what to say, Jack thought, *even when they're wrong.*

"Shall I take you to her room?"

"Actually, I'd rather see her out here."

Dr. Saunderson frowned. "I'm not so sure that's such a good idea."

"Why not? She's been cooped up for the better part of ten days. This is a pretty place, but it's still a prison." Jack smiled his most charming smile. "C'mon, Doc. You and I both know the fresh air will do her good."

"All right. I'll be right back." She was about to turn away when she hesitated. "Don't be surprised if Alli exhibits some erratic behavior, extreme mood swings, things like that."

Jack nodded.

Alone on the veranda, he had a chance to take in the antebellum atmosphere of Emily House, a large, rather overornate confection whose exterior might easily have been used for a remake of *Gone with the Wind*. Save for knowing its true purpose, Jack would not have been surprised to find himself mingling with couples drinking mint juleps and speaking in deep Southern drawls.

Emily House, named after a former president's dog, of all things, was a government safe house in the midst of fifty acres of Virginia countryside as heavily guarded as it was forested. Over the years, a good many heads of state, defectors, double agents, and the like had called it home, at least temporarily. It was painted white, with dove-gray shutters and a blue-gray slate roof. A bit of fluff on the outside, belying the armor-plated walls and doors, the bullet- and bombproof windows, and more cutting-edge security paraphernalia than Q's lab. For instance, there was a little number called ADS. ADS stood for active denial system, which sounded like something Dr. Saunderson might claim Alli was suffering from. However, there was nothing nonsensical about the ADS, which was to all intents and purposes a ray gun that shot out a beam of invisible energy that made its victims feel as if their skin were burning off. It wasn't handheld; it wasn't even small. In fact, it looked rather like a TV satellite dish perched on a flatbed truck or a Humvee. But it worked, which was all that mattered.

Jack, hearing a door open, turned to see Alli with Dr. Saunderson right behind her. It had been only three days since he'd last seen her, but she seemed to have aged a year. There was something in her face, a change he couldn't quite figure. It was another visual puzzle he needed to decipher.

"Hey," he said, smiling.

"Hey."

She ran into his arms. Jack kissed the top of her head, saw Dr. Saunderson nod to him, then withdraw into Emily House.

Alli was wearing a short wool jacket, jeans, an orange Buffalo Brand shirt, a screaming eagle with a skull in its talons silkscreened on the front.

"You feel up to a walk?" he asked her.

When she nodded, he took her down the steps, along the crushed gravel. There were a number of formal gardens around Emily House. This time of year, the low boxwood maze was the only one still green.

Alli ducked her head. "We can't go too far, you know, without catching the attention of the guards."

Jack listened closely not only to her words but also to her tone of voice. There was something sad there that touched the sad place inside him. This young woman had spent all her life at the end of a leash, watched over by stern men to whom she could never relate. He resolved to talk with her father about the new Secret Service detail that would be assigned to her when she came home. She deserved better than two more anonymous agents.

"How are they treating you?" he asked as they moved between the low hedges.

"With kid gloves." She gave a thin laugh. "Sometimes I feel like I'm made of glass."

"They're making you feel that way?"

Alli shrugged. It was clear she wasn't yet ready to talk about what happened, even with him. Jack knew he needed to take another tack altogether.

"Alli, there's something only you can help me with. It's about Emma."

"Okay."

Was he mistaken, or did her eyes light up?

"Don't laugh, but there have been moments during the past few weeks when I could swear I've seen Emma. Once at Langley Fields, then in the backseat of my car. Other times, too. And once I felt a cool breath on the back of my neck."

Alli, walking silently, stared at her feet. Jack, sensing that she'd had enough urging recently, chose to let her be. He listened, instead, to the wind through the bare branches, the distant complaints of a murder of crows, crowded onto the treetops like a bunch of old ladies at a funeral.

At length, Alli lifted her head, regarded him curiously. "I felt the same thing. When you were holding me, when that snake—"

"You saw the snake?"

"I heard it."

"I didn't realize."

"You were busy."

The words stung him, though that was hardly her intent. The wound his inattention had inflicted was still as raw as on the day he'd held Emma's lifeless body in his arms. There wasn't anything that could prepare you for the death of your child. It was unnatural, and therefore incomprehensible. There was no solace. In that light, perhaps Sharon's turning to the Church was understandable. There came a time when the pain you carried inside you was insupportable. One way or another you needed to grope your way toward help.

They had reached the heart of the maze, a small square space with a stone bench. They sat in silence. Jack watched the shadows creeping over the lawns and gardens. The treetops seemed to be on fire.

"I felt her," Alli said at last. "Emma was there with us in that horrible house."

And it was at that moment, with the utterance of those words, that Jack felt them both brushed by the feathers of a mystery of infinite proportions. He felt in that moment that in entering the boxwood maze, in finding their way to its center, they had both touched a wisdom beyond human understanding, and in so doing were bound together in the same mysterious way, for the rest of their lives.

"But how is that possible?" He spoke as much to himself as he did to her.

She shrugged. "Why do I like Coke and not root beer?" she said. "Why do I like blue more than red?"

"Some things just are."

She nodded. "There you go."

"But this is different."

"Why is it different?" Alli said.

"Because Emma's dead."

"Honestly, I don't know what that means."

Jack pondered this a moment, then shook his head. "I don't either."

"Then there's no reason why we *shouldn't* feel Emma's presence," she said.

"When you put it that way . . ."

With the absolute surety of youth, she said, "How else *can* it be put?"

Jack could think of any number of alternatives, but they all fell within the strict beliefs of the skeptics, scientific and religious alike.

And because he felt the wingtips of mystery still fluttering about them, he told her what he'd never been able to tell anyone else. Leaning forward, elbows on knees, his fingers knit together, he said, "After Sharon and I broke up, I started to wonder: Is this all there is? I mean life, the world that we can see, hear, smell, touch."

"Why did it come up then?" Alli asked.

Jack groped for an answer. "Because without her, I became—I don't know—unmoored."

"I've been unmoored all my life." Alli sat forward herself. "Sometimes I think I was born asking, Is this all there is? But for me the answer was always, No, the world is out there beyond the bars of your cage."

Jack turned to her. "Do you really think of your world as a cage?"

She nodded. "It's small enough, Jack. You've been in it, you ought to know."

"Then I'm glad Emma came into it."

"For such a short time!"

The genuine lamentation broke Jack's heart all over again. "And she had you, Alli, though it was only for a short time."

It was growing cooler as the shadows extended their reach across the vast lawns, hedges, and flower beds. Alli shivered, but when Jack asked her whether she wanted to go back inside, she shook her head.

"I don't want to go back there," she whispered. "I couldn't bear it."

Without thinking, Jack put a protective arm around her, and to his slight surprise, she moved closer to him.

"I want to tell you about Emma," she said at last.

Jack, stunned, said nothing.

Alli turned her face to him. "I think that's why she's still here. I think she wants me to tell you now. She wants you to know all about her."

THIRTY-EIGHT

IT TOOK the better part of an hour for Jack to convince Dr. Saunderson and the powers that be at Emily House that Alli wasn't joking when she said she couldn't spend another night there. In the end, though, he was obliged to call in the big gun.

"She'll be with me, sir," Jack said to the president-elect.

"That's what she wants, Jack?"

"It is, sir." Jack moved away from where Dr. Sanderson sat in a pool of lamplight behind her enormous ornate desk. "Frankly, I don't see any other way to get through to her. Every other avenue has been exhausted."

"So I understand," Edward Carson said gloomily. "All right, then. You have until noon tomorrow."

"But, sir, that's hardly any time at all."

"Jack, the inauguration is the day after tomorrow. No less than three top shrinks have evaluated her without coming to any conclusion except that she hasn't been harmed. Thank God for that."

"Sir, it's imperative we find who abducted her."

"I applaud your impulse as a lawman, Jack, but this is nonnegotiable. Alli has a duty to be at my and my wife's side at the ceremony. We didn't go through all this secrecy only for her to miss the most important photo op of her life. And after all, what's important is that Alli's safe and sound. I don't care to know about what happened to her, and frankly I'm not surprised she doesn't want to relive it. I sure as hell wouldn't."

It must be single-mindedness, Jack thought, that put such a hard, shiny shell around all politicians, conservative, liberal, or independent. He knew the president-elect's mind was set. No argument would sway him. "All right, sir. I'll deliver Alli tomorrow at noon."

"Good," Carson said. "One more thing. I must insist on a Secret Service detail."

"I understand how you feel, sir," Jack said, thinking their presence might not be a big problem, but it would have to be dealt with. "Just so you know, right now seeing a detail isn't going to be good for Alli. I need her to open up about what happened while she was in captivity. Feeling hemmed in is going to make that job more difficult than it already is."

There was silence on the other end of the line while Carson mulled this over. "All right, a compromise, then. I want them on the roads with you. They'll exit their vehicle only in case of an emergency."

"And then, sir, I'd like to pick her permanent detail. I've a couple of people in mind. I don't want a repeat of what happened at Langley Fields."

"You've got it, Jack, we're on the same page there," Carson said. "Now let me settle matters with Dr. Saunderson."

ALLI TURNED when Jack emerged from Emily House. She'd been standing on the veranda, watching the guards crisscross the lawns at random intervals. He saw the anticipation in her face, but also the fear.

"Well?"

Jack nodded, and immediately relief flooded her face.

On the way to his car, she said, "I want to sit in the backseat."

Jack understood immediately. On the way back to Washington, he kept one eye on the road, one on the rearview mirror, checking on the vehicle carrying the two-man Secret Service detail, and on Alli.

"Tell me where she was sitting," Alli said.

He knew she meant Emma. "To your right, just a little more. Okay, right there."

Alli spent the rest of the drive in that position, her eyes closed. A certain peacefulness settled over her, as if she had been transported out of time and place. Then, with a jolt, he realized that her near trance-like state reminded him of what had stolen over him after he'd killed Andre in the library. And he wondered whether he and Alli were two tigers, whether it was now his turn to lead her into the forest.

THE OLD wood-frame house stood as it always had at the end of Westmoreland Avenue, just over the border in Maryland. The house and its attendant property had resisted the advances of time and civilization. The huge oak tree still rose to a height above the roof; there was still a bird's nest in its branches outside Jack's bedroom. The forested area was, if anything, thicker, more tangled.

It was to Gus's house he took Alli. His home, the place Sharon had refused to move into, rejecting his past. In fact, she couldn't understand why he didn't sell it, use the proceeds to pay for Emma's tuition at Langley Fields rather than taking out a second mortgage on their house. "You own that horrid old thing free and clear," she'd said. "Why not just get rid of it and be done with it?" She hadn't understood that he didn't want to be done with it. Just as she hadn't understood that the house and property had been a place he'd taken Emma and, quite often, Molly Schiltz, when the girls were younger. They adored climbing the oak tree, where they lolled in the crotches of its huge trunk; they loved playing hide-and-seek in the wild, tangled woodland behind the house.

They'd spread out like sea stars on the huge living room sofas, listen to Gus's old LPs—Muddy Waters, Howlin' Wolf, James Brown, whose over-the-top stage antics they imitated so well after Jack showed them the electrifying concert video of him performing at the Apollo in Harlem.

On his way up the front steps, Jack noticed the Secret Service vehicle parked down the block, in front of the neighboring house. From that vantage point, the detail had an ideal view of the front and side of the house.

Jack padded into the kitchen, put the Chinese takeout on the counter. When he returned to the living room, he went over to the old stereo, selected a vinyl disc, put it on the turntable. A moment later, Muddy Waters began to sing "Long Distance Call."

Alli began a slow circuit, stopping here and there to peer at a photo, a book, a row of album covers. She ran her fingertips over an old guitar of Gus's, a stack of Jack's individually cased Silver Age comics of Spider-Man, the Fantastic Four, and Dr. Strange. His stacks of videocassettes of old TV shows.

"Wow! This place is exactly the way Emma described it."

"She seemed to like it here."

"Oh, she did." Alli looked through the cassettes of *The Dick Van Dyke Show, Sea Hunt, Have Gun—Will Travel, The Bob Newhart Show.* "She liked to come here when you weren't here. To be alone."

"What did she do here?"

Alli shrugged. "Dunno. Maybe she listened to music; she was nuts about the iPod you gave her. She took it with her everywhere. She made playlists and listened to them all the time." She put the cassettes aside. "She never told me what she did here. See, she had secrets from everyone, even me."

Jack, watching her, experienced a piercingly bittersweet moment, because as happy as he was to have her here, her presence—in a way that was most immediate, most painful—served to remind him of what he could have had with Emma. At the same time, he was overcome with a feeling of protectiveness toward her.

It had taken him some time after Emma's death to realize that the world had changed: it would never again feel safe, never have the comfort it had held when Emma was alive. Its color had changed, as if cloaked in mourning.

And there was something else. Through Alli, he was coming closer to Emma, he was beginning to understand that he and his daughter were not so very different. It seemed that Emma knew how similar they were, but Emma being Emma, she needed to go her own way, just as he had when he was her age. All at once, he experienced a jolt of pure joy. It seemed to him that he and Emma would have come together again, that they would have reunited, perhaps as soon as the day she had called him. She was coming to see him, after all. What had she wanted to tell him?

"Abbott and Costello." Alli was holding a cassette aloft. "Can we watch this? Emma talked about them, but I've never seen them."

Shaking himself out of his reverie, Jack turned on the TV, slid the cassette in the slot. They watched "The Susquehanna Hat Company" bit until Alli laughed so hard, she was crying. But then she didn't stop crying, not when the bit was over or when Jack popped out the tape. She just cried and cried, but when Jack tried to hold her, she shied away. He left her alone for a bit, going upstairs, sitting in Gus's old room, which, now that the bed was gone, he could bear to be in. He spent time thinking of Ronnie Kray, trying to imagine him, trying to imagine what a serial killer could want with Alli. Had he meant to kill her? If so, he'd had plenty of time to slip his filed-down paletta into her back. Had he meant to torture her before he killed her? If so, there was no sign that he'd begun. Besides, torture wasn't part of Kray's MO. And if there was one thing Jack had learned in dealing with criminals—even the cleverest ones—it was that once established, an

MO never changed. The same aberrant impulse that drove a person to kill another human being also ensured it be done the same way every time, as if it were a kind of ritual of expiation.

So, to sum up, at great jeopardy to himself, Kray had abducted Alli Carson from the grounds of Langley Fields. If it wasn't to kill her or to torture her, then what was his motive? And why had he abandoned her? Had they been lucky, had he simply been shopping for supplies when he and Nina raided the house? Could he have been tipped off? But how, and by whom? The more Jack worked the puzzle over, the more convinced he was that Alli was the key. He had to get her to talk.

When he came downstairs, she was sitting on the sofa.

"Sorry I freaked out," she said.

"Forget it," Jack said. "You hungry?"

"Not really."

"Let's have something anyway." Jack padded into the kitchen. Alli was right behind him. She helped him open the cartons, spoon out the food onto plates. Jack showed her where the silverware was, and she laid out neat place settings.

Alli was a carnivore, so Jack had ordered spare ribs, lacquered a deep-red, beef chow fun, roast pork fried rice, gai lan in garlic sauce.

Apart from the sticky ribs, they both used the wooden chopsticks that came packaged with the meal. Alli looked as if she'd been born with them between her fingers. Jack had been taught by Emma.

"I used to be a vegetarian, but that was before I met Emma." She managed a wistful smile. "She could eat more pork than anyone I ever met." She swirled the glistening noodles around with her chopsticks. "I made fun of her, you know? And she asked me why I was a vegetarian. So I told her about how animals are treated, and then slaughtered, all of that. She laughed and said if that was my reason for not eating meat, I was a hypocrite. 'Can I borrow your suede jacket? How about your leather skirt, or one of your belts? And how many pairs of plastic shoes do you own?' She told me about how small farms are breeding cows,

pigs, sheep, chickens in humane ways. She told me about slow farm-
ing, sustainable methodology, hormone-free raising. She said if I
wanted to be a vegetarian that was my business, but that I ought to do
it for the right reason. She was so damn smart. She'd done her research,
instead of just spouting talking points like me. What really amazed me
about her was that she never made a choice just for the hell of it. There
was always a reason behind what she did."

Who was this girl he was hearing about? "It never seemed like that
to Sharon and me. All we saw was chaos and rebellion."

"Yeah, well, there was that, too."

"I wish I'd taken the time to see more."

"Well, it might not have mattered."

"What d'you mean?"

"Emma was a master in letting you see what she wanted you to
see, and nothing more." Alli pulled her knees up to her chest, wrapped
her arms around them. "I'll tell you how it started with me. Emma
didn't have a lot of friends. It wasn't because other girls didn't try. They
did. Everyone wanted to hang with her, but Emma didn't want any
part of a pack, even though it would've been so easy for her to be a
leader. See, she saw herself in a totally different light. We both saw
ourselves as being different, Outsiders, you know, with a capital O."

The fact that his daughter had lived with the same sense of being
an Outsider that Jack had lived with all his life shocked him to his
core. Or maybe, if he was honest with himself, what shocked him was
that he hadn't recognized her as being an Outsider.

"The thing for me was that I always thought my being an Outsider
was because of my father's political ambitions," Alli went on. "From as
far back as I can remember, all he talked about, all he planned for was
being president. There were times I actually thought he'd started making plans to become president when he was in grade school.

"Anyway, it was Emma who made me realize that being an Outsider had nothing to do with my father; it came from inside myself."

Old Muddy had segued into the slow, rueful "My Home Is in the Delta," one of Gus's favorite tracks.

He said, "So Emma thought of herself as an Outsider."

"She didn't just think it," Alli said at once. "She *was* an Outsider."

Jack shook his head. "I'm not sure I understand."

"At first, I didn't understand it either." Alli gathered up Jack's plate and cutlery, put it on top of hers, took the small stack to the sink.

"Leave those," Jack said, "I'll take care of the washing later."

"That's all right." Alli turned on the water. "I like doing this because no one's told me to, no one's even expecting me to."

She squeezed some dishwashing liquid onto a Dobie, set about her job with some concentration. "I didn't understand it," she said, "until I took the time to get to know her. Then it hit me: Unlike most girls our age, Alli didn't define or judge herself in terms of other girls her age. She knew who she was from the inside out. And because of that, she had a kind of—I don't know—a savage energy."

Finished, Alli dried her hands, returned to the table, and sat back down. "It was Emma who introduced me to Hunter S. Thompson, a modern-day Outsider if ever there was one. But she also suggested I read Blake." She cocked her head. "You know William Blake?"

Jack felt a little thrill travel through him at Blake's name. He had read and enjoyed Blake during his time in the District's public libraries, which continued long after he was once again left on his own. But he couldn't forget the telling excerpt Chris Armitage had quoted to him and Nina the other day. "I do."

"Emma adored Blake. She identified with him intensely. And when I read him, I got her fully, because her favorite quote was this." She closed her eyes, her brow furrowed in concentration. " 'I must create my own system or be enslaved by another man's. My business is not to reason and compare; my business is to create.' "

"Emma wanted to create something."

Alli nodded. "Something important, something lasting."

"What, exactly?"

The tears came again, leaking out of the corners of her eyes.

A sudden awful premonition gripped Jack's heart. "What is it?"

Alli rose, paced around the room. Muddy was in the middle of "You Can't Lose What You Ain't Never Had."

She bit her lower lip, said, "Honestly, I don't know whether I should tell you."

"Alli, you've come this far," Jack said. "Emma doesn't need to be protected anymore."

"Yeah, I know, but . . ." She exhaled slowly, said, "She was going to quit school."

Jack was flooded with relief. "You mean she didn't like it at Langley Fields."

"No, I mean school—any school."

Now Jack felt bewildered. "But what was she going to do?"

"Oh God, I don't want to break a trust."

"But you said Emma wanted you to tell me," Jack said. He found that he was perfectly serious.

Alli nodded, but her expression was bleak. She came and sat down close to him. "She was going to do what she felt she had to do." There were tears in her eyes. "She was making plans to join E-Two."

THIRTY-NINE

THE IMAGE of Calla Myers hung in the air, the projector enlarging her face to Hollywood size. No one in the room, least of all Secretary Dennis Paull, failed to notice the resemblance to Alli Carson.

"Gentlemen," he heard the noxious Hugh Garner say in his most authoritative voice as he held up a bagged-and-tagged item. "We now have our smoking gun."

Paull was part of a very select audience seated in Sit Room W in the Pentagon. With him were the president, the Secretary of State, and the president's National Security Advisor. They sat around a polished ebony table. In front of each man was a pad, a clutch of pencils, glasses, and bottles of chilled water. After the meeting, all the writing materials would be gathered up and burned.

"This cell phone belonged to one of the murdered members of the Secret Service detail guarding Alli Carson," Garner continued. "It was found near Calla Myers's body. At the time of her death, the victim was employed by the First American Secular Revivalists. While it's a sure bet that the late Ms. Myers didn't kidnap Alli Carson, her implication is now all but assured.

"My guess is that she was getting ready to defect. She was going to the police with the cell phone. One of her compatriots found out about her act of heroism and killed her. She must've heard her attacker coming because she managed to toss away the phone. It was found in our initial search of the crime scene on the west side of the Spanish Steps, clear evidence that the FASR or E-Two is behind the abduction of the Alli Carson."

"Well done, Hugh," the president said. "Now if you'll excuse us."

"Yes, sir."

Garner marched out of the room like a good soldier, but not before Paull caught the sullen look on his face.

The president cleared his throat. "This little item combined with the documentation President Yukin has provided will spell the end of the missionary secularists in America."

He turned to Paull. "Dennis, I'm ordering you to begin taking members of the First American Secular Revivalists into custody. Since you have been unable to make any headway in identifying anyone in this underground E-Two, I want each one of the prisoners interrogated on the subject." He raised a finger. "I needn't remind you that my term of office is just about over. I personally won't feel as if our job was finished unless we bring these homegrown terrorists to justice. I certainly don't trust the incoming president to get the job done, so it's entirely up to us."

Paull, secretly fuming under the president's veiled rebuke, nodded, said enthusiastically, "Consider it done, sir. Now that we have the weight of evidence, we can attack in a more public way that was closed to us before."

"Good." The president, appearing immune to Paull's cleverly worded response, rubbed his hands together. "Now, to the business of what comes after January twentieth."

The Pentagon was built on secrets, but Paull observed that today there was about this room the deathly hush of secrets held close to the chest. On his desk, Paull had a rosewood plaque given to him by his mentor. On it was engraved in gold leaf the famed Benjamin Franklin quotation: THREE CAN KEEP A SECRET IF TWO OF THEM ARE DEAD. Paull was never more aware of the wisdom of that saying than he was now. As he looked around the room, it seemed to him that the atmosphere was rife with secrets. *Perhaps this is what happens when the skein runs out,* he thought, *when after eight years of hard decisions, close calls, and the need for frantic spin control, the trust among even the closest of colleagues turns rancid.* He'd been warned by his mentor that the last days of an Administration are gripped either by ennui or by desperation. Neither was healthy. Both revealed the corrosive workings of corruption. Each man had to face his moment of realization: Either the power had worn him down to a nub or he couldn't live without it. Over time, his mentor told him, all that's left to flush away is sewage, the entropy of power slipping through your fingers.

"Gentlemen," the president continued, "how goes our sub rosa campaign to ensure the continuance of our influence on Congress and the media when Edward Carson becomes president?"

Here, now, Paull faced the truth of his mentor's words. He was disgusted with the tenor of this meeting, the scrounging of Caesar facing the blade of the ides of March, railing against time and history. But he knew he couldn't allow the underlying wretchedness to blind him to the extreme danger of these last few orders. The desperate animal was the most dangerous animal. The question he had to answer, and soon, was which one of these three men was the most desperate and, therefore, the most dangerous.

It fell to Paull to discover for himself what form of damage eight years of power had worked on these three men. Which one was a nub, which one a junkie?

The Secretary of State, a large man with the flushed face of an inveterate drinker and the twinkling eyes of Santa Claus, was the first to take the president's challenge by the horns.

"If we stay the course, we have nothing to fear. The evangelicals are still our broadest base, though admittedly the NRA is less fickle."

"There's a growing problem with the NRA's power," the National Security Advisor said. He was a Texan, with a leathery face, a raspy voice, and the no-nonsense, faintly intimidating demeanor of a federal marshal in the 1880s. "Latest figures find an alarming decline in the number of hunters nationwide. Our concern has been given an environmental spin by our media outlets. We're worried because hunters keep the deer population in check, hunters are pro-environment, that sort of thing. Of course, the real worry for us is that faced with declining membership, the NRA is going to lose its clout on Capitol Hill."

"Now that would be a real shame," the Secretary of State said. "Can we find some way to funnel money in their direction to make up for the shortfall? By God, we don't want them running out of money to pay their lobbyists."

"I think we can twist some well-heeled arms in that direction," the National Security Advisor replied.

The president turned to his Secretary of Homeland Security. "Dennis, we haven't heard from you yet."

Paull tapped a pencil on the table. "I've been thinking on the evangelical issue. We have all the usual suspects tied up, but the growing influence of the Renaissance Mission Congress is a real concern. I've gone over the post-election breakdown a number of times, and each time I'm more impressed. There's no doubt its influence swung the election in Carson's favor. It got out the black votes in every state with appalling efficiency."

"What's your point?" the Secretary of State said. "Surely you're not advocating we turn Reverend Myron Taske into another Martin Luther King, Jr."

"God no." Paull poured himself some water to cover the wave of revulsion that washed over him. With all his heart, he prayed for God to protect him from people like the Secretary of State. "It happens that

Carson's own man, Jack McClure, has a relationship with Reverend Taske. With that in mind, I've been running a Secret Service special operative, Nina Miller, who I made sure joined Hugh Garner's joint-operations task force."

Once again, Paull paused to take a drink of water. As he did so, his gaze caressed the room like a lover, absorbing every texture, gesture, shift of body or head without seeming to do so. All these men were suspect; all of them, in one way or another, could have infiltrated his security measures. He was hoping one of them would betray himself—even by as little as the flicker of an eyelid—as he revealed the nature of the very operation his enemy had discovered.

"Now that McClure has found Alli Carson," Paull continued, "the task force is disbanding. However, following my orders, Agent Miller has formed a bond with McClure. She now has his trust." He turned directly to the president. "Here's what I meant to do from the beginning and now propose to you: Agent Miller will get McClure to use his influence on Reverend Taske to take our side."

"I've met with Reverend Taske several times," the president said. "He's as honest as he is black."

The National Security Advisor nodded. "We've vetted Taske thoroughly. He won't abandon Carson."

"He will if we convince McClure that Carson's values are not what they seem to be," Paull said. This was a total fabrication, one that his enemy in this room would discover when Jack didn't denounce the president-elect. But by that time it would be too late. All he wanted now was to buy enough time to get them all through the next couple of days. "What I've learned from my agent is McClure's an odd duck—loyal in the extreme, but quick to turn on a dime if he thinks he's been betrayed. I can use that to my advantage."

"He sounds unstable," the Secretary of State said. "I don't like it."

"Unstable or not," the National Security Advisor said, "I like the shot. Dennis is right on target as far as the Renaissance Mission Congress is concerned. It's powerful and getting more so every day. Of course, it would be ideal if we could wrap up the RMC and the Hispanic vote in one tidy ball, but I'm as much a realist as the next man. I know a goddamn pipe dream when I see one."

"I concur." The president nodded. "We'll give Dennis his head with the McClure mission."

"Dennis," the National Security Advisor said, "if there's any assistance I can provide, I'm only a call away."

"I appreciate that," Paull said. "That might be just the boost I need." *When there are ice cubes in hell,* he thought.

The president held up a hand. "Please, all of you, keep our accelerated timetable in the forefront of your plans. Dennis, McClure has to be wrapped up and delivered before the twentieth."

WHEN DENNIS Paull exited the Pentagon, he pulled out his cell phone, punched in a speed-dial number, said, "Latent," and rang off. A moment later, he ducked into his limo, which took him to the nearby Nordstrom department store. Paull strode inside, went immediately to the men's store. There, he spotted two of his men. While the first one covered his back, checking for tails, Paull went up to the second agent, took the large shopping bag out of his hand, proceeded to the entrance to the dressing rooms, outside of which another of his agents stood guard.

Inside, only one booth was occupied. Paull chose an adjacent booth, spent the next four minutes stripping off his fedora, midnight-blue cashmere overcoat, Brooks Brothers suit, Paul Stuart shirt and tie. He put his black brogues aside. From the shopping bag, he donned a pair of stovepipe-leg jeans, a blue chambray shirt, a pair of brown Lucchese cowboy boots.

Thus dressed, gripping a dossier he'd extracted from inside his overcoat, he knocked on the dividing wall between his booth and the other occupied booth. The fourth of his agents appeared with a brown shearling coat and a dun-colored Stetson for Paull. As the secretary vacated his booth, his agent, who was the same weight and height as Paull, entered, dressed himself in his boss's clothes. He was the one who exited Nordstrom by the same doors Paull had used to enter. He climbed into Paull's limo, which whisked him away. At the same time, Paull took a side door out to the mall, where an Empire taxi idled, waiting for him, its driver one of Paull's agents.

The taxi took off as soon as Paull climbed in, swinging onto Washington Boulevard, heading toward Arlington. On the corner of Fourteenth and North Wayne, Paull got out, walked around the block to make sure he was clear, then went up North Adams Street. Just past where it crossed Fifteenth, a Metro Police car sat waiting. Paull opened the rear door, got in.

"All clear," Paull said. "Do you have any news?"

"Yes, sir." The agent dressed as a cop nodded. "The captain of your boat reads lips."

"Damn it to hell!" Paull's fist struck the armrest. "Who's he reporting to?"

"It's a mobile number we can't get a handle on."

"That figures." He thought a moment. "How about a date and time the call was made?"

"That I can do," his agent said, then gave the information to him.

Paull stared out the window at the civilians hurrying past him on errands to buy fish or pick up flowers. Little People, the National Security Advisor called them, with an arrogance typical of this president's Administration. Of course, Paull himself was a member of the Administration, but right now he felt like a rat in the woodwork who suspected a slew of tomcats were waiting to snap off his head the moment he poked it into the open. "This is beautiful. Just beautiful."

He nodded. "Okay, let's get going." And he opened the thin dossier, reading it one more time and wondering at the paucity of genuine information on Ian Brady, the government's own crown jewel asset. But even in these few paragraphs, there was something for him, he was certain of it—trouble was, he was damned if he knew what it was.

HOWDY, COWBOY," Nina Miller said when he picked her up in the shadows of North Taft Street.

Paull shifted over. "I do look a sight, don't I?"

She tossed his Stetson onto the front seat. As she settled herself beside him, he said, "We've got a problem."

"Another one," she inquired, "or the same one?"

That made him laugh, despite his foul mood. "I think all our problems devolve back to one person."

"I only wish it was Hugh Garner," Nina said. "Him I can handle."

"He needs decommissioning, that's for certain," Paull acknowledged. "Any ideas on that score?"

"Jack told me he practically drowned Peter Link, one of the heads of the FASR. He would've done the same to Chris Armitage if Jack hadn't stepped in."

"Forget it. The president just ordered the arrest and interrogation of all FASR members."

"Then it's begun."

Paull nodded grimly. "Despite all our efforts."

"Jack's, too. He intervened, stood up to Garner to stop the torture by threatening to call the president-elect. It was no idle threat, and Hugh knew it, so he backed down. But now he hates Jack's guts."

"All useful bona fides," Paull said thoughtfully. "Is Jack one of us?"

Nina made a waffling gesture with one hand. "I don't yet know whether he has a side. He seems to be the most apolitical person I've ever met. Systems—any system—are abhorrent to him."

"So what is he, then?" Paull asked.

"Actually," Nina said, "from all the evidence, I'd say he's a humanist."

Paull seemed lost in contemplation.

The police car had taken the Curtis Memorial Parkway and was now on the Francis Scott Key Bridge, heading into Georgetown. The early morning fog had lifted, revealing a high sky filled with sunlight. There was only a light breeze. Paull, who hated overheated vehicles, had rolled down his window partway. He enjoyed the crisp air on his face and neck.

"The problem," Paull said, his eyes half-closed against the wind, "is that despite all my high-tech efforts at security, I've been undone by a very low-tech methodology: lip-reading."

"Someone on your yacht?"

He nodded. "The fucking captain, of all people."

"Wasn't he properly vetted?"

Paull shot her a pitying look. "We're talking someone inside the White House, very high up. All the vetting in the world is useless against being turned by someone of that stature."

The car took M Street, then turned north on Rock Creek Parkway.

"Surely you don't believe that the president recruited him directly?"

"I do not," Paull said. The car pulled to the side of the road within Rock Creek Park. "Walk with me. The driver will pick us up at the food shack two miles on."

They climbed out of the car and began to walk. The police car was soon gone. Paull had left his ridiculous Stetson in the front seat. The sun was but a sheen behind the tissue of white clouds. Nina pulled the collar of her peacoat up around her neck; Paull jammed his hands in his pockets as they set off together, surrounded by trees and brush.

"I've been thinking hard about your question," Paull said. "No, the president is too wily to initiate anything against me on his own. I'm not even certain that he's aware of the death of those two men who were following Jack to protect him. Therefore, he has to have a middle man."

"You mean a hatchet man."

"Call him what you will, Nina, we have a very potent enemy in the Administration."

"It's imperative we know his identity, don't you think?"

Paull nodded. "I most certainly do. Because the president is involved, even if it's on a nontactical level, our man has to be either the Secretary of State or the National Security Advisor."

Nina shuddered. "I wouldn't want either of them as an enemy."

"I hear you," Paull acknowledged, "but that's the hand we've been dealt."

They were nearing a fork in the road, and he directed them to the right, along a high embankment. A stream glimmered dully below. Apart from a smattering of passing cars, there was no one about.

"The good news is that I've worked out which one it is," Paull continued. "The message the captain sent was on the same day you and I met on the yacht. The time was a few minutes after you left. At that time, the president was on his way to Moscow to meet with President Yukin. He could have taken the call himself, of course, but that seems unlikely. The president maintains a high level of plausible deniability by using selected intermediaries he deems expendable."

"Both the Secretary of State and the National Security Advisor were with him on Air Force One," Nina said.

"So they were, but only one of them has knowledge of—and therefore access to—a specific high-level asset. I'm this asset's handler, that's how important he is. He's abruptly dropped off the grid, he hasn't made his dead drops in months. However, I have reason to believe that as recently as last week, this particular asset has been in touch with someone else in the Administration. I am very much afraid this high-ranking official is using this asset—a murderer without a speck of conscience—for his own purposes."

"What purposes?"

"That I'm not at liberty to disclose." *How about kidnapping Edward Carson's daughter so the crime can be labeled an act of terrorism and laid at the missionary secularists' door,* Paull thought. "At first, I suspected it might be the president himself, but now I think it might be the only other person who knows of the asset's existence: the National Security Advisor."

"So the National Security Advisor has been working, at the president's behest, against us."

Paull nodded. "It seems most likely. But I've bought us some time. I told him that I've been running you with an eye to getting closer to Jack McClure."

"That's too close to the truth."

Paull smiled thinly. "Have faith; that's as far as the truth goes. I sold them the story that I'm going to find a way to poison Jack against Edward Carson. Jack then goes to Reverend Taske, gets him to turn the power of the RMC against Carson."

Nina shook her head. "What I wouldn't give for fifteen minutes inside that brain of yours."

"Now that we know who we're fighting," Paull said, "we'd better rally the troops and man the ramparts."

"Good God, you're not talking about an all-out war, are you?"

"Not out in the open. But we've already felt the first shot across our bows—the turning of two of my men, plus my captain. Our first order of business is to root out any others. We can't mount a reasonable response if the opposite side knows every move we make."

"I'll get right on it," Nina said.

"Use the Secret Service facilities, not Homeland Security's."

"Gotcha."

They walked a bit farther, lost in their own thoughts.

"Now tell me what's new with our boy, Jack," Paull said.

"Sir, do you recall a double murder at McMillan Reservoir about twenty-five years ago?"

"That would be Metro Police territory, wouldn't it?"

"Apparently not this one. I checked Metro's records of the incident. There aren't any. According to Jack, there was very little in the papers. I checked out his story, and he's right. For that kind of crime, there was precious little ink spilled—not even the names of the victims. Everything was hushed up, so it must have been at a high government level."

"What's McClure's interest in the double murder?"

"I don't know, we haven't had time to talk about it at length," Nina said. "But he also has an intense interest in a local drug supplier working at the same time. Jack said no one knew who he was or where he came from, but that he had a tremendous amount of juice. No one could ever lay a hand on him, a man named Ian Brady."

For a moment, Paull thought that he'd been struck by a car that had jumped the curb. For certain he was having an out-of-body experience. When he was able to gather his scattered senses, he said, "Come again?"

"Did I say something—?"

"That name." Paull snapped his fingers impatiently. "Give me that name again."

"What? Ian Brady?"

"That's the fucking one."

Beside her, Paull stared off into the distance, his eyes seeing nothing. Brady was the key, the lynchpin to events unfolding all too rapidly. A serial murderer, a schemer, most probably a psychopath—this was the asset Paull had inherited. The most important intelligence asset stretching back twenty-five years. This was the monster he was forced to protect, whose whereabouts he no longer knew. Who did, then? His mind snapped into perfect focus. "Get Jack McClure," he said to Nina. "Bring him to me ASAP."

Nina took out her cell phone. "I'll call him right now."

"No," Paull said. "It's all too likely that our cell conversations are being monitored. I don't even want to use mine without prearranged coded signals."

"I'll find another way," Nina said.

Paull nodded gravely. "I know you will."

FORTY

GET IT into your head, Jack," Sharon had said in the ER. "We all
have a secret life, not just you." Now Jack knew the real truth of her
words. His daughter was living a secret life right under his nose. It
was as if he'd never known her at all—which was, of course, a defi-
ciency that Sharon had accused him of repeatedly. But, given what
she'd said to him, he determined that he had to know whether or
not she knew about Emma's radicalization, her secret life.

"If she felt so strongly about the blurring of religion and government," Jack said, "why didn't she join a peaceful organization like the
First American Secular Revivalists?"

"Because she was Emma," Alli said. "Because she never did things
halfway, because she was strong and sure of herself. Above all, because
she felt that the pack of evangelicals who had invaded the federal government were warmongers, that the only way to get their attention, to
attack them, to expose them was with a radical response."

"She hated the warmongers so she became one herself?" Jack
shook his head. "Isn't that counterintuitive?"

"The philosophers say fighting fire with fire is a legitimate response as old as time."

They were walking in the tangle of trees and underbrush behind the house. The sky was turning black, as if with soot, and a cold wind shivered the tallest branches. Jack was turning over what Alli had said because there was something about it that stuck in his mind, that seemed to loom large on the playing field he'd been thrust onto.

He stopped them at the bole of a gigantic oak. "Let's back this up a minute. Emma knew that your father would win the election, or at least that this current administration was on its last legs. Why not simply wait until the new regime came in?"

Alli shook her head. "I don't know, but there was an urgency in what she had to do."

"All right, let's put that aside for the moment. You said that she wanted to expose the Administration with a radical response."

"That's right."

"Did she tell you what she meant by that?"

"Sure. E-Two wants to provoke an extreme response from the Administration."

"But there's sure to be bloodshed."

"That's the whole point." Alli licked her lips. "See, the bloodier, the more militant, the more brutal the response, the better. Because E-Two is out to show the entire country what this Administration really is. They won't be able to round up the E-Two members easily. From what Emma said, they're all young people our age—no one over thirty. When there's blood on the streets, when America sees their own sons and daughters slaughtered, they'll finally understand the nature of the people who are exporting war and death to the world."

Jack was rocked to his core. "They're planning to be martyrs."

"They're soldiers," Alli said. "They're laying down their lives for what they believe in."

"But what they're planning is monstrous, insane."

"As our foreign policy has been for eight years."

"But this isn't the way."

"Why not? Sitting on their hands hasn't worked so well, has it? Anyone who has said or tried to do anything to protest faith-based initiatives has been ridiculed or, worse, branded a traitor by the talking heads controlled by the Administration. God, look at what wimps members of the opposite party have been through an illegal war, scandals, evidence that the government muzzles its scientists and specialists on the topics of WMDs and global warming. If the parties were reversed, you can bet this president would've been impeached by now."

Why was it, Jack thought, that he felt as if he were listening to Emma and not Alli? A strange thing was happening to him. It had begun when he and Alli entered the house and now had continued as they moved out into woods. There was the very curious sensation of the world finally starting to make sense to him—well, if not the whole world, then his world, the one he'd kept hidden from others and which kept him apart from them. Like his ability to sense Emma, though she was no longer in this world, at least by the limited understanding of man-made science, he felt as if his world and the one that had always been closed to him were beginning to overlap. Hope rose, completely unfamiliar to him, that one day he might even be able to straddle both, that he might live in one without giving up the other.

This gift he very badly wanted to bestow on Alli. To this end, he said, "There's someone I'd like you to meet."

Alli regarded him with skepticism. "Not another shrink. I've had my fill of probing and prodding."

"Not another shrink," Jack promised.

Rather than return to the front of the house where he'd parked, he took her through the underbrush. On the other side was parked Gus's white Continental, which Jack kept in pristine condition.

Alli laughed in delight as she climbed into it. Behind the wheel, Jack turned the key in the ignition, and the huge engine purred to life. With the lights extinguished, he rolled away without the Secret Service detail parked on Westmoreland being any the wiser.

He turned on the tape player, and James Brown took up "It's a Man's Man's Man's World" in midsong.

"Wow!" Alli said.

Yeah, thought Jack. *Wow.*

Ten minutes later, when they arrived at Kansas Avenue NE, they couldn't get near the old Renaissance Mission Church building. Barriers had been erected on the street and sidewalks on either side of it. There must have been more than a dozen unmarked cars and anti-terrorist vans drawn up on the street within the barriers.

Jack's heart seemed to plummet in his chest. Telling Alli to wait in the car, he got out, flashed his credentials to one of the twenty or so suits milling around. Then he saw Hugh Garner, who was spearheading the operation, and put away his ID.

"Hello, McClure," Garner said. "What brings you here?"

"I have an appointment with Chris Armitage of FASR," Jack lied.

Garner pulled a face. "So do we, McClure. Trouble is, we can't find him, or his pal Peter Link." Garner inclined his head. "*You* wouldn't know where they've got to?"

"If I did, I wouldn't be here talking to you," Jack said. "I'd like to speak to someone else in the FASR offices."

"I'm afraid that's impossible." Garner looked smug. Hailed by one of his detail, he turned, gave a couple of orders, turned back to Jack. "No one's here. This office has been shut down."

Jack thought of all the busy, dedicated men and women he'd seen on his way into Armitage's office. "Where is everyone else?"

"In federal custody." Garner grinned. "They've forfeited their rights to due process. They'll be held as long as necessary. Neither you nor anyone else can see them without a written order signed by the National Security Advisor himself."

Jack rocked back on his heels as if struck a blow. "What the hell are you talking about?"

"The president went on the air an hour ago with evidence supplied by the Russian president himself that the FASR and E-Two are being funded by Beijing." Garner's grin widened. "Under the Anti-Terrorism Act of December 2001, they've all been charged with treason."

JUST SOUTH of where the sawhorses blocked off the avenue was an alleyway. Jack drove the car around to Chillum Place, parked in a deserted lot. Alli said nothing; he knew she understood perfectly well what had happened.

"Why are we here?" Alli said at last. "Sitting in the dark with the lights out and the engine off?"

"We're moving to the edge of the world," Jack said quite seriously. "We're heading off the grid."

"What'll happen when we get there?"

"Tell me more about Emma."

Alli felt a familiar terror clutch her heart. Ever since Jack and Nina had rescued her, she had felt as if she had a fever, racked by bouts of anxiety, cold sweats, dreams of menacing shadows whispering horrible things to her. She saw Kray everywhere, as if he were stalking her, monitoring her every move, every word she said, every breath she took. Often, alone, she shook, chilled to her bones. Kray had become the sun, the moon, the clouds in the sky, moving as she moved, the wind rattling through the trees. He was always with her, his threats mingling with his ideas, the strange and powerful openness and freedom she had felt with him. These contradictory feelings confused and terrified her all the more. She no longer knew who she was, or more accurately, she no longer felt in control of herself. Something eerie and horribly frightening had happened to her in that room with him. Truth to tell, there were moments she couldn't recall, which was a relief. She so didn't want to probe beneath the unfamiliar surface of that vague unease at not remembering. Something had slipped away from her, she felt, and something else had been slipped into its place. She no longer was the Alli Carson who had lain sleeping in her dormitory room.

On the other hand, there was now, there was Jack. She liked him immensely, and this led to a certain sense of trust. He made her feel safe as no other human being—armed or otherwise—ever had. She envied Emma now, having this man for a father and then, realizing all over again that Emma was dead, shook a little, felt ill with shame for even having the thought. Even so, the thought of talking to him about Kray, about what had happened, set off a panicky feeling she was unable to understand, never mind try to control.

"Emma once said to me that we never really see ourselves," she said in an attempt to calm herself as well as to answer him. She felt that as long as she continued to speak about Emma, her friend wasn't truly dead, that a part of her—the part of Emma they saw and heard—would remain. "She said all we ever see of ourselves is our reflection—in mirrors, in water. But that isn't how we appear at all. So we had this game we played at night. We'd sit on the bed facing each other and we'd take turns describing each other's faces in the most minute detail—first the forehead and brow, then the eyes, the nose, the cheeks, the mouth. And Emma was right. We got to know ourselves in a different way."

"And each other," Jack said.

Alli stared out the windshield into the emptiness of the lot. "We already knew each other better than if we'd been sisters. We'd found each other; we loved each other. We shared the night with all its loneliness, its subversiveness, its secrets."

All at once, it was as if Emma were sitting there beside her, and with a sob, she began to cry. *She should be here,* Alli thought. *She'd understand what happened to me, she'd be able to tell me why I'm feeling so strange, why everything feels threatening. Everything except Jack.*

"Secrets like who Emma met under the oak trees outside Langley Fields?"

There was a silence for a moment as Alli squirmed in her seat. Inside her mind, a pitched battle was in progress between what she wanted to say and what she felt compelled to hold back. "Okay, I lied to you about that, but it was only to protect Emma, the part of her life she'd entrusted to me."

"So you know who she met?"

Alli bit her lip. As a cloud skims across the moon, a shadow came over her, her eyes lost their focus, her gaze seeming fixed on a distant shore. Her stomach was tied in knots; she could feel the cold sweat breaking out under her arms, at the small of her back. She couldn't backtrack now, and yet she knew she mustn't tell Jack Kray's name. If she kept to what Emma had told her, she thought she'd be all right. Talking about her friend, feeling closer to her was just about the only thing that calmed her. So she continued the process already begun by Kray himself of cleaving her thoughts in two: talking about the acceptable, pushing down the forbidden.

"Emma said his name was Ronnie Kray."

Until this moment Jack had thought the phrase "made his blood run cold" was merely a literary one. Now he experienced it literally. Emma had met with a serial killer, the man who had abducted Alli. Did Alli know that? He judged that now, as she was just beginning to open up, was not the time to tell her.

"But she suspected from the get-go Ronnie Kray might not be his real name," Alli said.

Every strangely wired synapse in Jack's brain was singing now. "Why would she question that?"

"Emma had done a lot of reading on the pathology of being an Outsider. In fact, she'd practically memorized a book called *The Outsider*, by Colin Wilson. That's where she got the term, that's how she knew she was one. She also read another book of Wilson's called *A Criminal History of Mankind*, I think. Anyway, she'd heard that name Ronnie Kray and looked it up. He was one of a pair of murderous twins in the East

End of London. Their pathology fascinated her, and I think that was one of the reasons she even listened to this guy in the first place."

"They shared E-Two's point of view."

She nodded.

Jack felt the tug of his daughter. This important history had happened while he was obliviously going about his job. His daughter's life had slipped through his fingers like grains of sand. "Didn't she understand the potential for danger?"

"Of course she did," Alli said. "That was the lure, that was why she wouldn't back off. Then she began to suspect that Ronnie Kray was keeping secrets, so she set out to discover what they were."

"I can't believe this," Jack said, because he truly couldn't.

"Why not?" Alli said. "It sounds just like what you'd do."

There was no point mentioning that he was an adult with years of training. "I knew she didn't follow Kray blindly."

"Emma never did anything blindly."

"Not even drugs?"

"*Especially* not drugs. For Emma, taking them was a kind of, I don't know, social experiment."

"How d'you mean?"

"She wondered whether being stoned would allow her to approach another level of being an Outsider. To touch—I don't know—the infinite."

"And did it?"

"Uh-uh. It disappointed her. She was so sure there was something just out of reach, but so far out there, it was beyond our comprehension."

"I've had the exact same feeling," Jack said.

Alli nodded. "So have I."

He had a thought. "So did she really want to join E-Two or did she want to find out more about Ronnie Kray?"

Alli shrugged. "Emma's motives were never simple. One thing I do know: She was far too smart simply to follow the pied piper. Her bullshit alarm was totally scary."

Jack thought of the times she'd busted him on his screaming matches with Sharon, how he'd let her words go in one ear and out the other. Why had he done that? Why had he devalued her opinion? Or was the truth of what she was saying too difficult to face?

"There's something else," Alli said. "I got the feeling that because she knew how dangerous her being with Kray was, she kept a journal."

This interested Jack immensely. "I searched everything after her accident," he said. "I couldn't find anything."

Alli's fear returned full force. "Maybe I'm wrong. It's only a hunch. I mean she never said anything to me directly."

Still, it was something to ponder, Jack thought. Maybe he'd over-looked something.

"C'mon, let's go," he said, getting out of the car. When she'd joined him, he took her down the alleyway and around behind the buildings on Kansas Avenue. They had to be careful as they approached the rear of the FASR building, as it was lit up like an airport runway, criss-crossed by federal agents in flak jackets, riot helmets, and assault rifles loaded with rubber bullets.

Jack moved them back into the shadows of the hulking warehouses on their right, crouched down, making their way past the activity. As they moved farther down, the light continued to fade until they were once again engulfed in deepest shadow. At the back of the building that used to house the Hi-Line, they crept along until they reached what looked like a windowless wall. Jack moved his fingertips along the wall until he found the join he was looking for, the outline of the door Gus's detective clients used to come and go without being seen.

Slipping a credit card out of his wallet, he slid it into the join on the left side. A moment later, though Alli heard no sound at all, he gripped the join with the tips of his fingers and the door opened outward.

They slipped in together and Jack immediately closed the door behind them. They were in almost complete darkness. Ahead of them was a thin line of warm light coming through the crack between an inner door and the floor.

Stepping up to the door, Jack turned the knob and, opening it, crossed the threshold. Chris Armitage whirled around, grabbing for a length of pipe.

Jack said, "Down, boy. You could get yourself killed that way."

Armitage had the look and posture of a hunted animal. "How the hell did you find us?"

As he said this, Jack looked behind him at Peter Link, asleep on the sofa. "Let's just say that I know these buildings were the haunts of bootleggers in the thirties, complete with escape routes to outwit the police."

Armitage's mouth twitched sardonically. "Seems nothing much has changed since then." He sighed, put aside the pipe. "I suppose they enlisted you to take us in."

"I had to dodge a Secret Service detail to get in here unnoticed," Jack said. Then he turned and beckoned.

Armitage's eyes opened wide. "Good God."

"Chris Armitage, this is Alli Carson, the soon-to-be First Daughter. Alli, Chris is the co-head of the First American Secular Revivalists."

"What's left of it," Armitage said. "Hey, Alli." Then, to Jack: "Why on earth did you bring her here?"

Jack smiled. "I thought you and she ought to meet."

"My organization has just been smeared by the President of the United States with the help of the Russian president." Armitage let go a bitter laugh. "This is hardly the time for a get-together."

"I don't see that you have anything better to do," Jack said.

Armitage nodded. "I can't argue there." He lifted an arm. "Sorry I don't have much in the way of conveniences to offer you." He pointed at a half fridge. "There're Cokes in there, a couple of cartons of juice. And frozen food."

Jack and Alli shook their heads as they sat on facing chairs. Armitage perched on the edge of the sofa.

"How's Link?" Jack asked.

"Out like a light, as you can see." Armitage ran a hand through his hair. "He'll be okay. Thanks for asking. Thanks for everything."

Jack waved away his words. "I'd like to ask you about a former member of FASR. A man you know as Ronnie Kray."

"Oh, him." Armitage rubbed his chin. "Interesting guy, actually. Very smart, very intense. And he'd done his homework—he knew all the ins and outs of every argument we're propounding. He was so well versed, in fact, that Peter and I wanted him to make some personal appearances with us, you know, to get the word out."

Armitage opened the half refrigerator. After offering them a drink, he took out a can of Coke, popped the top. "Above all, Kray had a quality about him—he was quite charismatic. That was another reason we wanted him to take a more active role. But he turned us down." He gulped down some soda. "He told us he could only spare us a couple of days a week. Plus, he said he was strictly a behind-the-scenes type of guy."

"Did you believe him?" Jack said.

"Interesting question. In a funny way, I did. He had trouble interacting with the other FASR members. He lacked—what?—for want of a better phrase, social graces."

"In what way?"

Armitage rolled the soda can between his palms. "He had no tolerance for people who didn't do things his way—and at the speed of light. He pissed off more than his share of coworkers because he didn't seem to have an inhibitor switch. Whatever was on his mind, no matter how harsh, he'd just say it. I recall one time, I brought him into the office to talk to him about the effect he was having on the people he had to interact with. 'Good,' he said. 'Maybe they'll get their act together.'"

"I'd like to fill out my mental picture of him," Jack said. "Would you mind describing him to me?"

"Not at all." Armitage thought a moment. "To begin with, he was a good-looking guy, but in an interesting way. Dark, smoldering—and charismatic, as I said. He was tall and slim. He was in good shape. He looked like he was in his late forties, but I got the feeling he was older than that, certainly in his mid-fifties."

Jack's mind was engaged on two levels. While he was using Armitage's description to build a mental picture of Kray, he was watching Alli for signs of anxiety or nervousness. After all, the man Armitage was describing had abducted her and held her captive for a week. But she seemed oddly detached, as if her mind was far away.

Armitage swallowed the last of the Coke, set the can aside. "I think he was actually popular with the women. The men felt they had to defend themselves against him."

"Did you know," Jack said, "that Ronnie Kray also goes by the name of Charles Whitman?"

"What? No. Of course not." Armitage looked and sounded genuinely shocked.

"Do you vet people—do background checks?"

"Sure. We don't want anyone with a record to be on our rolls. But frankly, it's rudimentary at best; we're all chronically overworked."

Jack nodded in sympathy. "I imagine he was counting on that. I doubt those two names are the end of Kray's deception." He turned to Alli. "What d'you think?"

"Alli," Armitage said, "you know this man?"

Panic gripped her with such force that for a moment she could scarcely catch her breath. "A friend of mine did," she squeaked. "Jack's daughter, Emma."

"I wonder," Jack said in a perfectly neutral voice, "whether you don't know him, as well."

Alli's panic escalated to an almost intolerable pitch. It was all she could do not to jump up and run out of the room. "Me?" *He knows,* she thought. *He knows Kray took me.* "I never met him."

"Haven't you recently been with someone who fits Chris's description of Ronnie Kray?"

Alli said nothing, but Jack observed a certain tension take hold of her like an invisible hand.

Jack shrugged. "Perhaps I'm mistaken." He turned his attention to Armitage, who had been following that byplay with a certain confused interest. "We'd best decide what to do with you and Peter. You two can't stay holed up here forever."

Alli was thrust back into the midst of her mental battlefield. On one side was Ronnie Kray, terrifying in his omniscience; on the other was Jack, her savior, who understood her in the same way Emma had. And thinking of Emma, she felt her friend's great strength and courage flow into her. Would Emma lie to Jack? Alli knew she wouldn't, so how could she herself do it?

"I was," she said faintly.

"Have you thought about how to get yourself out of this prison?" Jack said to Armitage.

Alli's guts were churning. "That was the man who took me from Langley Fields," she persisted.

Jack turned to her. "You don't say?"

Alli's expression was stricken. "I . . . I'm sorry. I know I should've told you sooner."

"I'm curious why you didn't." Jack knew it was crucial to keep any admonition out of his voice. He could see the terror shimmering in the faint sweat on her face.

Alli put her head down. "I was keeping Emma's secret. I thought if I said one thing, it would lead to the rest."

"But then you told me about Emma wanting to join E-Two. You could've told me about Ronnie Kray any time after that."

Alli wedged her hands beneath her thighs, her arms as straight as boards. "He said if I told anyone about him, he'd come after me and kill me."

"How would he know?"

Alli was crying again; she simply couldn't stop. "I don't know, but he knew everything about me, right down to what I did with a boy-friend, my doctors, what hospital I was born in."

Jack wanted to take her in his arms, but he intuited this was the wrong time, the wrong place. He'd read that victims of abduction or rape often react negatively to being touched, even when that's what they really want.

Alli panted as if she'd just finished a hundred-meter sprint. *Emma,* she thought wildly, *please help me be strong.* Then, with a start, she real-ized that she had Jack. In many of the important ways, Jack and Emma were alike, which was why she trusted him as much as she did, why she could talk to him on some level about her very private dread. "He's in my dreams. He's always there."

Jack felt his stomach contract. "What does he say? What does he want?"

She sobbed. "I can't remember." A tremor went through her like an earthquake. "Whatever he wanted, you got to me first—you saved me."

He could see how terrified Alli was of this man. How could she not be? He had held her entire life in his hands. Suddenly, he had a vivid mental image of the photos taken of her with a telephoto lens that had hung in the Marmoset's house, especially the one of her and Emma walking across the Langley Fields campus.

How, he asked himself, had Ronnie Kray—or whoever the hell he was—come to have all that info? Some of it, like the hospitals and doc-tors, was a matter of public record, but other things, like intimate de-tails of her personal relationships, certainly weren't. If this guy was a spook, Jack could see it. But a civilian? He'd have to be psychic.

In the back of Jack's mind, his oddly aligned synapses had been playing with the 3-D puzzle he was assembling in his head. Now the puzzle turned in a different direction, and he saw the shape of a miss-ing piece.

"Alli," he said with his heart pounding in his chest, "do you recognize the name Ian Brady?"

"Sure." She nodded. "He and his partner, Myra Hindley, were
responsible for what were known as the Moors murders. They went on
a two-year killing spree from, I think, sixty-three to sixty-five."

Ka-thunk! Jack could hear the missing piece fall into place. Proof
that the man who abducted Alli, who killed her Secret Service detail,
was the same man who, twenty-five years ago, had murdered the two
unnamed men at McMillan Reservoir and, shortly thereafter, the
Marmoset and Gus.

Jack had gone after the wrong man; Cyril Tolkan had been responsible for many crimes, but murdering Gus wasn't one of them. So
how clever was Kray/Whitman/Brady to have used a hand-honed paletta to kill, knowing full well that it would lead investigators to the
wrong man?

Come to think of it, didn't this serial killer use the same MO now,
twenty-five years later? He'd left clues to lead investigators to FASR
and E-2 and away from himself. Everyone had taken the bait—except
Jack, whose mind was already hard at work fitting pieces of the puzzle
together. At first, it simply hadn't felt right, and then, little by little, as
more pieces of the puzzle appeared for him to manipulate like a Rubik's Cube, he had started to gain an inkling of his quarry.

Now he knew beyond a shadow of a doubt: This man was his personal nemesis. Kray had played him for a fool once; Jack would track
him down this time, or die trying.

At that moment, his cell phone buzzed. He'd set it on vibrate before they'd left the house. He was getting a text message, just three
letters: WRU. It was from Nina, but what the hell? Jack never texted,
had no idea of shortcuts.

He showed the phone's screen to Alli. "What does this mean?"

" 'Where are you?' " Alli looked at him. "She needs to see you."

Jack thought a minute. Having slipped the Secret Service detail, it wouldn't do to show up at a meet with Nina with Alli in tow, and he certainly wasn't going to drop her off at the house, SS detail or no SS detail. They'd blown their coverage once; he couldn't afford to take the chance they'd do it again.

What location could he give Nina that wouldn't seem suspicious? He was about to ask Alli to text Nina back, but then reconsidered. It was odd for Nina to be texting him, rather than phoning. Given the specter of the Dark Car, Jack wasn't in any frame of mind to take a chance. He logged on to the Web, called up Google Maps. He already had several saved. Choosing the one he wanted, he sent it to Nina. It wouldn't show up as anything useful to potential eavesdroppers.

"Okay, we gotta go." He and Alli rose. "For the time being, sit tight. You have enough food for a week?"

"I think so, yeah." Armitage crouched down, opened the half fridge. "Plus, when the Coke and juice run out, we've got plenty of water." He glanced up. "But that's really all academic, isn't it? The minute the people who run this place return in the morning, we'll be screwed."

"No, you won't. I know them." Jack still owned the building; because he charged his tenants way under the going rate, they'd do anything for him. "Trust me, they won't bother you." Jack shook Armitage's hand. "I'll get you out of this, Chris."

Armitage nodded, but he looked less than sure.

FORTY-ONE

JACK'S FIRST choice would have been Egon, but who knew where he was at this hour. Jack wasn't about to call the house to find out. That left him but one other option, so he took Alli to Sharon's.

He wanted to call her to warn her, but at this point, he was afraid to use his cell phone. Instead, he stopped at a drug superstore, bought a burner—a cheap cell phone with a pay-as-you-go plan. After setting it up, he dialed Sharon's number.

As soon as he heard her voice, he said, "I need to come over. Is it okay?"

"After what happened the last time?"

"It was just an argument. Don't make a big deal over it."

"Big deal? Jack, don't you understand? Emma was the central argument of our life together."

She was right, of course, but he didn't have time to get into it with her. "Listen to what I'm saying, Shar. I need your help. Now."

There was a slight hesitation. "Is everything all right?"

"Not quite."

"What's going on?" A different quality in her voice. The saber had been sheathed, the charger's hooves stilled. "You're scaring me."

"We'll be there in fifteen."

"*We?* Jack, who are you with?"

"Not on the phone," he said, and disconnected.

He got into the Continental and took off.

Paranoia running at peak level, Jack checked out Sharon's neighborhood within an eight-block radius. That seemed excessive, even to him, especially since he could think of no reason why Sharon should be under surveillance. But since he still didn't know who had sicced the Dark Car on him—or even why—the more thorough he was in his security check, the better he'd feel.

Having ascertained there was no surveillance in the area, he pulled into Sharon's driveway. Alli hadn't said a word since she'd translated the text message from Nina for him.

With the engine still running, Jack turned to her. "You okay?"

"I guess." She put a hand to her temple. "My head hurts."

"Sharon'll get you some Tylenol as soon as we get inside."

"You guys broke up, didn't you?"

Jack nodded.

"Are you going to get back together?" Alli asked.

Jack sighed. "I'd be lying if I said I knew."

"Yeah, I know."

"What d'you mean?"

"Emma talked about you guys a lot because what upset her the most was the fighting. She couldn't bear it."

Jack opened the window a crack. The heated canned air was getting to him.

"Plus, she thought it was all her fault."

"That's not true!"

"That's funny, because she said you were always fighting about her."

Jack shut up then. There was a peculiar feeling in the pit of his stomach, as if he'd just overeaten and now had to get rid of the food at any cost. He opened the car door, got out. Leaning against the car, he realized that he was having trouble breathing.

Alli slid out, came around the front of the Continental to stand beside him. "I'm sorry if I upset you."

"Don't give it a second thought."

There had come a moment when, looking back, he saw that their fighting had been incessant. And about what? Nothing. They fought because it had become a habit, because they were locked in combat, like ancient enemies who no longer knew how their enmity began. He was sick of it. There had to be a better way to deal with each other than through the armor of anger.

He nodded. "You're just telling me something both Sharon and I should've realized long before now."

SHARON LOOKED scared out of her wits when she opened the door.

"Alli!"

"Hello, Mrs. McClure."

"Come on in." Sharon took a look over their shoulders before closing and locking the door behind them. "Now what's this all about, Jack?"

They went into the living room, sat down on the L-shaped sofa.

"I'll get you something for your headache," Jack said.

"No," Alli said. "It's gone now."

Jack regarded her for a moment before turning to Sharon. "I need a safe haven for Alli," he said. "Just for a short time while I take care of some business."

Sharon looked skeptical. "Alli, why aren't you home with your parents?"

"It's a long story," Jack began.

"I'm asking Alli, Jack."

"It's not for her to answer that question."

"I think it is," Sharon persisted. "Alli?"

Alli looked down at her hands. "This is what Emma said it was like, being with you."

"What?" Sharon said. "What did you say?"

"You wanted her to answer," Jack said softly. "Hear her out."

Sharon glared at him, but remained silent. Perhaps the rattle of sabers was all she was prepared to deliver. Still, Jack could hear the snorting of her warhorse champing at the bit to head into battle.

Intuiting the silence as a tacit acknowledgment that she should go on, Alli took a deep breath. "There's no use arguing over this," she said softly. "Jack's right. If he can't tell you why I'm not with my parents, I can't either." She lifted her head. "But it's important I stay with you, that he's free to do whatever he has to do."

Sharon sat back, looked at Jack. "Did you put her up to this?" Seeing the expression on Jack's face, she raised her hands defensively. "Sorry. Sorry." She nodded. "Of course you can stay with me, Alli." She smiled. "As long as you want or need to."

Alli ducked her head. "Thank you, Mrs. McClure."

Sharon's smile widened. "But only if you call me Sharon."

JACK FOUND Nina's car idling at the curb outside Sharon's house. Before he could open the door, the passenger's-side window slid smoothly down, and Nina, leaning over from behind the wheel, said, "Backseat, Jack."

Curious, Jack opened the rear door. Sliding onto the seat, he found himself next to a rather short barrel-chested man with a neatly trimmed beard and the calm demeanor of a sage.

"Jack," Nina said, "meet Dennis Paull, Secretary of Homeland Security."

"Jack, it's good to finally meet you," Secretary Paull said as he briefly enclosed Jack's hand in a hearty grip. "Nina has told me a great deal about you."

"Has she?" Jack caught Nina's eyes in the rearview mirror. "Spying on me?"

Paull laughed. "Keeping an eye on you is how I see it. Nina works for me undercover. She's a damn good operative."

"I'm in no position to dispute that," Jack said.

Paull laughed again. "I don't trust people without a sense of humor, Jack. And d'you know why? Because nothing murders a sense of humor faster than keeping secrets."

"Nina's a barrel of laughs, I can vouch for that," Jack said. "She's the only one I ever met who used a chocolate-chip cookie as a missile."

That got an appreciative chuckle out of Nina.

"Okay, now that we're one big, happy family, let's get down to brass tacks," Paull said. "Jack, I think you're looking for some answers, and I have them. I sent out the Dark Car manned by two of my agents in order to keep an eye on you. They had orders to protect you should anyone make a move against you. Unfortunately, the National Security Advisor—perhaps with the blessing of the president— countermanded those orders."

What have I gotten myself into? Jack asked himself. "Why would anyone want to make a move against me?"

"We'll get to the details in a moment," Paull said. "Now, suffice it to say that you're Edward Carson's man. As you might imagine, the president-elect is seen as something of a threat to certain individuals in the Administration. There's an initiative to get certain matters the president deems pressing sewn up before the twentieth."

"Like rounding up the First American Secular Revivalists."

Paull nodded. "Among other suspect groups."

"The FASR's only crime is that their philosophy is in direct opposition with the current Administration's," Jack said.

"As you no doubt understand, Jack, this Administration has serious perception issues. The world—and the players in it—are what it says they are, no matter the reality."

"Don't you understand that the FASR is being made a scapegoat?" Jack said. "You guys can't find E-Two, so you're going after the easy target."

"Please don't confuse this Administration with the truth, Jack." The secretary shifted in his seat. "Now, I think you may have an answer for me. You know a man named Ian Brady."

It wasn't a question, and Jack's eyes sought out Nina's again. "Yes, sir. Twenty-five years ago, he was a major drug supplier in my old neighborhood."

"Which was?"

"Not far from McMillan Reservoir."

Secretary Paull passed a hand across his brow. It was clear Jack had delivered his answer; trouble was, it was the answer Paull had been afraid of because it confirmed his dark analysis of who Ian Brady really was.

"You need to forget McMillan Reservoir, Jack."

"That's a bit hard to do, sir. This man, Ian Brady or Charles Whitman or Ronnie Kray, whatever he's calling himself today, is the one who abducted Alli Carson and murdered her Secret Service detail in cold blood."

"Nevertheless, you must forget him."

Jack would have said, *What the hell are you talking about, sir?* except he knew exactly what Paull was saying. The last piece of the puzzle he'd been assembling in his head—the most crucial one—had just fallen into place. No wonder the IDs of the vics at McMillan Reservoir were never revealed. It was the same reason that the crash of the Dark Car and the deaths of the two agents in it never made the news.

Jack's mind replayed the moment at McMillan Reservoir when he'd followed Gus and Detective Stanz, when Gus's snitch said, "I guarantee you'll never get the name of the murderer, either from me or anyone else."

"Brady's protected," Jack said to Paull. "You're protecting a serial murderer, a kidnapper."

"Not me, Jack. The government. That's why the order to my Dark Car agents was countermanded at the highest level. There was concern that you were getting too close to Brady."

"A legitimate concern."

The secretary's face looked like you could pass a steamroller over it without making a dent. "This is a matter of national security."

"How many illegal acts have been committed in the last eight years in the name of national security?"

"Jack, please. This is a friendly memo—the *most* friendly."

"I understand, sir. But I have to do this."

Paull breathed out a long sigh. "Look, I'm trying to protect you, you do understand that?"

"Yes, sir, I do, but that won't change my mind."

Paull looked away. He hadn't for a moment thought he'd change Jack McClure's mind, but he had to be absolutely certain of this man.

"From this moment on, you're on your own." Paull said this very softly, very distinctly.

"I'm prepared for the risk." Jack knew nothing would be settled inside himself until he hunted down Ian Brady and either brought him in or shot him dead.

FORTY-TWO

"HOW I wish you and Jack were my parents!"

"Good Lord!" Sharon was standing in the kitchen. So astonished was she by Alli's statement that she dropped the egg she was transferring from its carton to the heated pan. The yellow yolk burst like a water balloon, slowly threading across the stove top, through the clear, glutinous albumin.

She'd gone with her first instinct, which was to make Alli something to eat, so they had repaired to the kitchen, a room that always made her feel secure. If she was being honest with herself, Alli's presence here unnerved her, though her nervousness had nothing to do with the fact that Alli was the president-elect's daughter. It was all down to the fact that Alli had been Emma's best friend. They were the same age, and though one would hardly be taken for the other, it was difficult for Sharon to look at Alli without seeing her own daughter. She was beset by a profound ache she thought she had put aside. The poisonous stone of Emma's death was still inside her.

Mindlessly, she turned off the burner, began to sponge up the mess. "Why on earth would you say such an extraordinary thing?"

"Because it's true."

Sharon wrung the remains of the raw egg into the sink. She held the broken shell in her cupped palm. "But I'm sure your parents are wonderful people."

"Excuse me, but all you know about my mom and dad is what you see on TV or read in magazine articles," Alli said.

She stood with her back against the pass-through into the living room. She appeared to Sharon to be poised beyond her years—certainly more poised than Emma had ever been. *What I wouldn't have given for a child like this,* a voice inside her wailed. And immediately she put a hand to her mouth, appalled at the thought. *God forgive me,* she moaned silently. But her quick prayer of penance made her feel no better, just dirty. She panicked for a moment; if prayers no longer worked for her, what would? *The truth of it is that prayers are only words,* she thought, *and of what comfort are words at a time like this? Hollow things like the shell of an egg with the inside drained away.*

"You're right, of course," she said, desperately trying to soothe her way back into normalcy. "Please forgive me."

"There's nothing to forgive, Mrs.— Sharon."

Alli came and took the glistening shell out of Sharon's hand. In that moment, their hands touched and Sharon began to weep. It took only an instant for the dam to burst, for all the feelings, methodically and efficiently tamped down and squashed, to reassert their right to life. Father Larrigan's assurances of "It's God's will" and "Emma's death is part of God's plan" crumbled beneath the weight of hypocrisy. Sharon, queen of denial, was quite unprepared for the abyss, so that the dam not only burst but disintegrated entirely.

She rocked back and forth with inconsolable sobs. *Knowledge comes through suffering* was one of Father Larrigan's favorite bromides. But in a flash of knowledge, she saw that it wasn't a bromide at all; it was yet another way for the Church to maintain control over its increasingly unruly flock. *We all must suffer because of Eve's First*

Sin, we all deserve to suffer in this life so we may be redeemed in Heaven. What better way to keep people yoked to the Church? Surely God didn't mean these con artists to speak in His name. Oh, the insidious cleverness of it!

Now her sorrow was joined by her rage at being duped, her terror at life's random cruelty. All was chaos, uncontrollable, unknowable. With this came the stark realization that Jack was right. Her newfound religion was nothing but a sham, another way to deny her feelings, to convince herself that everything would be all right. But deep down where she was afraid to look, she knew nothing would ever be right again because Emma had been snatched from her and Jack for no good reason. And then she thought, despairingly, what possible reason could justify her daughter's death? None. None on earth or in heaven.

Gradually, she became aware of Alli holding her hand, leading her into the living room, where they sat quietly side by side on the sofa.

"Can I get you something?" Alli asked. "Some tea, a glass of water, even?"

Sharon shook her head. "Thank you, I'm feeling much better now."

But what a bitter lie that was! In her mind's eye, she could see the inside of her church, the gloomy atmosphere, the confessional, where priests heard and absolved your sins if you recited the canned blather of Hail Marys or Our Fathers. But Father Larrigan wasn't full of grace, nor was any priest. The flickering candles mocked those whose prayers they carried in their flaring hearts, the paintings of Christ, bleeding, dying while angels fluttered like so many moths over his head. And the gold! Everywhere you looked were gold crosses tinted rose or moss green by the saints in the stained-glass windows. And old-lady tears, old-lady prayers, old ladies with nowhere else to go, their lives over, clustered in the doorway, complaining about their backs and their bladders. She was not an old woman! Her life wasn't over. It wasn't too late for her to have another child, was it? Was it?

Wrenching herself away from her pain, she smiled through her tears. "Anyway, never mind me." She patted Alli's knee, and there it was again, that astonishing electric sensation that had made her weep. She managed to hold back the tears this time, but it wasn't easy. "It's you we were speaking of. You live a life of such privilege, Alli. You're admired and envied by so many young women, sought after by so many young men."

"So what?" Alli said. "I hate that privilege means the world to my parents. It means nothing to me, but they don't get it, they don't get me at all."

Sharon regarded her sadly. "I never got Emma, you know. All that anger, all that rebellion." She shook her head. "There were times when I thought she'd surely burst from keeping so much from us."

"The secrets we keep."

Sharon clasped her hands together. "I think secrets deaden us in the end. It's like having gangrene. If you keep them long enough, they begin to kill parts of you, starting with your heart."

"Your heart is still beating," Alli said.

Sharon looked away, at the photo of Emma on a horse. She could ride, that girl. "Only in a medical sense, I'm afraid."

Alli moved closer to her. "You still have Jack."

"Seeing you here . . ." Sharon bit her lip. "Oh, I want my daughter back!"

Alli took her hand again. "Is there anything I can do to help?"

Sharon looked into Alli's eyes. *How young she looks,* she thought. *How vulnerable, how angelic.* She felt all of a sudden a great, an overwhelming desire for solace, for a peace inside her churning self. She wondered whether she possessed the strength to find it. The Church couldn't provide it, nor all the prayers spoken by all the faithful in the universe. In the end, there was only what she could summon up from inside herself.

"Yes, please," she said. "Tell me about Emma."

SHARON CONFOUNDED Jack utterly when he returned to the house.

"I have an idea," she said brightly, "why don't you and Alli spend the night here? Alli can have the spare bedroom, and this sofa is very comfortable. I can't tell you how many nights I've fallen asleep on it."

Jack, mindful of the Secret Service detail he'd left behind, his brain turning over the problem of how once and for all to track down Ronnie Kray, heedlessly said, "I don't think that would be a good idea."

Sharon's face fell. "But why not?"

Seeing her stricken face gave him pause. He saw her on the sofa next to Alli, both women, torsos twisted, turned toward him. It was their proximity to each other, as if they were intimates, as if they had been talking of intimate things when he walked in. There was something about Sharon's face, an expression he felt certain he'd never see again.

"It would be so nice," Sharon said, "all of us together."

Jack, his mind changing gears, thought she might be right. "Why don't we all go to my house? It's larger and—"

Seeing the change come over Sharon's face, he stopped in midsentence.

"Jack, come on. You know that house gives me the creeps."

What was the use? he thought. No matter what he said, she'd never agree to go there, let alone spend the night.

"Alli and I have to go," he said.

Sharon stood up. "Why, Jack? I know you're not comfortable here, but just this once, stay here with me."

Jack shook his head. "It's impossible, Shar. Alli's Secret Service detail is expecting her to be at the house."

"You mean you deliberately ditched them to bring her here?" The sabers were rattling again, the warhorse stamping its huge hooves.

"It was necessary," Jack said.

"As far as you're concerned, it's *always* necessary to break the rules."

"Not always." How easy it was to fall back into the old patterns. "Sometimes I bend them."

"Stop, please!" Alli cried.

They both turned in her direction.

"This isn't anything to fight about," she said. "You're just fighting for the sake of fighting."

"Alli's right," Sharon said. "Half the time I don't even remember what we're fighting about."

"Then come with us," Jack said. "Spend the night."

"I'd like to," Sharon said. "Really I would." She shook her head. "But I'm not ready, Jack. Can you understand that?"

"Sure," he said, though he didn't, not really. If it wasn't for the Secret Service detail, he would have consented to stay here tonight. What was it about Gus's house she despised so? He couldn't work it out. He'd asked her so many times without getting a satisfactory answer, he had no desire to go over that old turf again. Besides, like her, he was sick to death of fighting.

"I guess it's time for you to go, then." Sharon embraced Alli, and they kissed. She stood in the lighted doorway, watching them as they went down the walk to Jack's car, and she shivered, as if with a premonition, or a feeling of déjà vu, as if she'd experienced this helpless moment of sadness and loss before.

FORTY-THREE

THERE WAS, no question, a certain gloom about Jack's house, a fustiness manifested by huge odd-shaped rooms, old gas lamps gutted and wired for electricity, massive furniture, not a stick of it built after 1950. Perhaps it was all this Sharon objected to, why she had opted for predictable square rooms, low ceilings, modern furniture—a house gaily lighted but without charm.

But there was also history here—chaotic, warty, fascinating. It was, as Alli had recognized, the residence of an Outsider, past and present. Could that be why Emma liked it here and Sharon didn't? Jack asked himself as he climbed up the stairs with Alli. Sharon wasn't an Outsider—that kind of life, often in conflict with rules, regulations, even, sometimes, the law, both baffled and frightened her. She was comfortable only within the well-defined bounds of society. That was why she'd been so hell-bent on Emma going to Langley Fields, which was so Establishment. And it was why Emma had gotten into continuous difficulty there. A round peg in a square hole. Outsiders never fit in; you could never change them. But until the day Emma died Sharon hadn't given up hope.

Jack showed Alli into the guest room, which was next to his. In all these years, he'd never been able to sleep in Gus's bedroom. Years ago, he'd hauled the bed Gus had been murdered in out back and burned it. More recently, he'd turned the bedroom into a media room with an enormous flat-screen TV on which he watched James Brown concerts as well as baseball and films he bought on DVD. He felt certain Gus would've liked that.

"The bathroom's fully stocked," he said. "But if there's anything else you need, it'll be in this closet here."

After they said good night, he watched her go into her room, close the door behind her. He thought about what might be going on in her head, all the things she had told him, all the things she hadn't. In his room, he called Carson, told him all was well and that he was slowly making progress.

Jack turned off the light, lay on the bed with his clothes on. He felt bone-weary, sad unto death. The experience of learning about Emma's secret life was a two-edged sword. Gratitude and remorse flooded him in equal measure. Tonight he felt an outsider even from himself.

He must have fallen asleep because suddenly he opened his eyes and knew time had passed. It was the middle of the night. Traffic sounds were as scarce as clouds in the horse latitudes. He felt that he lay on the bosom of the ocean, rocked gently by wave after wave. He was aware of an abyss beneath him, vast, lightless. Light filtering in through the window seemed like the cool pinpoints of ten million stars. He was as far from civilization as he had ever been. Unmoored, he had said. And Alli had said, *I'm unmoored, too.*

It was then that he heard a sound, like the wind sighing through branches, like moonlight singing in the trees. Rain pattered on the roof, and a voice whispered, "There's someone in the house."

Sitting up, Jack saw a slim figure silhouetted in the open doorway.

"Alli, what is it? What did you hear?"

"There's someone in the house," she whispered.

He rose, took his Glock and went toward her. She turned, retreated into the hall, as if to show the way. Shadows lay against the wall like wounded soldiers. The silence was palpable, even the house's normal creaks and groans were for the moment stilled.

"Alli, where are you going?" he whispered at the receding figure. "I want you to go back to your room, lock the door till I come for you."

But either she was too far away or chose to ignore his warning, because she went down the stairs. Cursing under his breath, he hurried after her. A strange form of peacefulness came over him as he followed the slip of a shadow down the hallway, through the dining room and kitchen. Off the kitchen was a pantry that Gus had used for a storeroom and a half bath situated between the kitchen and the mudroom.

The mudroom was a space that was never used, either by Gus or by Jack. It seemed the oldest part of the house mostly because of its chronic disuse. It hadn't been painted for years. There were cobwebs in the corners with the desiccated corpses of unidentifiable insects who'd met their end in their sticky strands. An old chair rail hung half off the wall, and an old-fashioned wooden hat rack leaned drowsily in one corner. The floor was constructed of ancient slate tiles, eighteen inches on a side. Many were cracked, some fractured entirely. One or two were missing.

As Jack crossed the kitchen, he could see Alli unlock the back door, disappear outside. Jack followed her. At once, he was engulfed by the odors of rotting wood, roots, and the mineral tang of damp stone. He pushed through into a deeper darkness as he moved into a patch of the forested area behind the house.

"Alli," he said softly. "Alli, enough. Where are you?"

The tangle of branches, dense even in the dead of winter, kept the city at bay. The sky, grayish pink like old skin, was intermittently swept away by the wind. Rain seeped down, bouncing off twigs and vines, taking erratic pinball paths. Save for this, all was still. And yet there was the sense of something stirring, as if the wild area itself were alive with a single will, had turned that will to a specific intent.

Jack, his anxiety rising, peered through the rain, through the Medusa's hair of the thicket. It was impossible to know which way she'd gone, or even why she would lead him here. In and out of faint lozenges of city light he went, turning this way and that, searching, until he seemed to be in a maze of mirrors, where he kept coming upon his own reflection.

He was certain he hadn't dreamt that whisper, certain that Alli had been standing in his doorway. After all, who else could it have been? Then, the fine hairs on his forearms stirred, because he heard the voice again.

"Dad . . ."

DENNIS PAULL, climbing the open stairs of the Starlight Motel in Maryland, was nearing the end of another grueling day. Part of it had been taken up by a meeting with Calla Myers's parents. He could, of course, have had one of his assistants meet them, but he was not one for delegating difficult assignments. Calla Myers had been killed on his watch. There was no excuse for her death; its dark stain would be etched on his soul forever, to take its place alongside many other similar tattoos. But somehow this one seemed darker, deeper, more shameful, because she was a civilian. She hadn't put herself in harm's way as the two Secret Service agents had. That she'd been murdered in precisely the same way as the agents was no longer a mystery to him.

Paull had no illusions about going to heaven, but since he believed in neither heaven nor hell, it didn't really matter. What concerned him was the here and now. He had conjured up all the right phrases of sympathy for the Myerses. He had even sat with them afterwards, while the mother wept and the father held her blindly, even after he'd run out of words of brittle solace. He tried not to think about his own wife, his two sons, tried not to wonder how he would react if someone came to him with unthinkable news. He'd had a brother who'd died in the Horn of Africa in the service of his country. Even Paull hadn't known the details of his mission. Nor had he cared to know the details of his death. He'd simply buried him with full honors and gone on with his work.

Having checked three times for surveillance, Paull walked along the open gangway on the second floor of the motel, inserted a key in the lock of a room at the far end, opened the door, and went in.

Nina Miller was sitting on the bed, her long legs stretched out, crossed at the bare ankles. She'd kicked off her sensible shoes and now looked fetching in a pearl-white silk shirt. Her dove gray wool skirt had ridden partway up her muscular thighs. She was a fine tennis player, as was Paull. It was how they'd met, in fact. Now they played mixed doubles whenever they had a chance, which, admittedly, wasn't often.

Nina put down the book she was reading—*Summer Rain*, by Marguerite Duras—a first edition Paull had given her last year for her birthday. It was her favorite novel.

"You're looking luscious."

She smiled. "I could have your job for workplace sexual harassment."

"This isn't the workplace." Paull bent, kissed her on the lips. "This isn't harassment."

"Flatterer."

Paull pulled over the desk chair, sat down beside her. "What have you got for me?"

She handed him a thick manila folder. "I back-checked the dossiers of every member of the D.C. Homeland Security office. Everyone's clean, so far as I can tell, except for Garner."

"Hugh's my deputy." Paull shook his head. "No. He's too obvious a choice."

"That's precisely why the National Security Advisor recruited him." She pointed at the open file she'd compiled. "Over the past eight months, Hugh has met five times with a man named Smith." She laughed. "Can you believe it? Anyway, Mr. Smith is Hugh's acupuncturist. He also happens to be in the office adjacent to the National Security Advisor's chiropractor."

Paull, paging through the file, said, "I see their appointments overlapped on those five occasions."

Nina folded her hands in her lap. "What d'you want to do?"

Putting the folder aside, Paull leaned over her. "I know what I *want* to do."

Nina giggled, took his head between her hands. "I'm serious."

"I couldn't be more serious." His lips brushed the hollow of her throat. "How's your friend Jack McClure?"

"Mmmm."

Paull raised his head. "What does that mean?"

She made a moue. "You're not jealous, are you, Denny?"

"I have no idea what you're talking about."

She pushed him away. "Sometimes you can be so starchy."

"I only meant that considering Hugh Garner hates McClure's guts, perhaps between us we can work out a way for him to take care of Hugh for us."

Her mouth twitched. "What a Machiavellian mind you have."

Paull laughed appreciatively as he manipulated the tiny pearl buttons down the front of her shirt.

Tossing the file on the floor beside the bed, she said, "I've gotten as close as I can to Jack. He's carrying a Statue of Liberty–size torch for his ex."

"Poor bastard."

"Nothing *you'll* have to worry about," she said. "You don't have a heart."

"Birds of a feather." He made a lascivious grab for her. "Anyway, what could be better than an affair with no strings attached?"

"I can't imagine." She gripped his tie, pulled him down to her.

JACK TURNED and saw her, framed between two trees, her skin pale in the ghostly light.

"Dad . . ."

"Emma?" He took a step toward her. "Is that you?"

The rain, gaining strength, beat down on him, water rolling into his eyes, mixing with his tears. Could Emma have come back to him? Was it possible? Or was he losing his mind?

He moved closer. The image wavered, seemed to break up into a million parts, each reflected in a raindrop spattering black branches, glistening brown bark, pale gold of dead leaves. She was all around him.

Jack stood in wonder as he heard her voice, "Dad, I'm here. . . ."

It wasn't the voice of a person or a ghost. It was the sough of the wind, the scrape of the branches, the rustle of the brittle leaves, even the distant intermittent hiss of traffic on faraway streets, avenues, and parkways.

"I'm here. . . ."

Her voice emanated from everything. Every atom held a part of her, was infused by her spirit, her soul, the electrical spark that had animated her brain, that made her unique, that made her Emma.

"My Emma." He listened for her, to her, heard the wind, the trees, the sky, even the dead leaves call his name, felt her close all around him, as if he were immersed in warm water. "Emma, I'm sorry. I'm sorry. . . ."

"I'm here, Dad. . . . I'm here."

And she was. Though he couldn't hold her, couldn't see her, she was there with him, not a figment of his imagination, but something beyond his ken, beyond a human's ability to comprehend. A physicist might call her a quark. Werner Heisenberg, architect of quantum mechanics and the uncertainty principle, would understand her being here and not here at the same time.

JACK RETURNED to the house dripping wet, feeling at once exceptionally calm and subtly agitated. He couldn't explain the feeling any more than he could the last half hour, nor did he want to. Heavy-limbed, he wanted only to return to his bed and sleep for as many hours as he could until sunlight splintered the oak tree outside his window and roused him with warm and tender fingers.

Before he did so, however, he peeked into Alli's room, saw her sleeping peacefully on her side. Silently closing the door, he tiptoed back to the bathroom to dry off. Then he stumbled into bed and, after pulling the covers up to his chin, passed into a deep and untroubled sleep.

FORTY-FOUR

JACK FELT as if he were walking a tightrope. On the one hand, he had promised Edward Carson to deliver Alli at noon today; on the other, he needed to find some way to get Alli to open up about Ian Brady because she was his only link to him. She'd been with him long enough; it was possible she had seen or heard something that could lead him to the murderer.

"Alli, I know how hard this must be for you," he said as she came down to the kitchen, "I know this man is scary."

Instantly, she turned away. "I don't want to talk about it."

He ignored the deer-caught-in-the-headlights glassiness of her eyes, plowed relentlessly on. This might be his last chance to get her to talk about her ordeal. "Alli, listen to me, we need to know why Kray abducted you. He didn't do it for a lark, he had a plan in mind. Only you and he know what that is. You're the key to what happened."

"I'm telling you I don't *know.* I can't remember."

"But have you tried?" Jack said. "Really tried?"

"Please, Jack." She began to tremble all over, absolutely certain that she was close to something terrible, that she was approaching a pit of fire into which she could not help but walk and be consumed. Even Jack couldn't save her now. "Please stop."

"Alli, I'm sure Emma would want you to—"

"Don't!" She spun around, her face flushed. "Don't use Emma that way."

"All right." Jack held up his hands. He knew he'd gone too far. "I'm sorry. I didn't mean to upset you." The more he pushed her, the more agitated she became. He wasn't going to get anything more out of her this way or any other way he could think of. Like it or not, he had to back off.

He smiled at her. "Are we good?"

Alli tried to smile back, but all she could do was nod numbly.

THEY WERE just sitting down to breakfast when Jack heard a car pull up outside. Assuming it was the Secret Service detail, he crossed to the front door, stepped outside to tell them not to come into the house. Instead, he saw Egon Schiltz's maroon classic station wagon, a superlative 1950 Buick Super Model 59 Estate Woodie Wagon, with its unique Niagara Falls bumper, real birchwood side panels, the original straight-eight-cylinder engine with 124 horsepower and GM's then-innovative Dyna-flow automatic transmission. In truth, it should have been in a showroom or bombing down Victory Boulevard in L.A., but it was Egon's second child, and he drove it everywhere.

He raised an arm as he got out of the woodie. "Finally. I tried all yesterday to reach you, but you weren't answering your cell phone, and Chief Bennett gave me a number for the task force that's no longer in service."

Jack came down off the porch. The mild air was still in place; there was only the hint of a chill in the air, low sunlight already melting silver hoarfrost.

"How are you, Egon?"

"Ask me in a month." Schiltz gave a wry smile. "I came clean with

Candy. I think she would've moved out, except for Molly. Molly must never know, that's something the two of us absolutely agreed on."

"If you agree on one thing, more will follow. You two should see someone."

Egon nodded. "I want to. I'm sure Candy does, too. She just needs some time." He scratched the back of his head. "You're a good friend, Jack, thank you. I feel . . ." He sighed heavily. "It turns out you know me better than I know myself. Living a lie isn't for me, which is why I've stopped going to church for the time being." He leaned back against the mottled trunk of a tree. "It's not so bad. Truthfully, I don't think Molly misses it at all. I tried to make her see the light, but it's no good, you see. It doesn't work. You want for your child everything you yourself didn't have, only to discover she wants only what she wants. And in the end, you're meaningless, really. It's her life." He rubbed his hands briskly. "She never really got God. Either you believe or you don't. There's no point going through the motions."

"I hope you haven't stopped believing, Egon."

The ME produced a rueful smile. "That would make my entire life a mockery. No, no, I still believe in God, but what you made me realize is that there are many paths to redemption. I've got to find mine. The Church can't help me."

Jack clapped his friend on the shoulder. "Everyone needs the freedom to make up their own mind." He gestured with his head. "D'you want to come in? I can fix you some breakfast."

Egon glanced around. "Not if you have guests."

"In that case," Jack said, "let's take a walk."

They went around the north side of the house. It was colder here; the green Bilco doors were still rimed with a thin layer of ice, the fallen leaves stuck together with the glue of winter.

"Something mighty queer is going on," Egon said.

Jack was automatically on alert. "In what way?"

"You heard about that girl, Calla Myers, being stabbed to death on the Spanish Steps the other day. The District ME is an old bridge buddy of mine. He called yesterday morning, and I met with him. He told me that the stab wound was in the same place as the ones on the two agents guarding Alli Carson. I showed him the photos of the wounds, and he confirmed the one that killed Calla Myers was identical."

"Did you confirm it on her body?"

"Well, that's the thing," Egon said. "The body wasn't in his morgue. The feds whisked it out of there along with his preliminary findings."

Jack was hardly surprised, since it was clear that Calla Myers was Ian Brady's latest victim. But the very fact that he'd targeted her set Jack's synapses to firing overtime. Another Rubik's Cube was forming in his head, and he didn't like the shape of it one bit. He'd heard the president's address. Direct evidence linked Calla Myers, a member of the FASR, to the murders of the SS agents. That was part of the rationale used to close down the Kansas Avenue office and take its members into custody. What did it mean that Brady—a federally protected person—had murdered Calla Myers? Brady had killed the Secret Service detail. In the initial briefing, Hugh Garner had told him that the detail's cell phones hadn't been found. In an instant, the Rubik's Cube in Jack's mind slid into focus. Of course the phones hadn't been found; Brady had taken them. And now he'd planted one with Calla Myers to implicate her and, by extension, the FASR.

Egon broke into his thoughts. "Jack, are you still with me?"

Jack nodded. "I was just thinking about Calla Myers's murderer. I think I know who it is, but I have no idea what his real name is or where to find him."

"I just might be able to help you there." Egon took out a small pad, flipped it open. "As I said, my friend hadn't finished his autopsy on Calla Myers when the feds took her away, but he did note something interesting. He hadn't yet put it in his prelim, because he needed to check it out, so the feds don't have it."

Schiltz consulted his pad. "As per the MO, there were no finger-prints whatsoever except for the vic's, which leads us to the inescapable conclusion that the perp wore gloves of some sort. My friend found traces of a superfine powder on Calla Myers's coat, in the place under her left arm consistent with where someone who had his arm around her would place his hand.

"It took him some time to figure out what this powder actually was." Egon glanced up. "You'll like this, Jack. What was on Calla Myers's coat was logwood powder. Logwood is a heartwood extract from *Haematoxylon campechianum,* found in Central America and the West Indies. When mixed with a carrier, such as ethyl alcohol, glyc-erine, or Listerine, it becomes a black pigment used for tattooing." He snapped the pad closed. "And, by the way, Calla Myers had no tattoos."

Jack's heart leapt. "So the logwood powder came from the perp."

Schiltz nodded. "Whatever else this sonovabitch is, he's also a tat-too artist. But here's the best part. Almost all tattoo artists buy pre-mixed pigments. None of those use logwood as an ingredient. Your man mixes his pigments by hand."

I LIKED the white Continental better," Alli said as she slid into Jack's car.

He laughed as he put the car in gear. A moment later, he picked up the Secret Service detail in his rearview mirror. It was 11:20. The minutes were counting down to when he'd lose his access to her. It was now or never.

"Alli, there's something I've been wondering," he said. "Did the man who abducted you have a tattoo?"

Alli went rigid. She stared straight ahead.

"Alli, honey, it's all right for you to tell me."

"I only saw his arms." Alli slowly shook her head from side to side. "He didn't have any tattoos."

Jack, heading for the Carsons' house in Chevy Chase, did his best to keep to the minimum speed. He didn't want this drive to end yet.

"Alli, I know Ronnie Kray frightened you terribly, but it would be helpful if you could tell me something more about what you saw. Anything at all."

Alli, still sitting rigidly, said nothing.

"I want to catch him, Alli. You want that, don't you?"

She bit her lip, nodded.

"You're the only one who can help me."

Tears began to run down her cheeks. "I wish Emma was here. She could tell you what you want to know."

"You can, too."

Her eyes squeezed shut. "I'm not brave like she was."

Despite his best efforts, they'd entered Chevy Chase. This was it, then. The end. Jack relented. "Alli, your father has agreed to let me pick the detail guarding you."

"I want you," she said at once.

He nodded. "I'll be there, just not the whole time. But you can absolutely trust Nina and Sam. I know them, I've worked with them. They won't let you down."

He turned onto the Carsons' street, a cul-de-sac, saw more Secret Service agents in cars and on the sidewalk. They all watched him as he drove toward the large federal-style brick house at the end of the cul-de-sac.

"Home," he said.

"It doesn't feel like it." Alli shifted in her seat. "Nothing feels right."

"As soon as you get back to your routine, it'll all feel as familiar as it did before."

"But I don't want to get back to my old routine!" She sounded like a spoiled child.

Jack pulled into the driveway where Edward and Lyn Carson were waiting. He shut off the engine, opened his door, but Alli made no move to open hers.

"Alli . . ."

She turned to him. There was desperation in her eyes. "I don't want to leave you!"

"You have a responsibility to your parents. Tomorrow you'll be the First Daughter. From now on, you have to act like the First Daughter. The whole country will be watching."

"Please don't make me."

"Honey, it's what has to happen."

"But I'm afraid."

Jack frowned. "Afraid of what?"

"To leave you, to be here, I don't know."

By this time, the Carsons, concerned, had come up to the car. Lyn Carson opened the passenger's-side door, leaned in.

"Alli? Baby?"

Alli, still turned toward Jack, silently mouthed, *Please help me.*

Jack felt torn into a thousand shreds. He had failed Emma, he didn't want to fail Alli as well. But what could he do? The president-elect had given him an order that he was powerless to ignore. Alli wasn't his child. So he did the only thing he could do. He leaned over, whispered in her ear, "I'll see you later, I promise. Okay?"

As he pulled back, he saw her nod. Then she turned, got out of the car and into her mother's arms.

"Jack."

Edward Carson was at his side as he got out of the car. The president-elect pumped his hand then impulsively embraced him.

"There are no words." His voice was clotted with emotion. "You've brought our girl back to us safe and sound, just as you promised."

Jack watched Alli. Her mother, arm around her waist, walked her up the brick steps to the open front door.

"That's right," Lyn Carson said. "Random House wants you to write a memoir about growing up to be the First Daughter."

"She's a special young woman," Jack said. "I want Nina Miller and Sam Scott assigned to her permanent detail. Nina and I were partners in finding Alli. I worked with Sam at ATF until he transferred to the Secret Service three years ago."

Carson nodded. "I'll make the necessary calls right away." He looked at his wife and daughter for a moment, before turning back. "Jack, Lyn and I would like you at the inauguration, up on the dais with us. You're like a member of our family now."

"It would be an honor, sir."

In the doorway, Alli turned, gave him a tentative smile, and with a sweep of her mother's arm, vanished into her world of privilege and power.

FORTY-FIVE

WHO WAS Ian Brady? In other, more normal circumstances, Jack would have been preoccupied with finding that out. However, this case was anything but normal. What concerned him now was not who Ian Brady was but why he had chosen that name. Clearly, his other aliases—Ronnie Kray and Charles Whitman—followed on in a straight line from the first.

It was Jack's experience—the experience of any knowledgeable lawman—that criminals, even the highly intelligent ones, chose their aliases for a reason. An FBI profiler who had been brought into the ATF office on a case some years ago had said that giving meaning to an alias was a subconscious urge criminals found irresistible. In other words, they couldn't help themselves. Of one thing Jack was certain: The name Ian Brady held special meaning for this man. The trick was to find out what that meaning was.

With his paranoia at full mast, Jack bypassed the computers hooked up to the federal network, which included his own at the ATF office in Falls Church. What was required, he thought now as he made his way out of Chevy Chase, was a public cybercafé. Twenty minutes of hunting from behind the wheel of his car unearthed one on Chase Avenue, in Bethesda. He sat down at a terminal, typed the name Ian Brady, but all he got was a bare-bones recap from Wikipedia and About.com. On the other hand, after some false leads, he found a distributor of logwood, the substance Brady had inadvertently left on Calla Myers's coat. Taking down the address and phone number, he walked outside, checked the environment for tags. In the shadow of a storefront, he got out his cell burner, punched in the number of the distributor. He got nothing, no automated message, no voice mail. He wasn't all that surprised. The distributor was so small and obscure, it had a rudimentary Web site. Customers could order its product online, but other than that, the site looked as if it hadn't been updated in months.

S&W DISTRIBUTION was on the outskirts of the curiously named Mexico, Pennsylvania, 160 miles north of Chevy Chase Village. It took Jack just under three hours bombing down I-83N and US-22W to get there. By the time he exited PA-75S, it was already late in the afternoon. The sun, low in the sky, was bedded on thick clouds into which it expanded and slowly sank. Shadows lengthened with the beginning of winter's long twilight.

S&W occupied a ramshackle building a stone's throw from the railroad tracks that brought Mexico all the business it was going to get. It was impossible to tell what color the structure had originally been painted or even what color it was now. Jack's heart sank because at first sight, the place looked abandoned, but then he saw a young woman come out the front door. She wore cowboy boots, jeans, a fleece-lined denim jacket over a ribbed turtleneck sweater. As he pulled up, she settled herself on the clapboard steps, shook out a cigarette, lit up. She watched him with gimlet eyes as he got out of his car, walked toward her. She had an interesting, angular face. Its slight asymmetry made her appear beautiful. She was slim and small. She appeared to be in her late twenties.

As he approached, he heard a train whistle. The tremor in the tracks built as the train thundered toward them. The unsettled air of its bow wave crashed over them like a hail of gunshots. The young woman, her long hair flying across her face, sat as calmly as if the only sound to be heard was the crunch of Jack's shoes on the pebbly blacktop. Smoke dribbled from the corner of her mouth, and now that he was closer, he could see the tattoos on the backs of her hands, either side of her neck: the four main phases of the moon. She must have dyed her hair black to match her eyes, but the tips were golden. She wore a silver skull ring on the third finger of her right hand. The skull seemed to be laughing.

In the aftermath of the cinder swirl, Jack flashed his ID, watched as her eyes tracked uninterestedly to the information. He began to wonder whether it was tobacco she was smoking.

"Do you work at S-and-W?" he asked.

"Used to."

"They fired you?"

"The world fired them. S-and-W is history." She jerked a thumb. "I'm just cleaning out the place."

Jack sat down beside her. "What's your name?"

"Hayley. Can you believe it? Ugh! Everyone calls me Leelee."

"How long did you work here?"

"Seven to life." She took a drag on her cigarette. "A fucking jail term."

Jack laughed. "You're a hard piece of work."

"It's self-preservation, so you can be sure I try my damnedest." She watched him out of the corners of her black eyes. "You don't look like a cop."

"Thank you."

It was her turn to laugh.

"How far along are you with the—" He jerked his thumb. "—you know?"

She sighed. "Not nearly far enough."

"I'm trying to track down a customer of S-and-W's," Jack said. "He's a tattoo artist who mixes his own pigments. I'm hoping he ordered logwood from you."

"Not too many of those," Leelee observed. "It's why S-and-W was overtaken by history. That and the fact that the owner never came around. The fucker stopped paying his bills altogether—including my salary. If I wasn't hired by the mail-order company taking over the building, I wouldn't even be here now." She shrugged. "But who cares? Odds are the new company'll go belly-up, too."

"Do you know something your new bosses don't?"

"That's the way the world works, isn't it?" She stared at the glowing tip of her cigarette. "I mean, we're all sheep, aren't we, persuading ourselves that we're different, that we're beautiful or smart or cool. But we all end up the same way—as a little pile of ashes."

"That's a pretty bleak outlook."

She shrugged. "Par for the course for a nihilist."

"You need a boyfriend," Jack said.

"Someone to tell me what to do and how to do it, someone to leave me at night to go out with the guys, someone to roll over in bed and snore his way to morning? You're right. I need that."

"How about someone to love you, protect you, take care of you?"

She tossed her head. "I do that myself."

"I see how that's working out for you."

Through her armor, she gave him a wry smile.

"Come on, Leelee, you need to believe in something," Jack said.

"Oh, I do. I believe in courage and discipline."

"Admirable." Jack nodded. "But I mean something outside of yourself. We're all connected to a universe more mysterious than what we see around us."

"Think so? Here's the truest thing I know: Don't for a moment let religion or art or patriotism persuade you that you mean more than you do." She took another deep drag, gave him a challenging, alpha-dog look. "That comes from a play called *Secret Life*. I bet you never heard of it."

"It was written by Harley Granville-Barker."

Leelee's eyes opened wide. "Shit, yeah. Now I'm impressed."

"Then give me a hand here."

"I could bust your hump, but you've taken all the fun out of that." She swept her hair behind one ear. "Does your tattoo artist have a name?"

"Ian Brady," Jack said. "Or Ronnie Kray. Or Charles Whitman."

Leelee took the butt from between her lips. "You're shitting me."

"He was a customer, right?"

"More than." She didn't look as if she was interested in smoking anymore. "Charles Whitman owns S-and-W."

THE EVENING was furry with sleet, but as Jack worked his way south toward the District, it became an icy rain his wipers cast off either side of his windshield. The roads were slick and treacherous, peppered with spin-outs and fender benders, which slowed him down considerably. He returned from Mexico with an address for Charles Whitman. He had no way of knowing whether this was Brady's current residence, but he wasn't going to take any chances. The approach had to be thought out in detail.

As soon as he entered the house, he turned on the stereo, along with the lights and his stove top. But the only meat he had—a steak—was frozen solid, so he turned off the burner, sat down at the kitchen table with a jar of peanut butter and one of orange marmalade. Using a teaspoon, he scooped out mouthfuls from one jar then the other.

Afterwards, he went through his LP collection without finding anything he wanted to listen to. That's when he came upon Emma's iPod. He'd stuck it on top of a Big Bill Broonzy album that contained two of his favorite songs, "Baby, Please Don't Go" and "C C Rider." Tonight, he didn't want to hear either of them.

He took up the iPod, plugged it in because the battery was low. Using the thumb wheel, he browsed through Emma's collection of MP3s. There were the usual suspects: Justin Timberlake, R.E.M., U2, and Kanye West, but he was startled to see tracks by artists he loved and had played for her: Carla Thomas, Jackie Taylor, the Bar-Kays.

Searching through the shelves that housed his records and video-cassettes, he found the box containing the iPod dock he'd bought but never used. He took it out, plugged it into the aux receptacle in the back of the stereo receiver. Then he put the iPod into the dock.

He decided to listen to something of Emma's at random. This turned out to be an album for some reason called *Boxer,* by a band called The National. He thought of Emma, imagined her listening to these muscular songs—he particularly liked "Fake Empire"—wondered what would have been going through her mind.

As the music played, he fired up his computer, went online. According to Leelee's records, the address where Brady had his logwood delivered was on Shepherd Street, in Mount Rainier, Maryland. He pulled up Google Maps, punched in the address, and clicked the HYBRID button, which gave him both the map and the satellite photo of the area. The address was only five or six miles southeast of where he was born. The thought gave him the shivers.

Forty minutes later, he got up, rummaged around the house for several items he thought he might need, stuffed them into a light-weight gym bag. He checked his Glock, shoved extra ammunition in his pocket, grabbed his coat. On the way out the door, he called Sharon. There was no answer. He disconnected before her voice mail picked up. With a sharp stab of jealousy, he wondered where she was. What if she was out with another man? That was her right, wasn't it? Yes, but he didn't want to think about it. He climbed into his car, his heart hammering in his chest. Driving to Shepherd Street, he thought, this could be it, the end of a road twenty-five years long.

FORTY-SIX

WHAT WERE the odds that Ian Brady lived in a hotel just four miles from Jack's house? Yet this was what Jack saw as he cruised by the address Leelee had given him. RAINIER RESIDENCE HOTEL. SHORT-TERM AND LONG-TERM CORPORATE LEASES AVAILABLE the sign out front read. He didn't stop, didn't even slow down until he turned the corner onto Thirty-first Street, where he pulled into the curb and parked. The first thing he did was to check out the rear, which was flat, save for a zigzag of tiered black iron fire escapes. It gave out onto a concrete apron and, just beyond, a modestly sized blacktop parking lot, lit by sodium lights, from whose hard glare he kept his careful distance. But there was no rear entrance, most likely because of the same security concerns that had led to the installation of the parking lot lights.

Walking back to Shepherd Street, he found himself across the street from an ugly U-shaped structure hugging a courtyard with four withered trees, a Maginot Line of evergreen shrubs, fully a third of which were as brown and useless as sun-scorched newspapers. The hotel itself was three stories of pale yellow brick. Access to the apartments was via metal staircases at the center and either end of the U, along raw concrete catwalks that ran the length of the building. There was a coarseness about it, a glittery shabbiness, like a Christmas present wrapped in used paper. Had it been painted turquoise or flamingo, it could have passed as a down-at-the-heels Florida condo.

Jack kept away from the occasional dazzle as passing cars lit up sections of the sidewalk. He crossed the street, found his way to the manager's apartment. Even through the door he could hear the blare of the TV. Waiting for a seconds-long silence, he rapped hard on the door. The blare started up again, louder this time, which meant a commercial had come on. A moment later, the door was yanked open the length of a brass chain.

Dark eyes in a square, heavy-jawed face looked him up and down. "Not interested."

Jack put his foot across the doorjamb, flashed his ID even as the door began to swing shut. "I need some information," he said.

"What kind of information?" the manager said in a voice like a pit bull's growl.

"The kind you don't want to give me while I'm standing out here."

The dark eyes got small and piggy. "You're not from INS? All my workers are legit."

"Sure they are, but I don't care. I'm not from Immigration."

The manager nodded, Jack took his foot away, and the door closed enough for Pig-Eyes to unlatch the chain. Jack walked into a low-ceilinged apartment with small rooms made even smaller by enough sofas, chairs—upholstered and otherwise—and tables of all sizes and shapes to furnish the Carson's Chevy Chase mansion. The manager muted the TV. Images of Fred Flintstone and Barney Rubble chased themselves across the screen.

"You have a tenant here by the name of Charles Whitman?"

"No."

"How about checking your records?"

"No need," Pig-Eyes said. "I know everyone who lives here."

"How about Ron Kray?"

"No Kray here."

"Ian Brady."

Pig-Eyes shook his head. "Uh-uh."

Jack considered Brady's propensity for misdirection. Alli had told him that the real Ian Brady had a female accomplice. "How about a Myra Hindley?"

"No," Pig-Eyes said, "but we got a Myron Hindley. You think he's the one you're looking for?"

"Do the apartment doors have peepholes?" Jack said.

Pig-Eyes seemed confused. "Yeah, why?"

"Are all the door locks the same as yours?"

"You bet. House rules. I gotta be able to have access to all the apartments."

"I need a broom, a wire hanger, and the key to Myron Hindley's apartment," Jack said. As the manager went to fetch the items, Jack added, "If you hear any loud noises, it's just a truck backfiring."

MYRON HINDLEY'S apartment was on the third floor, at the far end of the building. Hardly a surprise, since that's precisely where Jack would have situated himself if he were in Brady's place. He had two choices: The first was to go in the front door. The second was to climb up the fire escape to the apartment's two rear windows. Since it would be far easier for Brady to flee out the front door than climb out the window, he decided to make a frontal assault. He wished Nina were here to take the back of the building, but she was with Alli. Besides, ever since the explicit warning he'd received from Secretary Paull, he'd decided to continue after Brady alone. This was his fight, not hers.

Every six feet, bare bulbs were screwed into porcelain fixtures in the ceiling of the catwalk. On the third floor, Jack took off his shoes, covered his right hand with both socks. Reaching up, he unscrewed each lightbulb as he progressed down the catwalk. The circles of illumination winked out one by one. After he'd disabled the last bulb, he put on his socks and shoes. His feet were freezing, and he had to wait several minutes for the warmth to come back so that he had full maneuverability.

With only the ambient wash from streetlights and the odd passing vehicle to illuminate the catwalk, Jack set the gym bag down on the concrete, opened the zip, took out a small can of WD-40 and a pair of bolt cutters. Then he took off his coat, hung it on the wire hanger, buttoned it, put the collar up. Then he twisted the top of the hanger so it wound around the butt of the broom handle. He stood this makeshift scarecrow against the railing of the catwalk directly opposite the door to Myron Hindley's apartment.

Standing to one side of the door, he sprayed the key Pig-Eyes had given him with WD-40. It slid right in as he inserted it into the lock. But he didn't turn it over. Instead, he picked up the bolt cutter. He rapped on the door, very loudly. Just as he pulled his fist away, three bullets exploded through the door, ripping holes in Jack's overcoat. The broom crashed over onto the catwalk.

Jack turned the key, opened the door. As at the manager's apartment, the door opened only to the length of the chain, which Jack promptly snipped in two with the bolt cutter. Drawing his Glock, he kicked open the door. Expecting another salvo of shots, he held his ground. When none came, he pitched himself across the threshold curled in a ball, came out of it with his Glock aimed into the room.

"Relax," a voice said. "I've been expecting you."

Jack found himself confronting a figure sitting at his ease in an upholstered chair that had been pulled so that it faced the front door. Only one lamp was on, so that he was cast in half light, enough so that Jack could see the handgun gripped in one hand. It was lying on his right thigh, the barrel aimed casually at Jack.

"Sit down, Jack," the figure said. "It's been a long run. You must be tired."

Jack could feel the power of the man as a fish is drawn to the baited hook. "I don't know whether to call you Myron, Charlie, Ronnie, or Ian."

The figure shrugged. "What's in a name?"

"Who are you?" Jack said. He was struggling against an unnamed fear that had spread its black wings inside him. "What's your real name?"

"I didn't invite you here to answer questions," the figure said.

Jack felt a laugh forced out of him, but it sounded brittle and shaky. "You *invited* me?"

Brady shrugged. "Leelee told me you were on your way."

Now the fear took flight; he was in its shadow. As if he'd received a blow, he took an involuntary step backwards.

Brady bared his teeth. "Where d'you think she got all her ideas?"

Feeling a chair behind his knees, Jack sat down dazedly.

"Truth to tell, I've run you like a rat in a maze." In a trick of the light, Brady seemed to have inflated, to be larger than life. "Every time you got to another point in the maze, I moved your cheese." He waved the hand with the gun. "For instance, Calla Myers called me the moment you left the FASR office. I knew it was only a matter of time before you followed the clues I left to the Marmoset's house. Oh yes, I'm familiar with Gus's nickname for him."

Jack felt poleaxed. All the hard work he'd done to get here, the arduous path he'd followed, had been created by this monster. "It was all to get me here?" he said like a pupil to his professor. "Why?"

"That question I'll answer. I'm as tired as you are, Jack. I've had a good run, but now, like the president, my term has come to an end. And like the president, it's time for me to look to my lasting legacy."

He shifted slightly, and Jack could see him better now. Chris Armitage had described him well. He was handsome, distinguished even, with the kind of sexual magnetism he imagined Leelee would go for. Jack found him as sinister-looking as his horned viper and twice as terrifying.

"Your term stretches back far longer than eight years."

"All the more reason for it to come to an end." Brady leaned over, reached for the neck of a bottle of liquor, which he lifted into the light so Jack would be reassured. "Polish vodka. The real thing, not the watered-down crap you get here. Care to join me?"

Jack shook his head.

Brady shrugged. "Your loss." Hoisting the bottle, he took a long swig, then smacked his lips.

"Okay." Jack rose, gestured with the Glock. "Time to go."

"And where would you be taking me? Not to the police and certainly not to the feds." He possessed a crooked grin that gave him the aspect of a crocodile. There was something primeval about him, immutable, like a force of nature. This elemental quality was the source of his power. "You're the one they'll lock up, Jack, not me."

Jack stood, the Glock pointing at the floor. "Why did you kill Gus?"

"No questions, remember? Not that it matters—you already know the answer to that one. Gus wasn't going to give up looking for me. That idiot detective, Stanz, would have finally let it go, but not Gus." Brady lazily tilted his head to one side. "But that isn't the question you really want to ask, is it?"

An icy ball formed in the pit of Jack's stomach. "What d'you mean?"

"C'mon, Jack. I killed Gus inside his house. You were asleep down the hall. You want to know why I left you alive."

Jack, realizing he was right, said nothing.

"It's a mystery, Jack, like many others in this life destined to remain unsolved."

Jack aimed the Glock at him. "You *will* tell me."

"Are you going to shoot me? That would be a blessing. My term would end in a blaze of glory because my bosses would lock you up and throw away the key. Lawyer, what lawyer? You wouldn't even get a phone call. No, they'll stick you in solitary in a federal high-security penitentiary." He gestured with his gun, careful not to point it at Jack. "So sit back down, have a drink."

Jack stood where he was.

"Suit yourself." Brady sighed deeply. "We're both orphans, in our own ways. I murdered my parents, as you should have."

"If you're trying to say we're alike—"

"I must say you made up for it, though, when you killed that street thug, Andre." Brady chuckled. "In a library yet. Brilliant." He took another hit of the Polish vodka. "I'm going to tell you a secret, Jack. I have not one grain of faith in me. Early in life I wanted to get past all of life's tricks, small and large, to get to the heart of things." His eyes lit up. They were the eyes of Ron Kray, Charles Whitman, Ian Brady. "Sounds familiar, doesn't it, Jack? That's your search, too." He nodded. "Instead, what have I become? Life's ultimate trickster. You see, there's nothing left of me but tricks. That's because I discovered that there is no heart of things. I think there used to be, but that was a long time ago. Life's hollow, like a tree full of burrowing insects. That's what humans are, Jack. They've burrowed into life with their frenzied civilization, their running after wealth and fame, their attempts to deny the body's decay. They're all insane. What else could they be, making such an unholy mess of things? They've hollowed life out, Jack, till there's nothing left but the shell, the illusion of happiness."

"I don't believe you."

"Ah, but it's true, and your daughter knew it. Emma heard what I had to say, and it drew her like a moth to a flame. Too bad she died so young—I had big plans for her. Aside from killing, mentoring's what I do best. Emma had real potential, Jack. She could have become my most ardent pupil."

With a savage cry, Jack launched himself at Brady, crashed into him with his leading shoulder. The chair tipped backwards, and they both tumbled head over heels in a tangle of arms and legs, fetched up against the wall under the rear window. Jack punched Brady in the nose, heard with satisfaction the cartilage fracture. Blood spouted out, covering them both. At almost the same time, Jack felt the Glock being ripped from his hand. He felt around blindly for the other gun, saw Brady raise the Glock. A moment more, he'd shoot Jack. But then Jack saw where the Glock was pointed and, in a flash of insight, knew that Brady meant to shoot himself in the head with Jack's gun. He meant what he said about going out in a blaze of glory. He was going to end his reign by ensuring that Jack would spend the rest of his life in prison.

With a desperate swing, Jack knocked the Glock from Brady's hand. It went skittering across the floor. He hauled Brady to his feet, but one foot trod on Brady's gun. It was, like everything else in the area, slippery with blood. Jack lurched forward, taking Brady with him as they pitched through the window in a blizzard of shattered glass. Brady teetered for a moment with Jack over him, the two of them in stunned equilibrium. Jack tried to pull back, to right himself, but Brady was too far. Without Jack's weight to hold him in place, he began to slide headfirst out the window. Jack made a grab for him, but Brady slapped his hands away.

Brady stared up into Jack's face without expression of any kind. "Makes no difference. You'll never stop it."

The next instant he plummeted down three stories to the concrete apron. Jack, covered in blood and shards of glass, scooped up his Glock, ran out of the apartment, along the catwalk. He clattered down the stairs three at a time, around the side of the building.

Brady lay in a grotesque heap. He might have survived the fall, but the impact had broken his neck. His handsome face, under the harsh sodium glare of the parking lot lights, was a patchwork of seams, as if over time it had been stitched together. The eyes, devoid of their animating spark, were only buttons now. Stripped of charisma, he was nothing remarkable to look at. He was dead, Jack was dripping blood, and twenty-five years of rage, sorrow, and feeling abandoned drained away like grains of sand.

FORTY-SEVEN

WALKING INTO the vast hushed public library on G Street NW put Jack immediately at peace. The dry, slightly dusty scent of books came to him like a breath of fresh air, bringing back memories of so many hours happily poring through books to his heart's content. There was a certain kind of quiet here that calmed and stirred him at the same time. It was like being in the ocean, feeling your body light and buoyant and, at the same time, attuning yourself to the galaxy of unknown life that seethed beneath the surface. The knowledge of the world lay before him, the wisdom of history. This was his cathedral. Here was God.

IT WAS the morning of January 20. Inauguration Day. For a few hours, Jack had slept in his car before waking up just before dawn stiff and tired, his eyes full of grit. He went home, stripped off his bloody clothes, climbed into a hot shower, and putting all thoughts aside, stood under the cascade for fifteen blissful minutes. Then he scrubbed himself with soap, rinsed, dried off.

Fighting the urge to call Sharon, he dialed Alli's cell.

"I'm sorry I wasn't able to come by last night."

"That's okay." Her voice sounded furred with the remnants of sleep. "I missed you." There was a slight hesitation. "I had another dream last night." She meant about Ian Brady.

"Can you remember it?"

"He was talking to me, but his voice was all gauzy. It—I don't know—I had pictures in my head, like a movie. I was walking through a crowd of people."

"Were you trying to get away from him?"

"I don't know. I guess."

"Alli, you don't have to worry about him anymore."

"What d'you mean?"

He heard in her voice that she'd come fully awake.

"This is just between the two of us, right?"

"Right."

"That's why I couldn't come see you," Jack said. "I was with him. And now he'll never hurt you again."

He heard her sharply indrawn breath. "Really?"

"Really. I'll see you at the inauguration, okay? Now let me speak with Nina."

After a short pause, Nina came on the line.

"Good idea not contacting me on my cell. Are you calling from a pay phone?"

"A burner I bought a couple of days ago." He paused to stare out his bedroom window, where the branches of the oak tree reached toward the sky. "Listen, Ian Brady's history."

"What?"

"I tracked him down last night to a residence hotel in Mount Rainier, Maryland. He's dead."

"What a relief."

"Brady wanted to die, Nina. I'll give you the details after the inauguration, okay?"

"It's a date," she said. "Now I've got to get back to work."

Downstairs, he pulled the suit Chief Bennett had waiting for him those long weeks ago when he was being prepped for his assignment to Hugh Garner's joint task force. He stripped off the dry cleaning bag. He turned on Emma's iPod. He wanted to hear more of her music while he dressed. Alli had said that she was always making playlists. Seeing a playlist category in the iPod screen, he clicked on it. Oddly, there was only one, called Outside. He set it to play. Immediately, "Life on Mars?"—David Bowie's famous song about alienation—started up.

As Jack listened, he put on a freshly laundered white shirt, buttoned it up. "Life on Mars?" segued into the Rolling Stones' "Sympathy for the Devil." As he knotted his tie, on came Screamin' Jay Hawkins singing "I Put a Spell on You," a good deal more raw and powerful than subsequent versions.

After reknotting his tie three times, he got it right. He slipped on his jacket and was about to turn off the iPod when he heard Emma's voice coming out of the speakers. He stood, transfixed, listening to the aural diary of her three meetings with Ian Brady. This was how the entry ended:

"Finally, I said to him that if he saw me as his Myra Hindley, he was sorely mistaken because I had no intention of either fucking him or falling under his spell. This was the one time he surprised me. He laughed. I had nothing to fear. He said that he already had his Myra Hindley."

YOU'LL NEVER *stop it.*

Stop what? What had Brady planned?

Jack walked through the library's stacks. With each book he touched, he sensed a new door open to him. This was the place where his disability vanished, where he could read without the tension and frustration his dyslexia usually caused him. In the shadowed aisles he recognized Andre, Gus, Ian Brady, Emma. Each of their lives had meaning, a certain force that would remain with him even after death; of this, he was absolutely certain. Though they were beyond him now, still he sensed them, as an animal scents spoor and in its mind forms an image of what had once been there and has since moved on.

The truth was, Jack still felt the spoor of Ian Brady's mesmeric power, even though he was quite certain Brady had lied about his connection with Emma, had in fact been baiting him. Of course, this was precisely what Brady had meant to plant inside him, but Jack was only human, prey to human doubts and fears, just like anyone—anyone save Ian Brady perhaps.

Without quite knowing how it happened, Jack found himself at the section of the library that held the books of Colin Wilson. He ran his finger along the spines of the books until he found the intimidatingly thick *A Criminal History of Mankind*. Taking it down, he went over to a trestle table, sat down, and opened it up.

He was astonished to discover that the introduction was all about the real Ian Brady. Wilson had had a ten-year correspondence with Brady in prison. Wilson's conclusion was "that even an intelligent criminal remains trapped in the vicious circle of his criminality, and cannot escape."

Brady was involved in what Wilson termed a "dominance syndrome" with Myra Hindley, a young woman he seduced, deflowered, and somehow coerced into being his accomplice for a horrifying string of rape/murders over a two-year period. It was Myra who lured the teenage victims into her car so Brady could perform his acts of extreme cruelty and degradation. The real mystery was how he converted a young innocent like Myra Hindley into a criminal.

Jack paused. He could not help thinking of his Brady and Emma. *Emma heard what I had to say, and it drew her like a moth to a flame. Too bad she died so young—I had big plans for her. Aside from killing, mentoring's what I do best. Emma had real potential, Jack. She could have become my most ardent pupil.* What had he wanted with a Myra Hindley? So far as Jack could tell, Brady was a loner—whatever missions he performed for the government were strictly on his own. Anyone with him would have been a liability. So what, then, was he up to?

Jack went back to reading. On page twenty-nine, he came across the most heinous of Brady's crimes. He and Hindley picked up a ten-year-old girl. They took pictures of her (Jack couldn't help but think of the photos of Alli and Emma on the wall at the Marmoset's house), recorded her pleas for mercy, then killed her and buried her on the moor, where another of their young victims was buried. "Later," Wilson wrote, "they took blankets and slept on the graves. It was part of the fantasy of being Enemies of Society, dangerous revolutionaries."

Sickened by what these two people had done, Jack looked up. Into his head now came something else that his Brady had said to him last night: *I've had a good run, but now, like the president, my term has come to an end. And like the president, it's time for me to look to my lasting legacy.*

Jack understood that Brady had wanted to die last night: he'd tried to shoot himself with Jack's Glock, he'd brushed Jack's hands away when Jack tried to save him from his fall. Might it be that this was why Brady had kept Jack alive that night, because he suspected this moment in his future would come, that he wanted someone worthy to finish him off? *Truth to tell, I've run you like a rat in a maze. Every time you got to another point in the maze, I moved your cheese.* Jack had not only successfully negotiated the maze, but he'd also survived the horned viper's attack, the fusillade of bullets coming through the apartment door.

So Brady knew he was going to die last night, and yet he was looking to his lasting legacy. What might that be? Not his clandestine work for the government. A lasting legacy involves notoriety—a very public display. And he had very deliberately invoked the president. Why had he done that?

Another three-dimensional puzzle was forming in Jack's head as his brain made connections with the speed of light. Brady's MO was misdirection; he'd used it time and again. What if there was a second reason for him talking about Emma being his disciple, besides wanting to enrage Jack? Emma was never meant to be his Myra Hindley. What if—?

You'll never stop it.

Jack stood up so fast, he nearly overturned the table. The sound of its legs banging back on the floor was like a thunderclap in his mind. As he ran out of the library, he checked his watch. As usual, he'd lost himself in thought and reading. It was far later than he'd realized. The inauguration was about to begin and, with it, Ian Brady's lasting legacy.

FORTY-EIGHT

ALLI, IT'S time to go," Nina said gently.

Sam opened the door, stepped out into the wan January sunshine. Alli could hear him whispering into his mike, listening intently to security updates. When Sam nodded, Nina urged her charge forward, and Alli emerged from the plush cocoon of the limo into the seething crowd of politicians, foreign dignitaries, celebrities, the talking heads of worldwide media outlets, religious leaders, including Reverend Taske, head of the Renaissance Mission Congress, her father's special guest, military personnel in full-dress uniforms, Secret Service details crisscrossing the area with the concentration of marines landing in enemy territory.

Alli took all this in as if she were watching a film. Ever since she'd heard the first bars of Arcade Fire's "Neon Bible," she'd felt as if she were back in her dream with Ronnie Kray whispering in her ear. She felt detached and at the same time marvelously clearheaded. She had one mission to accomplish; everything else fell away as if off a steep cliff, vanishing from view. Her life was simple; all that was required of her was to remove the vial she somehow knew was basted into the lining of her coat and, at the proper moment, open it. What could be simpler? Her mind hummed along on the track Kray had set for it, using a combination of persuasion, fear, and a drug cocktail that included an efficacious dose of the horned viper's venom to metabolize the chemicals out of her system so quickly, it would be undetectable.

She was nearing her parents now. Her mother kissed her; her father smiled through her. The fanfare was playing, the Speaker of the House was preparing to take the podium for the Call to Order. Among the columns of the Capitol building hung three huge American flags. Above them, the dome glittered in sunlight.

Jack, snaking his way through the crowd, used his credentials at various Secret Service checkpoints. Approaching the dais was like negotiating the nine circles of hell—the closer he got, the slower his progress. The last bars of the fanfare faded, and the Speaker of the House took the podium for the Call to Order. Jack passed the final checkpoint and was admitted to the short flight of folding stairs up to the dais. He saw Reverend Taske, Secretary Paull, the National Security Advisor, the outgoing president. He looked past them for Alli, saw her between her mother and her father. She had a kind of faraway look on her face he'd seen a number of times before, and now all the tiny bits of strange behavior that he had observed, that had taken up residence in his brain, fell into place: her behavior when he'd taken her to see Chris Armitage, her dream. And afterwards: *Nothing feels right,* she'd said to him. *I'm afraid. . . . Please help me.* What had Brady done to her? Had he hypnotized her, drugged her? Perhaps both. In any event, he'd turned her into a time bomb. The fuse had been lit, and now, as he saw her reach into the lining of her coat, he made a beeline for her.

He saw Sam, who turned at the movement Jack made across the dais. Sam's eyes met Jack's, and he smiled until he saw Jack pointing. The vial was out, Alli's hand was curled around it. Sam saw it at the same moment Jack did. With a practiced move so smooth as to be virtually undetectable, he wrested the vial out of her hand, put his free arm around her, held her firmly against his chest.

And that was it, Jack thought, as he moved at a more leisurely pace toward them. Ian Brady's legacy had turned to ashes. Whatever substance he'd instructed Alli to release remained safely in its vial. The Speaker of the House finished the Call to Order, and the Reverend Dr. Fred Grimes began his fervent invocation and benediction.

"Let us pray. Blessed are you, O Lord, our God. Yours, O God, is the greatness and the power and the glory and the majesty and the splendor; for everything in heaven and earth is yours. Yours, O Lord, is the kingdom; you are exalted as head over all."

A stir began behind him. He turned in time to see Hugh Garner and three of his minions mounting the dais, heading directly for him. Clearly, Brady's body had been found. No doubt the pig-eyed manager of Brady's apartment complex had ID'd Jack.

"Wealth and honor come from you; you are the ruler of all things. In your hands are strength and power to exalt and to give strength to all."

Jack, zigzagging farther into the crowd on the dais, kept his eye out for Nina. She'd give him some help, provide cover for him while he slipped away. She should have been on the other side of Alli. There was still part of the last Rubik's Cube missing.

"As President Lincoln once said, 'We have grown in numbers, wealth, and power as no other nation has ever grown. But we have forgotten God. It behooves us, then, to humble ourselves before the offended power, to confess our national sins, and to pray for clemency and forgiveness.'"

At last, he caught a glimpse of Nina, moved toward her. She was standing on the other side of Edward Carson. He risked a glance behind him. Garner, in a classic pincer move, had ordered his two agents to the other side of the dais in order to intercept Jack while he closed from behind.

"O Lord, as we come together on this historic and solemn occasion to inaugurate once again a president and vice president, teach us afresh that power, wisdom, and salvation come only from your hand."

As Brady himself would understand better than most, what Jack needed now was a bit of misdirection. He tried to get Nina's attention, but her gaze seemed fixed on Edward Carson. Beneath the reverend's words, he could hear the commotion closing in behind him as Garner pushed through the dignitaries packing the dais. The missing piece of the last Rubik's Cube was this: Why had it been so easy to stop Alli? No one's lasting legacy—let alone Ian Brady's—would hinge on the actions of a coerced twenty-year-old.

Then, in his head, he heard Emma's voice as clearly as if she'd been alive and standing beside him. *He said that he already had his Myra Hindley.* That was *before* Brady had abducted Alli. So if he wasn't grooming Emma to be Myra Hindley and she wasn't to be Alli, who was his accomplice, whom would he trust to carry out his legacy after his death?

"We pray, oh Lord, for President-elect Edward Harrison Carson and Vice President–elect Richard Thomas Baer, to whom you have entrusted the leadership of this nation at this moment in history. We pray that you will help them bring our country together, so that we may rise above partisan politics and seek the larger vision of your will for our nation."

Jack felt Garner's grip on his shoulder, trying to turn him around. He saw Nina leaning in toward the president-elect. But her mouth was closed, her jaw set. She reached into an inner pocket of her coat, and at that moment Jack knew. The last piece of the Rubik's Cube fell into place. The real Ian Brady had used a woman younger than he for his accomplice, but not so young as his victims, not so young as to be unreliable. Someone just like Nina Miller.

Jack drew his Glock, fired one shot into Nina's heart. He saw her mouth open in shock, saw her body spin around; then Garner slammed him to the floor of the dais. Someone kicked the Glock away; Garner struck him a blow to the back of his head.

"Use them to bring reconciliation among the races and healing to political wounds, that we may truly become 'one nation under God,'" the Reverend Dr. Fred Grimes intoned just before the screaming began and all hell broke loose.

FORTY-NINE

SOMETIMES WE all need luck in addition to skill," Secretary Dennis Paull said. "And you, Jack, had both today."

Jack was sitting in a small cubicle inside the offices of Homeland Security. Across the table from him were Secretary Paull and Edward Carson, the new President of the United States. It was eight hours after the incident. Since then, Jack had been under arrest, in isolation, just as Brady had predicted.

"That was quite a heroic thing you did today, Jack." Carson waved Paull's protest to silence. "You saved not only my life but the lives of hundreds of people, all vital to the running of this country. That was a vial of anthrax Nina Miller was about to open."

Jack moved his head from side to side with some difficulty. His body still throbbed and ached from the beating Hugh Garner and his cohorts had delivered in the aftermath of the shooting. "And the vial Alli was carrying?"

"Confectioner's sugar," Paull said. "Thank God."

Personally, Jack didn't believe God had anything to do with it, but this was neither the time nor the place to say it. "Is she all right?"

"In light of what's happened, she's being evaluated more carefully this time," the president said.

Paull opened a slim file. "The doctors found a small bit of matter encrusted in the fold behind one ear."

"So Brady did drug her."

Paull nodded. "So far, the lab has identified Sodium Pentothal and curare. There's another, more complex substance the techs are still trying to analyze, but they figure it must be something that caused her to metabolize the other substances with unusual rapidity."

"Jack," Carson said, "do you know how he got to Nina Miller?"

"No, but I can make an educated guess," Jack said. "Nina was traumatized early in life. Her brother molested her."

"We know all about that," Paull cut in. "It's in her file. Her psychological profile was perfectly normal."

"Profiles, like Alli's medical exam, can be faulty," Jack pointed out. "Even more so with psych tests. Nina couldn't bear the fact that her brother was a successful married man."

"Wait a minute." Paull held up a hand. "Nina's brother was killed twelve years ago in a drive-by in Richmond, Virginia. One shot through the head."

"Why would she lie to me about that?" Jack's synapses began firing again. "Did the cops ever find out who the killer was?"

Paull shook his head. "Apart from the bullet, there was no evidence—no motivation either. They gave up, said it was a case of mistaken identity."

"What if it wasn't?" Jack said. "What if Nina met Brady twelve years ago? What if he proposed a plan: He murders her brother, and in return, she becomes his accomplice."

Paull began to sweat at the thought of the terrible mistakes he'd made professionally and personally.

"Brady was like a chess master—he planned his moves far ahead of time," Jack continued. "The night he went out the window, he told me he'd killed his parents. At the time, I thought he was simply goading me, but now I can see a pattern. He felt he was justified in killing his parents, for whatever reason. Taking a look at Nina's file gave him his opportunity. My guess is he sought her out. Nina felt that there was a privilege in loneliness. She said it made her feel alive, introduced her to herself. People like her are split off from themselves. They'll pass even the most stringent psychological testing because at the moment, they believe what they say."

Paull winced. He could feel Nina's sweat-slicked body moving against him, her breath in his ear, her deep groans. He felt quite faint.

Jack shifted to rid himself of a stab of pain. "In the course of my investigation, I met a young woman, tough and smart—in many ways a younger version of Nina. Brady got to her. She was a nihilist just like him. I'm betting he found the darkness in Nina and pried her open. He was a master at mentoring."

In his mind's eye, Paull saw an image of himself walking into the bookshop where he'd ordered *Summer Rain,* Nina's favorite novel. The dealer insisted he examine it before he bought it. It chronicled the struggle of an immigrant family, rootless and uneducated, marginalized by an indifferent society. He'd thought nothing of it then, but in light of what had happened since, he agreed with Jack. Nina's love of the book was a reflection of her inner darkness. Why hadn't he recognized it? But of course he knew. He'd blinded himself to the signs because her detachment, her rootlessness, her lack of desire for commitment or a family made her the perfect mistress.

"Good God." President Carson ran a hand through his hair. "This entire episode is monstrous." He turned his telegenic eyes on Paull. "My Administration will have zero tolerance for psychopathic agents, Dennis. You and your brethren are going to have to devise an entirely different yardstick to measure your candidates." He stood. "Excuse me, I'm going to deliver the same message to the new director of national security."

He leaned over the table, gave Jack's hand a hearty shake. "Thank you, Jack. From the bottom of my heart."

After he'd gone, Jack and Paull sat across from each other in an uncomfortable silence.

Jack leaned forward. "I'm only going to say this once: For the record, despite his best efforts, I didn't kill him, he killed himself."

"I believe you." Paull's voice was weary. "What went wrong, Jack?"

Jack rubbed the back of his head. "Brady—or whatever his name is—was no good to you anymore, sir. All he wanted was to impose a lasting legacy. He wanted to make a statement of the greatest magnitude. I imagine you'll agree that obliterating virtually the entire U.S. government at a time when the reins of power were being exchanged, when the country was most vulnerable, more than qualifies."

"Are you saying he was making a political statement?"

"I doubt it. Brady had moved beyond such considerations. He despised humankind, hated what he felt civilization had done to the world. He felt we were heading toward a dead end."

"You have my personal thanks." Secretary Paull stared at Jack for a long time. At length, he cleared his throat. "On another note, you'll be pleased to know that there's no sign of the organization known as E-Two. Frankly, I suspect it never existed. The former Administration required a domestic bogeyman to go after its main objective—the missionary secularists. Maybe E-Two was fabricated by the former National Security Advisor."

"Or maybe Brady came up with the idea," Jack said. "After all, misdirection was his forte, and those FASR defectors had to go somewhere."

"A bogus revolutionary cell? Could be." The secretary shrugged. "Either way, I've ordered the members of the First American Secular Revivalists released and reinstated. And, by the way, I protected them while they were in custody. No one interrogated them or harmed them in any way."

"I know you did what you could."

Paull rose, walked to the door.

"What was his name?" Jack said. "His real name?"

Paull hesitated only a moment. "Morgan Herr," he said. "Truth be told, I know precious little about him. I'd like to know more, but for that I'd require you and your particular expertise. If you're interested, come see me."

February 1

UNDER THE buttermilk sky of an early dusk, Jack stood at the front window of his living room, staring fixedly at the bleak view of his driveway. All the crispy leaves were gone. Overnight, a bitter front out of the Midwest had nailed shut the coffin of the January thaw. All day long, the District, home to mild winters, had been shivering.

Earlier in the day, he'd driven the white Lincoln Continental down Kansas Avenue NE. Parking outside the Black Abyssinian Cultural Center, he hurried across the pavement and through the door. There, he collected the month's rent, minus an amount for the time Chris Armitage and Peter Link occupied the back room. The leaders wanted to pay the full month's rent, but Jack said no. He drank a cup of dark, rich African hot chocolate with them, thanked them, and left.

Trashy wind, full of cinders and yesterday's newspapers, followed him down the block to the FASR office. Inside, everything looked more or less back to normal, except that Calla Myers's desk was unoccupied, wreathed in black ribbon. A number of lit candles clustered on the desktop in front of a framed photo of her with some of her co-workers. They were all smiling. Calla was waving at the camera.

Peter Link was out on assignment, but Jack spent a few minutes chatting with Armitage. He knew he'd made a friend there.

JACK ABANDONED the window and its bleak view to put a Rolling Stones record on the stereo. "Gimme Shelter" began, simmered to a slow boil. "War, children," he sang in a melancholy voice along with Mick and Merry Clayton, "it's just a shot away."

He returned to the window, waiting. Tonight, he had a date with Sharon. He had no idea how that was going to go, but at last she had agreed to come to the house, Gus's house, the house of Jack's adolescence. If he and Sharon didn't kill each other, then next Saturday the two of them would spend the afternoon with Alli. It was Alli's idea; maybe she wanted to play matchmaker—or peacemaker, anyway.

He thought about Alli and her effect on him. There was a time when he didn't know himself or the world. Worse, he couldn't accept that he didn't know himself, so he kept pushing everyone away. Without intimate mirrors, you have no hope of knowing yourself. So he kept Sharon and Emma—the two people best equipped to be his intimate mirrors—at arm's length, while he deluded himself into thinking his job came first, that saving strangers was more important than allowing anyone to know him.

He recalled his first encounter with Hermann Hesse's *Steppenwolf.* He hadn't liked the book, because he was too young to fully appreciate it. But with living comes wisdom. Now a line from the book surfaced in his mind. There's a moment when Steppenwolf is struck by a revelation. In order to understand himself, and therefore the world, he needs to "traverse, not once more but often, the *hell* of his inner being." This, Jack understood, was the most difficult thing a human being could attempt. Simply to try was heroic. To succeed, well . . .

He heard the soft crunch of the gravel, and then Sharon's car nosed into the driveway. She pulled in to the right, parked the car, and got out. She was wearing a black ankle-length wool coat, black boots, and a tomato-red scarf wrapped around her throat. Aching to see her long legs, he leaned forward until his nose made an imprint on the glass and his breath turned to fog.

She stood for a moment, as if uncertain which way to go. Jack held his next breath, wondering if she was contemplating getting back in her car and driving off. That would be just like her—or at least just like the woman he had known.

Low, cool sunlight came through the branches, speckling her face. It shone off her hair, made the color of her eyes clear and rich. She looked young, very much as she had when he'd first met her. From this distance, the lines of worry and grief weren't visible, as if time itself had been obliterated.

Jack saw her gazing at the house, taking in its shape and dimensions. She took a step toward him, then another. As she moved, she seemed to gain momentum, as if her intent had focused down. She looked like someone who had made up her mind, who knew what she wanted.

Jack understood that completely, and his heart swelled. His love for her was palpable, as if he'd never loved her before, or even knew what love was. Perhaps he never had. It was all too likely that the consequences of pain and loss had driven love from his heart. But not, it seemed, from him altogether. This was Emma's gift to him. She had taught him not only to recognize love but to seize it as well.

Sharon mounted the steps. He left the window and never again thought the view through it was bleak.

He felt Emma all around him, like the collective shimmer of stars on a moonless night.

There are many paths to redemption, he thought. *This is mine.*

He heard the knock on the door, and opened it.